# Rolling
# Thunder

# Rolling Thunder

a novel

by

## William Simmons

THE PERMANENT PRESS
SAG HARBOR, NY 11963

**Library of Congress Cataloging-in-Publication Data**

Simmons, William
    Rolling Thunder / by William Simmons
    p. cm.
    ISBN 1-57962-019-1
    I. Title.
    PS3569.I4773R65 1999
    813'.54--dc21

THE PERMANENT PRESS
4170 Noyac Road
Sag Harbor, NY 11963

For Barbara Elizabeth Simmons

Heartfelt gratitude to Barbara Braun, Martin and Judy Shepard, and Isadore Seltzer. Special thanks to friend and poet Michael Dodge. Cheers to the Emergency Cocktail Society, Lower Manhattan Chapter. And all my love to Anna Ancin-Simmons.

# 1

JUST in case you aren't one of Velez & Oldham's legion of listeners and have wandered in here by mistake, let me begin by telling you that Velez & Oldham pretty much *is* FM rock morning radio here in New York City.

We've been here at WRTR—Thunder Rock to you, of course, or 'The Thunder', as Velez prefers it—for eleven-and-a-half years now. Eleven-and-a-half years. We took over for one of the all-time rock radio icons. You know who I'm talking about: the guy who once ruled the rock airwaves, who borrowed 'Rolling Thunder' from Dylan back in the days before FM radio stations felt the need for nicknames and christened this place 'Rolling Thunder Radio,' who made himself a legend sucking up to the greats and anointing the comers, but whose epic drug proclivities gradually toasted him and one fine day—the day of the storied vomiting-on-the-air caper—became too untidy for the *corporados* to abide. You probably know every gory, dissolute detail by heart. Velez and I have discussed this on a number of occasions, and, for the record, our consciences are clear. If it hadn't been us, it would have been somebody else—it was time.

Yet thus it is said of our fabled predecessor with more and more reverence as time passes: his flameout marked the end of an era; with him went the pure sweet passion for rock. And I do not deny this because let's face it: the music we play on the Velez & Oldham Show morning after morning, day after rainy, sunny, snowy, blustery, sweltering, asphyxiating day, is not the stuff of passion.

My own credentials as a senior minister of the rock establishment owe entirely to my entrenchment at the right hand of Roberto Velez. In fact, I might as well confess right now, since things are bound to come out in the open here: I stumbled into rock by accident back in the old days, for motives that had plenty to do with passion but little to do with the music, so you can imagine how I feel about the remixed, remastered, regurgitated, market-tested, demographic-targeted, mind-numbingly derivative version we're paid to shovel your way every morning here at the Thunder. Now, Velez—he is the authentic music maven. Can tell you the names of the session guys on records you've never even heard of.

Shut up and pretend you like it, Velez tells me.

Velez covers for me.

I am in my day's first shift. The first shift goes from a little before five in the morning—the time of day when the fallen angels were cast out of heaven—until two or three in the afternoon. Second shift starts around nine and stretches until, well . . . depends.

Last night, for instance, I take in an early-season Rangers game at the surprise invitation of Sally Wallach, an invitation proffered with no evidence whatsoever of romantic intent. Sally is WRTR's college intern, and figures, I fear, to play a role of substance in this tale. Sally is studying broadcasting at Cornell and I decide a Rangers game will be a good opportunity to talk her out of it. Broadcasting—not Cornell. I have nothing against Cornell; anyplace that can lure the likes of Sally Wallach must have some major things going for it.

Sally is a nice kid. She's bright. No, really—I don't mean that to sound the way it did. You can see right away she deserves, and is no doubt ultimately in store for, a far loftier calling than rock radio. But in this, my first chance to exchange a little meaningful conversation with Sally Wallach, I see immediately that Sally has the disease.

No sense, I tell myself, trying to reason with a twenty-year-old woman—oh, please: girl—a twenty-year-old girl who's got the disease. There's not all that much sense trying to be rational with a twenty-year-old girl—yes, but undeniably on the lubricious cusp of womanhood—about anything. In my experience.

So I don't try.

Sally Wallach, who has selected an ensemble for this hockey contest that makes the Italian crooner at center ice forget the words to the Star Spangled Banner, is better positioned than the average nymphet to break into big-time radio—see how it trips so easily from my cynical tongue: big-time radio—because her father owns enough stock in WRTR's parent company's parent company that Sally Wallach could get Velez and me fired and herself installed as the morning man tomorrow if she wanted.

Wait: false modesty will get us nowhere, will it? The cold, hard fact is that neither Sally Wallach nor anybody else below cabinet level could get Velez and me fired. We are a money machine. The *corporados* virtually soil themselves in our presence.

No, the only thing Velez and I have to fear is Velez and I ourselves.

It takes Sally Wallach exactly half of the first period to recite for me everything she knows about radio, which she clearly thinks is a great deal. Sally is fairly pregnant with insight. She knows that 'programming' is the secret word that qualifies the utterer as a serious radio insider. *Artistic integrity, syndication sellout, market share, digital media, alternative rock, where are the important new artists*, blah blah, yaddayadda—these are also helpful phrases to remember if you want to ingratiate yourself with grizzled radio professionals, like Sally no doubt thinks I am. Let me let you in on a dirty little secret, Sally: from what I hear, the radio people in the sixties were just a bunch of horny pothead scammers doing it for the rush and the money and the easy-access babes. Just like Velez does.

The Rangers and the other guys can't keep track of the puck under the smoke-machine-quality steam rising from the humid Garden ice and so I sit and listen to Sally, partly because that is perhaps the thing I do best. Partly, too, because I suddenly have an ominous urge to know what's on Sally Wallach's mind.

Yet, girding up now for my first shift of the final workday of this resplendent autumn week, I can report that the Rangers game led to nothing I need to feel small about. Sally will come in today, about halfway through the Velez & Oldham Show like she always does, with a new gleam of admiration for me in her dizzyingly beautiful eyes. Because after Rangers and pasta, you see, I take Sally to her East Eighties apartment that her old man probably owns; I scurry around the cab to open the door for her and—I swear to God—I kiss her hand goodnight.

Velez is feeling chatty today. "Call us and tell us what you think of this new Pumpkins cut. We'll take the fifth caller at random and give you . . ." Jesus, Velez, can we just shut up and let the music play itself? It's too early for this. On the six-to-ten slot, it's always too early.

The problem is that I've got to be on my toes when Velez feels like chatting since I am, in addition to quasi-newsman, Velez's all-purpose foil, and Velez will jump me in the middle of one of these exercises just to be a malicious prick. And then there are the phones, which our engineers have not quite mastered.

Velez leaps without warning into a tale of drug use among the rich and famous. This is where I am supposed to leaven the show with stern editorial responsibility; on cue, I usually say something about how nobody of consequence in the music business fools around with drugs anymore. But today I'm more prepared than usual, because there's a news tidbit in the paper this morning about the seizure of twelve hundred pounds of cocaine hidden in a banana truck slinking its way north from Baja California.

"How would they . . ." I make the mistake of speculating out loud.

"Easy, Coolie. They stick the cocaine in condoms, which, when they're loaded, are about the size of guess what: bananas! 'Cept when I'm wearin' 'em, of course. So they suck out the banana meat, slip in a condom of coke, an' *vamos,* you're on your way."

"Wonder how they caught the bad guys," I ask, since I've waded in this deep already.

"I bet it was the tarantulas," ventures Velez.

"The tarantulas?"

"Yeah, Coolie, tarantulas love bananas. Them border guards, they probably seen a buncha tarantulas cartwheelin' around the back of that truck, sittin' up on their fat fuzzy backsides doin' the *macareña,* divin' off the truck like Peter Pan singin' 'we can fly, we can fly, *we can fly!*'"

We have this rhythm, Velez and I. In our rhythm I play the back-beat: I am the voice of moderation and responsible, aging-boomer sensibilities. Velez is the unrepentant rocker, the ageless child of glamorous adolescent decadence. We thus cancel each other out, a zero-sum glib frappé that has kept us at the top of FM New York since practically the day we parachuted in here.

Velez, at five-fifty-five this morning while I'm trying my best not to pour coffee on anything electric until my first news recitation is over, wants to know how things went with Sally Wallach after the Rangers game.

He knows better, of course. Like Velez himself, I wouldn't shoot my mouth off even if anything newsworthy had transpired. I don't kiss and tell, as I trust others not to do unto me. Velez accuses me of sparing myself the embarrassment of how little there is to tell. Nothing, I allow my righteous silence to insinuate, could be further from the truth.

If I thought my words would have carried any weight, I would have counseled Sally Wallach in a direction other than rock radio. Except perhaps for professional football, there isn't a business around that chews people up and spits them out like radio. Radio's not as tough on the knees, I suppose. Except for the groupies, that shameless, delectable legion of rock bottomfeeders whose knees have been known to take a fearful thumping.

By virtue of her wise selection of parents, though, Sally is hardly in the category of music-business fodder. Entry-level for Sally will be a station manager spot somewhere in a non-crucial market where the sun shines a lot and she can wear her bathing suit to work. Sally, in short, will be giving career-boosting oral gratification to nobody.

A five-tune marathon. There is a God. See you in ten minutes, Velez.

The six-to-ten a.m. slot has its blessings. At the top of the list is that I rarely run into anybody else who works at this station. Even better, I virtually *never* have to lay eyes on the record promoters. Since we, Velez & Oldham, are the top-rated FM program in one of the two most important markets on this forlorn planet, we command lusty attention from promoters. Now I personally couldn't be less relevant in the craven business of music promotion, you understand; but Velez and I are a package deal. I am nothing without Velez—his patronage, his social wake, and, oh yes, his friendship. Velez needs me no less, in ways that may become apparent as we progress through our adventure.

You may be curious to know that for my labors at Thunder Rock, I am given a yearly compensation approximately equal to the purchase price of a shiny piece of Bavarian rolling stock. Velez make more. A whole lot more. Station managers, who consider me excess baggage that Velez keeps around to irritate them when he's in the mood, and who wildly over-estimate my self-respect, have stooped to using Velez's lavish compensation in attempts to make me quit. But facts are facts: Velez is worth more. If you paid us by the word, Velez would get about four times what I do. Which he does, and then some. If we got paid on the basis of enthusiasm, the differential would be off the chart. More to the point, I have no skills, much less one that somebody would pay me this kind of cash for.

So this seventy-five thousand dollars per year, which is roughly what a certain discount electronics outfit will spend advertising on Velez & Oldham during our time together, is redistributed into the American economy thus: twenty-two thousand dollars in federal, state and city taxes; twenty thousand in rent; twenty-seven hundred in used-Volvo payments (plus fifteen hundred to park it); couple of hundred for food; zero for clothes; two or three thousand sundry gaming expenses, a grand or two for liquor. And twelve thousand dollars in child support.

This leaves roughly fifteen thousand dollars unaccounted for, I see.

I must call my accountant, who is due back from Nicaragua soon. Until then, I'm sorry; that's the best I can do.

How does such profligacy position me with Sally Wallach?

The fact is that unless events take a drastically unforeseen turn, I'm going to be keeping my hands off Sally. I am a curiosity to the sweet girl right now; she's thinking that beneath this melancholy mask lies a caring, sharing, sensitive man. My heart, however, has been calcified by the venom of female disillusion to which time and again I have bared my self-destructive veins in the past. I can't take another one; not just now.

Especially not Sally. We'd have dinner. She'd get me past the troglodyte cyclops faggot doorman at Nell's. I'd get silly on champagne and ask her to try to think of me as the older brother she secretly desired to be incestuous with, and she'd be touched by my vulnerability and take me into her lilac-dappled embrace, and pretty soon . . .ah, you know how it goes.

So I'm playing it safe with Sally. I'm determined.

On the other hand, it would drive Velez, who no doubt has designs on fair Sally, nuts. Velez is in charge of the lion's share of getting laid in this partnership. And not on merit. I dismiss the facts that Velez is semi-dangerously sly-looking and has every pussy-stalking move ever devised down to the level of surgical precision. He gets his women because he is a star. That's all. If I wanted to prostitute my own celebrity, I could do just as well.

Ten-thirty a.m. The week's time has been petrified on tape; we have, as usual, been marginally entertaining in fitful spurts. I troop behind Velez into the station manager's office for a staff meeting. The fact that we are having a staff meeting today, or any day, testifies to the latest palace coup. Our new program manager is a woman named Arielle, and she is brimming with hard-charge.

Arielle hit the beach a week ago, halfway through a Velez & Oldham Show, disembarking from the very same elevator car as Sally Wallach, of whom I have made recent mention. An engineer of ours, in his single salutary contribution to the morning's broadcast, offered Arielle his seat. Velez, tipped off as usual to the change in regime, pretended to turn the soundbooth intercom off and yelled to me, "Who the fuck is the chick?" so Arielle would accidentally hear him. Later, Velez would feign profound embarrassment and invite Arielle to lunch, her treat. She is, after all, the boss. For now.

Arielle—poor, misguided Arielle—tips her hand early by drooling about how much she has admired our work over the years and how privileged she feels to be heading our team. While sycophancy is the proper tack with most radio people, this preamble of hers merely qualifies Arielle as the new resident doormat.

Velez and I make our customary bet: my hundred has her out of here by Christmas. This is Arielle's first staff meeting. Velez insists we show up, and on time. I'm not sure what to make of this except the obvious: Velez is keeping his options open for the day when Arielle is no longer the quarterback of the Thunder. This strategy is laced with irony, since Arielle's inevitable trampling will in all likelihood be Velez's doing.

Arielle, a woman who was once no doubt amiably petite but who now sports Nautilus shoulders and the cow-punching gait of pumped-iron thighs, has redecorated the program manager's office—her office—which doubles as our conference room. Touching gesture, symbolizing the new WRTR team spirit. Her radar has not yet picked up the gale-force winds that gather just beyond her horizon even as she calls us to order.

The turnout, at least, must encourage her: eleven on-air talent, which is more or less everybody, wait in polite silence. It is the nature of radio that most of us co-workers are virtual strangers to each other; only at station parties and promotional events do we do any meaningful mingling. So the very notion of togetherness that Arielle has confided to Velez to be her top priority here at the Thunder just betrays her for the ingénue she is.

The meeting commences and the only piece of business on the agenda that in my book sounds potentially catastrophic is our new program manager's announcement that we will be doing more remote broadcasts. This is where we leave the splendor of WRTR's perfectly serviceable studio to set up impromptu shop at, say, the Asbury Park boardwalk or some other place where a raucous teen crowd can be conned into thinking that Springsteen might show up. During remote shows we spend lots of time interviewing normal people, an exercise of interest only to the families and friends of the interviewees.

We babble on about how happy and excited we are to be wherever we are, sitting at our rickety card table grappling with rotten equipment and a serpentarium of wires and wearing, Arielle now informs us, our new WRTR Thunder Rock sweaters, copies of which we'll be selling this Christmas for charity, instead of being safe and sound up in our eighteenth-floor aerie surrounded by more sound equipment than anyone here can figure out what to do with, and with the world—at least the Sixth Avenue glitter-and-snarl portion of it—at our feet.

Arielle has the salt of a post-feminist woman. Which is to say that she's too young to have been in on any of the serious gunfire, and is now reaping the benefits of revolution in childlike ignorance of her political heritage. Lucky for her, she has chosen a field in which jealousy and career-garroting are so wanton that rationales for treachery—

like the inherent incompetence of women, for example—are super-fluous. She appears to assume that she's wearing a bulls-eye on her back simply because everybody in radio does, without regard to race, creed, sexual persuasion or orientation. Good for her.

And Arielle, to her further credit, is not tip-toeing: she's letting us know that she's here to take her best shot. Which she proceeds to do now by announcing that more of the station's marketing budget will be going toward entertaining current and prospective advertisers.

To the extent that I can still be stunned, this stuns me—only because I had assumed that one hundred percent of the station's marketing money was already being spent caressing clients' private parts.

But, truth be told, I know about as little of the workings of radio as a business as anyone possibly could who's been in it as long as I have. I might glance through the trades two or three times annually, usually trying to catch Velez in a lie. This gives me just enough grist to inter-ject into meetings like these an occasional "All right!" or an "Ah, shit" at not altogether inappropriate moments.

Arielle now produces a colorful chart about something. Do I respond with an "All right!" or with an "Ah, shit?" I find myself unqual-ified to judge. I gaze at the chart intently and wait for Velez to give me a hint.

Velez, meanwhile, is sitting beside me, to the windward side of the powers, hands folded schoolboy style and hanging on Arielle's every word. Christ, it looks like he might start taking notes in a minute. Everyone in the room takes this for theater; even the ones who resent, envy or just plain loathe Velez are choking back their guffaws. Sitting here in Velez's shadow, I wonder if the art of cruelty is about to reach new frontiers all over poor Arielle.

Arielle's concept, she explains to her team, is to factor us heavily into the station's invigorated assault on the moral fiber of New York's advertising managers. "Let me be honest," Arielle says—a phrase that out of anyone else in radio will induce mass Pavlovian ass-puckering—hunching over and laying her hands flat on the conference table, her chrome-piston shoulders congealing like a piece of firewood strapped across her back. "For clients and agency people, having drinks with our checkered suits is enough to bore the balls off a brass monkey!"

Malicious silence implodes the room; just when it looks like the density of it will crush Arielle's ringlet-tressed skull like a beer can in three thousand feet of water, Velez, of all people, saves her with a howl of laughter. Arielle instantly dissolves in DayGlo-cheeked gratitude that

*Señor* Morning Radio has decided to grant her provisional one-of-the-boys status by laughing at her brass monkey's balls quip. Now everyone, with greater or lesser enthusiasm, joins in; we're evidently taking prisoners today.

"What they really want to do," Arielle lurches on with renewed confidence, "is to shoot the shit with WRTR's stars. Meet the glamour people—" she spreads her arms maternally, "—*you* guys!"

I, for one, am so imbued with team spirit I could vomit.

And it doesn't take long before the bottom line of this announcement begins to sink in amongst the company: Arielle is putting the arm on us for more goodwill appearances. Hendy Markowitz, who is no doubt secretly delighted at the prospect of acting like a celebrity despite his Siberia slot, makes a play at annoyance. "When will we find the time, Arielle?" I don't think we've actually been told Arielle's last name, so we're cornered into familiarity. Velez chortles privately next to me; Markowitz spends exactly six hours a week here at the Thunder unless somebody comes down with dysentery, and he spends the rest of his time looking for work. Hendy will find the time.

Velez and I, on the other hand, have a legitimate gripe. Dinners with clients generally occur, I suppose, right in between my first and second shifts. And Velez, who seldom if ever sleeps and then only when heavily tranquilized or fucked into a torpor, has a demanding schedule of his own, what with his personal appearances, some *cum* Oldham, mostly *sans* Oldham, his guest stints on the VH-1 and MTV circuit, and the other tentacles of his showbiz empire.

So let's watch, shall we, as Arielle tries to talk Velez into this.

Yet, confounding the experts, Velez shouts, "Excellent! I've been saying for years that we could push revenues through the roof if only we pull together."

And thus hypocrisy scales new summits here at the Thunder. Not six months ago a Yale MBA sat in the very chair now warmed by the arduously toned behind of our own Arielle and issued the same proclamation, to which, if memory serves, Velez told him he could snort mouse shit through a firehose before Velez would lower himself to play grab-ass with the advertising geeks. Isn't that, Velez had argued—persuasively, in my opinion—why we have geeks of our own?

The circuit of furtive glances is lost, mercifully, on Arielle, who sits basking in the togetherness of her new ball club. She is a woman utterly in command; she is high on triumph. Some people are born for the fast lane, and some people, no matter how far in front of me they finished in business school, just won't ever have what it takes, down here in the guts. All this tracks across Arielle's flat kabuki-on-Ritalin face like the running message board at Madison Square Garden. The sense of impending tragedy at this table is positively fucking operatic.

Velez passes me a note I didn't see him write: "Save your pity; the young are resilient."

There remains the question of the division of labor. The sexier the clients, the sexier the personality Arielle will want to heave at them. This, I see right away, could bury Velez and me, and probably Adrian Boe, our senior rocker and sole survivor from the station's rock-format inception back in sixty-something. Adrian tries to avoid personal appearances of any kind because Adrian looks like what he is: an old man. And nothing will turn an adolescent crowd itchier than a rock DJ who looks like their Uncle Howard. So Adrian confines himself to cranking out his nine-to-midnight, which he can and frequently does in a trance, and lending his venerable reputation to this young man's game.

But no one grills Arielle on the ugly details, so Arielle doesn't volunteer. Just so I know we're all pulling together on this. 'Cause money in the station's pocket is money in our pockets—right gang? God, protect this little flower.

I guess it's time I told you a little about my partner Velez, since, after all, that's probably why you're reading this. Robert, Bobby, Roberto Velez, depending on the constituency of the moment, is somewhat Puerto Rican, sort of like Geraldo Rivera, the man who made geek tele-journalism a viable minority franchise, is somewhat Puerto Rican.

Velez can ladle on the Latino at a second's notice. The Velez *barrio* persona fairly croons: all this class, all this style, and Puerto Rican all the while. Not that Latinos tip the scales of our vast demographic melting pot of an audience; but as community pillar material, Velez's blood plays well.

Political aspirations may lurk in Velez's heart. He's never said as much. In so many words.

Velez is a homeboy. Born and raised in Washington Heights, an outpost that, for your own safety, will not appear on your Manhattan celebrity tour map. Washington Heights is about as north and gruesome as the Isle of Manhattan gets. From certain neighborhood rooftop promontories, one can observe caravans of late-model shoppers streaming day and night across the George Washington Bridge and down the Henry Hudson Parkway and across the various Harlem River bridges on

errands of narcotic exchange, the only viable commerce currently prac-
ticed in Washington Heights. I have spent time in Velez's mother's
home. We are close in many ways, Velez and me. From me, Velez with-
holds fairly little, I like to think. Nor I from him, except those funda-
mental little terrors with which no one would burden a true friend.
Immaculata Velez cooks on holidays, and I am invited.

Velez's father dwells in roughly the same existential plane as my
mother. His father turned up missing hard on the heels of Velez's conception. My mother willfully smoked herself into a Baltimore mausoleum when I was thirteen.

Occasionally my dad will light down in New York. He works for a
computer company or defense contractor or perhaps even the CIA in a
non-shooting capacity—I get them confused. There is a distinction, I
suppose. It's just that my world view is too terminally apolitical to
appreciate it. But he is not the kind of man who should be held responsible for corporate dastardliness—I'll tell you that.

When Richard 'Buddy' Oldham comes to town, Velez and I take
him cruising, showing the old man the type of stuff we absolutely never
do on our own. We take him to the Rainbow Room. To the Carlyle to
listen to Bobby Short. You know—Buddy-era stuff. And Buddy always
starts out game, but he is over sixty years old and he's usually been up
working all day besides—on a one-shift schedule, no less. So he'll beg
off before midnight, feeling good about hanging out with his only son,
the grown-up.

How Velez came to radio is well-enough chronicled that I won't
bore you with a lengthy rehash. A few faltering stints with rooftop
bands in high school convinced Velez that his talents lie elsewhere than
in actually *making* music. From that revelation, he started promoting.
Anything. Dances, concerts, bands, the works. The essential perks of
the music business appealed to Velez: money and women. He hooked
up with a smalltime uptown radio station, using his night show mainly
as free promotion for his motley music enterprise. But gradually the
radio got under his skin. When he couldn't crack the big time in New
York—too Puerto Rican, not Puerto Rican enough—he took to the road,
knocking off a string of gradually larger markets until one day he landed
in . . .well, let's wait a while for the rest, shall we?

The big mystery to Immaculata Velez, a wiry, noble woman with
knuckles callused from a life of beating back a creeping voracious slum,
was where her Roberto learned to sound *Anglo*. For it's true: Velez
sounds more standard mid-Atlantic than the whitest Presbyterian in

New York City. I myself have no explanation other than plain determination.

Sally Wallach is not part of the staff meeting, since she's basically a production gofer and an intern besides. So I have no opportunity to assess our new relationship this morning. By the time we get out of here, Sally will be too busy doing whatever the daytime crew has saddled her with to exchange endearments with me.

I know I said I'm keeping my distance from Sally, and with good reasons. What reasons? There's age. Sally is twenty goddamned years old, as I may have mentioned. I, meanwhile, have already stepped into the shadows that my future throws. So to speak.

Besides the age barrier, there is the transience of the situation: Sally is slated to be Big Apple history in a few scant months. Yet even as I speak, I begin to realize that, in my list of pros and cons, I have entered this factor in the wrong column.

The real reason I should—*should?* yes, see how my resolve weakeneth already—steer clear of Sally Wallach is that my history with women, pre-marriage and post, is not a pretty tale. Actually, I guess you'd be correct in pointing out that considering my marriage, I've fared poorly with women, period.

Velez, my friend, continually encourages me to climb back on the horse. "You're a victim of your own shitty choices," Velez counsels me. I don't think this is true; if anything, the few women I've been involved with have been too good for me. Unless that's what Velez means.

Sally, as I feared, is already somewhere in the vault. The vault is the Thunder Rock record library, where WRTR has more records and tapes and CD's than anyone outside radio could possibly conceive of. Most of these will be played once a decade. But our afternoon guy, Kenny Appleton, has this feature between 3:00 and 4:00 p.m. where he plays obscure tunes that no one in New York gives the slightest shit about hearing. Kenny wonders why his ratings suck. Anyway, Kenny's producer sends Sally into the vault with a list of records every morning, and she does the best she can.

I'm not going into the vault to look for Sally because I don't want to be obvious and because the dust in there is murder up my nose.

Sally, I want to mention, came in this morning wearing one of those black pants deals that look like tights, with a great big cobalt shirt blousing all over her. Sally has a lot of auburn hair and wide-set eyes of a color I won't even attempt to describe to you beyond calling to mind a

Maxfield Parrish fountain fantasy; Sally's eyes have most of those colors in them.

I tell you this only because this budding situation could, if history is any indication, make an ass of me before long, and I want you prepared to sympathize.

I check my messages before fleeing WRTR, the Thunder, for another week. There will be some calls that I'll probably want to return. They'll be from listeners who call regularly to talk to me. Not to get all pee-pantsed about being on the radio, but just to talk to me. This is the difference between Velez and me, and possibly between me and almost everybody else in radio. I know that there are actual people on the other end of the wireless, and for some of them, listening to the radio is the most important thing they do all day. And many of them—the desperate ones and the mere junkies—know I know it.

It might be something in my voice; I don't know.

# 2

WHO are these people—my children of radioland?

Most of them are just first names. That's all I need.

I know them. Got 'em straight, even though there are five or six Bobs and the Cathys are in double figures.

Knowing Velez as you do, you might be tempted to suppose that my children are people who'd rather be sharing their thoughts and secret yearnings with the real star of Velez & Oldham but who settle for me because Velez is too busy or doesn't give a shit—both of which are true enough. There are a few cases, I'm sure, that started out that way.

But look: what would the average listener say to Velez if he actually got *Señor* Rock & Roll on the phone? What would *you* say? How's the family, Velez? How 'bout that Stones concert?

C'mon. Velez, who lets it be known in innumerable subtle ways that he is virtually too hip to show up for work here at the 'Thunder?' Velez, who desecrates this venerable rock institution every morning since he found out how much it pisses off the greybeards? Never mind swapping gossip with the unwashed.

I, on the other hand, guess I radiate a brand of airwave karma that fairly begs communion. Been that way ever since my virgin radio days in college, back in the police-action years.

There stretches between us, my children must sense, a network of spiritual synapses, open and beckoning.

Alicia writes poetry for the approval of my disembodied voice. Reads it to me on the phone after we pull the plug on Velez & Oldham at ten a.m. She won't send it to me, oh no; has to read it to me in her gulping gullet-to-nose turkey gobble, and then listen to the Oldham voice she hears on her radio tell her, private and personal, what it thinks of her poem.

To Alicia, the Oldham voice is a person of its own. If she wrote down a poem of hers and actually sent it to me, then my voice, she fears, would have to show it to that mundane stranger: the everyday Oldham. The one with the smelly sneakers and the unremarkable countenance and the empty uncertain time to pass, just like her own.

"Dennis. Hey. Dennis, that you?"

They're following me home.

"Hey, Dennis. Glad I caught ya."

"Hey," I say, "glad to be caught. Who is this?" I jab buttons on my remote control to cut through the curtain of noise. Nothing happens. This must be the remote control to something else around here. The Venetian blinds maybe.

My caller manages to outshout the sound system. It's Bennie. Ah, okay. "Bennie, me lad. How's them blue margaritas, Bennie?" Bennie is currently a bartender at a previously trendy bar on currently trendy lower Broadway. The cognoscenti had rained all over Bennie's place at first but they dried up quick when a new bar with even ruder doormen and dirty movies in the ladies' loo opened up across the street.

"So," says Bennie, who didn't expect me to answer my phone and is unprepared for actual discourse. "You, uh, comin' in tonight, Dennis?"

Bennie knows I'm not. I haven't been there in over a month. This has nothing to do with Bennie's bar's fall from grace. His place was always a sad sea of retro kitsch and I harbor little sentiment for the fifties, an era I remember just well enough to know better. Plus, Bennie's crowd—what's left of it—is a pimple and shoe-polish-black-hair crowd. No, I'll pass, *mercury hubcaps*.

I ask, "How's your lady, Ben?" since I know that's why he called, besides the despicable desire to snort celebrity.

"Christ," Bennie says, blissful that I asked. "She says she's quittin' the bar, Dennis. Movin' on."

"Smart girl. So should you," I say. Kindly.

"I know, I know. But Dennis," he bleats—I hate it when Bennie bleats—"she's talkin' symbolism. Symbolism. Leavin' here, leavin' the whole experience behind. 'Experience,' she's sayin'. To her I'm a fuckin' experience—something to tell her future shrink an' her hairy armpit lesbo girlfriends about. She's talkin' baggage, Dennis. I'm emotional baggage."

"How's work, Bennie?"

"Baggage, man. I'm baggage."

Bennie has already decided, as if you had any doubt, that he'll crawl through medical waste for the chance at another night or two with this woman. This much is abundantly clear. My insight, which would be to cut bait, is worthless on Bennie—though out of deference to my celebrity status he would make blustery pretense of weighing it. "Bennie," I say, "you'll do what you have to do. Just . . ." Ah, what the hell. "Just listen to what she's saying is all I'm asking you, Bennie."

"Her girlfriends—they're the ones talkin' her into it."

"Don't jump to a conspiracy theory. This may not be a case of feminine wiles, Ben. She might just need some growing-up time. Don't forget—she's young."

"Young?" Bennie bleats. "She's twenty-goddamn-two, Dennis. That's not young."

Bennie, you dopey bastard, can't you feel the noose around your dick? "Look at you," I try. "What're you worried about? You need a woman with a little more stability, my friend. Somebody a little bit, say, older."

"I'm twenty-six, Dennis. How old you sayin'?"

Twenty-six. The age of infinite possibilities, of a conquerable world. A fine age to be married, and nurturing vague notions of family. Of contemplating jobs of respectability.

Here's my chance. "Bennie, have you ever thought about all the women in this town in their thirties, prowling for a solid, fun-loving, down-to-earth guy like yourself?" Do you think I'm making a dent? "Now, this waitress of yours—"

"Marnie," Bennie reminds me.

"—Marnie, yeah. Listen, Bennie, while I explain something to you. This Marnie, she's the age and the looks where she's just interested in running a city-wide television game show, and she's the prize. You want to compete with every sleaze who blows toot up her nose at a bar? C'mon, Ben. You're too big a man for that."

Somebody's at my door.

I jab some more buttons, to no avail; the door is evidently not on remote control yet. I must do something about that soon. And I'm not expecting guests. Are they really following me home?

"Hold on, Bennie."

Well—Mrs. McMichael.

That Mrs. McMichael and her toilet water have graced my doorbell with a poke on the way in here is out of character. Mrs. McMichael is my downstairs nanny. Now she ambles past me and heads for the kitchen. She is short and immutable and charitable to distraction. She might straighten up my kitchen now that she sees I'm not holed up with some chippy—one of her favorite words—this soupy Friday eve.

"I'm gonna give her an ultimatum," I catch Bennie saying. Bennie sounds like we kept right on talking in my absence. I feel confident that I'm up to speed anyway. "Time she grew up, Dennis. I want her to move in with me. That ain't askin' too much commitment, right Dennis? Dennis?"

The tea kettle hisses. I hear Mrs. McMichael taking stock of the cupboards. They're not bare, but Mrs. McMichael won't be pleased.

"I thought she did move in with you."

"Nah," says Bennie. "I mean, yeah, she did—but she stays with her girlfriends half the time and if she has any stuff I'll be damned if I know where she keeps it 'cause all she's got here is a drawer full of jeans and underwear."

"You looked through her drawers?" Ah, Bennie.

"I was lookin' for keys," Bennie says lamely.

Mrs. McMichael calls, "How about some tea, dear?" and I say sure, even though I'd rather have a beer.

"Bennie, going through people's drawers is not a healthy sign. Believe me. I think maybe you lost a little perspective on this whole relationship."

"Awright, awright," Bennie says, and I think maybe I've gone too far. Bennie didn't call me to be told everything's his fault. He knows whose fault things are.

"Hold on a minute," I tell Bennie.

"Where ya goin'?" Bennie bleats, voice echoing in the cold Marnieless void.

Mrs. McMichael has assembled a counter full of bowls and things. Where did I get all this stuff? Anyway, I foresee chocolate in my immediate future, and I feel positively swaddled in the expectation. The kettle's commotion grows more rambunctious as Mom-like activities percolate in the kitchen.

So where did it all begin, this thing between me and Mrs. McMichael? Since Bennie seems not to be losing any momentum, I can put him on speakerphone and reminisce for a minute.

Mrs. McMichael is a bridge-painter's widow. She is the same age as my real mother, Elizabeth Reilly Oldham, would be—possibly to the day. I know her birthday's in May like my mother's is. Was. Well, still is, I guess. Unlike people, birthdays are forever.

Right off after moving into this charming little West Village relic a few years ago, I fell epically ill. The doctors consulted their tarot and came up with mononucleosis. I wasn't too sure about the diagnosis, but even in my less hallucinatory moments I didn't much care about the fine print.

So I spent the better part of that autumn in what that cheery asshole Roberto Velez liked to call my walking corpse mode. Velez would play graveyard organ music as background for his daily on-air call to me, to let our loyal legions know I hadn't secretly died like Paul McCartney. In the belly of the siege I think I was racked for two solid weeks.

My new landlord, not anxious to have to fumigate and repaint his crummy (though spacious) apartment so soon if I died of mononucleosis or whatever I really had, assigned the building's senior resident, Florence Mary Constance McMichael, to look in on me. Velez, I'll tell you, was thrilled to get out of daily visitation duty.

"C'mon, Dennis, you must have to deal with young girls all the time. How do you talk to them?" Bennie shares this popular image of radio people that each day is a new pussy barrage. What the hell, is my policy: issue no deflating denials that could undermine the glamour of the industry as a whole. I allow Bennie and others to coddle their assumptions that I get a lot of female attention.

Mrs. McMichael, to make a long and dreary story short, nursed me back to health, submitting me to a welter of Irish folk remedies that seemed not to be doing me any harm. At length she confessed that she missed having someone to care for. And whatever my officially documented shortcomings, I am not the sort to deprive the Mrs. McMichaels of the world their snippets of fulfillment, however Kafkaesque they might seem to you. I acquiesced in being cared for, part time.

I wish . . . oh, I wish a lot of things. But right this minute what I wish is that I had some better advice for Bennie, who, unlike many listeners who call me, I have encountered on a face-to-face basis. I think, by the way, that I may once have made the acquaintance of Bennie's girl, the obscure object of his anguish. I do remember a thin peripatetic waif with one of those cutesy side-mounted ponytails buzzing Bennie's end of the bar once. Did I just imagine her wide-bore flirtations? Or was there an attachment to Bennie in some remote proportion to Bennie's yearning? It's so hard to say with these Method waitresses.

Bennie talks on. Happily, I remembered to pigeon what was left of Mrs. McMichael's scratch-baked coffeecake this morning. Light as Immaculata Velez's ambrosia, that cake, but too much to eat by myself before it gets stale on the outside.

"You'll keep some for Jane," Mrs. McMichael says.

"Jane won't be here this weekend, Mrs. McMichael," I say. Even so, Mrs. McMichael gets a heavy lower lip when she comes across leftovers. I can't afford to have Mrs. McMichael heavy of lower lip; I'll starve. And if I ever get mononucleosis again, I'll die.

Bennie, meanwhile, is saying, "I never felt like I could really give a woman pleasure before. What if it just works with her? I mean, what if she's the one woman in New York that I'm the perfect lover for? Huh? Then what?"

"If that's the case, Ben, you'll find her back on your doorstep with her tongue hanging out."

"Okay. Sure. But meanwhile, while she's out finding this out—that I'm the only perfect dude for her—Christ only knows what she, you know, might . . . you know."

"You'd just have to be careful for a while—"

"Careful? You mean, like, use a rubber? After all she and I have been to each other?" Bennie's bleating climbs an octave. "Would *you* use a rubber with someone you loved, Dennis?"

This is a perfect example of why the one-wayness of radio is so much better than actual conversation for dealing with people like Bennie. Once you give them a chance to talk, they don't want to listen anymore.

What I'd like to tell Bennie—and stick around, I still might—is that he should be more like Velez, my partner at the Thunder. You remember.

I'd say: Bennie, Velez would lay it on the line for this babe. Step off the fast track, honey, and you might not ever have a chance to hop back on again. Not many girls get even one shot at a guy like me. You want out? They're standin' in line to take your place; don't let the door hit you in the ass.

It might be fun to tell Bennie this, except Bennie might figure: What the hell? If that's how the great Velez handles women, why not? After all, everybody knows that Velez gets laid about every twenty minutes, right? And then Bennie would go to the blue margarita bar and start in on his girl with this Velez rap, and she'd sock him in the eye.

The way Velez comes by his own women in real life, by the way, is that they're more or less presented to him like John the Baptist's head on a platter.

For instance: We're at this Upper East Side hang called Mortimer's—I don't know what we're doing at Mortimer's, nobody I know has ever set foot in Mortimer's except for an occasional Betty Ford Clinic welcome home party, but okay, we're there—last Thursday night, when down from a grapevine swings Kiwi Corcoran, a particularly cloying member of the pre-*sapiens* entertainment-industry subspecies known as record promoter. By way of example regarding Velez and how he comes by his women.

Kiwi, who, I suppose I should mention, is a guy, orders Velez a drink. Velez wiggles his finger at my glass too and Kiwi Corcoran doesn't protest. What does he care; it's not his money.

You might expect Kiwi to be pretty anxious to talk music at Velez, since a slot in our playlist is candy in Kiwi's nose. Music, however, seems to be the last subject in the world it would occur to Kiwi Corcoran to broach. "Got this new lady in promotion," Kiwi is saying instead, trying to sound street-Latino for Velez's edification. "Total shirtfull of girl, man. Want you to meet her, Roberto. Want you to take her out, man." Kiwi is flourishing his drink in time to himself and oozing lascivious implications all over Velez's shirt.

"You go out wit' her, meng?" Velez asks cagily, talking street Latino back at Kiwi Corcoran.

"Shit, man. This woman is class. I can't get bitches like her. I ain't a star. But if I tell her who you are, she'll get real excited 'bout goin' out with you."

"She doesn't know who I am?" Velez says.

"Oh, yeah, *shit* yeah! Comom, man, *everybody* knows the Man. But see, like, you're larger than life. So I gotta tell her you're a nice, regular guy. I tell her that, tell her she gettin' a shot at Roberto Velez, man, she gonna get *all* excited."

"I don't know," Velez says, and hooks the bartender for another round on Kiwi's bottomless expense account.

"I'm tellin' you, Roberto my man. She looks . . . God, I ain't even got words. An' she got this breast situation, man. Lemme explain about the breast situation." Kiwi cozies up to Velez, as if anybody close by actually gives a shit what he's saying. "Empires have changed hands, Roberto, for a look, a *look*, at babies like those."

Now Kiwi Corcoran is massaging my partner's drinking shoulder. "She fucks hard, man. I swear on my mother's eyes."

"How do you know?" Velez says "I thought you never went out with her."

"No, no, man," Kiwi backpedals. "Not me. Not personally. But I got it on excellent authority."

Yeah? Who? I'm dying to ask, but Velez beats me to it.

"A major recording artist on our very own label is who."

"Cut the bullshit, Kiwi," says Velez. "Who? I want references."

Kiwi's hand, festooned with a glitter of willfully tasteless jewelry, goes to his heart. "I'm tellin' you, Roberto, a very major star who if I was at liberty to tell you who, your ass would fall off but I ain't at any such liberty because his wife is a dear personal friend of mine an' I ain't the type to besmirch a woman's reputation in the community by blowin' the whistle on her old man. I got too much integrity for that. But believe me . . . major. A major star."

Velez lets a little line play out so Kiwi Corcoran can paddle around Mortimer's a while longer. "This major star," says Velez at length, "he wouldn't happen to have white hair and a couple of pathetic country cuts on his newest sorry-ass CD for old Black Rock Records, would he?"

"Sorry-ass?" Kiwi Corcoran mouths in deep emotional pain to his filmy reflection in the bar mirror. At least now that somebody else brought up the subject of music, he can go to work. "Sorry-ass? Lemme tell you, that CD is goin' to the fuckin' moon, Roberto my man, an' you just better jump on my single, or you gonna be the only DJ in town that everybody be tunin' out 'cause they don't wanna hear nothin' but my boy's new sorry-ass single from his sorry-ass CD that's gonna sell about a bazillion copies, man."

Velez turns to me. "Try talkin' babes with this guy, all he wants to talk is music."

"I'm tellin' you, man," says Kiwi. "Forget platinum. They gonna have to invent a new precious metal when this record sells a gazillion copies. A diamond record, man. A fuckin' kryptonite record."

"Kryptonite," I tell Velez.

"Hey," says Kiwi Corcoran, throwing an unsuspecting stock-holder's hundred at the bartender. "This new chick in promotion. I'll set somethin' up." He puts his hand on Velez's shoulder. "You go out with this lady, Roberto. Twenty, thirty years from now when you drop dead an' go to heaven, guess what? Your dick is already there waitin' for you."

So now you know. This is how Velez gets women.

And they go out with him, fully expecting to find him a shallow self-absorbed celebrity asshole with a whole lot of money who's only interested in showing them off around town and then diving into their laundry. For a girl with radio or television or music ambitions, as what other kind is there in this town, a date or two with Roberto Velez is a simple and painless transaction in return for an evening of reflected glory with potentially blazing career ramifications. It is a tribute, I suppose, to Velez's instincts for the female psyche that he seldom even tries to transcend their tawdry expectations.

I hear the rustle of baking pans in my kitchen. Is it possible that Sony will soon offer a remote control with a chocolate chip cookie button? Not for nothing do we live in New York, the world capital of instant gratification. Point at the kitchen and shoot, and wait for that McMichael magic to come wafting into nostril range. Any hour of the day or night.

Bennie, meanwhile, seems to have forgotten why it was he called me and is winding down with an expression of gratitude for the advice he's sure I must have dispensed at some point over the course of the last half hour. I counsel Bennie, finally, to let time have its way with Marnie the Method waitress. I don't know what I mean by that, exactly, but from my high ground as an established authority on things, it probably has the sound of poetry in it. Tonight, Bennie will be at the bar, ruining perfectly serviceable tequila with that revolting blue stuff and telling his confidants that Dennis Oldham, his friend, counseled him this very night to let time have its way with his chick. In the retelling, it will sound profound.

It is Friday night.

The kitchen, *my* kitchen, is humming under the baton of Mrs. McMichael, who likes to tell about how her husband made the cover of the *Daily News* with his tumble from the Queensborough Bridge in '69. Great year, 1969.

Mr. McMichael—whose first name, Duane, has been perpetuated in a string of Mrs. McMichael's dogs, the incumbent a mangy arthritic schnauzer—managed on that fateful July afternoon to shimmy out of his official Bridge & Tunnel Authority harness while slapping still another coat of rust-proofing red lead paint on the creaky strutwork of the old Queensborough. Duane McMichael was near the top of the Manhattan-side tower; it must have taken him quite a while to hit the East River. Faithful artisan, Duane McMichael was still clutching his gnarly red paintbrush when the police frogmen hauled him out. Mrs. McMichael recounts this with pride.

With the kitchen in capable hands, I consider paying a visit to Bennie's bar. Instead, I look in the phone book for Sally Wallach's number. Playing it aloof this morning by not hunting her down in the Thunder vault seems like not nearly so great an idea right now. She is not listed. I could call the station. Somebody there'd give it to me, and then make the appropriate notations on the john walls. Maybe later.

I leave Mrs. McMichael in charge and head downtown. Bennie is not behind the bar.

Around me spins a shuffling and unconfident mating ballet of costumed youngsters drinking designer beers out of bottles or slurping goblets full of crushed multicolored slime. Children don't drink whiskey anymore.

I, however, do, and order a Dewars from Bennie's replacement, a tall female of twenty or thirty with American southwest-colored half-moon cheeks that proffer themselves for inspection under the general blue malaise of Bennie's bar. "Bennie quit," she informs me. What happened? "He had a fight with this waitress who's sorta staying with him. Giving her his typical male deal. She has other ideas. Bennie got upset. He took off."

I should check my machine. Bennie might be trying to reach me.

I must look worried, because the bartendrix with the half-moon cheeks—which, I notice now, are finely and almost aristocratically beveled away from generous lips and look slightly not right only because their owner is so gangly that there abides in her a general disproportionality to everything around her—reassures me now with what I take for a guileless smile, though I myself am too guileless to tell for sure. "Hey," she says, "it's no big thing. Bennie quits all the time." The solicitousness of motherhood creeps into her voice. "He'll be back by midnight." She sets my scotch on an Evian water coaster and says, "Quitting is good therapy for Bennie. It's, like, an emotional safety valve."

Well, she's right. I consider displaying a little male solidarity by sticking around for the return of Bennie. I ponder Half-moon Cheeks' subtext. I consider calling the station for Sally Wallach's phone number and audition a couple of pretexts. I consider the odds that Sally Wallach sits forlornly unengaged this Friday evening by her princess phone, awaiting my call. There is no television in this bar. No MTV for Velez to do some guest mugging. In so desolate a place as a bar with no television it's hard not to look bored when you are; hard to pretend you're killing a little time instead of looking like you're on the skulk with no place else to go.

I go.

All right. Maybe 1969 wasn't such a great year, even though just about everyone worth assassinating had already been assassinated.

Richard Nixon took his oath of office to kick off the 1969 festivities. But then there were the Jets, and the Mets. There was also Vietnam, laying in wait for the likes of me to emerge from the cover of higher education. There was a college radio station in the heart of Springsteen country—Exit 9, to be precise—that featured Ellen Larkin late at night five nights a week. My segues are not always logical, but simple minds are easy to follow.

I'm tempted to spare you this part about Ellen Larkin and her late-night rock radio show. But if I do, you may be tempted to keep looking for some grand unifying theme to all this instead of accepting the perpetually simmering chaos that seems to clog the filters of my existence, as perhaps it does yours.

So here we go: Ellen Larkin.

Those were the heady days of Allison Steele. The Nightbird. Oh, dear, departed Allison—God, how she'd purr and whisper her whiskey-voiced incantations over these very FM airwaves, draping all that scruffy rock in silk stockings and garter belts. Oh, we loved the Nightbird. Allison, that dreamy fusion of the '60s iconoscape: sex and rock. To me, the music was mostly senseless, pretentious, self-absorbed noise, no better or worse than it is now. But I was willing to listen to whatever turned Allison Steele on. Night after night. And I was not alone.

Allison Steele was one of the chief reasons, though by no means the only one, why almost nobody listened to our college radio station, except during Ellen Larkin's slot. I know I'm being coy about which college, but Velez's current attorney, Fat Tom the Lawyer, is constantly after us about naming names. "Why give some avaricious slimeball like me a shot at suing you?" is Tom's line of reasoning, so for once I'm going to follow Tom's instructions and just say it's nestled in the sooty underbelly of New Jersey and was renowned in those days primarily as the weekend mecca for chaste Georgian Court girls and besotted Fairleigh Dickenson girls and even the stray militant Douglass girl—though Princeton women couldn't look far enough down their noses to bring us into view—and leave it at that. Investigate if you must.

I spied Ellen Larkin during the sweltering dusty dawn of 1969's fall semester. Ellen was manning a recruiting table for the college radio station, WRSU. I, the jock, manned the recruiting table for the crew team. Yes, I rowed crew back then, before it came to me that there were other roads to self-fulfillment besides freezing my ass off in the choppy embrace of a stinking riverlet full of beer cans and environmentally contaminated fishoids. Little did I suspect that very day how closely lurked just such a shot.

I must interrupt here to call Bennie's bar. It's after midnight. No messages on my machine. I sort of hope that the moon-cheeked girl—Hope, incidentally, is her name, so you can remember easily in case she makes another appearance in these pages—answers instead of Bennie. Hope seems to possess some wellspring of moist and mother-earthy openness that manages not to smother her overall targetworthiness, I've decided. If Hope answers, I am prepared to suggest we meet.

But no, it's Bennie.

And boy, is Bennie flabbergasted that *I* called *him*. I guess I don't go around calling listeners all that often, though I don't think anyone could accuse me of celebrity assholedness. Anyway, Bennie is a special case; after all, I've actually met him. Also, I'm feeling for Bennie tonight, and for all of us who suffer the stupid compulsion to come to terms with women.

"You were here?" Bennie demands. "You stopped in?" he keeps saying.

"I hear you had a fight," I try to interject.

"Shit, I'm sorry I missed ya," Bennie answers.

So I ask, "Straighten things out with your woman?"

"Huh?" Bennie says, "What? Oh, sure. Right." This plunges Bennie back into the miseries, where I expected to find him in the first place and where he is most comfortable. "The bitch. You know, it was me set her up with this fuckin' gig here. Me!"

Hey, Bennie. Welcome back.


To Ellen Larkin, I was a jock. That was all she needed to know. A woman with a consciousness as elevated as Ellen Larkin's had no time for frivolity.

Don't get me wrong. I would have bailed on the crew team sooner or later, even if I hadn't decided to scam Ellen Larkin. Maybe not right then, not that very year—but eventually.

So I began going to concerts sponsored by the station. Ellen Larkin would be a co-emcee. Concerts weren't just for music in those days; they were anti-war drug-and-beer fests with spasmodic tossing of arms and hair as the inclination arose. Some people danced. I stalked the periphery of things and put a stealthy, steamy peek on Ellen Larkin.

She wasn't hard to keep track of, even in strobe-slashed semi-darkness. Her hair was screamingly, outrageously red, and she made little attempt to steer any of it in common cause. She wore tight black shell tops under a floppy Air Force airman's coat. When she flipped her hair out of her eyes, a maneuver that required the coordinated effort of most of her upper musculature, her breasts would find their way out from under the lapels of the military coat and beguile me in whatever corner of the room I had set up surveillance.

But Ellen Larkin was only interested in talking to musicians and an anemic, sepulchral cabal of politico-poets. Them I considered uniformly shallow and affectatious; she, their dewy-eyed acolyte, I knew in my restless bones to be deep and passionate and wise.

There was a better than even chance, I had to admit, that Ellen Larkin was fucking anyone who had something nasty to say about Richard Nixon. I took the obvious course of action: I bought a G.I. field jacket and a guitar.

Once fixated, some people will pursue their object of desire against all reason. Take Bennie. "How do I get her to see what an ass she's making of herself?" Bennie asks me. How, I ask Bennie, is his girl making an ass out of herself?

"You ready for this, Dennis? She wants to go back to school."

I wait.

"She wants to study economics," he says, as if that explains it.

I bite.

"Can't you see? She's so impressionable. She'll wind up another Wall Street asshole MBA."

"I see what you mean," I tell Bennie, and in a way I do. She will certainly be an irretrievable case, from where Bennie sits. "You've got to let her make her own mistakes," I grit my teeth and say.

And I know what Bennie's going to say next. He's going to say, "But Dennis, the intimacy! The sex! Ya just can't expect me to write her the fuck off. We were in love, goddamn it!"

No, Bennie won't say this, because Bennie, sturdy steeltown stock Bennie, is hardly aware of the quicksand he's wading into, even as he speaks.

No, this is probably what *I* said, or thought, when the aromatic days of Ellen Larkin had come and gone.

# 3

INSIDE the glass tile wall resides a glow. It is neither warm nor triumphant nor even particularly conspicuous. Just a peculiar, diffident protrusion from beneath the scabrous concrete crust of New York City.

Two unornamented rectangular portals are all that relieve this slab, this translucent communal gravestone. From too far away to make out the inscriptions, the wall seems satisfied with its own noble obscurity.

I, who have hardly any business feeling emotion in its presence, come to the wall down here on the water once in a while. Not to reflect, but to check up on Lyndon McDonald, the closest thing the wall has to a permanent resident.

Dawn's gray imminence is Lyndon McDonald's time of preference for political pontification. Lyndon stands on a brick rampart overlooking the glowing glass altar, under a frail canopy of recently-planted swishy blue trees, and addresses the empty courtyard below him. He takes for his theme one of the glass wall's inscriptions—bits of letters composed by Vietnam's soon-to-be-dead to the folks back home. There are, I don't know, maybe thirty or forty of these battlefield farewells etched in the wall's glass blocks. None are ascribed to Lyndon McDonald, but Lyndon McDonald can recite them all.

Soon the bankers and traders and cocaine dealers and lawyers will begin the day's scavenge down here, the daily munch. But for now, for another hour maybe, Wall Street is the property and province of Lyndon McDonald and the leviathan mutant roaches that promenade from restaurant delivery chute to restaurant delivery chute before surrendering, with Lyndon McDonald, their nocturnal sovereignty. A few of the truly white folks are already at work, e-mailing to London and Zurich and all the other financial wonderlands where the sun and money wake up first. And at least some of them have surely heard Lyndon McDonald's honey-drip baritone creeping in off the East River waterfront and wafting into the crevasses of power with its melodically insane recitations. They don't have the numbers at this hour of the morning to venture too near the edge of civilization that Lyndon McDonald inhabits. These are the hours where finely-tailored suits and car service and President wristwatches lose their daytime currency and leave their preening owners as defenseless as if they were in the middle of the real jungle. Happily, the truly white folks seem to recognize and accept this, which suits Lyndon McDonald, who likes to be left alone with his audience of ghosts. For me—one of the truly white folks, I suppose—it's simply a term of co-existence between madmen and rogues in a place with plenty of both.

It's Wednesday. A few days since last we spoke. Don't worry. You haven't missed much.

It's hard sleeping in the middle of the week. I'm sure that my two-shift existence accounts for this; that, and the jet-lag jolt my bioclock suffers on weekends. Sometimes I wake up for the second shift—nine or ten at night—and there's just no going back to sleep later. Since I only drink socially now—that is, only in the presence of witnesses—I don't allow myself the luxury of sour-mash anesthesia. Most times I stay in and wait out the morning.

Tonight, I go out to wait it out.

There's a steady wind crackling its way across the East River from Brooklyn. Things look clean down here in the financial capital of the world. It rained a half-hearted rain for most of the night, managing to hose down this scrungy city and to wake me irreparably up. Lyndon McDonald appears not to have taken note of the precipitation. He's soaked.

I approach Lyndon from the south—South Ferry, up Water Street. Lyndon is standing under a soggy sapling reciting one of his favorite passages—a letter from a scared infantry boy to home somewhere in Kansas. It doesn't come right out and say so on the wall, but one is given to believe that these thoughts of his on the grimly inspiring fraternity of jungle patrol are the last his people in Kansas will share.

Here is Lyndon McDonald—truculent malodorous hulking bear, with a voice so sensually, mellifluously mismatched to the physical density of him that it almost makes you want to laugh except that no one in their right mind would give Lyndon McDonald occasion to suspect he was being laughed at; there's an elemental scent of barely bridled violence about Lyndon, though he seems mercifully oblivious to his own forbidding presence.

Lyndon stops talking as he hears me approach.

He doesn't normally; I guess he just stopped to catch his breath.

The back of Lyndon's fatigue jacket, not unlike the one I once bought to demonstrate my orthodoxy to Ellen Larkin, is merely damp. The front—the river side—is sodden and encrusted with spilled or regurgitated food. Faint echoes of Lyndon's voice seem to come back to us from across Water Street, where the fluorescence of finance begins to twinkle. Lyndon regards me, impassively.

And down below, in the center of the modest plaza, sits Lyndon's friends' tombstone. Against one of the portal jambs Lyndon has piled his sack of junk.

I wonder for a minute what the trickle of Wall Streeters would make—*are* making—of this surreptitious meeting between me and Lyndon McDonald. No doubt I am taken for a retail shopper in search of medication.

I have to be at work soon, at the Thunder.

Arielle, our new program manager, has announced that we'll be doing a remote from down here in a couple of weeks. Veterans Day. I think I'll have Lyndon McDonald, who is a veteran if there ever was one, as a guest; I'll sneak him on early in the program before anyone of corporate consequence is listening. If he does well, maybe Velez can make him a guest jockey on one of his teen-screamer video shows. From there it's just a short jump to syndicated television or maybe a local news show. Vietnam's human wreckage is hot box office these days.

And if he goes crazy and yells *fuck* over fifty thousand watts of FM airpower or grabs a technician and garrotes him with electrical cable, Velez will think of a way to blame it all on Arielle.

If Lyndon McDonald realized I was standing here plotting his show business debut he'd probably take my head between his supple scarred black killer hands and crush it like a pumpkin. This I imagine as I climb up onto Lyndon's rampart, struggling not to slide down the slippery stone incline on my shivering ass.

I take a taxi uptown. Dawn is taking hold, which means I'm late. My Rasta cabdriver is not inclined to tarry on the traditional side of the sound barrier, though, so I needn't fret about the time. I practically have to beg him to stop for a *Times*, so I can compose the opening newscast of the Velez & Oldham Show.

Oh—you were under the impression that I write my own newscasts?

Well, we at the Thunder are internetted to the world, of course, but computers give me hives and what's the use, anyway, of living in the very village where they publish the *New York Times* if you can't steal your newscast from it? What am I going to do, dream up *better* news?

Once we're settled in for the morning and I finish my first newsreading, I'll pick up a token rock item or two from *Rolling Stone* or

*Spin.* Most of our producers hold that no Thunder Rock newscast is complete without a chronicle of the music scene. Of course, Arielle hasn't dealt with the issue of a new producer for Velez & Oldham yet, so technically we are unproduced and I can include more or less whatever the hell I feel like in my news, bearing in mind as always that our audience represents a pretty short-throw worldview. Lyndon McDonald, who stores the detritus from his nose in the recesses of his hairlocks in the event of future use, probably represents the top-end of our audience's political awareness. Or would, if he listened to the radio. Which he actually does sometimes, when he can scavenge batteries for his discarded transistor. But I don't think he tunes in to the Thunder very often, preferring instead a Cuban nationalist station that broadcasts from some New Jersey slum.

Arielle has had a bulletin board installed in the one place nobody can claim to have missed it: the Thunder Rock crapper. With touches like this, I'm starting to come over to Arielle's side—tentatively. Arielle has hung a magic marker on a string next to the bulletin board; we're supposed to initial official notices in transit.

Thus on my way back from making room for more coffee I discover and initial a notice for a promotional party at a late-night club for fat Arabs and thin models located just below midtown Manhattan's welfare hotel and crack district. Everything here has its district. Attendance mandatory for Velez, me, Kenny Appleton, Cheryl Mann and Adrian when he finishes at midnight. I pencil in Hendy Markowitz's name at the bottom and scribble HM next to it.

I am small-minded and ungenerous at this hour.

Oh Christ, I forgot: we've got a guest today. A late-sixties meteor who vaporized a good three albums short of immortality. Just the kind of guy who has to get up at this hour to get any attention.

The guest will disrupt things, but that's later. Right now a dentist's office smell of too-clean permeates the premises; the overnight cleaning banshees flame-throw disinfectant everywhere as an expedient alternative to actually removing any of the crud, and here I am to inhale the toxic consequences. I kick Mr. Coffee in and light a cigarette—the minimum daily backroom sensory feedback we seedy mortals need to goad us on our frivolous way.

An unfamiliar engineer is fiddling with switches that she—*she!*—is undoubtedly unqualified to tamper with. Now, as I crib from an election story in the paper, I spy her running head-cleaning cassettes through the tape decks. Next she'll probably—oh, Christ, there she goes—straightening up Velez's leftover shit from bygone days. There will be hell to pay here at the Thunder, and I hope this denim-dreary doesn't look for me to cover her eager beaver when Velez gets wind of things.

Hendy Markowitz is stumbling through another of his cloying segues from a Fillmore-era block; he's squeaking through my earphones as they lay in patient anticipation on my newsdesk. Hendy sounds pretty psyched to be this close to the Velez & Oldham Show, timeslot-wise. He probably figures someone corporate will be tuning in right about now to listen to the flagship station's flagship show. I wouldn't put it past Hendy Markowitz to run accidentally past 5:56 a.m. just to make sure somebody up there is aware of his miserable existence. At the digital passage of 5:57, Hendy's ass is off the air; this, gentle reader, I personally guarantee.

It's 5:48. No sign of Velez.

Wednesday morning; yes, we are supposed to be working today. I tap on the window that separates our box—a starship amphitheater of gadgetry surrounding our two high-tech swivel stools—from the unadorned white cubicle where I retreat half-hourly to recite the news. The reason I have a separate place to read the news is that Velez's protomaniacal screwing around is beyond my capacity to maintain newsmanly decorum for even three-and-a-half minutes. As you probably know.

The new engineer finally looks my way. I give her a signal to flip on the studio intercom. She can't find it. I point. She still can't find it. I pantomime-scream at her and pretend to slam my fist down on my little coffee-ringed table in front of me. I watch her jaw drop. I jab my finger again toward her intercom button. She hits it.

"Good morning," I say. "Would you do me a favor and stick a tape into C-deck, just in case the star of the program doesn't show up in time to do it himself?"

"What tape?" she asks uncertainly. I've got her where I want her.

"Heeeyyy," I smile, "suit yourself. Whatever you like. By the way, how about sitting there while I read the news, and then hit *play* for me?"

"Play for you? Yeah—what do you want me to play for you?" It is 5:51. People all over this decaying metropolis have set their radios to rev in six minutes. No one will be surprised if Velez is not on the case at 5:57 but it would sure be nice if *something* came out at them from their radios besides me struggling with this sleepy, baggy enginette. I scoop up the *Times* and my news notes and hustle into the Velez &

Oldham box. At 5:56, if there's no sign of Velez, I'll lock myself and this enginette in here and fire the solid boosters.

I have about three minutes worth of news, plus the weather and a concert schedule to read if I need to kill some time. It's 5:55 and sure enough Hendy Markowitz is deep into reminiscing about being backstage at a Crosby, Stills, and Nash concert that I'll bet he wasn't within a thousand miles of. I think about our listeners; radios are warming up throughout the land. Waking up to the granny-glassed prattle of Hendy Markowitz is like waking up and finding out it's April 15th.

I'm not kidding, folks: in ninety seconds I'm pulling the plug on the little slammer.

An ear of mine cocked for shuffling in the outer sanctum, but no: Velez will not be answering the bell this glorious October morning. Son of a bitch. I'm glad there's a window in this place. Probably not another big-league soundbooth in the civilized world has an honest-to-God window in it. Must be Eichmann-witness-booth-gauge glass to keep out the city's sonic assault. I crane to see the street. It would be a simple matter to spy the Velezmobile prowling around down there on Sixth Avenue at this empty hour before the great urban munch spawns its no-prisoners Hong Kong-style traffic gnarl. If the Velezmobile is down there, which it very likely is not.

Okay, 5:56.40. Hendy has scant seconds to finish whatever the hell he's talking about. My trigger finger already caresses the toggle that will shortly send Hendy Markowitz to the fucking ether where he belongs.

The secret telephone rings.

"Hey, Coolie!" It's Velez, live from the Velezmobile. "Ya hear me?" Velez crows. Yeah, I say.

5:56.56. "We're on the air in four seconds, asshole," I advise my partner Velez.

"Cue me, Coolie. I'm ready."

Ah, why not? I slice Hendy Markowitz's throat mid-sentence, hit Velez's microphone, whisper "Go!" into the telephone and hold the earpiece up to the mike. Monitor needles jump comfortably up to near-red. I wrestle to pull my headset on with one hand; the enginette appears and helps me. I take back for now what I said about her before, but I reserve the right to reinstate.

" . . . from Sixth Avenue, where the traffic is just exactly like Oldham is always telling you: it *sucks!*" This Velez is saying from the crushed velvet of his varsity limousine. I just look out my window of privilege down onto the deserted boulevard and listen, wondering where Velez *really* is. Before long, my arm starts to get tired holding the phone up to Velez's microphone. The enginette, who at point-blank range now doesn't seem nearly so unredeemable, catches on and starts to dink around with things.

" . . . our special guest, Judd Tate of the legendary Standard Band, will be joining me in, ah, I dunno, probably an hour or so, unless he's stuck in the same damn mess I am. . . . If he is, then God only knows—"

The enginette has patched the phone line into one of those little jack holes that Velez is always putting his cigarettes out in on the input board—I know it's the input board because a sign on it says 'input board'—and now I can hang up the receiver and rest my arm; Velez is now mainlining directly from the back seat of his car to one-point-three million listeners who probably think this is too cool for words.

5:59.

"Now," Velez is saying, "let's go back to the palatial studios of WRTR, where I'd be right now if this city wasn't so screwed up all the time, to Dennis Oldham with news, sports, traffic, weather, and probably some other stuff. Dennis?"

So, "Thanks, Bobby," I say, the opening beats of that metronomic drone that ritualizes yet another day-beginning for all my children—Bennie, Bennie's ex-chick Marnie, the Bobs and Cathys and Alicia the poetess and all the rest—out there on the other end; and with "Here's what happened when we weren't looking," my trademark news sign-on, I launch into my cribbed capsule of the world's latest tumultuous spin.

Was it just a half hour ago that I left Lyndon McDonald, he simulating with swoops of his burly paws and whining whistling sound effects the progress of Colonel Elmo through a screaming incendiary thicket of North Vietnamese SAMs, me bundled and rushing as if I had something more important than that to do?

Well, I didn't have anything more important to do, and here I sit doing it.

The sun is up now and Lyndon has disappeared, I'm certain, into the nether regions to wait out the day. Night will be back and so will Lyndon. And so, sooner or later, will I.

I play the last news-slot commercial, one of those cutesy bantering boy-girl jobs where the characters sound like they just quit fucking long enough to let us know how great it is to bank at Chase. In the meantime, I confer with my partner Roberto Velez.

"How's the sound, Coolie?" Velez wants to know. I put our enginette on the line. She tells Velez that, against all odds, the sound isn't bad. "Kind of like a concert remote," is what she tells him, with more assurance than I would have guessed. Sure enough, Velez gets me back and says, "Hey Coolie, here's what we're gonna do: an impromptu remote broadcast from right here in the Velezmobile. I drive around all morning, you man the studio, let that babe take care of the music. Whaddaya say?"

I scramble. "What about Judd Tate of the legendary Standard Band?"

"Ah, shit," says Velez. "He showed up?"

And on cue, an emaciated Lone Star boy with a motel tan, more or less arranged inside elbow-worn buckskin and pegleg jeans that precede his deflated torso in a slooping roll comes bumping into the outer sanctum.

"Oh, you bet. He's here—body and soul," I report.

"What kinda shape?"

"About what you'd expect," I say. I'm not inclined to babysit this Judd Tate, and I'm sending Velez vibes to that effect.

"Okay, okay," Velez says. "You send him . . . wait a minute. Hey, where are we?" And to this I hear a female voice holler something in response.

"New driver?"

"Um, no, Coolie. See, it's like this: I gave Mario the day off. He said something about thinking about getting married today, so I let him skate in case he decided to go ahead with it. In command of the Velezmobile this morning—" I have Velez on the air now, ever vigilant for an inopportune 'fuck,' "—is my good friend Michelle. You remember Michelle, Coolie?"

"Gee, I dunno, Bob," I say. "How 'bout you, out there in radio-land—anybody remember Roberto mentioning his new buddy Michelle?"

"Ah," Velez scolds, "you little dickens, Coolie. Sandbagged me again, you bastard. You'll get your own show when you grow up, don't worry. Okay, Michelle, we're on big-time radio now so watch your mouth. Now, Dennis, I'm sure you remember hearing about Michelle. Our good friend Kiwi Corcoran from Black Rock Records told us about her at that dump Mortimer's last week."

Ah, the shirtfull; let there be light. "So, you driving around looking for a trailer hitch?"

"Jealousy is an ugly emotion, Coolie. Hey, Michelle—where the hell are we?"

Muffled squeaks.

"She old enough to drive that thing?" I ask Velez.

"How many times I gotta tell you—age is in the eyes of the beholder. An' I gonna be holdin' her everyplace she let me . . . ." Crackly cellular interruption for a moment; then: "Well, well, Dennis, it looks like we're passing through your very own neighborhood. Greenwich Village, the mincy whiteboys' barrio. How about that?"

Imagine: respectable businesses are paying a lot of money to sponsor this drivel.

"My neighborhood is not on your way to work, Velez."

But now comes the voice of the Velezmobile's guest pilot. "Hi, Mr. Oldham!"

Oh Jesus.

"Oh yeah—hi, listeners!" Velez is coaching her from the back seat. I say, "Let me talk to—"

"Oh, right, I almost forgot! I wanna say hi to all my new friends at Black Rock Records, and to all my old Phi Delt sisters—c'mon, wake up, sleepyheads! Oh, I *always* wanted to do this. Oh, this is the best, Mr. Vel—Bobby, I forgot . . . Jesus Christ, I'm *so* excited." A sudden swerving sound and a chorus of horns; as a gesture of solidarity, no doubt, Velez too utters the Lord's name in vain.

The enginette is cramming a tape into a deck. C'mon, I pray: bail us out.

"Hey, Michelle," Velez is saying now, *"are* you old enough to drive this thing?" I can't make out her response but Velez says, "Ah, don't worry about it. Neither does Mario, and you're a *way* better driver than he is. You haven't hit anybody all morning."

I spy Sally Wallach rushing in. Yes, one-point-three million people are gorging themselves on this fiasco, but here, provocatively flush of cheek and fervidly animated of brow, is my Sally—and in the eye of the storm I feel myself sucked ever nearer the black hole of inevitable, profound humiliation. Hot on Sally's tail is an apoplectic Hendy Markowitz, toting around his outraged countenance for all to inspect. I watch Sally swivel her way through the accumulated junk of the outer sanctum, Hendy Markowitz fishtailing after her like a derailed caboose. The radio god has a macabre sense of humor.

The enginette gives me thumbs up and I goose Velez. "We'll be right back to you in a while, Roberto, right after I play four or five CDs." My enginette, my spunky new comrade-in-arms, hits it.

Now that the initial hysteria has worn off, it occurs to me that this is actually a pretty funny idea. Why not have Squire Roberto cruise Manhattan in his limo, checking in from time to time from his $125,000 rolling window on the world? We could have a promotional contest: the Find Velez Sweepstakes. I have the power to provoke the sacking of every stretch limo in the city this morning. Some real *Day of the Locust*-quality destruction.

I peek beyond my enginette to the lounge, where Hendy Markowitz is gesticulating in cocoon-weaving semblance before Sally Wallach; Judd Tate has atrophied into wallow-eyed narcosis, cantilevered across the corner of the desk behind Sally. Sally, while I have a moment to digress, has braved this crisp autumn morning in a skirt short enough that when she shifts her weight from one leg to the other those sleek unblemished thighs can, from my fortuitous vantage point, be observed to flex beckoningly—one, then the other, then the first one again…oh boy.

Markowitz locks eyes with me, drilling me with his perm-festooned, designer-framed Westchester evil eye. Now he's moving in my direction. Hendy is not frail, exactly, but he's short in the most thoroughly undignified way and so comically unmenacing that I'm sure Sally Wallach could smack him around in my defense without too much difficulty. I jump up and reach the heavy soundbooth door just ahead of him and I jab the lock button. This is a common ploy on the Velez & Oldham Show; Velez barricades us in on a fairly regular basis. The soundproof door barely flinches when Hendy Markowitz kicks it. Behind him I watch Sally Wallach's eyes smile at Hendy's dervish and I begin to vow things that I vowed I wouldn't vow about Sally.

Does this surprise you at all?

Judd Tate has summoned the animation to open his guitar case, which I see is brimming with personal effects; he fishes out a nasal spray bottle, cocks his head back and fairly empties it into the cobwebby recesses of his cranium. I pick up the Velezmobile hotline: "What do you want me to do with your guest?"

In response, I hear rustling sounds. "Womphh. Humphh?" says Velez. Moments pass. "Hey, sorry. Michelle and I, we figured we'd stop at McDonald's and score ourselves a couple of McMuffs. Since we're stopped anyway. We got any McDonald's commercials on the slate?"

"No," I lie. We don't need to piss off Ronald McDonald with a restaurant review this morning.

"Okay," Velez says. "Tell you what. You get Judd Tate in the box. You ask him how his new CD is doing. If he has a new CD, which I doubt. Ask him about the legendary Standard Band and if any of his old boys can still find their ass with both hands, which I also doubt. Let him play a couple of tunes. He got a guitar with him?"

"He's got a guitar *case* with him. Hard to tell if there's an actual guitar in it."

Sally Wallach, WRTR's temporary Mother Theresa, has fetched coffee for Judd Tate, which is probably as close as Judd Tate ventures near actual food. Judd seems utterly unstirred by Sally's close-orbiting topography; I take this as not such a positive augury for an animated interview.

"Listen, Velez," I say. "Why don't you take Michelle back to her Mommy and get the hell in here and interview this crispy critter yourself?"

But I'm just pouting and Velez knows it. There's no reason why I shouldn't do this interview. I've interviewed easily twice as many fried musicians as Velez has, and plenty of them were in worse shape than old Judd Tate here. I high-sign Sally to steer our guest in the direction of the box. She'll have to get rid of Hendy Markowitz before I unlock the door, though.

I have two more minutes of music on the deck; Sally pulls in an extra chair while I shake the hand that in better days made guitars cry and dampened a generation of girls in their nether regions. Judd Tate appears at this range to be in overall command of his facilities and even manages to give me a dopily amiable grin. I brief him quickly. Live, we exchange some perfunctory grab-ass and then go to a digitally remastered Standard Band classic.

God, I think in spite of myself: those guys could play.

I ask Judd Tate what song he feels like treating us to.

"Whatever ya got words to, man," says Judd.

I look quickly at Sally, who pales. I say, "Uh, we didn't . . . look, why don't you just play an old standard. You know."

"Sure, man, no *problemo*," Judd Tate's head bobs. "Only thing is, see, I ain't got any words to nuthin' with me. Whatcha got words to?"

We're under thirty seconds. "Just do something you, you know, *know* the words to," I say.

"Oh, Christ, man," Judd Tate grins a leathery, once-cute dimpled grin at me, "I don't know the words to *nothin'*. Not, like, by heart."

I look at Sally, Sally looks at me. I wish I had more time for this. Judd Tate aw-shuckses us down to ten seconds. "Ah'm real sorry. I thought you'd have some words layin' around is all."

At eight seconds Sally, dear Sally, utters the magic words: "Album jackets."

"Goddamn!" Judd Tate and I say in respectable harmony. "Sally, why don't you show Judd here to the vault." Four seconds. The door squeaks open. The enginette has something cued; I don't give a shit what. Two seconds. The door squeaks closed. "We're back," I tell one-point-three million listeners, more than a handful of whom, I hope, are too young to care about Judd Tate, "with Judd Tate. And in just a few minutes, Judd will be laying down a few for us. But first—" And the enginette, to whom I suppose it's time to assign a name, kicks in with some new-release junk from a whiny Gen-X white girl with a what-else-is-new chip on her shoulder.

And as I settle back down and prepare to call Velez again, I watch Sally Wallach tow her charge, Judd Tate, across the lounge toward the Thunder vault. I watch Judd Tate put his hand lightly, sort of gallantly even, around Sally's waist. I watch Sally Wallach blush and smile.

# 4

My windows, except one, face the street. Not far down the street is a firehouse. The immediate neighborhood is lousy with restaurants and minimalist storefront boutiques catering to the leather underwear crowd, and magazine stands where *Backstage* is the hot paper. And Korean markets. Let's not forget those.

The street has trees on it; old defiant ones. Some have shown the fatalistic humor to twine themselves through fence iron and fire escape trestles, and to rut up the most treacherous efforts of generations of paving brigades. Theirs is an obstinacy emblematic of this chunk of New York City, steadfast in the teeth of relentless urban underplowing. Buildings here are old, mostly. My building is old.

The wispiest twigs of the chestnut tree at the entrance to my building brush up across this window. It is far and away the most charming feature of my apartment, and it is free. There is absolutely no charge for the soothing and unobtrusive caressment that presses its nose up against my insular existence. In the dead of winter, the chestnut's ice-encrusted branches do seem to threaten to punch their way through my steamy windowpanes, but now, this morning, the leaves in their generous autumn yellow make me thirsty for the cool breeze that insinuates them back and forth across the glass.

It is early and I sleep, in spurts, like a dead man. Yanked awake by the sentry's paranoia; nestled back down in the indescribable warmth that, for a few more hours, is mine.

The back window is cradled under what looks in my bedroom like a simple dormer and probably once was. But now a door, adjacent and perpendicular to the window, leads to an enclosed staircase to the roof. This entirely suitable piece of patched-together carpentry allows me almost exclusive access to the flat tar roof that overlooks a teeming garden courtyard below. Tomatoes are grown down there, and fat ponderous sunflowers and assorted green things that cannot help but find their way into the cuisine of Mrs. McMichael, who shares proprietorship of the garden with two Italian spinsters on the ground floor.

The sun, I see, riseth.

I'd like to take Jane up there with me right now, to watch the sunrise. She likes to peer down over the roof's creaky iron railing to the courtyard garden. She likes to smell the secret smell of things growing down there in the middle of all this stone and high sooty hardness.

But I don't want to hurry the day along. It will close itself down soon enough. I'll stay here and listen to the leaves fiddle, and maybe sleep some more, and let the sun take care of climbing out of the East River on its own.

In my unscrubbed news cubicle, I regard the undulations of Velez's shoulders in time with music unheard through the bulletproof glass partition and I contemplate violence. As an accredited newsman, I have plenty of violence to contemplate. It comes over the AP line, where I'm supposed to compose my news; it leaps from the slimy *New York Post* and the despicable *New York News*; and if you look in the right places you can even find a clipped chronicle of Big Apple depravity in the *Times*.

But what the hell; one man's senseless violence is another man's normal course of commerce. Like that fat guy who got blasted not long ago while having linguini with some nineteen-year-old nymph; you saw him on the front page of the *Post* in all his blood-and-sauce-soaked glory. Scharff, I think his name was. Weighed about three hundred pounds, which must have been a treat for the five-foot-three Puerto Rican Emergency Services guys to haul out of the little Italian restaurant. Scharff, it is generally assumed among us accredited journalists, trafficked with a dangerous element. Those who got a close-up look at his dinner companion have advanced some alternate theories, and who's to say it wasn't some Jesus-crazed cousin trying to rescue this little flower from the easy life? Nobody examined the babe's shoulder blades for calluses, but it's safe to assume she was sitting ankle-deep in olive oil with this revolting enormous diamond-studded sleazebucket for business-related purposes.

You just never know, as I frequently remind listeners of my newscasts. This Scharff fellow . . . victim, or creep in timely receipt of his just desserts? Look at the startled-kitten eyes of Mr. Scharff's dinner companion—what do you make of that look? Innocence lost? Please. Check out the vampire eye make-up and tell me she isn't calculating lost fees even as the wiry Puerto Ricans wedge themselves between the corner wall and the beached decedent in preparation for removal. I can hear the Spanish epithets flying as Mr. Scharff, God rest his soul, leaks bountifully into the custom lining of his big-dollar suit. The maitre'd offers Mr. Scharff's dinner companion a business card and a monogrammed linen napkin, into which she blows her cocaine-scorched nose and hands it back to him. I feel sure a tableau like this probably played itself out, though I couldn't swear.

My partner Roberto Velez observes from time to time that a newscast on a rock radio show is about as worthwhile as Mother Teresa's tits and if this were the Nightbird's heyday I'd tend to agree, but the fact is that it isn't kids who're listening to us anymore. At least, not many; while we weren't looking the *avant-garditude* of this place vaporized. The people who listen to us are 60's and 70's children—yuppies with a token sprinkling of nostalgia-starved throwbacks who, like us, manage to convince themselves that they're still unrepentant rockers under all the Brooks Brothers. And we indulge this mass self-delusion shamelessly, in the interest of doing the big numbers for the big dollars, et cetera.

While Velez and Cheryl Mann and Adrian and the others make like next week's Crosby, Stills and Nash reunion is the paramount event in our listeners' lives, I am in charge of the reality therapy: our listeners number among them the generation that is taking over the world, for Christ's sake, and they need to know what's happening in it. We run call-in contests on Velez & Oldham, and half the calls are by goddamn carphone.

Ringo Starr is a grandfather.

Nobody in rock—okay, except Keith Richards, the old buzzard—gives good, credible danger anymore. Anybody worthy of the reputation drugged himself to death long ago in the interest of the mythology. Yet on we go, pretending our generation hasn't been asleep and having babies and becoming their former worst nightmares for the last twenty years.

So my job is to deliver a distillation of the world's events and not sound like somebody's old dad. I do an okay job of this. It is not hard, even though in real life I am somebody's old dad, two weekends a month.

Jane is piddling around in what becomes her room two weekends a month; it's almost nine o'clock on this Sunday morning. Five or ten minutes ago it was Friday night and Jane was sitting in my Volvo heading down FDR Drive, identifying skyscrapers for me. This is a favorite hobby of hers, and although she is only five years and five months old she can name more New York City landmarks than I can.

On Sunday mornings she wakes up weird. Saturdays she'll be up by seven, comfortable in the completeness of the day we have ahead of us. Sunday, she pretends not to be awake until ten or sometimes eleven. I tell myself it's because she thinks the sooner our day officially begins, the sooner it will end. Am I imagining a subtext beyond the five-year-old psyche? She's effectively blown me off by midafternoon on Sundays, and the countdown to her mother's arrival is excruciating.

I hear music. Jane has been nuts about hi-fi stuff since the first time I brought her to the Thunder studios to screw around with the buttons while Velez and I taped a show for a subsequent fraudulently live broadcast. We do this more often than you think; you wonder why the line's always busy when you call in to win a pair of concert tickets? It's because the program was taped days ago, Velez gave the tickets to some woman, and there's nobody home at WRTR. Anyway, Jane made her Thunder Rock debut and now I spoil her by packing her twice-a-month bedroom with gadgetry of every description. Jane's room could qualify for an FAA control tower license. And the goddamned thing is that she knows how to use most of the stuff.

She's keeping the volume down so I won't know she's awake. I think today we'll go to Mohammed's Electronics and buy her a set of headphones. Let her mother be a prick and say no to her. I'm going to spoil the shit out of this little girl. Two weekends a month isn't enough time to say no.

But Sunday will end, bless it. The Giants, a collection of what Velez characterizes as notorious homosexuals masquerading as a National Football League franchise, will lose to the spread and cost me money. And yet all is not lost, because tonight is WRTR bowling night.

Bowling night is a howling, blistering workout for a number of reasons. One is that Velez's monstrous ego cannot brook defeat in even so stupid a game as bowling, which I suspect was invented by Norse warriors using bound and gagged Irish prisoners as pins. Velez chooses the teams so that they are heavily weighted in his own favor, and then he insists on playing for beers. Ultimately, bloated on Bud and triumph, Velez will pick up the tab for our three lanes and the liquor anyway.

We bowl in just about the hippest room in town: the Bowl-Mor Lanes on University Place in the Village. It occupies two floors of a building erected by cave dwellers at the time of the most recent thaw. You get there by shiny freight elevator, and in the event of fire the plan is that you burn to death. Management serves alcohol and looks the other way. Beer puddles provide an interesting variation on regulation bowling. And, of course, we are treated like celebrities, even by the real celebrities who come to Bowl-Mor.

My own enthusiasm owes to the recent attendance of Sally Wallach, a womanchild closer in age to Jane Oldham than to her father, me. Sally stinks at bowling, and it is only as a favor to me that Velez picks her for our team. We ameliorate her ineptness by cheating on the score sheets. I've been giving Sally Wallach some bowling pointers in recent outings, and I sense her appreciation even if it's getting her no closer to knocking down those pins.

Fat Mr. Scharff, if that was his name, friend of high-rollers and players for keeps, was about my age, I remember noting as I cribbed the story from the *Times*. I couldn't fathom at the time that somebody my age could weigh three hundred pounds. Scharff's dinner companion was a year shy of Sally Wallach's age, though light-years ahead in turned stones. There's an uncomfortable symmetry to this.

In fifteen years some three-hundred-pound pig will be lusting after Jane Oldham is what I guess I'm getting at. And are my intentions materially loftier toward Sally Wallach? Are my intentions honorable? They are not, I have to tell you, as we sit here on these molded plastic benches watching Sally wrestle a ball off the return rail and hoist it to her bosom. Her legs are strong and her shoulders are broad; she's not overwhelmed by the mass of the ball as much as its offensive unfamiliarity. Jeans and a sweater is all I need to tell you; hair ponytailed, not a single hit of make-up. She rolled out of bed looking like this, I have no doubt.

Do I want to treat her with respect and dignity, so that in three months when they haul all the Christmas crap off the streets and Sally leaves, she'll say, "I never met anyone like you, Dennis. I've never felt so respected, so . . . dignified."?

No! I want her to say she's never going to leave my side, that age is nothing, that she's never met a man like me. Then I can take her cold, fluttering fingers in my hands and tell her how it's best that she move on, that what we shared was precious in its time, a moment in two lives never to be recaptured but never to be forgotten.

I'm no better than Bennie from Bennie's bar. Another sad delusionary. No wonder I work in radio, where just like my partner Velez I can pretend to be anything you one-point-three million people want me to be.

Not two hours ago Jane's mother made the pick-up. I probably have five-year-old smells on me yet. Sally Wallach plunks down next to me—this has become automatic. Paranoia roils: I feel Jane peering over my shoulder to see for herself what her father considers all right for her to allow men two decades her senior to do to her. I give Sally Wallach a congratulatory pat on the leg. Not the knee, exactly, but a circumspect distance from her intimate portions. Sally leans in and her ponytail finds its way onto my shoulder. I glance around like a car thief and catch ill-concealed accusations from the station women and foamy-mouthed encouragement from Velez. Any one of these friends of mine could one day be sitting in an Italian restaurant, I realize, sucking linguine and flashing his cheap pinkie ring into Jane Oldham's impressionable eyes, patting her strong, muscular thigh under the guinea-checker tablecloth, peeking down my daughter's top for a look at a heart-stopping turn of flesh.

There's bowling going on here, incidentally. I take a rejectionist posture and feign embarrassment when my tosses knock down pins. I am not unathletic—you'll remember that I rowed the highly toxic Raritan before my rock epiphany—but bowling isn't a sport. Bowling is something for people whose cemetery plots aren't yet paid for in full to do in the meantime. Taking pride in knocking down bowling pins is a particularly abject form of self-deprecation.

Except for professional bowlers, everyone feels the same way I do about bowling until they've had something to drink, smoke or snort. After that, bowling takes on whole new nuances. People seem to taste life-metaphors in the careening of giant plastic balls down the green gutters of failure, while preening white pins the shape of corporate receptionists stick their tongues out at each ball's impotent passing. And quite beyond the symbolism, there's the ritual cycle of sitting, rising, shuffling, wiggling, creeping, crouching, swinging, heaving, twisting, shouting, swearing, gesturing, retreating, scribbling, and sitting to refresh oneself with beer and dope. Bowling is not a whole lot different from the standing, sitting, kneeling, ingesting and processioning that goes on in church, is it? Abetting a different sort of high, but pretty much the same drill.

The scoring of these contests is a work of fiction. Of the entire Thunder Rock crew, only Hendy Markowitz could possibly know how to keep a bowling score, with all that carrying over of 10's from one inning to another. And Hendy works Sunday nights. Sunday nights are Hendy's only shot at an audience; he doesn't mind missing out on the camaraderie and the grab-ass of the Bowl-Mor excursions. Hendy hopes the old building that houses the Bowl-Mor lanes, as well as a dinky little tennis court and a parking garage, will choose one of these Sunday nights to collapse. Then Rolling Thunder Radio will be all Hendy's. It's not much of a plan, but it's a plan, and it's all Hendy's got.

Jane, my daughter, weighs heavily on my mind. When I go home, my apartment will still smell of her, and of the anger and confusion attending her departure, like the smell lightning leaves in the summer night sky. I'll wander around my apartment and wait for it to go away. Round about three or four a.m., after I've asked and answered all the usual questions and endured the mandatory bi-weekly self-flagellation, it will.

An alternative is not to go home at all.

"I think," says my friend and partner Roberto Velez, who is, as is his custom, unescorted for tonight's bowling excursion, "you're staring at a solid opportunity to get the old weasel waxed." I don't need to ask; Sally Wallach is preparing to negotiate a ball down the alley. There's an odd absence of salaciousness in Velez's observation; it's Roberto Velez at his most admirably analytical. Neither is there the slightest hint of competition. Velez wouldn't dream of hitting on Sally Wallach once he's put the issue of her and me on the table. No 'you nail her or I will.' Such is the depth of Velez's loyalty.

Sally is perched, stiff-backed, at the top of the runway or whatever you call the place where you slip and slide your way toward the pins. She cradles the ball under her chin, like a deco statuette caressing a glowing globe. Her entire being defies the gravity of city existence. She's a girl in a bubble. Unafflicted by the New York need to be perceived as brilliant and neurotic. Soot and vulgarity deflect away from her. Look at her.

This is not the first time I haven't known what to do about a woman. Take Ellen Larkin, who I haven't told you much about yet but I'm working my way up to. The big difference here at the Bowl-Mor lanes on an early autumn Sunday night is the age thing. I am afraid of women older than I; I am afraid of women my age. Now I discover that I am, if possible, even more afraid of the young and unscarred.

If I had a regular schedule, I might have a better sense of the passage of my life's time. Do you think? A week goes by; I know this because Velez and I have knocked off five programs—not because I've gone to bed five times and gotten up five times and brushed my teeth five times and had five sets of meals. If I only had a reliable dividing line between one day or year and the next, things might start getting more . . . I don't know.

I don't need reminders of the passage of time. Just the benefits.

Sally Wallach gives every evidence of being oblivious to my turmoil. Velez would sound her out if I asked him but I'd be smacked-ass embarrassed to admit that I don't know how to proceed, even though I know that Velez knows that I don't know how to proceed or whether to proceed. Velez won't embarrass me that way. He plays along with the aloofness I wrap my neuroses in, just like I play along with his hippest-spic-in-town persona. He probably finds chivalry in my reticence.

But what about Sally, who has sidled clumsily down the runway and spun her ball on its irresolute way down the alley and now waits to see if the alley is short enough for the ball to take out a few pins before it tails off into the gutter or just runs out of gas and comes to a stop on one of its finger holes in front of the scornful fat-assed pins? Is it conceivable that she doubts my craving? What can she be making of the front I'm putting up in my own defense? Do I sound more and more like Bennie? Do you begin to understand why I'm so good at talking to the thousands of Bennies in this town?

We leave before the Bowl-Mor closes. I'm not sure if the Bowl-Mor ever actually closes. It might be the bowling equivalent of the Empire Diner, which has been open every single minute since the late 70's, and where we—seven of us, including Sally Wallach—now find ourselves. Velez's limo sits in the fluorescence of the Empire twenty feet under our noses. There are plenty of people here, as the clubs flush out for the morning. Two technicians, boys Sally's age, flank her on one side of the table, but that's okay. Something's happening here, something that may be about to transcend the adolescent jockeying for position at a table in a diner. Velez has observed it too, and remarked on the way over in the limousine that Sally would soon be my slave.

Velez drives. The management of WRTR gives its drivers strict orders not to relinquish command of the limo to Velez. Velez gives them the night off or, if they resist, fires them. Velez loves to drive the limo. I sit in the front seat next to Velez. Behind us are Sally Wallach, the two techie boys, the young woman engineer who saved the Velez & Oldham Show's ass a few days ago when Velez and Kiwi Corcoran's friend Michelle spent the morning joyriding in this very vehicle, and a tall female in torn jeans and a biker jacket over an 'Elite Models' tee shirt that she doesn't appear to have had to steal from anybody.

"You're confusing her, Coolie," Velez tells me. "Good boy. She's in your pocket."

# 5

THE Empire Diner, a place even more confused than I about the passage of time, since it has never once closed in all the years of its existence, is a congenial location for the temporary suspension of events. Here, then, we sit, the seven of us, waiting for burgers and eggs, glasses half-raised to or half-lowered from lips—which are the optimists?—while I take you back to when I first learned how little I knew about women. The people around me seem to be resisting this digression; they persist in moving ahead with their breathless and yet weary multilogue on bowling and rock radio. Their voices, the collective voice of this third Formica-topped table to the right of the Empire Diner's front door, including the voice of Sally Wallach—though by no means do I wish to lump dear Sally in with the pimply twin techies or our game, winsome enginette or the Elite model—seem to have thickened into an aural pudding, eddying and lapping gooily at my waist. If they'd just shut up then poor Sally wouldn't feel as though politeness, one of Sally's most fastidious qualities, required her empathetically juvenile responses.

Something pink has begun up in the sky. We'll be going straight from the Empire Diner to work, not for the first time.

To me and the rest of the uninitiated, student political activists were creatures of a loftier social order. They were people with a fully cultivated comprehension of what in life was essential, what was worth spending passion on, and what was superfluous or worse: bourgeois bullshit. They were not reluctant to share their views. They argued well, irrespective, I've since realized, of the merits or even relevance of their positions. They were crusaders and polemicists and elitists and conspirators and paranoiacs and they abided by an intricate political canon with profligate druggery and intracause fucking as the principal sacraments.

They were celebrities, and they cleaved to celebrity—the ultimate bourgeois bullshit institution.

To be a student political activist of consequence, however, you had to assume a pose of disdain for the intrigue and notoriety that, during the latter years of Vietnam, couldn't help but swirl up around you like some narcotic incense. You secreted importance from every pore; it stained your clothes and you wore it proudly. The minute you started acting like a celebrity, though, you could count on losing your political legitimacy like poop through a goose.

No doubt there were those who felt a part of grand purpose, and I think a few of them probably read passages from some of the trendier leftist treatises. But, like today, attitude was where it was at.

Ellen Larkin put out attitude in generous, fulminating gales. Physically, she was a billboard of radical chic: defiantly uncut and uncombed red cascading mottles of glorious hair; the ever-present Airman's coat, even when it was too hot to wear much under it; standard-issue uniform torn jeans, with red bandanna patches under both ass cheeks that looked like a crazy-quilt push-up bra. Tie-dyed caressment of that impertinent bosom. Studied grubbiness—oh, but it was all a sham, because how could she be oblivious to the trail of men and boys who scampered along behind her, pitching her with politics and music and that self-conscious pubescence passing itself off as poetry until somebody strumbled up a tune for it and sold it to a frat-house party band for a six-pack and a joint?

Nor, I found out, was this some unconscious emission of colorless, odorless mating potion on Ellen Larkin's part. For Ellen was to turn out to be a creature of political convenience; a sorceress in camouflage. Which was a good thing for me, now that I think of it, because if it were otherwise, if Ellen Larkin were what she had advertised, then I wouldn't have had a shot in hell.

So dense was the human orbit around Ellen Larkin that catching her in an isolated moment was not a realistic strategy. But it was the only one I had, so I started gravitating toward the political whirlpool. I checked billboards for notices of meetings. I made notes. I may have flashed a number of peace signs in the course of my ricocheting rounds. I told my friends I was too busy to conduct what up until then had been my normal existence, consisting mainly of basketball and alcohol and sorties across the singed, dilapidated demi-city that separated our campus from the University's far more politically-conscious—well, militant actually, as I remember—women's college. I showed up for meetings, late enough that I didn't run the risk of being engaged in political discussion and thus unmasked for the horny fraud I was.

Ellen Larkin's presence could be counted upon; she'd be seated on the epicenter of this real and manufactured emotional tumult, lending the kind of self-denying glamour to these disarrayed proceedings that Jane Fonda was concurrently providing to more ambitious goings-on country-wide. I suspect that Ellen Larkin kept more than a casual eye on Jane Fonda's comportment in the eye of the anti-war hurricane, picking up style points and a sense of the boundaries separating the movement celebrities from the colorless troops. And it would be none other than Jane Fonda who would soon season our modest campus with the necessary atmospherics to round off Ellen Larkin's heels for me.

It took me four or five organizing committee meetings before Ellen Larkin bestowed upon me her first nod of recognition. From then, however, things slipped and slid their way along at a pace that even today is difficult for me to credit as happenstance.

I entered into our formal relationship in the capacity of pack mule. A meeting of the organizing committee—what organizing committee, you ask? Well, in the utterly *ad hoc* world of campus politics, plenty of organizing needed doing just to keep pace with the Richard Nixon juggernaut, never mind the fringe activities like women's rights rallies and union solidarity rallies and politico-poetry readings and teach-ins where white college students ventured into the inner city to explain to poor blacks the evil of having white politicians sending black children to Southeast Asia, and even the regularly scheduled beer barrel grab-asses that all of a sudden took on the highmindedness of a Bastille storming. The self-anointed organizing committee took all this in hand.

The calendar was a prime topic of conversation at this particular organizing committee meeting. The calendar, as I recall, seemed to be conspiring against most of what was trying to get organized. The problem, as Ellen Larkin and I heard separately but from close enough range that the lines of her face, previously unapparent to me, poured more fuel on my clandestine lust, was that the school year was about to end, and all the marchers and chanters and sitters-in who demonstrated mainly because they had to be here another couple of weeks anyway and it beat studying for final exams—which were on the verge of being canceled because the faculty felt an institutional gesture was in order—would bolt for the Jersey shore the instant they got the green light, leaving the organizing committee with only its elite, paltry self to organize. Ellen Larkin and I could appreciate, from our titillating proximity, the urgency of the problem.

I remember Ellen's face as if it were yesterday. In the too-close hallway headquarters of the organizing committee, the accumulated body heat had produced a sheen on Ellen's freckled forehead, and random red hairs filigreed their way back and forth across it like an hallucinogenic Triple-A highway map. It took no great imagination on my part to picture her looking exactly this way after intercourse, eyes and nose wide to drink in the vapors and pigments of its aftermath, those thin blue lips parted in the serenely self-satisfied decelerating rhythm of her breathing. Oh boy, how I longed to be the perpetrator of such a moment.

From behind my cover as a student activist, I sat and calculated how many people in the room had fucked Ellen Larkin, or, to be more precise—since I viewed Ellen as the absolute master of her existence—how many people in the room Ellen Larkin had fucked. It was, I judged, a safe bet that the three or four scruffiest and most roisterous of the organizing committee ringleaders had shared moments of intimate political communion with my Ellen. This meant nothing to me. Actually, it meant everything to me, because these stringy kamikaze poet-bombasts had all the credentials that I hadn't. It was not, for me, an encouraging organizing committee meeting.

But then opportunity presented itself to me, cloaked in the most banal of circumstances. Ellen, you see, was on the agenda at the end of the organizing committee meeting, after the most consequential of the pissing had been contested, after representatives of one or two factions had stormed out with just the sort of shouted imprecations that I bet had earned Leon Trotsky a hatchet in his goofy head.

Ellen, as the most listened-to radio DJ on the college station, was a central cog in the movement's propaganda effort; it was Ellen who would exhort and seduce the stolidly apathetic into showing up for this or that quasi-political happening. Just prior to this particular organizing committee meeting, in fact, Ellen Larkin had been broadcasting remote from outside the main dining hall, and had been forced to haul several armloads of broadcast equipment along with her.

Up bounced Ellen to make her announcements. She displayed a verve that was, sadly, no longer matched by those organizing committee members who had remained and were not busy horning their jargon at each other. I paid her my rapt respect, and hoped she noticed. I felt fleetingly sorry for her; she couldn't see, poor Ellen, how irrelevant women were in the heat of such revolutionary combustion. Perhaps, I began to think, I had overestimated Ellen Larkin's canny.

There was, I knew by now, an unofficial concluding signal to the organizing committee's proceedings: when members began inquiring of each other about the availability of dope, you knew that all that could be accomplished had been accomplished. Such rumblings now undercut and all but drowned out Ellen Larkin's final announcement: that she needed help humping her sound stuff back up to the WRSU studio.

A lone soldier—a newcomer to the fight, perhaps, but pure of spirit and broad of shoulder—heeded Ellen's plea for help. I was beside her so fast that I kicked a small hole in the fabric cover of a speaker cabinet in Ellen's pile of electronic things; it went unnoticed. She looked at me blankly for a moment, uncomprehending, I suppose, of my intentions; then past me around the room for volunteers among the cabal. I looked around with her, giving anyone who noticed to understand that this particular revolutionary initiative was under control.

"Hi," she sighed. I was not foolish enough to read anything into this sigh.

"Need help?" I suppose I grinned stupidly.

Ellen flapped her hands, signaling her abandonment by the organizing committee and her acquiescence to my offer. I told her my name and, in keeping with her celebrity, it didn't occur to her to tell me hers.

Unbeknownst to me, the college radio studio was on the top floor of the very building where the organizing committee was, as we spoke, disappearing into the woodwork like cockroaches before the light. It didn't matter; I'd have carried Ellen's stuff to New York on my back if she'd told me to. But it wasn't ten minutes later that her gear was redeployed around what struck me at the time as a rubble heap of a studio—today, I know what a rubble heap of a studio is—and, after a few indecisive shuffles on my part, yes! Ellen Larkin asked me if I felt like sticking around for a while.

Welcome to radio, Dennis Oldham.

Back at the Empire Diner, things feel like they're getting ready to happen. A WRTR driver has found us out, and now sits at the wheel of the Velezmobile. This one is a brawny-shouldered, no-nonsense beast of the species generally assigned to produce Velez for work in the morning. In the back seat of the limousine, Ms. Elite is making a few phone calls while our two techie lads sit across from her, watching her lips move. Our enginette has gone home to bed. Inside the diner, Sally Wallach is dozing, her head resting gently against the grimy window of morning. Velez is cooking something in the kitchen; there is no limit to the tolerance these people show celebrity here at the Empire. I sit and observe the flattening of Sally's auburn hair against the streaked glass; occasionally I look outside into the ominous good humor of the morning sun.

The DJ team from a nearby dance club now plunks down into a nearby booth. One, a heavy-breasted girl armed with an ammo-belt, recognizes Velez's cackles from the griddle and bounds over the counter to join him. Our driver is taking all this in, not approvingly. He eyes me, taps his watch, and does this thing with his shoulders that's supposed to look like, "Don't make me get up and come in there after you clowns." I give him a surreptitious sneer, cloaked in deniability. I can't be absolutely sure that this guy knows I'm protected, after all. I don't know where they get these guys, but I'm willing to bet this particular one has done time.

I'm not in the least bit tired. My body has long since given up trying to calculate when it's supposed to feel like going to sleep, except for the post-Velez & Oldham Show narcosis that tends to take hold around one p.m. But right now, at five-fifteen of this October morn, I'm pretty ready.

And, I have to report, I'm feeling vapidly parental toward the lavishly proportioned lass now lightly snoring across the glittery Formica from me. I wish it were otherwise because the backwash of Jane Oldham's monthly visit has, as usual, left me in need. And I wish what I needed from Sally Wallach was an immediate and incautious coupling; believe me, I'm this close to being able to wallow in the prospect of secret, shared adolescent intimacies with her, like heavy eyebrow work between us from across the Thunder studio, and glances in the full and requited expectation of return glances on a knell unheard by the rest of the troupe. I have a history of easy self-delusion and I think, soon, I may fully delude myself into messiness with Sally. But of that I am not, right this second, in need.

Here comes my partner Roberto Velez. He has spilled something Mexican on his tie and he looks kind of wired. His hair glistens with the brilliantine potion of cooking-labor sweat and vaporized griddle crud. A casual follower of gossip journalism might observe the half-sentence movements of my partner and draw some conclusions regarding drug use.

We pile into the Velezmobile—Velez, me, and a sleepy, dewy Sally—more or less on top of Ms. Elite and the techie twins. The uncontested center of gravity is Ms. Elite, pressing up against the Mexican-stained tie of my partner Velez, angling. For what? Gold dust? Angel dust? Notoriety? Wrong, friends. The limo.

"Bobby," she says, "I gotta be at Battery Park in exactly one half hour or it's my ass. I wonder. . . ."

Velez knows what's coming, and I know she'll get what she wants eventually but it won't come cheap. Velez reaches for the phone and pretends to call the station, so he can feign distraction.

"Hello, Arielle?" Velez dissembles into the phone.

"We're shooting at goddamn dawn, Bobby, which it's already past—what's, what the hell—" she's discovered a wet Mexican stain streak down the breast slope of her Elite tee shirt. She snatches a WRTR Thunder Rock ballcap from the head of techie two and rubs furiously at the streak, with an effect something like having her tit fingerpainted by an angry first grade class. This mindless eroticism instantly renders the techie boys spellbound and I can't say I blame them. There's nothing under this Elite tee shirt except five feet and eleven inches of efflorescent Kansas childflesh, thoroughly oblivious to the puddles of worship at her feet; I study this person from my vantage point, wedged between Sally and the limousine door, and I can't put my finger on it but there's something about her that's not quite right. Even by model standards. Especially by model standards. Some of the usual stuff is missing here, like the vacuous self-absorption and telltale teen locutions. Now she fishes in her floppy leather backpack and pulls out a silky shirt and leans forward on the seat in front of Velez and hauls her stained black Elite tee shirt up over her shoulders and off. And for the couple of seconds it takes her to ball up the dirty tee shirt and stuff it into the depths of her leather bag and then angle herself into her silk blouse and tie it in front, Velez and techies one and two and Sally Wallach and I pay silent homage to two of the most gloriously gravity-defying breasts that one could hope to encounter at this or any other time of the day.

Sally, I notice, seems very impressed with this facile little gesture of Ms. Elite's.

I, I notice, am impressed with Sally Wallach's reaction to the momentary display of Ms. Elite's two-hundred-or-so-dollar-an-hour anatomy; no evidence whatever of envy or competitive pique or abashedness or fluster. She thinks Ms. Elite is cool. Not that she, Sally Wallach, would be likely to follow Ms. Elite's lead and bare herself in casual company, even for so understandable a reason as a Mexican-slathered tee shirt.

And notwithstanding the celestial engineering of Ms. Elite, who at two hundred dollars an hour is the best bargain in New York City this fall, the amused crinkle in the corners of Sally Wallach's eyes, amethyst in this breezy crisp morningrise, tells me that she wouldn't trade her own.

Now our driver launches us into the morning. The Velezmobile's g-force sucks me forward in my seat, as if I'm maneuvering for a last glimpse of Ms. Elite's chest. I plump presently back into my seat, next to Sally Wallach, feeling the sex-charged ion cloud slowly, very slowly, dissipate around us. Then the phone rings and Velez, who's frozen in the middle of his bogus call to Arielle, pretends to put her on hold, only to find the real Arielle on the other line. Fortunately, nobody is paying the slightest attention to any of this.

We skid to a stop at a red light on Twenty-third Street and I jump out and make a dash for a corner newsstand. The driver begins to edge out into the intersection while I dodge early morning traffic back toward the limo; I detect a sneer on the driver's face. Velez kicks open the door and I just about hurl myself through it as the driver wheels out and up Sixth Avenue. It's five-twenty-one a.m., Monday morning. Somebody tunes in Thunder Rock on the Velezmobile's ear-rupture sound system; we are greeted by Hendy Markowitz's dippy whine. Velez and I reach for the console but Sally Wallach anticipates us and punches up a teen screamer—*"If you ain't crankin' it, you must be yankin' it!"* You know.

Of the six of us bouncing around in our crushed velour Velezmobile passenger coach, I reckon only Velez and I have contemplated mortality on a personal level. I may be underestimating my young friends here. And this doesn't include our driver, who may have more intimate experiences with mortality than I really want to hear about. But when you're, say, Sally Wallach's age, or Ms. Elite's—roughly the same—the cosmic significance thing is a pretty remote consideration day-to-day. I was their age once upon a time; pathetically short-term and shallow as I recall, with instant corporeal gratification at the very top of my list. Can I expect more from them, especially since they don't have a TV war to give their existence a little context?

So Ms. Elite's breasts, for one immediate example, must at this point in her life seem to her to be an immutable fact of her person, instead of the highly transitory commodity that they really are. It's useless to point this out to her. Intellectually, she'd accept it, but it's hardly a reason for her to make life changes. Her reaction, if she's anything like I was that late afternoon in the WRSU radio studio with Ellen Larkin, introducing myself to the impenetrable gadgetry of broadcast, would be: "So what?" She'd have a point. So what. So she's not going to look like this forever. As far ahead as she cares to foresee, those breasts are going to last her plenty long enough. The mere exercise of considering a post-world-class-breast existence denies, in a way, the legitimacy of her life now. The moment is the thing—and the breasts are here, now, where and when I need them. Anything beyond that is boring.

All this occurs to me—I swear—in about the fifteen seconds between the time I notice on the second page of the *Times* business section that the corporate monolith that WRTR, the Thunder, calls Daddy is about to cut bait on all subsidiaries not related to their core business—which is ensnaring the Third World in indentured servitude—and the explosive instant when the same intelligence, via our station manager Arielle, registers on my friend and partner Roberto Velez.

"To whom?" Velez asks through clenched teeth; this is how I know we're on the same page.

"When?" Velez just about whispers into the receiver. The WRTR junior staff in attendance just now—techies one and two, Sally Wallach—seem to know something is not right. Ms. Elite is kneeling forward between Sally and me, making pliant conversation with our driver.

"He can't do that," Velez says next, unconvincingly.

I search for more in the *Times*, but the *Times* is just doing its reportive duty and seems to care every bit as little about the crumbling ramparts of WRTR as Ms. Elite. So hypocritical of this fucking newspaper, where so much ink is dedicated to accusing the *Wall Street Journal* of worshipping corporate avarice, that there's not even a hint of compassion for the lives facing upheaval at the Thunder. "Tough shit," the spare, matter-of-fact story seems to be saying directly to me. "Who cares about a radio station anyway, beyond its commodity value? No different from a pair of temporarily extraordinary breasts, except that ownership is transferable. Nothing of lasting value to work up a sweat about. It's just people talking and music playing; all very forgettable stuff compared with about three hundred other events recorded in these pages today alone."

Well, all that may be, and now's a pretty cynical time for me to be questioning the judgment of the *New York Times*, from whom I've been stealing the substance of my livelihood for more than a decade, but the issue does somewhat intrude on our otherwise gentle excursion up Sixth Avenue: What about Velez and me?

But while Velez hyperventilates and importunes at Arielle, threatening immediate job-action—hah!—it occurs to me that a guardian angel sits no more than a hair's breadth from me. It's one of those moments where all of a sudden you start spotting tiny little 'redemption' signs on the highway to hell. I refer, of course, to Sally Wallach's father's equity position in what seems soon to be the ex-parent company of WRTR—the Thunder.

# 6

BETWEEN 27th Street, the wholesale plant district, and here, creeping through the 50's, the Rockefeller district, much has transpired, none of it good. Velez, for instance, told Arielle that Hendy Markowitz can have his—our—morning slot beginning right now, which will be convenient for the prospective new ownership of the Thunder, since Hendy is, as we speak, wiping the snotty nose of his graveyard show; Velez hung up on Arielle, as if any of this is *her* doing. Our last several hours in the Empire Diner notwithstanding, Velez sent techie one into a Wendy's for a couple of bags of breakfast, whereupon the light outside Wendy's changed and our driver screamed away into traffic, leaving techie one scrambling up Sixth Avenue in hot, gangly pursuit. Our driver took it upon himself to assure Ms. Elite that he'd chauffeur her to her shoot at Battery Park, whereupon Velez fired him at the 38th Street red light, ordered him out of the car, and turned command of the Velezmobile over to techie two—a good thing for techie one, since this gave him the opportunity to catch up. Velez called Arielle for some clarification and then hung up on her again.

Sally Wallach and Ms. Elite are conferring, *sotto voce*. I sit, leaning into the reassuring solidity of the Velezmobile's passenger door, giving ideas room to ferment on the Sally's dad angle. One thing seems certain: any belated romantic advance on my part toward Sally will now look calculated, which, as I trust you know, it wouldn't be. There are real life situations in which one should be allowed to introduce character witnesses; this could be one.

What, it occurs to me, if Sally's dad is *behind* this? Maybe he's engineered this whole thing; and, for that matter, maybe his daughter is a corporate spy! Highly trained undercover operative, placed in an innocuous, low-level position to assess the long term profit and loss prospects of WRTR-FM, the Thunder. Now a tornado of Wendy's wrappers engulfs the interior of the Velezmobile; Sally Wallach has taken charge of dispensing handfuls of breakfast while techie one gasps his way back from the brink of exhaustion in the front seat next to techie two, our pilot. Ms. Elite pitches in, sugaring and creaming coffees to our respective specifications. Do you feel something evanescently familial in this sharing of our Wendy's breakfast? For a moment I allow myself to imagine a common bond in the face of the disaster before us.

As for imagining, I can just imagine the reports Sally might have been passing along to her father. Oh boy.

But who says this is such bad news? What difference can it possibly make who owns WRTR? What can happen? I'll tell you what can happen: Hendy Markowitz can get fired. Adrian Boe can get sent to an old folks home. Cheryl Mann and Kenny Appleton can take their vanilla personalities anywhere in radioland, though probably not for nearly the money and not with nearly the audience, which is currently furnished to them in large measure by the Velez & Oldham Show. And what of Velez and Oldham? If you're going to buy WRTR, what you're buying *is* Velez and Oldham. We've been bought and sold before, and always at a handsome profit to us. Especially Velez.

Velez, however, doesn't seem to be taking my emerging wait-and-see attitude. He's on the phone, talking to one of his lawyers.

One of *our* lawyers, I guess I should say, since Velez sees to our contractual arrangements and he's the only one who ever gets sued. He even selected my divorce lawyer from among his stable of specialists.

Ms. Elite passes coffee to Velez. Velez passes his half-eaten egg sandwich to Ms. Elite, who tends it patiently.

"Don't we have a say in this?" Velez wants to know. We don't hear the answer, and don't need to. Velez is ranting incoherently; this phase will pass pretty soon.

"How can they sell us without even *telling* us?" Velez wants to know. "Well, *fuck,* Tom," Velez says.

I hazard a peek past Ms. Elite at Sally Wallach. If she's an undercover agent for her corporate father, she's very good at it; all she looks like right now is a succulent twenty-year-old neophyte radio junkie enjoying the barely comprehensible maelstrom around her, basking in the celebrity tantrum unfolding across the Velezmobile from her, joyfully doling Wendy's junkfood back and forth, giggling with Ms. Elite at my partner, Roberto Velez.

"Tom, all I'm saying is, this is no way to treat a couple of corporate assets like me and Dennis. *Assets,* I said. What kind of a fucking radio station are they going to have if Oldham and I take a walk? Huh? They ever think of *that?* How much they gonna sell the fucking Thunder for without me and Dennis? Huh? How much they gonna get for Appleton and Adrian and, and . . . whoever else we got there! Huh? Just ask somebody who the *fuck* they think they're jerking around!" Velez listens and munches egg sandwich. "Well, Jesus Christ, Tom, you're a lawyer . . . threaten somebody!"

Even if Sally Wallach isn't a spy for her father, this is turning into a conversation that Sally shouldn't be privy to. But how do I give Velez a high sign without making Sally feel like a spy? I don't want Sally to feel like a spy. I want her to feel just like she looks like she feels right now: a junior comrade-in-arms.

But Velez seems to read my mind—or Tom the Lawyer has momentarily placated him. "Okay," Velez says. "Just let's find some good news this morning, all right? 'Cause I'm really goddamn depressed right now and I have to go on the air in six minutes and I just ate a fucking McPoison breakfast and one-point-three million of my personal friends are going to listen to me barf all over Oldham's pants, so you can see how important it is, Tom, that somebody find some *good news* for me— soon!"

5:56:20. We—Velez, techies one and two, Sally Wallach, me, and Ms. Elite—disgorge from the elevator on the eighteenth floor of this black shiny building of ours. Our enginette, who not four hours ago was trooping gamely into the Empire Diner behind us, is calm and competent at the controls behind aviator Ray-Bans. I have mentioned to Velez that we need to keep an eye on this young woman; we need her. If we wind up walking from WRTR, she's walking with us—whether she likes it or not.

Before Hendy Markowitz's last nasal whimper evaporates into the New York morning, Velez launches his—our—directionless campaign. "From WRTR-FM, this is Roberto Velez with my partner, Dennis Oldham—two loyal employees about to be orphaned by what I had previously considered the sweetest, kindest multinational corporation that a couple of guys like Oldham and me could ever hope to be owned by—"

I have made newscast notes on a Wendy's breakfast bag and now I slide into my white, sterile, Velez-proof newsbooth and unwrinkle it on my desk. Ms. Elite whispers into Velez's ear mid-harangue, and he nods hastily. Thus does Ms. Elite close the deal on the use of the Velezmobile for the morning, although I don't know who she thinks she's going to get to drive it for her. If I had more time right now to reflect on Ms. Elite, I would; let's just say that I think she's not going away easily and that she makes me uneasy for Velez's welfare. But enough of this, because our enginette is giving signals to red-faced Roberto Velez, pumping her arms like one of those airport guys in goggles and earphones who wave taxiing jets into position with a pair of giant red flashlights, and Velez swears, ". . .you haven't heard the last of this!" to one-point-three million groggily amused listeners just before our enginette slices his toes off and pops it to me.

"Thanks, Roberto," I say to Velez and our listeners. "Valium's in your upper right hand drawer; why don't you help yourself to three or four while I tell the nice folks what happened while we weren't looking. . . ."

The hours creep ahead and the news is conspicuously thin—not the news of the world, which is hot and tilted toward disaster, natural and man-made—but news of the fate of WRTR. Roberto Velez veers from one unfounded supposition to another in his public display of petulance, but at what? At not being consulted, I suppose. I give our one-point-three million listeners their 9:30 dose of news and, in the temporary absence of Velez, stretch out my time with some lame explanations about the results of my pro football picks of yesterday. Just one of the public services offered by the Velez & Oldham Show is sports-wager counseling, compliments of me. I try to sound off-handed and tongue-in-cheek enough about this that few of our listeners, I bet, realize how inveigled I am in the whole ugly business. I have no doubt that pockets of fanatic listeners risk good, hard-earned money backing my selections each week.

Velez has been on the Velezphone for a good portion of this morning's show. You've noticed that Velez has named many of the accouterments of our daily lives after himself—we have a Velezphone, direct and uneavesdroppable by WRTR reception; and, of course, the Velezmobile. Roberto has been burning up the Velezphone line this morning, no doubt in connection with the impending sale of WRTR. Options, he explained to me at 8:46 this morning, must be explored.

I've gone as far as I can with my post mortem on yesterday's picks, and Velez is ignoring the entreaties of our Ray-Banned enginette to come back to work. "Velez had to go to the bathroom," I tell one-point-three million people, who at this late hour number substantially less than one-point-three million but are still a lot of folks, and our enginette pops a CD. Rock music, nineteen-nineties. Like Geritol—cain't do you no harm.

I should confess right here that I know there aren't one-point-three million of you out there. As the diligent and delectable Thunder intern Sally Wallach would tell us if we quizzed her, there aren't one-point-three million people in all Christendom who listen to anything but Howard Stern these days. Those are not sour grapes you're smelling, and to all the pulpit-pounding about shock radio defoliating the moral landscape, I feel I can speak for Velez when I say: bullshit. Besides, I seem to remember people with short haircuts and thick glasses saying the same thing about rock & roll back in the day when Ozzie and Harriet and June and Ward bestrode the realm, before rock & roll calcified into its own sorry shell of middle-aged respectability.

No, even if you include the remotest reaches of our nuclear deathray broadcast tower here atop the Too Tall Jones building where we work, we're probably lucky to cadge a half-million people on the best day of the week. The one-point-three million is a scurrilous fiction perpetrated by the weasels who sell our advertising air time, with the full collusion of the agency punks who buy it for their gullible clients. What they're really buying is the Velez and Oldham cachet at a shamelessly inflated per-thousand price tag and, more to the point, a guaranteed steady flow of personal invitations to Thunder Radio promotional parties where for a few fleeting hours the punks can cavort in close quarters with Velez's rock-video-babe pals, who would normally cross the street to avoid them. If they want to quibble about six or seven hundred thousand phantom listeners who manage to elude the official ratings radar, well, the next half-dozen guys lined up to buy thirty precious seconds of Velez and Oldham won't be so scrupulous. And as long as Mister Hyundai and Mister Sony see Velez's mug on the sides of buses when they come to town, it'll never occur to them how rapaciously they're being hosed. So we pretend we're selling one-point-three million golden demographic exposures, as the weasels call you nice people behind your backs, and the agency punks fudge the ratings and pretend to believe us.

What do they care; it's not their money.

Sally Wallach is acting like she got ten hours of sleep last night, instead of the zero hours I happen to know she got, not counting the nap she took against the window of the Empire Diner while Velez was making Mexican flapjacks. There she is, brewing tea, conferring with Kenny Appleton's alleged producer, who's about to send her off on another jackalope hunt in the vault for Kenny's oldies deal this afternoon. I admit it—she's been looking in here a lot this morning.

Tonight is the promotional party at that Eurotrash disco on Twenty-first Street. I buzz my partner. "What?" Velez says, covering the mouthpiece of the Velezphone.

"We have a party tonight."

"I know," Velez bluffs. "What party?"

"Arielle's promotional deal."

Velez appears to ask whoever is on the other end of the line about this, and then indicates that we will attend.

So it's come to this: a forty-something-year-old divorced father of one sits in his high, narrow white cubicle in front of a dead microphone, looking through his partial reflection in streaked glass, feeling the deadness of soundproof tiles pressing down and in on him, ignoring the lights blinking on his telephone console and the assorted, dissociated amblings outside the booth, wondering what will be worse: to vogue through another night as Velez's unescorted appendage, or to make overtures to the girl Sally Wallach.

At 10:01 Sally is nowhere to be found. That's not so; I know perfectly well where to find her: the vault. She's there with her hand-scribbled list of old tunes, many—most—from before her time, rooting through stacks and stacks of albums and tapes. The door to the vault is directly off main reception, in plain view of the receptionists, the production assistants, whom Sally Wallach theoretically works for, and directly aligned with the perpetually open door of our new program manager, Arielle.

One of the production assistants is Raylene McDonald. Raylene is, as she puts it, a 'sort of sister' to Lyndon McDonald, resident of the Vietnam Memorial Plaza and its surrounding downtown catacombs. Raylene's mom could be Lyndon's mom; it's possible, I guess. Raylene is my age, give or take, and has walked in the valley of the shadow of death—she was born there, like Lyndon, like Roberto Velez—and she has overcome. She is short and broad and attractively buoyant, you could say, even though she wears around her eyes the evidence of what I imagine she's seen. Raylene has two daughters. One is Jane Oldham's age; they have played together at the Thunder Rock consoles on more than one Saturday morning. The other of her daughters is ten or so. Their dads are gone and forgotten, Raylene says.

Roberto Velez got Raylene McDonald her production assistant job here at WRTR, but this was no stroke of charity. Raylene could manage this entire station better, no doubt, than Arielle, and certainly far better than a half dozen of Arielle's predecessors.

It is on Raylene's behalf that I look occasionally in on her putative quasi-brother Lyndon, who cannot abide Raylene's presence, or, I think, who cannot abide himself in Raylene's presence.

So now Raylene McDonald gives me my messages before I escape. I have had calls during the morning from assorted Bobs and Cathys,

Bennie from Bennie's bar, Alicia the faceless poetess, and a half dozen more that draw me a blank. "Now don't you forget about tonight, you hear?" says Raylene McDonald, who knows how much Velez and I love it when she talks to us like a mom. "Don't worry," I say. "I'll be there."

"You, ah, been downtown lately?" Raylene asks.

"Last week," I say. "He looks okay."

"What does he say?"

"Not much. He was giving a speech and telling about Colonel Elmo's last flight again."

"He clean?" asks Raylene, and "Yes," I lie, "he looks like he's taking care."

"So," Raylene says; 'so' is the way she ends our conversations about Lyndon. This doesn't get any easier, I think. Ever.

By noon I have answered the calls I'm going to answer, done my logging, made the FCC happy, and I'm ready for a nap. Most days Velez will long since have fled but today he is lashed to the private-line Velezphone. Strategizing.

But downstairs, surprises await. Here at the curb hunkers the Velezmobile, which I had deemed lost for the day. Not only has the Velezmobile been returned, but Ms. Elite has returned with it. And not only does Ms. Elite sit in the back seat, door open to this singularly aromatic morning, but who sits across from her but our WRTR intern, Sally Wallach.

I make inquiries. The morning has gone expeditiously and profitably for Ms. Elite. Innocent conspiracy seems afloat, and sure enough, Ms. Elite presently mentions a Thunder Rock promotional party. Has Velez invited her? So it would seem. I'm not sure. And what about Sally Wallach?

Then, as at more times in the past than I could possibly recall, Velez materializes to take over, slapping me on the ass and ordering me into the Velezmobile. "C'mon, Coolie, we got some plotting to do!" And to Ms. Elite, whom he seems not at all surprised to find back here as she promised, "Party tonight?" Ms. Elite smiles yes, and Velez starts to pull the Velezmobile door closed before Sally Wallach makes a jump for it. "Hey, I'm working!"

Now she's on the curb saying her goodbyes and I have only seconds more to score. But it's Velez who says—to me—"Sally's coming tonight, right?"

So Sally Wallach will, indeed, be filling out our foursome for the

Eurotrash disco promotional party tonight, thanks to my partner Roberto Velez.

An hour or so later I am deposited outside my building by Velez and Ms. Elite. Mrs. McMichael, sitting on our stoop with one of the twin Italian spinsters who occupy a first floor apartment and share the backyard garden with Mrs. McMichael, tells her companion that her husband worked hard all his life—right up to the day he took his dive off the Queensborough—and never got to ride in a car like the Velezmobile until *after* he died. But she says this with affection, and I know she takes pride in even the hollowest trappings of my success.

How much plotting could we possibly have gotten done in an hour, you wonder? Plenty, although I can't vouch yet for its coherence. Tom the Lawyer has emerged as a temporary hero for finding out that Velez's contract with WRTR is about up, and that Velez's contract is probably non-transferable. Tom the Lawyer has given Velez to understand that there's money to be made.

And who's buying WRTR from the conglomerate in which Sally Wallach's father is a major league presence? A sleazy British newspaper tycoon named Harold Fish, that's who.

"So?" I ask Velez on the ride home. Velez gives me a condescending grimace, thinks for a minute, and then punches numbers into the carphone.

"Tom the Lawyer, please. Roberto Velez." Ms. Elite appears to be dozing lightly, although her head is elegantly erect. Since the Empire Diner, she has acquired a pair of snakeskin cowboy boots, but the jeans and the tied-in-front silk shirt are the same. Among her more endearing peculiarities is that she doesn't exhibit the clawing tenacity to *stay put* that many wayfaring females, once aboard the Velezmobile, do. She's not counting the seconds until her celebrity bubble pops all over her face, and it occurs to me that perhaps she's even more famous than Velez, and I'm simply too clueless about the fashion scene to realize it.

Tom the Lawyer is on. "This new owner," says Velez, "Oldham wants to know: So what?"

Velez listens and relays. "Tom the Lawyer says the new owner is lower than whale shit," says Velez.

"So is the present owner," I remind Velez.

"Tom says the new owner has no journalistic integrity."

"Neither do we."

"Tom says the new owner buys companies and sucks the brains out of the old employees through their nostrils, and pours rotten sushi into their skulls, and turns them into sleazoid zombies to do his bidding."

"Is that illegal in New York?" says—are you ready?—Ms. Elite. And she says it in this self-possessed, chillingly familiar way, like she's been Myrna Loying back and forth at Roberto Velez since they were kids.

Soon Tom the Lawyer signs off and Velez summarizes. "It's Tom the Lawyer's legal opinion that we don't have a future with the new owner, Coolie."

"We're going to get fired?" I ask.

But "Hah," is as much as I get out of Velez.

And I kiss Mrs. McMichael on her powdered, downy cheek, and smile at her friend Rose, and I climb up through the cool, old, sweet-smelling stairways to my third-floor door. There is an old chain-latch skylight, unbelievably gritty, over the wide, winding staircase, and through the perpetual mustiness—stirred up today by the general open-ing of doors and windows—the early afternoon sun fairly trumpets its way down and around me here in the hallway. There is a concentrated geometry to this downpouring of autumn sun; in my mind I see Jane reach out to touch the edge of it; I hear her guffaw as her fingers pene-trate into the dusty radiance. I hear her not being fearful at the years this building has seen.

I am inside and tired. This is the only cyclically reliable event of the day: that I will need to crash a few hours after the show. I push open the front window, wrestling branches out of the way, and look down; there sit Mrs. McMichael and Rose, down through the branches and the cool sunlight. Their bare arms are brown from a summer of their stoop vigil. This place is theirs in ways it will never be mine, no matter how long I stay. Mrs. McMichael knows this and pities me discreetly for it.

Back into the infrequent room of Jane Oldham, I open the window-door that leads to the roof. Suddenly air exhilarates through the apart-ment, sending things flying.

I climb to the roof.

Jane Oldham and I spend time up here. She likes the secretness of this place in the same childish way that I do. Up here, you feel like you're getting away with something the grown-ups would never allow if they caught you. I have some dopey lawn furniture up here, including two of those hinged loungers with the woven plastic seats that can be made to lie flat out from one end to the other at a perfect height for a five-year-old to hide from the world under.

I have told Jane not to tell her mother that we go up to the roof, but I have been hectored by Jane's mother for taking her daughter up onto the roof of my building anyway. Jane has not mastered the art of judicious deceit yet, and it's not likely that she'll be able to put anything over on her mother for a long time. I wish Jane looked less like her mother. Not that those looks are a lamentable inheritance—oh no. I could simply do without the reminders.

Velez is without children—"I don't *get* married," is Velez's policy—and seems satisfied with the time he spends godfathering Jane Oldham. That Velez would be the godfather of Jane went without question; besides being my best friend, he ran with Jane's mother, introduced her to me, cautioned me against her, and reluctantly gave up in the face of my blind determination to marry her.

Yes, Velez has slept with my ex-wife. Before I knew her. Before I married her. After she divorced me, I wouldn't be surprised; and in between? I choose to think not.

An old blanket of mine is still up here under the lounger that Jane uses for her fort. Lucky it hasn't rained. It's an indistinct olive green, this blanket, the color of Army things. Mustard and pizza stains commemorate two, at least, of our rooftop picnics. I angle the other lounger away from the sun, toward the East River, and ease down beside Jane Oldham's fort. Sleep really insists, now.

# 7

In the hours of my sleep the day has turned nasty.

It's the wind that wakes me. The Army-colored blanket under Jane's fort has blown clear off the roof; I look down and there it is, spread-eagled over Rose's sister's tomato crop. The hair on my arms is standing up and I feel light-headed, like the onset of fever.

It will be hours before anything of consequence is required of me; today, specifically, my presence at Arielle's disco deal. Standard insomniacs, I imagine, feel at about 4:30 a.m. the way I feel right now. If I ignore the grinding insistent convulsions of the city under and around me, I could believe no one else existed at this odd, empty, still hour.

It would still be plenty light around here had this storm not slunk up over things. There'd be colors in here instead of this lead mist, billowing around where I fully expected to wake and find congenial October dusk.

Weather is tricky, whether you're living under it or, worse, forecasting it for one-point-three million New Yorkers. Weather comes from the south a lot, like this particular intrusion this afternoon must have. We in New York don't get much from the south that we wouldn't be a lot better off without.

And what if my listeners made their plans around the official Velez & Oldham Show weather forecast, which yesterday put scant stock in a vile low pressure system off the Carolinas? What if they listened in this morning and thought: Great, we can go outside and have fun this afternoon? How could I bear *that* responsibility?

You might well expect responsibility to be a centering force in the life of an accredited journalist—which, I believe I've mentioned, I am.

Where would you regular people be without journalists? Who'd tip you off to the sodomizing of civilization? Have you considered that today? No, probably not. It's all right; neither have I, up to now.

But okay: what if there wasn't the news? You'd have to go investigate official corruption yourselves, you know. You'd have to appoint community representatives to travel to distant lands, to check and see if anyone's having a war. You'd have to find human interest stories on your own blocks, and what if your own blocks aren't humanly interesting? How about if everywhere you ever go is so boring that no news happens there, huh? Then what? Give some neighborhood kid an assault rifle to take on the class trip, just to break up the monotony?

Wouldn't your lives be bereft without us journalists to tell you what's new where you don't live?

In my humble—but professional, don't forget—opinion: nah.

Which is why I can take my occupation—my job—as lightly as I do, free of anguish or guilt. If I were an irresponsible practitioner of a vocation that mattered, like teaching or day care centering, I am just moral enough to expect that I would feel guilt and anguish about it. But since the importance of what I do is completely illusory, what's there to feel guilty about?

I have a theory, speaking of illusion, that journalists have plenty in common with priests: interpreters of the unfathomable, packagers of reality. A stretch? Okay.

But tell me: do you agree that your lives would not materially change if all the newspapers and TV reporters and radio news readers like me suddenly vanished? Would you worry more? Less? I'll tell you what *I* think: we give you more things to worry about than you could possibly dream up to worry about on your own. Take radon, for instance. How many of you would have dreamed up radon, that frisky little dickens of a radioactive gas, by yourselves? I know I wouldn't have. And more of you—us—are going to die worrying about radon gas and similar one-in-a-jillion bogey things than radon gas itself could possibly kill.

You could say the same with regard to Sikh terrorists. Not the ones who own and operate the Manhattan storefront boutiques where my partner Roberto Velez buys his Hugo Boss suits; I mean the ones who borrow Libyan bombs and seduce stupid Irish girls into smuggling them onto planes and then sit watching the news yelling *"Allah ahkbar!"* while journalists play and replay the blowing up of airplanes and their gooey-hearted, freckled, unwitting saboteurs. I say, get rid of the televisions and see how many Sikh terrorists start signing up for vocational training.

But don't worry: even if all the Sikh terrorists send their bombs back to Libya and open Hugo Boss boutiques on every street corner in New York City, we journalists will find alternative catastrophes with which to traumatize you. And if we can't find any, you can count on us to make some up.

Which is why I most of the time really like being a newsman on rock radio, because our listeners can be counted on to take my news even less seriously than consumers of, say, the *New York Times*—where, I've mentioned, I steal all my non-rock-related news. Because of where

I ply my trade, my credibility is less than zero; so, consequently, is my culpability in the grand illusion of journalism. News hell is going to be a lot hotter for Dan Rather than it will be for me.

I choose these indistinct hours of waning daylight to howl at the moon like this in complete privacy, which might not make me a stand-up citizen but it does make me a tolerable neighbor in a city where the latter is of much more consequence than the former.

From the junk drawer in the sometime room of my daughter I find a barely used spool of audio wire. I fetch an unoccupied wire coathanger and a beer, and climb back up to the roof.

Three tentative tries already presage a fiasco. The pre-storm wind is twirling my makeshift fishing rig like crazy as I swing it out and around the backyard garden after the pizza-stained blanket. There's not enough heft to the coathanger, I fear; not the ballast to steady it. So far, all I have managed to do is savage a sunflower, and my deniability on this charge won't hold up for long if Rose or Rose's sister get wind of the damage.

The city, meanwhile, is cringing in the face of the gathering storm. Lightning smells like a possibility, even now in mid-October. What's left of Rose's sister's tomatoes better get themselves inside before too much longer; better hop into one of Rose's no-holds-barred spaghetti sauces. No fruits of real estate so dear can be allowed to wither on the vine.

Downtown glows wanly under the soupy evening dankness; a dismal green shrouds the island. I sense whipped-dog slinking down in the streets surrounding this warm inelegant building of mine. I am delighted not to be out there among it.

And while I daydream this, I seem to have hooked a whopper with my audio wire and coathanger fishing tackle. I peek over my iron rooftop rail, and oh boy—Rose's sister has extricated her tomatoes from *their* mustard-stained shroud, and has hooked my coathanger through a hole in the blanket. I hoist it up; Rose's sister storms inside.

Time passes slowly enough here in the western warrens of Greenwich Village, and in this, my most recent regressive stage, these sinking middle hours feel like an insolent weight congealing in the center of the apartment, so heavy that it depresses the floor, threatening to draw everything sliding down into this soundless drain in the center of the room, and I with it, right down through the second floor apartment and then the ceiling of Rose and Rose's sister's apartment, there to answer for my bumbling act of defoliation on my way down through the laundry room and the Eighth Avenue subway tunnels and on to hell.

Today's developments at Rolling Thunder Radio do not strike me as career-threatening. Three or four times before in my eleven-and-a-half-year partnership with Roberto Velez, such situations have presented themselves; yet here we are, aren't we, at the very top of FM radio in one of the two places where that matters most. We've been threatened; Velez for his willful malfeasances, I for—how shall I put it?—the subtleties of my contribution to the product. Our responses to management blandishments have been among the creative high points of our partnership; we play well off pinstripe hostility. I cannot think of a single reason why this latest deal, this purchase of the Thunder by the tabloid king of western civilization, should be any different.

And yet . . . and yet. More established institutions than Velez & Oldham seem to be going to hell on a regular basis these days. There used to be a lot more rock radio stations in this town a few years ago, for instance; none as hallowed as Thunder Rock, but outfits with barnacles of their own. Where'd they go?

Sally Wallach, student of media at Cornell University in upstate New York when she's not interning her heart out at the Thunder halfway up a shiny black building on Sixth Avenue in midtown Manhattan, could explain it to us: she'd say that the trend is toward talk radio. Look at Howard, she'd point out, look at Imus, and she'd illustrate with charts and graphs if we asked her that radio talk shows establish a much more compelling and immediate relevance with the 24-and-older segments, and that the 14-to-23's are visually-oriented in their musical consumption.

Well, thanks, Sally, but Roberto Velez doesn't need a senior media student from Cornell University to tell him that music video is here to stay. Velez has money in a number of music video production concerns and, as you all know, his is a familiar guest face on syndicated teen screamer videofests.

The tough part is explaining the symbolism in the videos to Immaculata Velez.

"Why they do that with the crucifixes?" Immaculata Velez demands. "What that deal for?"

Immaculata Velez is a closet fan of her thoroughly *Anglo*-accented son Roberto; that's how she comes to call everything a 'deal.' At home, where she almost always is, she takes pains not to let this on. Velez's youngest sister Margareta, who is twelve years, old and Velez and I both fervently believe, a legitimate candidate for escape from Washington

Heights, keeps close tabs on her big brother's upcoming appearances on MTV and Letterman and the local so-called news/entertainment magazine shows, and makes sure Immaculata Velez doesn't miss a single one. Margareta tapes my partner's appearances on the tapedecks Velez brings home and that his brother Nicolo hasn't had a chance to unplug and hot-foot down to the local sidewalk electronics wholesaler for crack money. Immaculata does not go on about her oldest son Roberto because, in part, she is a wise woman and knows that it will only make things worse with Nicolo and with Michael, who is Nicolo's junior by three or four years and is technically a sophomore in high school, but who is in fact a serious-intentioned apprentice to the drug trade and, from what I've seen and heard, is even more doomed than Nicolo because at least Nicolo is smart enough to duck when somebody's shooting at him, where the same, I fear, cannot be said for Michael. Larceny and filial cruelty are occasional visitors to Mama Velez's clean and determinedly sanctified home, but outright violence has managed to keep itself away, and Immaculata Velez figures that resentment of high and mighty Roberto, toast of the Big Apple, celebrity, star, is perhaps a final straw better not to be heaped upon Nicolo's back.

Now it's 9:30 p.m. in the thunderstorm's crisp aftermath; the city looks deceivingly docile in this fresh-scrubbed sheen as we roll away from Mrs. McMichael's and Rose's stoop in the Velezmobile. I am not surprised to find Ms. Elite in the back seat, her head haloed by the gooseneck reading lamp behind her. She greets me cordially, in the manner one greets a visitor to one's home. She is no longer a passenger in the Velezmobile. She is now something like its proprietress, and I am supposed to feel like I should thank her for stopping by to pick me up.

I am surprised, however, to find no Velez.

Where we head is uptown, to collect Sally Wallach. I bring myself en route to inquire about Velez's whereabouts and, without actually telling me that it's none of my fucking business, Ms. Elite manages sweetly not to answer, clearing up for me in an instant any naïve questions I may have had about who's in charge here. Ms. Elite seems to have decided that two sidekicks are one sidekick more than Roberto Velez needs.

Do I feel threatened? I do not. This is a phenomenon as ancient as celebrity itself. Velez, in particular, is a velcro personality, and he is as partial as anybody to the gratifying shiver of idolatrous tongues lapping his rectum. As far as Velez is concerned, Ms. Elite is a perk. Like the Velezmobile. I don't get jealous of cars, and I don't get jealous of pretenders to the innermost affections of my friend and partner Velez. The Velezmobile will get worn out, and so, quickly enough, will Ms. Elite. Then both will be traded in for shiny new models.

So I take the demure proprietary smugness of Ms. Elite this night with equanimity, and I hope you will, too. After all, here's a girl who, maybe six months ago, was an anthropology major or something in rural Kansas. What she knows about hitting it big in New York is what she sees on television and what she reads in the fashion magazines— images which, by their self-aggrandizing ubiquity, have become the art that life here grimly imitates. She looks in the mirror one morning and decides that Providence had bestowed upon her this body and this photogenic radiance for a fate far loftier than marrying a fat John Deere salesman and breeding jayhawkers or cornhuskers or whatever the inhabitants of that vast undifferentiated amber wave of grain between St. Louis and the ocean are pleased to call their spawn; she kisses her Pop and her Auntie Em goodbye, scruffs old Toto behind his ears, and catches the next stage east, ready to do whatever it takes.

I'm guessing at a lot of this. I know she's from Kansas, because I heard her tell Sally Wallach this at some point during the Bowl-Mor overnight where she first turned up. The rest you may consider a faithful composite of the tales brought to the banquet table of Roberto Velez in these, his halcyon days of rock radio celebrity. Velez should be given credit for the perspective he has managed to maintain; others have not been so strong. The oldies charts are littered with those who think they actually merited the affection of the likes of Ms. Elite; those who allowed themselves to be convinced of their specialness. Not Velez. Not me.

Moments later, I hop out of the Velezmobile like prom night to ring for Sally Wallach, who's out of the elevator and into the Velezmobile like a high-voltage discharge. I continue to look in vain for the slightest reassuring manifestation of cynicism on Sally's part; I would even welcome a snippet of the tedious one-liner irony that passes for wit among Manhattan's effete elite. Anything to ratchet down the looming age differential.

Sally and Ms. Elite exchange cheek kisses. These two are clearly pals. Sally, of course, has no need to dabble in Ms. Elite's intrigues; success happened to her at conception and all that's really required of her is not to spit in its eye. This is not to take away from Sally's talents and her intelligence, or to suggest that she couldn't make it on her own. It's only to say that tightrope walking is easier with a net.

Outside the club, here in the heart of the club district, stand the obligatory door-gargoyles: a tall, pear-shaped boy with a tiny bolero hat teetered on his buzz-burr head, and silky jodhpurs that give his lower quarters the appearance of parentheses at odds. In his chalky, pudgy fingers resides the fate of many a glamour-seeker this night: the clipboard. The clipboard bears illegible scribblings that this boy will allege to the unanointed to be reservations; this largely-fabricated list will be pored over often tonight in the imperious, masochistic ballet of doorly selection. Flanking this boy are a pair of extremely happening African-American bouncer types—the only things standing, at times, between the pasty-faced plumberry doorman and disembowelment at the hands of the maniacal rejected.

I will spare you a tour of this place; suffice it to say that this club looks like an oleaginous Iraqi's idea of a slick New York club—in other words, it looks like a Holiday Inn lounge in Columbus, Ohio. There are lots of bells and whistles, and all the homeless smoke machines from the 1970's have retired here. No one is who he or she seems; these places are a chance to be somebody else for a while in the assurance that, once you have finessed your way in, nobody will call you on it. Your admittance depends entirely on how erotically sepulchral and catatonically vapid you can manage to present yourself. The doorman can spot normal citizens in camouflage from across the street.

For advice on how to assault these places, I will only repeat the two recommendations that Velez and I have made on our show innumerable times. One way to get into these clubs immediately is to arrive in a limousine. The doorpeople will assume you have a glamorous job, and they are looking to be noticed by glamorous people—this is the beacon of their existence. Or they'll assume you're having sex with someone who has a glamorous job, which in a way is even better, since they presume you rose up from the same charnel heap where they currently wallow during the day and they might be able to pick up some style points from you.

The other surefire dodge past the doorpeople is to be Japanese. Japanese, it is said, lend an air of sophistication to a club. By sophisticated, club people mean that Japanese pay full freight to get inside instead of scrounging for comps, suffer the most imaginative of indignities in stoic silence, and dress in black uniforms that clash with nothing and that won't even require changing for a mass funeral in case a steam pipe ruptures inside and kills them all. Who wouldn't want guests like these hanging around?

We three—Sally Wallach, me, Ms. Elite—prowl for Velez. Picture an ordinary, unremarkably-attired man flanked by these two: Sally Wallach, her volcanic arrangement of auburn hair jouncing across the light dusting of freckles on her shoulders, which are bare except for the valiant shoelaces that struggle to hold her spangly scalloped top in place; and Ms. Elite, towering over us both, swathed in black cotton with sleeves that swing considerably closer to the floor than her skirt. Ms. Elite has stylishly looped her hand under my arm—an olive branch?—and Sally has done the same, and a lesser man would be tempted to issue a hearty kiss-my-ass to the entire ensemble.

Tropical flora bleeds color into the monochromy of the rooms. The decor intends to complement its regular Japanese clientele and succeeds. The guest list this evening consists of WRTR's three hundred most valued business associates and its half-dozen most bankable commodities. The Thunder personalities in attendance this evening—Velez and me, Kenny Appleton, Cheryl Mann, old Adrian Boe, and the new late-morning guy from Baltimore, Stevie Joe Adams—have a lot more years on us than most of our advertisers and agency leeches, not to mention the WRTR sales menagerie. Theirs are jobs that no grown-up could endure for long; and yet, think of the *millions* in the hands of this bunch! Here is a twenty-four-year-old fellow who, it is pointed out to me by the suddenly present Arielle, allocates the broadcast budget for one of Velez's favorite fast food chains—a vast pile of U.S. currency, no doubt. The point of this evening is to ensure that a substantial fraction of this youngster's pile of somebody else's money continues to be shoveled into the WRTR coffer, and Arielle seems to have orchestrated herself a level of high-intensity shmooze here at the oily Arab-Manhattan dude ranch.

Velez is here. Lawyers are here. Velez and the lawyers are surveying things from a strategically-elevated table above the main spotlit cattle-chute promenade and out of the immediate arc of the speaker rigs that corner the dance levels. The lawyers look concerned. Velez does not.

Sally Wallach and Ms. Elite have preceded me up to Velez's table; I tarry for no reason on the promenade and try to figure out if this is really tonight's promotion party or if it's a promotion party from, say, 1989, where I may have stepped through a looking glass and just now emerged to find that none of these people have aged, though many have died or had children—except me. I've been lurking behind the looking glass as promotion party after promotion party has clattered in and out of kitsch-dappled places like this. I've watched as boys in jackets with big shoulders have stared into my mirror and brushed away nose icing and girls with legs that go on and on, not exactly straight and sure but youthfully enticing anyhow, have unbuttoned buttons and checked themselves, this side and that, to see if enough is finally showing now to make a goddamned dent in the hopping crowd down below, and I've watched, unnoticed, while skirts have been hiked up and zippers have been pulled down and trousers have been lowered in back and a withering assortment of inconsequent couplings have thus presented themselves for my delectation, the unwitting participants borrowing their reflections from my looking glass, so to double their pleasure and to facilitate mine. There's a crypt-like refusal of time to pass here behind my looking glass, and an almost welcome redundancy to life back here, like the slavish following of a syndicated sitcom—see the cycle to the end and it starts, reassuringly, all over again, as many times as you have time to watch before you die, with the ever-increasing comfort of knowing just exactly where things are going. Is there any more drama to what will happen before my mirror in the next five minutes, where a lean boy with a crimson vest over a floppy untucked shirt has wrestled a tall, always tall—part of the Darwinian New York imperative of altitude and attitude and architecture—girl behind the glass-brick wall that not quite offers recluse for transient drugging or approximations of coitus? No, no surprises here. He spoons for her; he spoons for himself. She leans back against the wall, glances in my mirror, observes her own legs angling out around the feet of her bounding companion. She lets her shirt be pulled open for the sheer jolt of having her breasts manifested to this public place, to the salacious potential of discovery. She lets herself be handled, inexpertly, but so what? She's doing it in the big time now, like she used to read about as a girl—what, two years ago, in high school? She allows herself to be rutted up against, and watches the proceedings in my mirror. The profile of her ordinary breasts, illuminated into their own heady momentary celebrity against the shadows of movement—of curious observers?—passing in the background. From behind my looking glass I preside over the hauling down of another zipper, the reaching in of another hand, panting gratitude from the beneficiary of these furtive ministrations, another bout of comical flailing with an inventive twist: she doesn't take him out, but handles the operation inside. And in his moment, the one he'll cherish and recollect countless times throughout the remainder of his ordinary, ordered, inexorably attenuating life, she glances again into my mirror, to see what a sublimely detached and utterly proficient seductress looks like as she makes her boy come in his pants against the glass-brick wall under the smoky, gilt-framed looking glass where I think I've been held prisoner since 1989.

# 8

I must have wandered around this place for a while. It appears, in fact, as though I've been outside, too; somewhere damp and unkind, like the waterfront of Lyndon McDonald, where autumn is currently insinuating itself with nasty licking stealth. I'm standing clammily inside my club suit—my one concession, at Velez's strenuous insistence, to the stylishness that celebrities like us are supposed to vanguard. Certain things are clear: a number of hours have passed since our ceremonious arrival here at *Chez Smokemachine*; the crowd in here would now outpopulate many midwestern townships; the sunken dance floor looks, from my remote vantage, like a National Geographic film on the wondrous world of fly larvae.

Directly across the premises, from my elevation to theirs, I can observe the goings-on at the court of my partner Velez. A minor forest of champagne bottles has sprouted from the table, all emerald-glowing under the crossfire of spotlights. I can tell you from here that Velez is feeling like Vito Corleone at his daughter's wedding—sitting in ebullient cynosure, ringed by his lawyer-henchmen, decorated by Ms. Elite and, yes, by Sally Wallach too, giving an occasional condescending Windsor Wave to the processionaires below his table. Radiating the aura of his celebrity. Being the entire reason for this occasion.

For my part, I suppose I've been circling indecisively. Since I am known only in my capacity as Velez's appendage, I have my anonymity out here on the fringe. I'm sure the place is crawling with WRTR people but I'd recognize few of them, avoiding, as I make it a rule to, anyone connected with sales. This is really their night, their chance to drag time-buyers up the promenade to Velez's table for a few of the comradely insults and a moment in the glow. Roberto Velez has this uncanny talent for making each one of these advertiser-children feel like his existence is Velez's lifeblood—all without actually saying a single civil word to any of them. To our own sales maggots, Velez is appropriately unsparing in his contempt; I'll have to give him that.

Ms. Elite and Sally Wallach are the glorious adornments in this startableau of Velez's. Sally, game and enervated, seems to be playing the unofficial hostess to Velez's table, holding up the small talk with the parade of WRTR advertisers when Velez chooses to ignore them, pouring champagne, waving cocktail semaphores at the table-of-honor's squad of stewards. Ms. Elite, meanwhile, stands behind Velez, swiveling from one sultry pose to the next, serenely surveying the middle-distance flurry, occasionally resting a hand on Velez's shoulder—*attending* Velez for the world to see.

Are you in the mood to go back in time, or forward, my friends? Actually, it doesn't make any difference because whether we go around or we come around, we're doomed to end up right back here at Arielle's promotion party—the timeless, inescapable black hole of big-time radio. We can indulge the illusion of freedom for a while if you want but sooner or later if we don't die first we're going to be sucked, brain first, right back into this masquerade ball with the kind lights to conceal that other illusion—you know. What I'm melodramatically sneaking up on is this creepy bottomless feeling that only hours ago were manhood and radio thrust upon me, and I was not, believe me, ready for the radio part.

Ellen Larkin was a one-woman radio marathon. During the first fateful day of my novitiate, Ellen had hosted and engineered a remote broadcast from outside the campus's main dining hall, from where she plotted to rally the lunching hordes to the following dusk's antiwar tubthump on the campus green. Ours was not exactly a provincial studentry, but in the daily absence of what folks used to call coeds, a personal appearance by the likes of Ellen Larkin was big news; a hand-presented invitation to link arms with Ellen Larkin in her march toward peace was likely to be turned down by few.

After four or five hours of this, she had bundled her gear up to the organizing committee meeting where preoccupied ringleaders delivered her into my volunteering hands. And no sooner had we replugged this and that into their proper sockets than Ellen Larkin sailed once again out onto the airwaves, a shade late of her customary evening slot. I, invited to stay, sought justification for my presence.

It was over the low desk where a worn, snubby microphone seemed to sprout up from under a mulch of announcements, commercial copy, cassettes and music notes that I left her standing; there was a chair, but, as I would learn before long, this was much too early in the program for Ellen Larkin to consider sitting down. There was no separating her physical and mental output. She paced and pranced through a show; she danced and rocked her turbulent red hair to the tunes and she stroked that little gray microphone like she had to coax its arthritic compliance. At the door I watched her fingers play with the microphone,

one moment throttling it like a miscreant little neck and the next minute caressing it like—ah, you know. But mine, I yearned, mine!

I handled my first career radio assignment promisingly. Her pastrami was moist and pungent, heaped between thick sturdy slabs of seeded rye scumbled deftly by my own hand with deli mustard; her coffee was rich, aromatic, issuing forth beckoning curlicues of steam. If you want to be in radio, this is where you start. I felt competent; I sensed, in fact, that professionalism was not beyond my grasp.

For my reward, Ellen Larkin gave me a tour of her electronics. I studied hard and asked questions when I didn't understand, and sometimes even when I did. I volunteered to flip switches and feed cassettes when she found herself full-handed. I may even have straightened things up a little. As for Ellen Larkin, she forgot for long periodic stretches that I was present, and gave the same glazed-eye start when she'd go to a record and then turn to rediscover me.

A few dozen times I looked at my watch, affecting pressing demands on my own time. If she noticed . . . never mind. She didn't.

We cruised undisturbed through hours one and two of the Ellen Larkin Show, she deliciously focused on the rabid bounces between the music and the outpourings of her own personality, I puppily attentive and trivially helpful. The one interruption to our privacy came in the person of a muscular, mustachioed girl who palmed a plastic bag into Ellen's hand and retreated into the night without a word. To watch Ellen Larkin roll a joint one-handed while flailing the electronics to her will with the other was to witness the epitome of broadcast professionalism.

Her hair called to mind farming, somehow. Not that I've ever been on or near a farm, but you contemplate a windblown presence, utterly at home in the plainness and wonder of the outdoors, inattentive to the false adornments of civility, rejecting postmodernism's venal entanglements, blissfully unpretentious in the bosom of the communal ideal, and pretty soon you long for the aroma of sun-dried cow flop on boots of your own.

Most intoxicating of all was her dominion over her anonymous congregation, *out there*, living the large and small details of their nights, orchestrating a thousand dances in the dark. She absolutely knew that they'd be waiting, at the end of the tune, waiting for her to come for them with her sincere prepossessing intimacy; there when they needed it, rewarding and undemanding and, I couldn't help thinking from here at the giving end, grandly promiscuous. Ellen Larkin, I suddenly understood, was putting out for every single one of them out there. I allowed myself to wallow in the blinking darkness of the studio, to watch the swayback maestra stroke the presences in the night that she knew were out there dwelling in her voice, to soak in the vapors of what, at this point in the evening, seemed to me some kind of ephemeral, perpetually consummating gang bang.

But what did Jane Fonda have to do with all this, you—especially those of you too young to remember—might well be wondering.

It was into hour three of the Ellen Larkin Show, after dozens of exhortations on Ellen's part for a rousing turnout next evening against the Vietnam deal, accompanied by dozens of the current antiwar anthems, and Ellen was beginning to show signs of boredom with her company—me. Of course she had to answer her steady trickle of phone calls; putting listeners on the air was part of her show. But when she began *making* seemingly pointless calls of her own, I looked for an honorable escape.

Then Jane Fonda stepped in and, in retrospect, made my one and only career decision for me.

Shuffling irresolutely toward the door, as I remember it, I was waiting for Ellen to hit her next record so I could make my cool goodbye, when suddenly the telephone lines—all three of them—went crazy. Caught on-air, Ellen waved me to a phone. It was thus that I became the unwitting recipient of the first of half a night's calls from assorted wired, hysterical members of the absolutely official antiwar organizing committee.

I cannot help wondering, if you'll pardon a momentary digression, who the suits are who've just ascended to Velez's table—*our* table, except that I haven't been up there yet to display my territorial rights. Two gray eminences with matronly spouses as I make it out from here, where I find myself shoulder-to-shoulder with a pair of plunging necklines drinking champagne and weighing the evening's odds, pointedly oblivious to me. One, I have discreetly overheard, wouldn't mind fucking Velez; the other professes such profound indifference that I know her knees would rattle a Richter scale at the outsidemost opportunity. I've done my share of floor-working for Velez in similar situations in the days before we became media giants, panning the stream for the shiniest nuggets of an evening, presenting my anonymous self as the one and only fast track to Velez. Watching the instant eye-commerce between the two ladies in the crosshairs: which of us is for Velez himself? For me it remained to be a not-too-dispiriting consolation prize once Velez crowned the winner.

About these unidentified suits one thing is clear: Sally Wallach knows one of them intimately. Perhaps parentally is a better word, for I suspect I've just set eyes on Sally Wallach's pop, Boss Wallach, E. P. Wallach to be absolutely precise, for the very first time.

Dad Wallach, I may have mentioned, owns a very substantial chunk of the company that is about to unload WRTR-FM, the Thunder, on a billionaire British pustule of international disrepute. Over the years we've met plenty of suits, Velez and I, but we've never met Himself before that I can remember. E. P. Wallach is a fairly low-profile kind of guy in this latter-day culture of sexy executives. But he's reputed to have as handsome a collection of amputated penises as any of the Fortune cover-boys. And from loins of his own has issued forth Sally Wallach, who is neither spoiled, obnoxious, affectatious, overbearing, jaded, effete, nor stupid—in spite of all her childhood advantages.

The necklines and I observe the goings-on across the room above us. Warmth is being exchanged between my partner Roberto Velez and the sire of my date, E. P. Wallach. To the uninitiated, like these two percolating necklines next to me, it must appear that Velez and Pop Wallach are fishing buddies at the very least. Velez is on his feet. Sally rests a hand momentarily on Velez's sleeve but her important arm is crooked under E. P.'s. I wait for her to look around for me. I realize that it's been long enough since I've even been within waving distance of the table that Sally may be assuming I've left. I also realize that it's just this happenstance, this calling of me to account by some dour grownup for my intentions toward this young Wallach girl, that has kept me away from the table, hovering, skulking.

My paralysis is presently invaded by Hendy Markowitz. Hendy is dressed Japanese, which tonight I do not hold against him. My loathing for Hendy, it would seem, is relative to the proximate alternatives. Hendy may have spotted me first, but it's the electromagnetic field surrounding these necklines that has drawn him nigh.

"Dennis," he says to the two, assuming we are a momentary trio. "Great party."

The name Dennis doesn't register with the necklines; why should it? On the air, my partner Velez either refers to me by my last name only—"Here's Oldham with the news and stuff . . ."—or else by one of the manservant nicknames he plasters me with, like the current "Coolie." My whole name gets used on the air about three times a month, I'd guess. So when Hendy Markowitz clambers up into the wedge created by the two necklines and says, "Great party, huh Dennis?" these girls do not care.

But it's late, and I think it's time to make my way, finally, to the Velez table, so I say, "Hendy Markowitz! Listen to you all the time, babe! Hey . . ." Now the necklines sense celebrity in their midst— they've heard *of* Hendy, even though they've probably never exactly *heard* Hendy. Markowitz, meanwhile, senses trouble, but waits to see what will happen next.

What happens next is that I say to the necklines, "Hey, you know who this is?" And they say, "Sure!" And I say to Hendy, "Y'know, I always wondered: How do you manage to wake up so goddamn early?" And Hendy Markowitz grins nervously because he thinks he's about to be knifed in the kidney but I haven't got anything of the kind in mind. Instead, I say to Hendy and the necklines, "You won't believe . . . this is supposed to be a hip radio party, right? So I'm talking to a couple babes before, right? And they think Velez is a smokin' property, y'know, wouldn't mind puttin' the old—well, y'know." I look wide-eyed from Neckline One to Hendy Markowitz to Neckline Two. "God," I say, shaking my head, "I thought everybody knew about Velez and babes by now." And I shake Hendy Markowitz's hand and leave him to make of the situation what he can.

It couldn't have been that long, this diversion with Hendy, but now as I climb the steps to Velez's table I see Velez, a platoon of Velez's lawyers and other assorted quasi-official sycophants, and Ms. Elite, but no suits, no wives of suits, and no Sally. I slide in next to Velez, who looks restless.

"Where you been?" asks my partner.

"I'm allergic to lawyers," I say, not loud enough to give offense.

"You're supposed to be helping me give handjobs to our sponsors tonight, remember?" says Velez.

"Where's Sally?" I ask.

"Where's Sally?" Roberto Velez repeats. "Where's Sally?" he asks Ms. Elite, who now hunkers down by his shoulder. "Hey, Coolie, it wasn't my turn to watch her. It was *your* turn to watch her."

And Ms. Elite tells me, "She really does like you, Dennis," in a way that makes it unnecessary for her to finish the thought: "So why are you acting like such a bumbling asshole?"

But Velez winces at this, just like I do, and I know I'll get some commiseration from him when we're out of earshot. He knows. How could Ms. Elite appreciate such ambiguous circumstances? Christ, she's a teenager herself! She probably doesn't see any difference between her situation with Velez and mine with Sally Wallach. But Velez does and I do and maybe even Sally Wallach does.

I scan the scene from the battlements for a minute. "So," I say to Velez, "where's Sally?"

"Went out to breakfast with her Dad. You see Old Man Wallach?" Yeah, I nod. "I begged him not to sell," says Velez.

"Yeah?"

"Nah," says Velez. "I don't give a shit. Time for us to get out of this business, Coolie. Leave it for the hyenas. Leave it for the rabid dogs to eat Hendy and Arielle and the rest. There's just us and them, Coolie. The quick and the dead."

He says this with such weary conviction that Ms. Elite rocks backward, stunned. Could this be it? she must be thinking. Could I be in on the final chapter? Of course, this is the very first time Ms. Elite has heard such talk from Roberto Velez. It is definitely not the first time for me.

Ellen Larkin's first concern was to determine whether someone on the official antiwar organizing committee was full of malicious, cynical, manipulative shit, or if Jane Fonda had actually agreed to come and speak at the next day's rally. Her instincts, I remember thinking with admiration, were suspicious: somebody has decided that the only way to rouse the snoozing masses was to promise them Jane Fonda.

I suppose I'm assuming you know who Jane Fonda is; let me fill you in if you don't. Jane Fonda is a video fitness guru and the wife of a media mogul like the putative new owner of WRTR, the Thunder. But back in the Ellen Larkin era of our immediate recollection, Jane was a Hollywood star of many lumens. Jane had attached herself fiercely to the Vietnam War as the latest cause in a career of political crusading, and had recently paid a sympathetic and vastly publicized visit to North Vietnam, to predictably mixed reviews on the home front. I personally have never doubted either her sincerity or its transience. But in those heady days Jane Fonda was the undisputed gossamer glow on the celebrity antiwar road show, and, according to some on the official antiwar organizing committee, she was about to descend into our dismally apathetic midst.

As I mentioned, Ellen Larkin had her initial doubts. She'd been in on enough official organizing committee meetings, and had shared intimacy with who knew how many of its members, to be wary of such an unlikely thunderbolt. But circumstantial evidence lent credence: Jane Fonda would, in fact, be appearing at Columbia University tomorrow at 11:00 a.m.—cannily timed for the news at 6:00 p.m.—so said the *New York Daily News*. And Columbia was only ninety minutes—though several intellectual light years—removed from our own hallowed halls. So we had a clue at least that Jane Fonda would be in our time zone tomorrow.

Beyond that, it was the word of the organizing committee's politburo against—what? Against all odds, and nothing more. Maybe, Ellen Larkin decided after a contentious half hour, Jane Fonda would indeed show up. Wanting to believe is the most important thing.

Before my eyes, there blossomed in Ellen Larkin an arousal that exceeded my wildest imaginings. Droplets of passion sprung to her surfaces. Possibilities raced their way through Ellen's brain. How to make this happen? I heard her thinking. What to do first? What to say to Jane Fonda's face?

Well, *I* knew what to do first: get the music—"y'say y'want a revoloootion?"—off the deck and tell everybody that Jane Fonda was coming!

"Yes, yes, yes, yes . . ." I can still hear my Ellen chanting, half to me, half to herself, fingers and hair swirling around and above the junky console, full, earnest mouth buzzing the microphone like a bee on the prowl, trying to frame just the right first words to spring on the drowsy remnants of her scraggly audience.

"Okay—" is how she began. "I've just got . . . word has just come in . . . that tomorrow's rally will have an additional guest speaker—*Jane Goddamn Fonda!*"

Yes, that's how Ellen Larkin broke the news. Jane Goddamn Fonda.

There followed more of this, a jumble of enthusiastic fragments that, if followed carefully, added up to an ironclad guarantee that Jane Fonda would be here, in the flesh, next evening, disbursing glamorous agitprop to all comers and at no charge.

After ten minutes of all but commanding listeners to wake up everyone immediately—it was after midnight by now—and spread the word, Ellen Larkin ran out of breath. ". . . Be right back—" she gasped, and stabbed a tape into motion. She slumped into her chair for a motionless moment and then bolted up, facing me. "Fuck!" she announced, "nobody's gonna hear this now! We have to do something. Take action!" Ah, yes. Take action. The absolutely official organizing committee's prime tenet. Doesn't matter what action; just take some. But what was to follow would change everything.

Ellen Larkin decided that taking to the streets was the thing.

"You got a car?" Ellen asked, and as she asked this her fingers closed around my forearms and I felt something approaching religious zeal course through those freckly fingers.

"Yes. Sure!" I said.

"Okay. Okay. Go get it," Ellen said. Did I ask, What for? Did I wonder for a split second if I was about to sacrifice my Plymouth to the official organizing committee, all of whose members except one I despised? Did I question Jane Fonda's politics, or Ellen Larkin's? Ho ho.

Downstairs, I and my Plymouth idled, but not for long. The muscular girl who hours before had delivered Ellen Larkin's dope rapped her hairy knuckles on my window and said, "Hey, you Ellen's friend?"

Yeah, I thought. I'm Ellen's friend.

"Go upstairs," I was ordered. "Leave the car running."

In the broadcast booth, Ellen Larkin was pulling on her airman's coat and leaning into the microphone with renewed entreaty. "Tomorrow. The Green. If you care. If you know what's right. If you want to show how you feel. If you want to stand up to the White House. Be there. Now," she said, and pulled me down into her seat, "I'm hitting the street. We'll be cruising the campus all night. You'll hear us. Come out. Tell everyone. Tomorrow—Jane Fonda. Tom Hayden. Dick Gregory. You. Me." Behind me, some commotion; the equipment I'd hoisted up here for Ellen Larkin just hours before was being hauled right back out again. Ellen ignored my questioning look.

"Meanwhile, we'll be right here on WRSU all goddamn night, bringing you news as it happens about Jane, Tom, Dick—" I thought, Jane, Tom, Dick? That was quick. But then Ellen said, "—and plenty of rock, the best, from WRSU, with my friend . . ." and she whispered, "What's your name again?" So I said, into the mike, "Dennis Oldham." On her way out she kissed me—probably, I thought, as an apology for forgetting my name, but I didn't care. My upper lip was wet from her.

Music played. In between, I spoke. I watched the bouncing needle and tried not to trip it into the red zone too often. My rap was a parrot of what I'd listened to Ellen do for the last three-and-a-half hours: "Tomorrow. The Green. If you care. Six o'clock. If you have a watch."

Yes, dumb. Fumbling. Dopey. But here I was, on the radio.

And, I presently found out, some people actually were listening.

Because they started to call. Most wanted to know if this Jane Fonda bullshit was for real. Time and again I staked my professional reputation on her appearance. Some people didn't care about the war, but wanted to talk about Jane Fonda, who back then was widely considered to be—with apologies to all concerned movements—the most cold-blooded babe on the face of the earth. Some didn't care about Jane Fonda *or* the war; they just wanted me to play their favorite tune. I caught on; pretty soon I was even entertaining callers live on the air.

And where was Ellen Larkin? Well, she was motorcading through campus, town, and suburbia, leading the chase in my Plymouth, with its newly rigged megawatts of loudspeaker power. WRSU had been spray-painted in a shaky hand along both the Plymouth's rusty green flanks, and its hood stood adorned with scrawled *"Out Now!"* placards. I wouldn't find this out until later, of course, but even as I sat in her own broadcast studio, alone with her mike and her callers and her tapes and her quiet blinking lights and her night solitude, I felt the eeriest connection to her—sexual, without a doubt, but more. I had thrust upon me a battlefield commission in Ellen's underground society. I knew something that she and not many others knew. I knew about talking out into the faceless night, and feeling it listen. Okay.

# 9

"C'mere, c'mere. . . ."

"Where do you want these?"

"Forget them. C'mere."

"They're warm—"

"Yeah, that's great. Wait now . . . shhh." Into the mike-stump: "We're back, oh yeah, Doobie Brothers doin' it on WRSU where rock happens first, babies, and where you can get it anytime you want from me—Ellen Larkin. More tape from last night's *incredible, far out* happening on our own college green . . . love, music, voices against the war, and my own exclusive visit with a truly courageous lady, the remarkable Jane Fonda. So whatever you do tonight, whoever you're grooving with, don't forget to take us with you. Give a listen. Feel it, just like it happened right here. Tape it, so when your children ask you what you did to stop the murderous U.S. imperialist adventure in Vietnam, you can play the tape of Jane Fonda right here on this goddamn campus last night, when all of us—Jane, me, you, everyone—joined hands and said, 'No goddamn more! *OUT NOW!*' in one beautiful voice, loud enough so even the White House can't play deaf anymore.

"Now let's listen, and rock, and be together—just like we were, all of us, last night."

Music cued. Screech and thump, needles jump.

"Hi. Dennis. Hi." I march right up in my newfound familiarity. I am not merely a new member in this radio deal. I and my Ellen are one, fused by the soldering heat of Jane Fonda. We have been inseparable for twenty-six hours now; not alone, of course, except for those first few hours of her show last night, before Jane Fonda spread her magic beans all over our humble college green and made temporary crusaders of us all.

Ellen had been in the thick of things, though not exactly in charge of anything; the brotherhood of the official antiwar organizing committee wasn't about to put anything of weight into the hands of a girl. And yet Ellen Larkin was the campus personage that none of them were, and as late yesterday afternoon sunk into damp evening and the bloated, beer-sotted crowd began to grow surly at the non-appearance of Jane Fonda and company, it was my Ellen they pushed out onto the outdoor platform stage to keep the rabble at bay.

My credentials were these: I had Ellen's personal stamp of approval, I had not made an abortion of my six-hour marathon radio debut of the night before, and I had a car that worked and that I was willing to put, for now, at the movement's disposal. There wasn't time for anyone to question my qualifications, since Fondanoia had rendered the official organizing committee apoplectic *en masse*. Physical violence attended the discussion of who would be the organizing committee's official celebrity greeter; I, in fact, personally assisted in quelling a hair-pulling contest among two of the official antiwar organizing committee's ministers.

We hadn't slept in a very long time, my Ellen and I, and yet there seemed to be a residual seepage of adrenaline here in the WRSU broadcast studio. Afterglow is the sensation, I guess, although for the record the physical contact that had so far transpired between Ellen Larkin and myself had been limited to comradely bumps, touches and three hugs, the last of which left a profound impression on me, happening as it did minus Ellen's airman's coat. Loosened from the coat, Ellen's body breathed a sigh of relief. We hugged—this was upon our near-dawn retreat with equipment to this very studio—and Ellen's pungency flooded me; she was unwashed and unapologetic, and I stole a look through her tangled and, at this range, slightly moldy-smelling hair, and watched myself trace fingerlines in the dull sheen of sweat and grime on her freckly pink shoulder. Would my Ellen have considered my burgeoning erection politically inappropriate? So I feared; it was I who broke the embrace.

But did Ellen Larkin notice? No. Ellen never noticed anything. Sensitivity was not Ellen's strongest suit.

Nothing happened that next day, and I did not miss a moment of it. My debut of the night before had the unintended—though apparently not unwelcome, from where Ellen Larkin sat—effect of precipitating a mutiny among WRSU's non-activist on-air people. "Fuck them," was Ellen Larkin's emphatic reaction. "They just want to go home to their mommies and daddies early anyway." Holes abruptly opened up in the broadcast schedule. Ellen suggested I take some; I pounced on the offer. There was the little matter of an FCC license, but Ellen assured me that WRSU was the last outfit on the FCC's watchlist and besides, my minor gesture of civil disobedience would be serving a higher cause.

It was spring. Nitrogen atoms, yanked from plants by the electromagnetic turbulence of Jane Fonda, twitched about, working their mischievous vicissitudes on all who dared foray out into their murky midst. Few escaped the insidious intoxication, though the symptoms varied wildly.

The ministers of the official antiwar organizing committee, for example, seemed to be wandering the campus in victorious stupefaction. Little was heard from them here at 'RSU. On the other hand, little seemed left to be organized: the school year was about to be declared over, as even the recalcitrant science faculty had apparently been Fondacized into political action. Students who didn't give a shit—the substantial majority—were stuffing their bags and loading their cars. Sultry spring aromas infused the local beerhalls. People were horny.

We—my Ellen and I—had ensconced ourselves in the studio, wrapping ourselves in command-post attitude. People called. Are classes really canceled? What about grades? What about summer session? What about the Beatles?

We handled calls and dispensed information, making it sound official whether we knew what we were talking about or not. We did not, of course, speak for the university, but the university was in such disarray just now that *somebody* had to tell people *something*, and we were, after all, in control of the radio, which any student of history will tell you is the first objective of revolutionaries. Making up official policy was, for my Ellen and I, a delicious secret subversion that we had faith would somehow ripple its way south on Interstate 95, all the way to the Pentagon.

As for Jane Fonda, she did in fact appear, as advertised, although the other celebrities in her antiwar tour had split to other campuses. I wouldn't have wanted to be, say, earnest Tom Hayden, showing up and explaining to our throng that he was here while Jane had gone on to Princeton. Oh boy. But such was not the case; Jane struck at something after ten that night, rock time: four hours late.

Our campus green could nestle about three thousand students and their families comfortably for graduation; using that barometer, I'd put the Fondafest at about six thousand bruised and battered souls. By next day, Ellen and I had inflated it to ten or fifteen thousand for the gratification of our listeners. The first rows below the stage had been commandeered since noon by the antiwar faithful; by the time of Jane Fonda's arrival, the rest of the crowd resembled the hounds of hell at a British football match.

From my perch at the corner of the stage, helping Ellen Larkin's crowd-control efforts by goosing the music a notch louder every time an ominous new roar of impatience swelled the green, I saw the organizing committee ministers making like a jailbreak for the curb as three long cars screeched their way to a halt. It didn't take long for the crowd to catch on. Things took flight—beercans, bras, sneakers, shirts, shorts, a flock of Frisbees—and the noise rose like a dome, holding the thrown objects aloft, roiling up through the canopy of maples and sycamores, mushrooming out into the night.

The first thing that happened is that three large people got out of the car, propelled by a collective jet blast that knocked the entire organizing committee back fifteen feet. The *coup d'etat* was complete without a shot fired. Jane was in charge.

I gesticulated at my Ellen to make an introduction, but before we could kill the music Jane Fonda and her hulking anonymous retinue had overrun the stage. Jane embraced Ellen Larkin, to the fury of the scrambling, lacerated ministers below. Jane hoisted the microphone and said hi; the crowd lost what was left of its mind.

Her speech was a potent brew of passion, reason and rage. There was to it not a hint of contrivance. Some in the crowd—a crowd who had come not to rally against the war but to ogle Jane Fonda, pure and simple—found themselves following her words and being moved by them. These were in the minority.

Then, with the suddenness of a spring shower, it was over. I looked at my watch: Jane Fonda had addressed us for eight minutes. True, she had said all that needed to be said, fired all her guns; still—eight minutes. This had been a surgical strike, like Colonel Elmo's F-4 flying close-air support over Jane's last stop, Vietnam. In quick, hit hard, vanish. The sniveling organizing committee didn't even try to intercept her on the way back to the cars.

But on the way out, Jane Fonda latched onto Ellen Larkin, and bustled her into their escaping phalanx. Ellen thumbed me out onto the stage on her way out; I stumbled my way through the microphone wires and presently found myself staring down a bemused, blustering drunken multitude who'd expected to be spending more than eight minutes with Jane Fonda this evening for their four-hour wait.

So I made a speech. Not an eight-minute speech; not a lucid speech; probably not even an audible speech above the rumbling surge of discontent among the shortchanged. But a speech. Enough to close off the festivities, salted with antiwar exhortations and plugs for WRSU. I may have mentioned my own name, and I garlanded Ellen Larkin with the same type of heroic testimonial that the organizing committee's inner circle liked to shovel upon itself. And when I sensed a dangerous swirl of unfulfilled expectations looking to turn unpleasant, I made the traditional roadhouse move: turned off the lights and beat it.

What transpired in the brief moments between Jane Fonda and my Ellen Larkin? Nothing memorable, to be sure, and Ellen had the calculating presence of mind to capture every inconsequential second of it on her portable cassette recorder. And Ellen and I managed to slop the entire next day's broadcast around snippets of Jane and Ellen, Ellen and Jane.

What an interview. How many days on the road now? Where's Dick Gregory? How was North Vietnam? Do you resent your treatment at home? Will this do any good?

To which I think Jane responded: 'Eighteen; Yale; hellish and beautiful; goddamn right I do;' and, 'the people's voices must be heard.' This last part was the half of Jane Fonda's answer that we broadcast; her follow-up was, as I recall, unexpectedly and profanely pessimistic. Not in tune with the general mood, in Ellen's opinion, of galloping headless euphoria that Ellen Larkin and I were doing our blind stinking best to perpetuate. We stuck with the 'people's voices' part, and kreugered the rest.

Here we are. Others have done their bland little program stints, but Ellen and I have chosen to stay, and now yesternight has become tonight and it's the chemically assisted Ellen Larkin Show again. Where is the absolutely official antiwar organizing committee, so much in evidence up until last evening? "Fuck them," is the way my Ellen put it, from range of unprecedented closeness. Arms have found their way around waists and exploratory rubbing has commenced. As soon as Ellen cues up the next record, I remember thinking, I'm going to give this its long-awaited shot.

I don't know what I expected, but Ellen responded with exactly, precisely the same florid rush of breath and moisture that the first Jane Fonda warning shots produced just about this time last night. A course tongue fired into my mouth and jeans ground themselves into me. She was strong. That moldy smell from her hair welled up into my face and heightened, if possible, my desire. I can't explain it beyond pleading attraction to her unadorned physical candor. I began to hoist her shirt.

She stepped away but not in protest. Oh no. She stepped away to lock the door. To turn off the inside lights except for the desk console, which I suppose would have rendered us in silhouette to anyone outside the glass wall. To feed 'Volunteers' and others into waiting decks. To fetch me a rubber from her bag.

She stepped back to the console as the music ground to a halt. "The Dead, babies, here on 'RSU. It's the night after. Things won't ever be the same, will they? Hell, no." As she whispered this to the unseen, she unbuckled her biker's belt and kicked off her boots; holey socks held on as she wrestled her patchwork jeans to the floor. "It's nighttime, now—smoky and hot. The energy refuses to go away . . . I hope you feel it like I do." This she purred into her weary servile mike, leaning over it with her freckled and, in this absence of real light, creamily pellucid legs careened out and away toward me. Tiny green panties peeked out from under her weathered tee shirt; comically mortified socks drooped down. "Okay," she said, "the 'Plane. Do it, Grace." And music whined. She turned down—but not off—her microphone. I crept up to her and tried to turn her to me but she looked over her shoulder like the mirthfully scolding maestra and said, "Here, like this."

So next I went to silent frantic work on my shirt buttons. But again she stopped me. "In case somebody comes." I was not to undress beyond the essential. She unbuckled and unzipped me and ripped open her little packet and sheathed me and then turned again to the console and there I stood, pants at my knees, arms at my sides, my securely gloved and unabashed erection bobbing out into the night, staring with me at the back of Ellen Larkin.

Over the console she bent, down toward her faithful microphone. On played the music. She turned it down slightly, and her mike up a notch; this she sometimes did to soothe a rap out over a tune, making it a momentary background track for herself. An Alison Steele trick. The Nightbird. "Where are they right now, do you think?" whispered Ellen. Who? I wondered. "What are they doing tonight?" Is she talking to me, I thought—but no, she was talking to *them*. "I wish they were doing what *we're* doing, don't you?" Now she brought the tune back up—not all the way—and brought her mike down—not all the way. She looked up over her shoulder at me and nodded me toward her. I inched up and saw her slide the crotch of her greenies to the side, watched her haunch up for me. I pointed to the microphone; she smiled.

Even sleeved, inside felt delectable. She moved with me a little, but not precipitously. I teetered a bit for leverage. Ellen played with her hair, her mouth inches from the half-juiced microphone. We fucked tentatively.

Then she reached for the volume again. I froze, and she stopped short. She turned her lips up to my ear; I twisted and strained not to lose my place.

"Let them," she said, or something like that. "I want to let them think I'm getting off with them. They can't hear much . . . just a little of us, inside the music." Then she turned us up, and cupped my behind to encourage me on. I peeked over her shoulder and watched her freckly face, hair floating and flailing in unruly tails across her upturned cheek. I think she was whispering something into the microphone, to *them*, but I couldn't hear and didn't really care. My legs threatened to cramp and the efforts at silence were knotting my back, but I held off stoically.

Music ended and Ellen reached for electronics; I leaned with her. Balance was precarious. We threatened to topple each other. But Ellen Larkin managed, a professional in the circumstances. She did no intro, allowing one tune to crash headlong into the next. Secure for the moment, Ellen leaned down again, resting her head on the littered desk within whispering distance of the mike. She reached out over her head to the deskback and braced herself, then smiled up to me with closed eyes and the final invitation.

I listened to her breath; I watched the sound-level needle breathe with her. We were going to go through with this. Now.

She raised herself up on the balls of her feet for me and now things felt in proper form for the execution. Music and Ellen's breathing came faster; I couldn't help listening. Could *they* hear?

Ellen was talking to *them* all but inaudibly; I watched her lips form her commentary, I watched her face *show* them. I could make it out: ". . .sweet love we all need sweet love don't we, babies? Oh we do . . . now listen to your Ellen she's gonna show you all about sweet love . . ." It was then, I suppose, that I remembered that Ellen Larkin had breasts—those Gemini grails of my months-long voyage, those terminal images all the times we'd made it without her knowing it, or me. I lay my weight on Ellen's back and reached around under the shirt she wouldn't allow me to remove—in case someone comes!— and tried to imagine what they looked like by what I felt and soon I watched Ellen Larkin's lips tell the microphone, *almost* silently, "God, I love to fuck for you," and even though I knew perfectly well who she was talking to, I took her, for that moment, to mean me.

Contemplating those days of Ellen Larkin deep into this late night, after duties have been fulfilled and milk has been spilled, it occurs to me that Lyndon McDonald's ruinous excursion through Southeast Asia might well have coincided with the notorious Hanoi pilgrimage of Ellen's fleeting demigod, Jane Fonda. Giving succor to the enemy, our Jane was accused of at the time, and plenty worse; but those of us enlisted, passionately or otherwise, in the rear-guard campus theater of action couldn't possibly have had the same visceral reaction to the escapades of Hanoi Jane as a big, petrified New York black kid battened down in the belly of the jungle under a teeming monsoon, trying to elude the treetop attentions of barefoot teenage snipers sighting down their guaranteed rustproof Kalashnikovs, listening on scratchy transistor radios to perplexing dispatches from the North. Maybe Lyndon cursed our Jane for a traitor in chorus with his fellow foxhole captives, but I can't help thinking that deep down, Lyndon, or someone shoulder-to-shoulder in the same soggy, precarious boat but with a few more marbles still in play, might have thought, "Wish somebody would listen to that white girl and get us the hell outa here."

What do you suppose Lyndon McDonald would make of Hanoi Jane today, all these years later? Well, Lyndon, you'll be pleased to know that Jane took off her fatigues and came home and, by and by, she and her country pretty much forgave each other their trespasses. She got on with her life, as you might have gotten on with yours. An epic divergence of fates, I know, but this is not one we can pin on Henry Kissinger or Richard Nixon, because, as you know better than anybody, Lyndon, our Jane was born holding most of the cards before anyone ever heard of Vietnam.

# 10

WE are in the last long moments before paleness purges us of this October night. Our silver caravel cruises its pools of infernal light and peers past fugitives' corners. It's too late to sleep, and too early to go to work.

I am nestled in the womby recesses of the Velezmobile. Opposite me, Ms. Elite lies fetally curled and motionless across the forward seat. Her shoes are missing and my jacket cloaks her shoulders. Except for those legs, she could be a sweet child sleeping homeward bound from a day trip to grandma's. Except for those legs, which don't bring grandma's hearth immediately to mind. Solemnly ensconced at the helm of this pig is my partner Roberto Velez.

I can see the back of Velez's head, but not his eyes in the rearview mirror; it's too far away. Velez's hands white-knuckle the wheel but he pilots us smoothly through what's left of the night. Our graveyard cruise has taken us uptown this evening; we have prowled the streets of Velez's distant childhood and navigated the scabrous wards of Manhattan's outskirts. As Ms. Elite slept we parked, wordlessly, across the street from Immaculata Velez's walk-up; this splendid fatuous Cadillac loitering in the deep unbroken years of smothering night that Velez thinks he has managed to leave behind.

We might have stayed longer had not a police cruiser assumed the obvious: that this Cadillac is here on a commercial junket.

They wanted to search, the two cops. A man and a woman. Bristly Italian boy, workout type, a barrel-chested guido with hair curling way down over his collar; his partner a tired-eyed Hispanic girl, bottom-heavy even without her crammed, clattering service belt. Prowling their flinty precinct streets and what did they find? A rich radio badboy at the wheel of a limo, an unconscious very downtown-looking babe and an uncongenial other male in the back. But when Velez politely—deferentially—invited them to search the car, they lost interest and told us to beat it.

I am waiting for this whory, filmy residue from Arielle's promotion party to leach out of my skin. Velez and I are cold sober, except for the taste of cocaine that I think Velez may have finally accepted from one of our sales geeks. Economic aftershocks from tonight's party have surely reached Cali by now. Velez, despite the big talk, is ferociously temperate in his consumptions; as for me, once was scary enough. I am not strong like my partner.

The 24-hour sports channel stares, muted, at me. I have won money and lost money, all within the margin of tolerable exchange. Next week I think I will not make any bets on sports contests, to see how it feels. Success will depend, I suspect, on finding an appropriate substitute addiction.

At the curb across the street from Immaculata Velez's house, the street's streaming refuse—piles and swirls and disgusting rat-gray mottles—started to feel weirdly animate. There began to seem a feral meanness to the roiling filth under and around us: scaly hands and slimy gray tongues reaching up around our preposterous fat limousine, looking to reclaim us from our momentary exaltation. There seemed so little to buoy us; the unstanchable floe of decomposition seemed terrifyingly unimpressed with us three perched above. I envied Ms. Elite her sleep.

"You awake, Coolie?" This comes to me in a whisper, over the Velezmobile's intercom. I look up through the window slit that separates us—sleeping Ms. Elite and I—from Velez. I think he's looking back. I nod.

"How 'bout our friend?" I rest my cheek on the back of flat hands to indicate that Ms. Elite is out. Is it possible that Velez doesn't know her name either? I pick up the phone behind me; this cuts off the intercom speaker. "What's her name?" I whisper.

"Kendall," says Velez. "You hungry?"

"That her first name?"

"I'm not sure. She says, 'Just Kendall.' Lotta these model types go by just one name. You hungry?"

We pull up in front of the Moondance, a tiny '50s dinette in long eyelashes, sequins and falsies; at the deserted curb, the Velezmobile stretches from one end of the Moondance to the other. The Moondance has nothing to recommend it except that its door is open and its hearth inviting at 5:00 a.m. I lean forward to wake Ms. Elite but Velez waves me through the window to let her sleep.

We are presented some brackish ponds of breakfast. "We're going on strike," Velez says.

"Immediately?"

"Almost."

"You running out of money?"

"You want to work for that lowlife tabloid pederast Sir Harold crumpet-fucker Fish?" This Velez manages to squeeze past cheekfuls of guacamole and cereal. I love to watch Velez eat. He looks up. "Huh? Do you?"

"He might not be so bad."

"Not so bad?" Velez kneads a brittle hunk of roll. "Hey, Coolie, you're the fucking newsman; don't you read the news?"

"Ah, that's your lawyers talking."

"Hey, hey," Velez says, poking his oozing toast my way. "My lawyers—*our* lawyers—are smart guys. Don't let their fondness for little girls fool you."

"*Their* fondness," I say.

"Don't start," says Velez, "I have nothing to be ashamed of. Lately."

"Me neither," I say.

"So don't start."

The coffee edges my belly toward revolution. "How come we're going on strike?"

"To fuck up the sale."

I see. "Harold crumpet-fucker Fish won't want damaged goods."

"No Velez & Oldham, no shirtee."

This strikes me as brutally and unexpectedly logical. Provisionally, I like it. "Your lawyers think this up?" Velez shrugs and munches and checks his watch. "C'mon. Let's go to work."

It's still nighttime out here in the foothills of downtown. The moon, so wickedly resplendent above the evening's earlier, sorrier proceedings, has left us the black empty impassive acceptance of a denser, meaner day ahead. We approach the Velezmobile quietly so as not to disturb Ms. Elite. But Ms. Elite is gone.

I catch here a furtive passage of something across Velez's eyes— disappointment? Worry? Pique? I don't know. But he covers in a flash, and soon we're bounding up Sixth Avenue, scrambling the earliest of the dog walkers with their pooper scoopers and the can hunters and paper fetchers in our path. We pit stop for newspapers of our own and squeal on.

Velez has something on his mind; this I know because he hasn't started pulling on his game face for the show. A silly-seeming but deadly serious ritual in the hour approaching airtime, Velez pumps attitude—a deliberate, physical inflation of his energy level, his consciousness, designed to overcome exhaustion, cocktail flu, purple rain, chemical shrouds of all description and, most amazing of all, the masochistic repetitive monotony of eleven-and-a-half years of this: days, each like the last in all but the most peripheral of details.

This is the real reason, I suppose, why we go to such lengths to drive everybody crazy: it's them or us. Like Velez says.

"What?" I prompt.

"What about Sally Wallach?" Velez asks.

Ah, finally. But what to say? "God, man, I'm confused—"

"You should spend some time with her."

"I keep telling myself—"

"That way, you can find out if we're fucking up the sale."

"What?"

"Yeah," says my partner. "Y'know, a casual inquiry once in a while. 'By the way, Sally, is Harold Fish ready to shitcan this sale business with old E. P. yet?' Discreetly, of course."

"You want me to use Sally to spy on her old man?"

"Well, hell, Coolie, you're not using her for anything else, that I can see."

"Velez, you slimeball."

Velez makes simpering noises like I have hurt his feelings. "What? What?" he croaks. "What'd I say? Huh?"

"She's a nice girl is all," I say, "and I would prefer not to turn her into a spy—"

"Yes, yes, she's a nice girl. A nice, nice girl. She's so fucking nice, Coolie, that you should be taking her out anyway, even if she wasn't the daughter of the very Massa Wallach who's about to cut our aggots off because he doesn't *feel* like being in the radio business anymore." Velez backs off now, and says, "I'm not saying you should ask her to spy on her old man. Jeezus."

"Fine."

"All I'm saying is, you're a lonely, borderline pathetic old sack of shit and you could use some company and who better than Sally Wallach? Sooo, she's a little young. But hey, I bet she's been around. She's done the bop—trust me. An' she sure doin' a slam dance in *your* pants. Anyway, she's gonna be history soon; I'm not asking you to get married."

"You want me to get married, I get married. It's in the contract."

"Fuck you. And, while you're spending a little light recreational time with Sally, just see which way the wind's blowing with Harold Fishass. That's all."

While he's winding this up, he's winding himself up too, because now we're outside the Too Tall Jones building and it's about time for the Velez & Oldham Show. I have a newscast in less than five minutes. So, "I'll think about it," I tell Velez, and I start tearing and highlighting my *New York Times*.

Upstairs, Velez wastes no time declaring war: no sooner do I finish running down the football scores and apologizing for my guaranteed picks of the week than Velez announces on-air auditions for strike-jocks, the temporary replacements for Velez and Oldham, who are walking at the end of the week and—who knows—maybe never coming back. Unless certain demands are met. Lots of demands.

First to fly into coronary arrest is our fireplug program manager, Arielle. Arielle, whose home video collection no doubt features the complete fitness library of my old comrade-in-arms Jane Fonda, is late today, and I take her first call from her carphone within moments of Velez's announcement of our personal Starsearch. Arielle is waxed in on the Martha deck of the George Washington Bridge—not always a congenial perch for a cellular phone. Velez knows perfectly well whom he's talking to through the static, and pretends not to.

"Hey, we have our first caller for the WRTR Thunder strike team, Coolie!" Velez yells to me from three feet away. "Whatcher name? Huh? Adrian? L'Oreal? I can't hear you!" Well, *I* can hear her just fine, and she's telling Velez to stuff the strike team bullshit because there isn't going to be any strike because there aren't any problems and just *what* demands is Velez talking about? Ah, but we know Velez isn't going to listen to reason now, don't we? He's having fun. Besides, he'll have no pity on Arielle. The only reason she's still working here is that she hasn't fucked Velez yet; in Arielle's short-term favor, the advent of Ms. Elite has made the prospect of Velez and Arielle dim indeed.

Weekend approaches.

I have received new instructions from Jane Oldham's mother through her attorney. Jane's mother's attorney is a severely coifed and oversturdy woman with left-lane political ambitions. In spite of this woman's relentless orthodox belligerence, most responsible parents would not consider these new orders unreasonable: No more roof. No more R-rated movies. No more industrial-strength chili from Machito's. Just the type of earnest demands people pay attorneys to enforce.

But we're not going to pay much attention to these instructions, Jane and I; and even if we wanted to, Jane's godfather Roberto Velez wouldn't let us. It was Velez's idea that we—Velez, Ms. Elite, my daughter and I—attend this very afternoon a neighborhood showing of *Friday 13th, Part* . . . well, I'm not sure which part, but it's the one where Jason, the walking-cuisinart hockey-goalie psycho, kills some babes and their boyfriends. Perhaps you caught that one, too.

That Velez would foment rebellion among me, Jane's mother and Jane's mother's butch attorney shouldn't surprise you by now. Jane's mother and Velez have a history, don't forget, and the way things turned out I know Velez feels he should side with me in the more trivial subversions of this relationship's protracted epilogue. He knows that in the small matters he can call Jane's mother and mollify for the moment the pernicious little spews of pettiness that I seem so uncannily adept at evoking in her. To her he can say, "Ah, you know Dennis." To me, he can say, "Ah, you know Sarah."

Of course, he's stunningly wrong on both counts, but it works. Like a mantra. You know Dennis you know Sarah you know Dennis you know Sarah. He chants; the snakes go into a trance.

Here we stand in line with the regular folks. Velez has not been recognized—not so unusual. Would *you* know Velez if you passed him on the street, the way you'd pick out Woody Allen or Robert DeNiro or Spike Lee or the other Manhattan furniture? Yeah, I suppose you would. Anyhow, Ms. Elite is the one getting all the eyeworks from the twelve- and thirteen-year-old boys who have gathered with us outside this twelvetuple-screen movie palace to see Jason the hockey killer eviscerate all who cross his psychotic path. What would I think if I were thirteen, standing here on line for the Saturday movie, right next to the four of us? What would I make of this crew? Here's what I'd be wondering: Is the babe old enough to be the little kid's mother? Uh uh. Old enough to be one of the old guys' girlfriend? Maybe, but how come the best babes like to hang out with old guys? Money, that's how come. And the little girl. Can't be the Spanish guy's kid; not with the goldilocks. Maybe the other guy's. Fucking grownups, man. That's what I'd be thinking about Velez, Jane Oldham, Ms. Elite and me if I were one of these grimy little rodents in their Batman tee shirts waiting out here in the loud afternoon to chill with Jason.

Ms. Elite, meanwhile, is playing it cagey with Jane Oldham. While Velez is nearby, Ms. Elite stays cool and keeps her distance. As soon as Velez is out of sight, though, Ms. Elite melts down in delight at the touch and the smell of my Jane; the very feel, it seems, of my daughter's breath on her cheek makes Ms. Elite swoon. Ms. Elite manifests, for the private moment, a touching thirst for the kind of familial moistness that she hopes she hasn't left behind in Kansas forever. Then Velez resurfaces, as he did an hour earlier from my kitchen with a platter of Velezburgers for us four, and Ms. Elite's eyes and hands turn to marble. Jane Oldham, who seems knocked silly by Ms. Elite, is confused; I am not. Conspiracy theorist that I am, here's my analysis: Ms. Elite would, left to her own devices, like nothing better than to slather Jane Oldham with jayhawker affection for hours on end. But to let Velez get wind of this would be to betray mating instincts, a sure ticket, Ms. Elite figures, to instant exile from the obdurately single Roberto Velez.

This is not a stupid girl, Ms. Elite. I've told you that.

Inside the theater, Velez is flanked by Ms. Elite and Jane Oldham, who is scrunched down between her father and her godfather. We are brimming with barrels of popcorn and candy and soda—enough, if she found out, to make Jane's mother punch automatic dial for her attorney. Ms. Elite made the popcorn run, an anomaly of sorts since Ms. Elite does not eat more than trace quantities of solid food—ever—at least that I or Velez have witnessed. Yet here she came in search of us in the semi-dark among all this roiling adolescence, loaded with armfuls of junk food, gliding down the aisle with her carelessly pinned-up hair and her buckskin jacket and her frayed, painted-on jeans and her reflectors, looking like the all-time champion American teenager that she pretty much still is, when she thinks nobody's looking.

This package is not lost on the crowd: howling food fights screech to a halt in her wake, as teenage boys gape and marvel at Ms. Elite. And none of this seems incongruous to Roberto Velez is what I'm getting at. None of this is weird. All this is in perfect harmony with the underlying philosophy of everything Velez does: nobody told him he couldn't.

The mayhem on the screen doesn't disappoint. Blood flies and oozes and curdles and seeps and sprays; the audience is appreciative. In a land of undeliverable promises, there's something deeply satisfying about Jason up there. He is unaffected and uncomplicated, and he delivers. I glance at Jane Oldham from time to time and there she sits like an autumn squirrel with bulging cheeks full of popcorn, as if she has taken it as a personal mission to consume everything Ms. Elite has fetched her. The cartoon violence above us seems to be having no effect whatsoever. How about being a little scared, kid, so dad can throw a protective arm around your shoulder?

What happens instead is that Jane whispers to me that she wants to go sit next to Ms. Elite. I glance over but Jane is already out of her seat and scampering across Velez's legs. "You sit over there," my daughter orders Velez on her way across his lap. Ms. Elite cannot hide her delight. And it's not five minutes before Jane Oldham is fast asleep, her splendid, placid, gloriously unconcerned face lying against Ms. Elite's chest, strands of buckskin fringe fingering their way through my daughter's pale blonde hair. Velez makes like he's so utterly engrossed in the cinematic experience that none of this registers on him. He's not without his compassionate moments, you see. I, meanwhile, sit desperately glad to be in this tiny midst, whether I truly qualify or not.

My daughter is a fearless child. Among the things she is not afraid of are bugs, being alone, heights, school, grownups, rodents, motor vehicles, strange sounds, silence, and the dark. The only thing that spooks my Jane is the prospect of her parents crossing paths, as we must, twice a month, to hand her off between us. That's why Jane and I have such shitty Sundays; she knows that her mother will soon come for her. It's not that she doesn't like her Mom, oh no; it's just that the palpable weirdness that we bring out in each other, Jane's mother and I, poisons Jane's chemical balance in regrettable if completely understandable ways.

This lack of natural fear is a cause of concern to her mother Sarah, who would feel better if Jane were afraid of everything I mentioned above, and wouldn't mind a bit if she were afraid of me, too. Jane's unintimidability quietly infuriates her mother, who has come at this stage of her privileged life to define the world purely in terms of who can intimidate whom. Sarah has discussed this with Jane's teachers and her school psychologist—yes, at five years old great psychological boils are already festering, Sarah has repeatedly been assured. In this town, every ostensibly well-adjusted kid is assumed to be hiding a catalogue of vile neuroses and, according to Sarah, there is general agreement that the child has wrapped herself in a massive cloak of emotional denial that can be attributed directly to what a malicious cocksucker I am. This isn't a direct quote from Sarah, who no longer uses words like 'cocksucker.' But no one can make words like 'irresponsible' and 'infantile' and 'self-absorbed' sound so much like 'cocksucker' as my former wife Sarah can.

Among Roberto Velez's contributions as a godfather is that he has encouraged me to disregard most current child-rearing wisdom. Velez's theory is that the kid's heart will be thoroughly hardened toward me before long, so we might as well at least have some fun that Jane can remember for a while before she's old enough to be taught to hate me on principle. So we go to Jason movies and feed her anything she's willing to try to keep down—including beer, when she insists—and if we don't get around to putting her to bed until two or three in the morning we don't worry about it too much. We are at Machito's—Ms. Elite, Velez, Jane Oldham and I—and Ms. Elite points out that most five-year-olds are in bed by club-closing time. Velez puts her straight: "The kid can catch up on her sleep when she's older."

Velez has decided that our remote Veteran's Day broadcast from the Vietnam Memorial will be a great time to debut the Velez & Oldham Show strike team. Our strike deadline is thus penciled in for two weeks from now.

Velez figures it this way: Arielle and the Thunder Rock suits will have a tough time turning people away right out in the downtown open, whereas they could pretty well barricade us all on the eighteenth floor of Too Tall Jones. Velez also figures that some of my fellow Vietnam veterans could use some vocational assistance.

We spent this morning lining up auditionees. The WRTR switchboard, needless to say, had kittens; Velez decided, in the interest of fairness, that applicants could just keep calling all day, even after the Velez & Oldham Show was over. Thus were Stevie Joe Adams, Kenny Appleton, Cheryl Mann and even old Adrian recruited into our subversion. The most likely product of this exercise will be flame-throwing chaos; this will suit Velez and me just fine.

But I think a few private precautions are in order. I must visit Lyndon McDonald, whose deep-night amphitheater we're about to co-opt for our remote broadcast. Our people will be there at the plaza straight through for days before the morning of the broadcast, and who can say what such displacement will trigger in Lyndon? For although I haven't let on to Raylene McDonald, Lyndon's condition is lately taking some disquieting turns. His hands are perpetually bandaged now. Things rattle in his putrid pockets. His mania seems more focused, if only in bursts. And he has begun listening faithfully to the Velez & Oldham Show. All of these I see as signs that Lyndon McDonald's phase of benign and invisible craziness may be teetering to a close.

# 11

"An assassin," murmurs Velez. "Look. Look at that. A killer. An absolute merchant of death." The subject of this sanguinary litany is—guess who—Ms. Elite, that sashaying six-foot shadow sewn to the soles of Roberto Velez's goddamn feet.

Okay, okay. I'm sorry.

We seem to spend an awful lot of time these days worshipping the ground Ms. Elite walks on. That's all I'm saying. Ms. Elite gets a glob of pizza on her nose and Velez—not to mention Jane Oldham, my very own five-year-old daughter—immediately cell-phones Stockholm to inform the Nobel committee. Every time Ms. Elite lands herself a modeling assignment, which she does three or four times a day, for Christ's sake, and for which her only qualifications are her accidental architecture and her ability to walk on her hind legs without falling over, the rest of the day is canceled for a celebration.

But since I am an accredited journalist, in the interest of balanced reporting and despite my profound suspicions of her being up to no good where Velez is concerned, I suppose I must acknowledge that in this, her brief shining moment, Ms. Elite fills her role—slathering her blistering beauty all over the capitalist enterprise—as breathtakingly as just about anybody. There. Happy?

But tonight they can celebrate without me. I think I'll catch up on Bennie at Bennie's bar, where the women are taken at face value.

Ah, but first we have to finish this program and have lunch with Tom the Lawyer, and make an appearance somewhere that presumptuous little muscle toner Arielle promised we—promised *Velez*—would show up. Yes, I'll go; it will get me past those abysmal hours of the day between finishing the Velez & Oldham Show and my late-day nap. Besides, I am usually the designated sacrificial lamb at these appearances: we all cruise up in the Velezmobile, Velez pockets his humanitarian award, throws me to the squids and makes his sleazy getaway before anyone's the wiser.

News has been flat. The city is lurching through a mayoral campaign of incomparable boredom; accredited journalists like myself are reduced to baiting the candidates into newsworthiness. And while the nation's chief executive has recently and famously tread upon his presidential appendage, he and his bride provide only occasional relief for the kind of news vacuum seldom seen in the rollicking years of his predecessors. Perhaps California will choose this week to jump into the ocean. Californians can be counted on during slow news weeks.

So Velez and I have taken matters into our own hands and created some news. Velez has launched an on-air investigation of my gambling habits, calling friends and acquaintances and others, including my former wife's cloven-hooved attorney, posing as an FCC investigator looking into alleged Federal wire violations by one Dennis Peter Oldham. "Do you have any direct or indirect knowledge of Mr. Oldham moving sums of money across state lines for purposes of wagering . . ." is how Velez's line of questioning goes. "Would you be willing to arrange to meet with Mr. Oldham and wear a wire . . ."

For my part, I have been appointed talent coordinator for the strike team auditions. Applications, as you may imagine, are avalanching in. Unbidden, people are sending homemade tapes; I, as talent coordinator, have decided to get a jump on the auditions and play a few. These are voices gloriously uncleansed of their ancestry; these people sound like they're *from* somewhere. Sons and daughters of authentic wretched refuse from teeming shores. Not like Velez. Not like me. We—except when Velez figures it behooves him to sound Puerto Rican for a few minutes—ooze that synthetic mid-Atlantic white noise that has anesthetized you for so long now that people with authentic neighborhood in their voices sound ignorant and silly on the radio.

These auditions, by the way, are having the unintended effect of sending our ratings to Neptune. This is one of the things Velez wants to talk to Tom the Lawyer about, no doubt. Our strategy of subversion is not exactly taking hold.

The morning frolics on. "Dennis Oldham, please."

"This is Oldham." See? Even I do it.

"Is this where I get to audition?"

"This is the spot."

"Okay, okay, now, wait. Wait. Are you gonna put me on the radio, like, right now?" A strong boy with a voice not quite settled yet. Determined little scrub on his lip where an NYPD-style mustache will one day reside. Hair close on top, and maybe a swaggering little rat tail in back. His girlfriend runs a mousse factory and has the Doublemint jaw of a pitbull. How do I know all this over the phone? Ho ho.

"You ready?"

"No no no no . . . hold on. Should I, like, y'know, tell everybody my name an' everything? 'Cause some of these guys been auditioning, hey, haddahell anybody know who they are? Right?"

But the Grand Auditioner is heartless; you see, *this*, baby, is the audition, and the earnest young man has already flunked.

His public humiliation commences in the midst of this: three radio professionals, a paralyzing Kansas model and a sweet-smelling station intern of your recent acquaintance pack the official Velez & Oldham broadcast booth. The environs bear the blustery aftermath of a recent donut storm. Velez whispers to Ms. Elite, who whispers back. Enginette Casey looks to me, to see if we have enough. I point; Casey rewinds. I ask our auditionee if he's near a radio. He says yes. I advise him that it might be easier on him if he turned it off for a few minutes. The commercial ends: we have sold a few hundred more Korean cars. Enginette Casey gives me the finger. "Back with the strike team auditions, gang," I say to what's left of the one-point-three. "Next is a guy with a radio future—take that to the bank."

"With your football picks," Velez takes time out to say.

"Ah, welcome back, Roberto; I was beginning to think you were on strike already," I say to Velez and our listeners. You just love it when we banter, Velez and I; one marketing focus group after another tells us so. "I love when they rag each other," someone will say. "It's cool the way they break each other's balls." The Thunder pays immense sums to document such audience sentiments.

"Let's hear the guy," Velez says.

"Yeah, well listen closely, Roberto my man, because the next voice you hear is the future of American radio." I give it to enginette Casey, who rolls.

". . .this where I get to audition?" comes the gurgling gearbox of a voice. Sally Wallach stops to listen. Since Arielle's promotion party, Sally has shown me a new, sisterly face: all the touching, but none of the tension. I have blown it with Sally, which is just as well. ". . .put me on the radio, like, right now?" Everyone giggles; Velez howls. ". . . some of these guys been auditioning, hey, haddahell anybody know who they are? Right?"

And now uptown, to a Catholic school in Washington Heights not all that far away from the ancestral village of Roberto Velez. Velez will be presenting a public service medal to two students for writing a play about saying no to drugs. Velez will undoubtedly receive a public service medal of his own for presenting the kids *their* public service medal. Inflation is currently ravaging the public service medal market in New York and, I wouldn't be surprised, elsewhere. I report some of these awards on my official Velez & Oldham Show news. Recently, people have been getting a lot of public service medals for inventing worthy programs for the destitute that no one in authority has the slightest intention of funding, but they make uplifting counterpoints to the tales of Middle Eastern suicide bombings and millenialist cult shenanigans here at home that I feel it my responsibility to pass along to you.

Lunch happens in the Velezmobile. Velez has given our driver the day off, and has turned the wheel over to Ms. Elite. If this narrative ends abruptly, you will know why.

We—Roberto Velez, Tom the Lawyer, and me—are dining on Quarter-Pounders with cheese, french fries, and cocaine; the latter mostly for Tom the Lawyer and, yes, I suppose I must report it: for my partner Roberto Velez. But Velez's hit is roughly equivalent to the amount that Fat Tom the Lawyer will sneeze back onto his Armani lapels. Whatever is happening in Roberto Velez's sinus cavities just now is strictly a misdemeanor; he just does this to put Fat Tom the Lawyer at ease. When Fat Tom goes, and it won't be long now, they'll tell the family: "Heart attack. Can you imagine? And such a young man." And despite the fact that the fashion world has pushed aside the music industry as the undisputed new *avant-garde* of narcotic self-immolation as art form, Ms. Elite shows no interest in partaking of Fat Tom's lunch. No needle marks between this fair maiden's toes, I can practically assure you.

The school kids are cute; they wear uniforms of sorts, their hair is brushed for the newspapers and the TV cameras. This, we discover, has turned into quite a media event, remarkable for a neighborhood where it normally takes quantities of spilled blood and empty shell casings to lure the mainstream media. Lucky for us that our tiny entourage numbers among its ranks an accredited newsman of its own. The nuns who apparently run this place—a crumbling three-story affair in the midst of dwellings doubtlessly flagged on the fire department's 'let burn' map— would like it known that theirs is a drug-free school zone. Or was, at least, until Fat Tom the Lawyer managed to heave himself out of the Velezmobile.

We're doing this presentation business in a weary auditorium outfitted with basketball backboards and tall dirty windows with serious metal mesh gratings, and smelling of old school milk. It is a tableau designed to downplay the significance of the sun's progress across the heavens and the decay squatting just across the moat. The stage at one end is set up to look like a semi-squalid but clean tenement apartment— all too familiar territory for most of the kids who go to this school, I'm sure. The head nun whispers to Velez that the kids wouldn't mind doing part of their play for us, but Fat Tom the Lawyer puts the wood to that idea.

So here we stand—Velez, the chief sister, me, Fat Tom in the background blowing his nose, two kids with earnest brown eyes and skinned knees and elbows, all surrounded by gamely painted flats resembling an embattled ghetto apartment. Ms. Elite, not exactly attired for an encounter with women of the cloth, is hiding out in the car. Below us are three local news camera crews and about a hundred or so other kids. I am surrounded by junior high; what's that, twelve years old? Eleven? This crew is older and moldier than Jane Oldham, who in any event won't be seeing life from this angle when she reaches her eleventh or twelfth year.

Roberto Velez gathers the two kid playwrights to him and cameras roll; electronic flashes glaze our eyes. Velez says something about these two kids being the new saints of Washington Heights. Velez says he wishes his Mom could be here too, because she always says that the morning belongs to the children. The kids aren't buying, though, until Velez finishes and then repeats the whole thing in Spanish. At this the place goes crazy. "These babies are my people," Velez actually looks at me and says, loud enough for the TV cameras and everybody to hear.

Well, we've been in such a hurry to get here and dispense our good will that nobody remembered to bring the citations. The Thunder has this form-citation with blank spaces that the public relations department fills in with the appropriate fluff; only nobody did it. Fat Tom the Lawyer springs forward to shoulder the blame, and volunteers to call the station from the Velezmobile and have the citations rushed to the scene. Meanwhile, the chief sister gives Velez *his* citation; it's a calligraphed beauty that the sister informs us was done by another of her students. Velez makes like he is so moved by this that he decides we're going to bring the two student-playwrights back to WRTR and give them their citations right in the Thunder broadcast booth—"that's right, kids, on the air!"

So now we hurtle back downtown with a full coach: Sister Annemarie, a bespeckled assistant nun and designated chaperone, sits between Velez and Fat Tom in the back; I and the honorees face them. Velez and the sister are regaling each other in Spanish. I could probably make most of it out if I wanted. Tom is perspiring. The two kids are checking out the Velezmobile. A couple of hundred dollars' worth of gigantic, untied, multicolored basketball shoes draw designs on the carpet under us. One of the kids scrambles up on his knees for a look up to the front seat. Seconds pass, and he slides down and whispers in frantic Spanish to his partner. Up bounds the other one and now I realize that they've just discovered Ms. Elite up there, wearing a token leather skirt and what, for a pair of molting adolescents, must be a demented fairy-tale of a tee shirt. Sister Annemarie tells the kids to sit down and behave; I don't think she's had a glimpse of our pilot yet.

I call ahead and get Sally Wallach. Sally jumps on the case at once, promising to scrawl out a form-citation and to get Stevie Joe Adams, our new late-morning guy, to give us some air for the big presentation.

Velez tunes in WRTR. Stevie Joe is saying nice things about the two Washington Heights kids who are going to be his special guests during the next half hour, along with their personal friends, Velez and Oldham. The kids are sitting next to me, hissing back and forth about Ms. Elite's body and ripe *bodega* fruit. All is in order.

And it doesn't take long before we're all loaded into Booth B—the one Stevie Joe now shares with old Adrian Boe—for the presentation. By this time of the day Velez & Oldham's alleged—and highly suspect by yours truly—one-point-three million of you will have bottomed out at about two hundred thousand. Stevie Joe hasn't been here long enough to tell if he's going to be able to hold onto more of our listeners than the last late-morning guy could; his ass, needless to say, hangs in the balance.

Anyway: two Washington Heights kids, who five hours ago were probably tip-toeing over their cracked-up mothers and their latest mystery-uncles to get to school and meet their famous homeboy Roberto Velez, are just for right now living large. And Sally Wallach is giving them the royal Thunder business: she pulls a couple of Arielle's giant, hot-off-the-press WRTR sweaters over the kids' heads and gives them Thunder mugs full of hot chocolate and calls them *Mister* Salvinas and *Mister* Ramos and bends low and close enough to give them things to dream about until they're grown up and perhaps until they're dead.

The kids, to their credit, do not act as pee-pantsed as most of our strike team auditionees have been. They're cool. They're not kiss-Hillary Clinton's-ass types. They handle themselves. Stevie Joe asks them why they wrote a play about saying no to drugs and one of them tells about his older brother, the gist of which is that bro' is wearing a few extra holes these days as mementos of his sporting life. Velez goes momentarily quiet on us.

Then, quick as that, their fifteen minutes are up. Sister Annemarie is trying to herd them across what must look through her lifetime-guarantee specs like knee-deep pandemonium but is actually a pretty placid early afternoon around here. Ms. Elite has absconded with the Velezmobile and a driver, so Velez personally hails Sister and her playwrights a cab. Sister climbs in. Sally Wallach comes dashing out of Too Tall Jones with the kids' citations; Velez and the kids study them. I watch Velez edge the kids out of Sister's line of sight for a stealthy second and palm them each a fifty-dollar bill. They stare at the bills; Velez takes the rest of his money and stows it in his sock. They do the same, and clamber into the cab. Velez grabs the one with the story and whispers in his ear, "That ain't for your brother, you hear?" I think Velez is trying to teach these two something of the value of fame. It may work. We'll see.

The weekend before our Veterans Day remote, I have just realized, is my regular weekend with Jane Oldham.

In the beginning, there was Sarah and Velez and me.

No. In the beginning, there was Sarah and Velez. No—in the real beginning, there was me and Velez.

That's important to remember. Sarah came, technically, later.

The fact is, Sarah married me because Velez wouldn't marry her, although I think they never discussed the subject in so many words. I know all this now. Velez knew it then and he tried—maybe not as resolutely as he could have—to tell me. But Sarah and I wound up abruptly married one day, and that held the three of us together until Jane Courtenay Oldham came along and put a bullet right between the old nag's rheumy, betrayed eyes.

I suppose I had been marking time since college waiting for Velez to come along and tell me what to do. I guess you've pretty much figured that out by now.

First, though, there had been the little matter of Vietnam, which I and my classmates thought we had managed to wait out. But no: stapled to my diploma was an invitation to see the world. Happily, however, Henry Kissinger closed his Nobel Prize deal—literally, I would later calculate—during my severely reluctant unit's flight to the Philippines for assignment. So it came to pass that I spent a year in a part of Vietnam that could by then have passed for the cargo terminal at Kennedy Airport: very little gunplay, plenty of freight—including, even in the adventure's merciful twilight, a stray casket or two, bearing the remains of people who had stayed too long at the fair for transshipment to Arlington or other points east. I jockeyed my share of these at the wheel of a U. S. Army forklift, and soon enough gave up trying to explain to my passengers or myself by what fortune I was driving and they were riding.

Yes, in case it has occurred to you: I have wondered, down at the Vietnam Memorial, spying on Lyndon McDonald, if the incessant overhead sonic procession under which we rear-guard teamsters in the Army matériel wagon train labored might, once, or often, have included in its chorus the screaming afterburners of the vaunted Colonel Elmo himself, itching for one last stealthy sortie across the Cambodian border.

As the NVA waited for us to pack up and get out so they could conclude their business in the newly christened Ho Chi Minh City, I started hanging out at an Army radio station. When a heroic inflammation of the genitalia waylaid one of the incumbents, I taped a prophylactic sheet of plastic on the seat of the chair and sidled myself behind the mike. Let somebody else drive the forklift; I was back in radio.


By the time of my triumphant return from the fields of rice, Buddy Oldham's philosophy on parenting had more or less distilled itself to giving me sympathetic and uncritical audience and then, with that Buddy-tick of his brambly white eyebrows, saying, "Well, partner, you know I'm behind you. It's just you and me, y'know." It had been just Buddy and me since my thirteenth year and Buddy's forty-second, when Elizabeth Reilly Oldham smoked a final cigarette on our sepia sunporch, took a leisurely ambulance ride—no emergency, not much drama—to Johns Hopkins and coughed it all up.

Does this sound like the scraping of chewed fingernails on psychological scars? Forget it. My Mom smoked because she was afraid of guns, or, more precisely, of God—a woman who had allowed her hand to be given over in a moment of abject resignation to the ordinary and devoted Buddy Oldham, second-string school ballplayer and straight shooter, and had loathed herself for it from that moment on. From where I sat, it had *always* been just Buddy and me.

But that's not how Buddy saw it. The dopiness-about-women gene pool issues forth from Buddy's side of the family. Buddy was in love. For my Mom I must say this: she never tried to wring him out, never humiliated him. She just took the honorable Baltimore Catholic way out of a misbegotten union: she died as fast as she could within the ecclesiastical rules.

There followed Buddy Oldham's weird year. Buddy drank and, I think, whored around a little, in his abashed little way. Buddy didn't shave from Thursday to Monday. He watched TV. I, in my first year of high school, was able to lay low without much notice.

It was my nose that snapped Buddy Oldham out of his mourning. Buddy had spent a weekend like most others that year, privately and numbly intoxicated. I don't know how it happened but Buddy wound up barreling into a little table where Mom used to keep her cigarettes and her family pictures, and sent everything flying. Stale old orphaned cigarettes rolling around on the floor. Little silver picture frames with the usual immigrant railroad workers grinning and trying to hold still, steam rising off their aching backs. And Buddy Oldham straddling all this, teetering, when I chose to barge in and say something like, "Ah, fuck, dad"; Buddy wheeled around and socked me in the middle of my face and then, without pain, I was down there with the cigarettes and stained pictures of the life my mother once came from, flat on my back, staring up at Buddy Oldham, who kept looking back and forth between my now spurting nose and his fist—a fist that had probably never been thrown in anger before in his adult life and surely never was again.

I don't guess I need to deconstruct this tawdry little psychodrama for you. Even from down on the floor, leaking all over my shirt, I knew it wasn't me Buddy had swung at. It was the monumental accumulation of his life's colorless fortunes and unrewarded love, all cruelly crystallized by the clumsy defilement of this Philip Morris reliquary of Buddy Oldham's once-upon-a-time salvation.

We were both quietly sobbing by the time we got to the doctor's office, Buddy and I. Our doctor was a school friend of Buddy's and the three of us sat while Buddy bleated about breaking his son's nose for no reason, no goddamn reason, except that he was a drunk because his sweet Elizabeth was gone.

While I sat with a bloody handkerchief in my lap and heard my father's slobbery confession, the doctor snuck up on me and did something to my nose that hurt so much worse than Buddy Oldham's blind drunken roundhouse that I think I passed out because next thing I knew I was laying on a couch with an aluminum splint taped to my face and the whispers of Buddy Oldham and the doctor finding their way in from the next room. What the doctor said, I couldn't be sure; Buddy just kept whispering, achingly, "I know. I know."

When the subject of my vocation finally surfaced in earnest at the Baltimore dinner table of Richard 'Buddy' Oldham shortly after my unscarred return from the front at the beginning of what would be my final summer in my childhood home, what I came up with was, "I think maybe radio, Dad."

And Buddy Oldham was in no position to argue. What was he going to say? "Gee, son, I always dreamed someday you'd be traveling the Middle East with me, selling guidance systems to camel-pumping, dog-barbecuing, unveiled-daughter-ass-whipping, *Allah-ahkbaring* Shi'ites?" C'mon. Buddy was unsettled enough at the prospect of my Army adventure. In fact, I've suspected that Buddy may have placed a discreet call or two to his Pentagon pals just to make sure his kid would be tucked away in sufficiently Southeast Asia to stay clear of the serious gunplay. I have never in all the intervening years called him on this, and won't now, fraught as the subject would be with issues of manhood and duty and such.

No, Buddy didn't even offer token resistance. And so it was that I found myself marginally matriculated as a communications graduate student in the labyrinthine City University of New York, which exists mainly for unendowed sons and daughters of Gotham but was willing to accept hard currency from out-of-staters.

I had a feeling that night that Buddy would dump that house and its memories before long. But there, to this day, he stays—third row home from the corner, twenty minutes from the Harbor Tunnel, less than a mile from the gate of Perpetual Help Cemetery, where Elizabeth Reilly fled in terror of her ordinary existence back when Buddy Oldham was forty-two, and I was thirteen.

# 12

COLONEL Elmo looms large in the rabid declamations of Lyndon McDonald, who this deep night stands at stolid attention in the eerie, radiant green of the glass-block Vietnam Memorial Wall. I sit at a circumspect distance from the motionless Lyndon and listen. The only sounds that obstruct our communion are the anonymous sullen foghorns that issue at sporadic intervals from the veiled rivermouth, and the tinny, blustery thwack of business helicopters feeling their way through the murk down onto the pier helipad. Lyndon stops for both of these. I can just about see him cocking his ear riverward, straining, waiting for—what? A signal?

A signal that Colonel Elmo has made it after all. Against all odds.

Colonel Elmo straddles Olympus in Lyndon McDonald's Vietnam mythology. I have heard enough exerpts from Lyndon's Colonel Elmo routine to be able to report the following with some confidence: that Colonel Elmo—uncertain last name—flew the fast and nasty F-4 Phantom jet off U.S. Navy aircraft carriers as they sloshed their figure-8's and dipsy-doos around the South China Sea. The reign of Colonel Elmo in the Asian heavens would have been well before my own three-hundred-and-sixty-five-day sojourn as landlubber and tractor jockey and radio fill-in.

Colonel Elmo, if Lyndon McDonald's epic poem is to be believed, was a stealth pilot way before anybody thought of a stealth airplane. As Lyndon tells it, Colonel Elmo was invisible to Vietnamese eye and Russian radar alike. The Soviet SAM's couldn't touch him high, and the teenage VC girls manning their mutilated brothers' anti-aircraft guns couldn't touch him low. Colonel Elmo could feel things at sixty thousand feet and Mach-2 that were happening in whispers in wormy catacombs under the jungle floor. With his 20mm cannon Colonel Elmo could singe the hair off a monkey's privates and still leave its essential monkeyhood intact. Thus spoke Lyndon McDonald, with unabashed reverence.

I have searched in vain for mention of a Colonel Elmo on the Wall, down here near the gray water where Lyndon surfaces at night, and where he disappears God knows where during the day. Lyndon whispers to the terrified writers of the letters home that are etched into this wall of recollection as if to assure them that all is not lost—even now, all these years later—because Colonel Elmo is slotted down into the catapult of his heaving ship, pointed into harm's way, wings and cannon loaded heavy with screaming, sulfurous redemption.

I first encountered Lyndon McDonald at the end of one of his brief residences at Bellevue Hospital's psychiatric observation ward. Raylene, WRTR's all-purpose programming assistant and Lyndon McDonald's obscure relation, had been summoned for not the first time to take custody of Lyndon—one more fantastical exercise in bureaucratic capitulation among countless here in the national terminus of the roving insane—and little Raylene recruited me to ride shotgun.

They had cleaned him up, chiseled the ancient crusts of snot from his gaping bellicose nose, mined the crud from his bleeding ears, deliced and disinfected him and, funniest of all, had given Lyndon McDonald a prescription for anti-depressants. The orderly who escorted Lyndon into our care insisted on assurances that Lyndon would take his pills; we all—Raylene, me, the orderly—eyed the hulking intractable beast in our midst and we thought, probably in harmony, how absurd was the notion of Band-Aid therapy to pacify the screaming banshees lurking within the gnarled shell of Lyndon McDonald.

As for Lyndon, he played it cagey. He didn't say a word. He was giving them all the reassuring docility they could handle.

Then we were in Raylene McDonald's second-hand Japanese car, wheeling through the Dickensian Bellevue gates and back out into true bedlam. Cramming Lyndon into the back seat was a logistic impossibility, and so I pretzeled myself across the torturous driveshaft hump and kept my own mouth shut. For a while I wasn't sure Lyndon was capable of speech, but presently he garbled a barnyard medley and then launched a soliloquy on the prisoners of Bellevue Hospital that was quite amazing in two respects: one, that he sounded so utterly lucid and convincing despite the insanity of his convictions, and two, his creamy baritone voice—a voice surgically transplanted from a creature of culture and intelligence into this inscrutable coil of slumbering mayhem.

I craned for a peek at Raylene's reaction to all this, but she kept her head straight and her eyes focused and her mind curtained. There was almost a naturalness to this ritual of ransoming Lyndon, driving him to the outskirts, praying to God to protect him, giving him twenty bucks and letting him loose—for this is what Raylene McDonald did that day and what she and I have done since—that seemed to embody Raylene's acceptance of such a world without exactly surrendering to it. I watched for some glimmer of cognizance as Lyndon wrestled himself out of the tiny car and into the yellow swelter, welcomed by dust swirls drawn up around his hospital-issue charity pants like caressments of his element, a slow, sad colossus retreating into the tunnels of his warren. There was none.

Tonight Colonel Elmo is much on Lyndon McDonald's mind. It is a misty green night, the kind that might bring ghosts to minds far more even-keeled than Lyndon's. Lights peek through the fog from mysterious depths out over the somnolent old river; Lyndon turns to the private sounds and tries to fathom them. At one point I think I hear a fierce, prayerful "Don't let dese boys down, Colonel," and then Lyndon's eyes rifle across the impenetrably soupy sky, following the echo that is Colonel Elmo crackling down from combat air patrol to engage. I search the sky myself—it's a night like that. Back on earth, Lyndon is tracing the words a Lance Corporal scribbled during the Tet celebration, trying to soften the inevitable news that may even reach home before his letter. Guess time's up, Mom, but I ain't scared. You'd be proud.

I'm wondering what you're making of my partner Velez by this point in our tale. You must have your ideas, listening to him—to us—every morning on the Thunder. You can't spend eleven-and-a-half years listening to a couple of guys without thinking you're on to them, right?

It was at Bennie's bar tonight that I began to question the wisdom of this whole exposé. Velez doesn't know about it but I doubt he'd have any objections; hell, he'd probably *love* the idea: The Velez Story, as told by his trusty sidekick Dennis Peter Oldham.

The thing is, though, that now I suppose I have to tell you about Sarah and about how we got started, Velez and me, and I . . . well.

Hope, the earthy, moon-faced womanchild who tends bar at Bennie's, has worked up a lipfull of perspiration this night and her shoulders ask for pity. For since my last visit, Bennie's bar has transformed itself yet again: gone is the ubiquitous blue; gone are the movie posters. Gone is the conspiratorially subdued, grainy gravity of the place, the kind that emboldens the meek to sneak up on attractive strangers.

In place of all this is a stormy pastiche of bogus trinkets and street signs and cultural ephemera—yes, you've seen one of its legion clones at your favorite mall. These candy-light carnivals are the juiciest of sanctuaries for young refugees in their Manhattan suits and ties. It has, you see, apparently not escaped the attention of the shadowy eminence who owns Bennie's bar that pubescent bankers and brokers like to spend money lubricating each other's loins, and so Bennie's bar has come to this: a yuppie Mexican tequila stand.

To his credit, Bennie has resigned.

"For good?" I ask Hope, who used to have time to chat during Bennie's bar's previous incarnation.

"Yeah. He was embarrassed. Looka this," she says with a contemptuous grunt at the foaming hops and the swirling hormones. "Bennie takes things more seriously. He craves the aesthetics."

Don't I know. "How 'bout you?" I ask Hope, who's wrestling with the radiation-proof lid of an industrial-strength daiquiri vat.

She wipes hair out of her eyes and grins. "I made almost nine hundred bucks here last week. Last *week*. That's how about me."

Which is not quite half of what I made last week, before the bogeymen came: taxes and alimony and child support and the three-hundred-and-fifteen dollars I dropped off at the delicatessen of Morton the nine-fingered bookmaker and the payment on the car that I've used exactly twice since the spring. Net: a little less than Hope the bartender hauled to the bank. And I am a goddamn radio star. Of sorts.

I may dump the car. It's a pathetic Baltimore vestige and there's always the Velezmobile.

When I first laid eyes on Sarah, my misbegotten future wife and the eventual mother of Jane Courtenay Oldham, she was on the arm of Velez. Some other woman was on his other arm. Things were green and spinning that night as I remember, spinning mostly around Velez and me, then in the first blush of our rock radio notoriety. It was a promotion party, you won't be surprised to learn. It was, I think I remember, at a now defunct downtown dance sewer called the Ritz. Thunder Rock, as Velez and I had irreverently rechristened venerable old Rolling Thunder Radio upon our ceremonious arrival the year before, had just signed to co-promote its first summer concert series. Stations do this all the time now, but Rolling Thunder Radio started it, way back in the day.

Velez and I had been working together for less than two years, not a long road try-out for the big time, before we landed at WRTR, a desperate, shock-troop experiment in the ratings chase. How this all came about, we may get to. But right now Sarah is on my mind, tracing a trail before me across the dewy autumn sheen even as Colonel Elmo slices the vapor above.

When Velez and I were snatched from a mercifully brief minor league stint in Albany and enthroned in one of the two most treasured morning holes in radioland, WRTR-FM was a corpse. Suits came and suits went, but the Peter Pan air talent stayed, embalmed in full public view like Lenin in his glass box, losing the life-and-death struggle against the ravages of respectability. When disco hit—painful memory, I know, but music is a cruel game—WRTR, by then a pathetic husk of its rebellious, subversive, authentically counterculture self, dug in its purist heels and went to the bottom of the ratings cesspool. And there, for years, it would stay.

Finally, they—the suits—scoured the steppes and the moors and came up with a fresh, good-looking, smart-ass Puerto Rican rock DJ and his droll, mismatched newsman/sidekick and probably calculated thus: How much worse can things get? So it happened that Velez and I finished a Thursday taping for a show that would purport to be live on Friday morning, and marched into the station manager's office accompanied by two WRTR lawyers to announce that we were hopping the next stage.

"The fuck you are," was our station manager's answer.

Our Albany station manager was that not-uncommon rock mutant: a doggedly hip-dressing and talking and drugging and drinking dude whom fate had sentenced to a flamboyantly ludicrous body. The boy was fat. And smelly and sweaty and powerful and hyper and weasily— a trait he shares with most station managers—and so protrusive in his dimensions and demeanor that one would feel claustrophobic alone with him in an aircraft hangar. And to top this picture off, his name was Molly. I never cared to inquire how that happened.

So into the closetlike office of Molly, our obese, sneery-eyed yard-boss, trooped Velez and me and these two city lawyers who, Velez had been assured, would handle the contract stickiness.

The walls of Molly's confessional sweated brown and mean in sympathy with its solitary inmate. Molly invited us to sit down, a cheap taunt since there was room for only one chair and it lay buried under Molly himself. And when Velez crowed that we were headed to the Big Apple, Molly enshrouded us in reefer smoke and said, "The fuck you are."

The architecture of the situation was this: Molly hated Velez's entrails for many reasons, some of them rational. But Velez was the best thing that ever happened to Molly's shitty little radio station up on the icy forlorn riverbanks of Albany. Velez didn't hate Molly so much as disdain him, which prompted Velez to tattoo Molly remorselessly on the air. We were, as things broke that day, in the process of trying to register Molly with the New York Department of Transportation as a Class-3 motor vehicle, license plate and all; the final paperwork was pending.

That had been my idea, by the way. For the record. In case you're keeping score.

So it came as no surprise that, presented with a situation that would be so good for Velez and so disastrous for himself, Molly responded with a flat "The fuck you are."

Velez just laughed his mirthless, sideways chirp, and Molly said, "Who the fuck are these guys?"

Velez turned to me. "This one's my partner, Dennis Oldham. He reads the news on your radio station—"

*"Those* fuckin' guys," Molly said. "Who's those guys? Huh?"

"Federal agents, Molly," said Velez. "It's all over, babe. I told them everything."

Now, we didn't have anything of felony quality on Molly that I knew of, but Molly's fatty old heart plainly went supersonic for the moment it took to realize that Velez was bullshit. "I'm busy, Velez. See you at work tomorrow."

"Nope."

Molly pinched out his joint, stowed its drippy remains in the folds of his biker colors, and studied Velez. "Who are these fuckin' guys?" he asked Velez again.

"These are my new friends, Molly. They're lawyers, in the service of dangerous white people from New York City."

"Get 'em outa here," Molly said apprehensively.

Velez plowed on. "Molly, meet Lawyer Number One. Number One, say hi to Molly." A sturdy Ivy type began to reach for Molly's hand, but Velez waved him off. "Careful, Number One. You don't know where those fingers have been. Now, Molly, this is Lawyer Number Two." A puffy-cheeked three-piece suit nodded curtly Molly's way.

"Fine. I want *my* fuckin' lawyer, Velez."

"C'mon, Molly. You're not under arrest. In fact, we're bringing you the end of a truly shitty chapter of your life. You will be delighted."

"I got you for fourteen more months, pal, and your lawyers can kiss my ass and so can you."

"See?" Velez turned and said to me and the lawyers. "I told you he'd be reasonable, didn't I?" Now he leaned down into the toxic pale of Molly's reefer breath. "'Kay, Mol. Here's the deal. Lawyer Number Two is going to discuss with you your assorted breaches of my contract. He's going to review your legal liabilities with you, no charge. Unless I miss my guess, he's also going to offer you a couple of bucks. Who knows, maybe there's a genuine New York blowjob in it for you. Also probably no charge."

Lawyers One and Two, obviously no strangers to the indignities of show business clients, stood impassive.

"Now if you're still churning this 'contract' attitude after all that, Molly, Lawyer Number One—that's the big guy, Molly, just to review the numbering system—is going to reach up your disgusting clammy syphilitic asshole if he can find it and he's going to finger around till he finds your heart, Molly, and he's going to pull it out so fast that you're going to be able to watch him *fucking eat it*, Molly, just like in the Crusades, and then we're going to haul you over to the McDonald's on Front Street and turn you over to that little Eskimo faggot an' let him carve your whaleblubber ass into five thousand orders of Molly McNuggets. . . ."

We hit the beach at WRTR in New York the following Monday morning.

The Too Tall Jones Building was still an architect's fancy back then. WRTR was still broadcasting from an East 44th Street dump that looked like heaven to me and my partner Roberto Velez. For Velez, of course, this was a homecoming. No, more: it was a triumphal entry through the gates of the citadel after the cold mean years scraping at the outside of its glass and steel ramparts. Since we were still making this radio thing up as we went along, we felt no sense of reward or accomplishment. We had simply hit the lottery; found a goose that shat golden eggs.

Actually, they got us for a song that first year but theirs turned out to be the shit end of the stick, for they had hedged by signing us for one year only, and by renewal time WRTR was off the respirator and making a few bucks and other rock stations were calling Velez and making offers. Velez hired a new agent and a couple of new lawyers and he woke up one morning a rich young man. I, by that time, was a given in Velez's contract negotiations, much to the disenchantment of the suits, who were more interested in salary than in chemistry.

I didn't see much of Velez that first year in New York. In Albany we'd both been exiles, so we hung out together pretty much all the time. But New York was home for Velez, who at that point was still Puerto Rican enough to want to hang with his boys. And there were plenty of boys who wanted to hang with Velez and cash in on the celebrity and the easy pussy that buzzed Velez from morning to night. I'd have looked silly in the midst of such a crew, and Velez and I both knew it.

Besides, two years is two years—not a marriage. I still considered Velez and me a temporary arrangement. Without a better plan of attack, I was content to make a living jousting with this Velez character on the air, and to drink and posture and stunt with him in bleak Albany bars and to flag bleak Albany babes. I was in no hurry to make a move, so when the radio fairy threw Velez and me together one spring day I decided it would be okay enough to let Roberto Velez hurry for both of us. I wasn't even consulted about our escape plan from Albany, that I can remember; Velez and the WRTR lawyers just grabbed me in the parking lot that day and told me it was time to boogie.

But Velez snorted New York from the time we hit south on the Saw Mill River Parkway, as if the lane stripes were giant lines of Colombian candy.

So we went pretty much our own ways that first year; the parts of the city I got to know were, at first, of no particular interest to homeboy Velez, and vice versa. Velez lived up on Broadway and 93rd Street, where, then as now, signs in Spanish about equal the signs in English, but where civilization enjoys a far securer beachhead than in the thumped and cragged Washington Heights of Immaculata Velez and the remnants of her brood.

So while Velez played *nouveau* hotshot, I hopped from one sublet to another. And then there was Sarah, in pursuit of whom I leased a place I couldn't afford in a neighborhood chocked full of wrinkled white people among whom Sarah's parents wouldn't mind hazarding a visit, with rooms and luxuries designed to rival Velez's own. This sub-liminal bidding war did me no good; even if I could have kept up with my newly rich and voraciously acquisitive partner Velez, Sarah's tastes and expectations proved to be of a loftier magnitude entirely. But I had myself momentarily convinced that she was ready to give at least some of it up, you see.

And she conspired in the delusion. She did. In her deprecations of mommy and daddy. In her seeming amusement at the vacuous company Velez and I subjected her to. In her willingness to sit on dirty floors and drink out of bottles and wear trampy rock uniforms and teeter back and forth zombielike to the soundtrack of our existence and to do the things the bad girls do, out in the open, even if only to win some private dare. There she was, taking Velez's best shots and *seeming*, goddamn it, to thrive on it; so what was I to make of it when Velez decided to move on and Sarah didn't?

Which brought me, finally, to my one-bedroom-plus-roof in the

West Village, with its obstinate, scratchy chestnut tree sentry and its leaky, skylit staircase and its widows: Mrs. McMichael, Rose, and Rose's sister. From time to time Velez coaxes me to move to a faster part of town. But I see a measure of wisdom in keeping some geography between me and Velez. If only as a reminder.

# 13

IT was on a night as murky and unpromising as this, except in spring—yes, a cold spring evening in the mercifully waning months of the long-running Republican juggernaut, as I remember—that we headed north.

Those were obsessively spontaneous times. Velez felt image-bound to behave erratically, even to the point of blowing off the Velez & Oldham Show without proffering the slightest warning or the most disingenuous excuse. In those days, before our co-conspiracy had reached blood-oath depth, I often found myself holding the bag, doing solo stands that consisted of castigating my partner for his absence while he, holed up in some grimy byway of romance, listened and howled and sometimes called the station in lamely camouflaged voices to scorn me. As with everything else that transpired accidentally or otherwise on the Velez & Oldham Show, our dopey listener-minions couldn't get enough. *I* could get enough; but success is a potent pacifier and Velez is not an easy man to stay angry at. So I ranted and pouted and cajoled Velez out over the old waves to tickle the listeners and to work the bile out of my throat.

But the excursion of my immediate recollection was more premeditated than most. A Thursday, it was. Thursday, the day named after the ancient god of thunder and of flashing the bird at the authorities—begotten, I suspect, by the god of intercultural subversion and born to a harpy princess with leisure pursuits twisting heavily in the direction of human suffering.

Velez was curious to see if we could get away with taping Friday's allegedly live show on Thursday and then blowing town like we used to do with Molly in Albany. That's how the trip north was hatched.

And even then it might have turned out to be just one more excursion among many, a guerrilla-style royal slumming progress for Velez to show himself to his fans in venues cozy enough for personal expressions of adoration. We'd more or less descend someplace. A bar or a roadhouse or a disco—the dumpier the better, because the locals would fawn that much more shamelessly over Velez. Velez would allow himself to be courted and, much more often than not, he would wind up ambushing one of the local cheerleaders. One minute we'd be there, trading grab-ass with the crowd, our shirts clammy with sycophantic drool; next minute I'd notice the energy level seeping away, and I'd look around and find myself the only celebrity in the joint and, in most cases, not a celebrity with sufficient candlepower to hold things together for long. Once Velez had made his selection and spirited her away, chances are I'd be trapped in a rabid pocket of radio junkies. Occasionally a female of modest promise in the group, but mostly guys with stars of their own in their eyes, looking for the breakthrough insight, thinking I must have it stashed.

And I'd stay, partly in astonishment at how thoroughly brainwashed these people were by the Velez & Oldham Show. There was *nothing* they didn't know about the show, or, it seemed, about radio. Most knew more than I did. But I got to where I could fake it competently, and my exalted position gave me' all the cover I needed.

They never asked the *big* question, the one that their own mindless devotion begged: How's it feel to be such a big fucking deal to so many small, inconsequential people?

And it's a good thing they didn't, because how would I have fielded that one? What do I say now, when the indictment carries even more weight than back in the early days, before the suits gave Velez the Velezmobile to chase women and be famous in?

What, I'm asking, would be worse: to pretend we deserve their slavish obsession, or to smack them between their red clammy little eyes with the truth: that we don't? Do I share with them our own darkly guarded opinion that we're nothing but chewing gum, waiting for the inevitable day when you spit us out and stick us onto the bottom of New York City's chair in favor of a fresh stick? How do I tell somebody like Alicia the faceless poetess, whom I believe I've introduced to you in passing, that she has to stop spending so much of whatever time she has left writing poems to impress *me?* Because let me tell you, gentle reader, these poems will not see the light of day unless Alicia makes posters of them and glues them to every construction site barrier in New York.

What do I know about poetry, you ask? I, a mere accredited journalist and radio co-celebrity? I know this: Alicia's poems rhyme. Poems aren't supposed to rhyme anymore. That much I know.

Besides rhyming, Alicia's poetry betrays a trove of rather unholy preoccupations. Victim fantasies, you might call them. No feminist agit-prop for her. Alicia likes to explore the ethereal side of forcible, blood-soaked sex. And her allusions have included words like 'sacrament' and 'epiphany'—what am I supposed to make of business like this? An invitation? I don't think so, because Alicia, unlike many of my regular callers, has never as much as hinted at a face-to-face meeting. For all I know I have met Alicia, or passed her on the street. Sometimes I think I know everybody out there. Sometimes I think there are far, far fewer than seven-and-a-half million people in this place; they just keep running around the block, changing clothes on the run, looking over their shoulders again and again with every anonymous lap.

And then there's the barely-ponderable possibility that Alicia—or one of them—is truly, psychotically fixated. A stalker. Heavily armed and determined to express her devotion in a climactic, tabloid-treacly blaze of glory, like the twisted fan-club president of that Tex-Mex pop teenager kid—Serena, Selena, something like that. You know who I mean. I can only endure such ruminations by banking on the probability that Alicia the assassin will be a bad shot, thus not only sparing my hide but placing me in the enviable journalistic position of reporting live the gruesome details of my own attempted murder, there on the spot to interview the friends and family of whatever innocent bystanders have paid the price of celebrity worship syndrome.

Ah, you don't want to hear this. You want to hear about Velez, that radio rebel who somewhere along the line achieved institution status without once getting caught kissing anyone's ass. You want to know every infinitesimal pissant detail, don't you.

You can't get enough of Velez, can you?

In a way it's too bad Velez is on the radio; no one knows this better than Velez, of course. That's why a casual punch across the cable box buttons on any weekend evening can get you two or even three different views of the icily stylish Velez, crooking his smile over a slight but not weak-looking chin, drawing deep ingenuous creases down those smooth, clean-shaven cheeks, cranking up the wattage on his pussy-prowl smile, narrowing and wizening his wired-butterfly gaze. Here's Velez, summoning his garage-band riffs to the thin toleration of Letterman's band. There's Velez, doing his record review on one of the teen-pump music videothons. Here's Velez hosting a late-night stage show at the Apollo— "yo', wuzzup, y'all? Hey now, putcha hands together an' give it up for—". And Velez again, playing in a charity basketball game with some of the local sports heroes.

There might be something behind this. Radio, unless I miss my guess, may be starting to bore my partner.

But it would be hard—and stupid—for him to walk away. Look, the only reason all these doors keep flying open for Velez is because of the Velez & Oldham Show. He knows this. Fifteen minutes after he folds his tent—*our* tent—one-point-three million of his neighbors won't know him from any other slick Latino on the make.

Which is why Velez & Oldham isn't going porcelain anytime soon. And nothing is going to happen here unless Velez tells it to.

The trip north never would have come off if Velez hadn't been dallying with the assistant program manager of the moment. She was Greek, I think; at least, she was short and dark and wiry and full of snarl; doesn't that sound Greek to you? And she was devoted to Velez. She would tell you that she was the first to recognize Velez as a true, instinctive radio genius. This was not the sort of charge Velez went around denying in those days or these, and he found more than sentiment, I think, in the promotion.

This girl was not the first Thunder damsel to get bonked by Velez, but she was *a* first: the others, up to then, were of such a humble species in the radio food chain that Velez knew they wouldn't live long enough to make a commotion. This was before Velez found out how easy it is to have people fired on the grounds of screwing the star. But yes, Velez and the Greek assistant program manager were carrying on for a while there. An affair, you might say; which Velez defines as kissing a girl *after* you fuck her.

But the Greek assistant program manager was already on borrowed time when Velez hatched the plot for the trip north.

"I need you to help me out," I can still hear Velez saying to her.

"Sure, babe." Everybody was *babe* with this girl, not just Velez. Even I was *babe.* "What do you need?"

"It's my cousin. He's in a little jam upstate. Y'know?" And it was as easy as that. The Greek assistant program manager put her fragile little career on the line for Velez's slimy, not-even-flimsily-substantiated excuse, and agreed to spirit a taped show onto the air next day pretending it was live.

Why did Velez lie to the Greek assistant program manager, who had so earnestly warmed his bed and declared his genius to anyone who'd hold still long enough to listen? Ho ho.

Because yes, it had been just those few nights before that Velez had shown up for the promotion party that proved to be Sarah's debut. Where'd she come from? I didn't know. Her, hanging on one arm, and a girlfriend of hers on his other. I had them figured for just another pair of Velez's easy-access groupies out for a little star power. They seemed to occupy their evening in a heated tit-flash competition for Velez's edification—of that I am certain, and never, in subsequent weeks and years, even at the bleakest depths of my future with the lovely Sarah, has my recollection of those decadent first-night posturings and prancings failed to stir me.

But people came and went, you understand. I didn't ask Velez next day what happened to the pair of babes he'd shown up with the night before. I didn't ask if he'd bonked either or both because then, as now, Velez was curiously reticent about confirming—or denying—rumors. I didn't even wonder why he hadn't covered his tracks better; our Greek assistant program manager was back minding the store that night, but the rumor mill would have wasted no time. It turned out that Velez already had the Greek assistant program manager on final forty-eight hour countdown to oblivion, unbeknownst to her. Or me.

But I, as an accredited newsman, can occasionally put two and two together, and when we slunk out of our East 44th Street slophouse studio to find Velez's two companions of scant nights before waiting in traveling trim for our arrival, I could have sworn I heard the sullen *thwump* of the guillotine falling in the WRTR offices above us. It's gotten to be such a fixture, that *thwump*.

Pennsylvania Station and the overnighter to Montreal. That's where we headed.

Sarah's friend's name was Charly. A woman of endearing countenance and beneficent endowment—a serious shirtfull o' girl, Velez had assured me—which may be why it had seemed to me that she'd spent the better part of the promotion party showing Sarah and Velez her tits: it was, I now realized, all but impossible for Charly *not* to create that impression.

The weekend's pairings were not, at the outset, explicitly specified. We were a jumble, a pocket juggernaut of hooky-playing radio guys and their new friends. I tried, sitting at the window in one of those face-to-face four-seater arrangements next to Charly and across from Sarah, to get a reading on the orbiting electromagnetics, but Velez wasn't letting on.

Of course, now I know. He wanted to keep all three of us guessing. The slimy prick.

I was in love with Sarah before we crossed the Westchester County line. Before the first bottle of pirated champagne was drained, before the old black conductor with the pocket fob and the lapels dusted with an antiquity of cigar ash had even come to claim our tickets. I was in love with Sarah before the purple Catskill foothills stole the rose outlining of shapes from outside my window and turned the evening in on us, giving me a surreptitious window-mirror in which to study my Sarah. I was in love with Sarah without listening to her or studying her physical aspects; I was in the kind of love that bends sterling silver forks from across the room—irrational in a way I'd never been irrational before. No, Ellen Larkin wasn't an irrational pursuit. It was just the opposite: as calculating as someone as innocent as I could possibly bring myself to be. No. Sarah was a celestial force; an intravenous assault.

I was in love with Sarah before my partner Velez declared himself, in the subtlest of ways, with a whisper inaudible to either me or Charly, at which Sarah gave herself to a laugh not gay but conspiratorial and unmistakably lascivious, and the deal was pronounced: I was with Charly.

I don't, even now, trust myself to report accurately the events of the trip; a hypnosis had overtaken me and rendered me insensate beyond the tunnel that separated me from the gamboling, oblivious Sarah. Montreal was a blur of too new and too clean shapes and crowds, which is to say I didn't notice a goddamn thing beyond a droning civic self-conscious-ness against which Sarah spun her ethereal captivations. If Sarah took a turn, the entire city seemed to pivot in her wake; the entire metropolitan electron stream realigned in obeisance. When Sarah laughed, things qui-eted as they do in church. Do I sound like a fucking fool, a drooling ado-lescent? Well, that's undoubtedly how I acted; so Velez informed me, at any rate, many months later, after all the essential fluids had been drained from my heart.

And what of me and my date, Charly? Well, there was the guilt. I, after all, was in love with another. And it turned out that so, in modest proportion, was my date Charly. But not with Velez. Charly had a boyfriend, a frequent flyer who left Charly with plenty of time on her hands to keep Sarah company.

Charly was many things that Sarah was not: she was low to the ground and fluffy of body; she was stolidly but not unpleasantly earth-bound of disposition. She was a woman like many others in New York in that she came armed with an elaborate construct of social permissi-bility that, I discovered soon enough, revolved around her pantyhose.

"Charly take off her pantyhose?" Velez asked me on the evening of our first day in Montreal.

"What?"

"Sarah said she wouldn't. Said it's Charly's rule. She'll let you do anything you want, as long as you don't try to take her pantyhose off. Am I right?"

Yeah, of course he was right. Women talk. And although Charly, willing if not wildly enthusiastic during our hotel settling-in of the afternoon, hadn't offered any explanations, things were obvious enough to me. And just in case they weren't, I always had Velez to explain them to me. "Don't take it personally, Elvis. It's just her way of being sort of faithful to her boyfriend. Sarah told me all about it."

"Sarah take off *her* pantyhose?" is what I really wanted to know, and much more, but all Velez would say was, "Great fuckin' hotel, joo tink, Elvis?"

Despite my remorseless fixation on Sarah and notwithstanding Charly's dehosestration policy, we two managed a handful of serviceable encounters. Charly bore no illusions with her to Montreal: she knew that certain things were probably expected; that there's no such thing as a free weekend in Montreal. And she didn't begrudge her part. There was even something high-schoolishly titillating about roistering within threshold limitations. And there was the comic element: how many pairs of rinsed-out pantyhose are hanging in the hotel bathroom became a running gag among the four of us by weekend's end.

And I didn't want to go home because who knew when, or even if, I'd see Sarah again?

As for Charly, certain things were expected of *me*, too: the boyfriend situation had been made clear at the outset, and I, in return for her company and compliance, was clearly expected not to come back to haunt her once we lit back into town. And yet she was one of my only two connections with Sarah. And there was no guarantee Velez would have any interest beyond this Montreal joyride. Was that good news, or bad?

Look, Sarah was pleasant enough to me that weekend, as far as our contact went. Together we bombed around and ate and drank and squirreled back to our respective hotel rooms—not adjoining—for private congress. Room service figured prominently in the weekend. Sarah listened politely at those infrequent times when I mustered something to say, and her eyes didn't glaze that I could tell. But there was to this, the beginning of our relationship, a thoroughly dispiriting neutrality from her. Which wasn't surprising, since she was clearly in love with my partner, Roberto Velez.

"God, I'm gonna miss all you guys," Velez is saying to one-point-three million unbelieving devotees. It is Thursday. Within the next four days, if all goes as Velez is threatening it will, the following will transpire: we will set up for our Veterans Day remote broadcast at the Vietnam Veterans Plaza, turn the controls over to the finalists in our strike-team auditions, unplug ourselves, and march.

During all of which, Jane Oldham will be paying her scheduled weekend visit to her father.

Now, technically, we can't go on strike. After all, what're we, long-shoremen? We do belong to a union of sorts. But our union performs one function: to take money every month from people who aren't making enough to survive in their chosen line of work. Velez and I are notable exceptions, and we neither begrudge nor miss the dues. But principled labor relations is immaterial in this particular situation, as I'm sure you can see.

"So, Coolie," Velez says to the audience and me after I finish with the news, "what're your plans after our radio careers are over next Monday?"

I can't help noticing the complete absence of anybody giving the slightest credence to our threat to pull our own plug next Monday. Arielle, whose job rides on a ratings bubble that stands to implode on Tuesday, isn't even here where she should be, begging Velez to call it off. No suits have descended to bully us or to offer Velez a blowjob. People whose livelihoods are about to be *thwumped* are carrying on as usual. And why? Because nobody believes Velez.

Oh, sure, they believe we won't be here on Tuesday. Wednesday. Maybe the whole week. This is just another cheap dodge, they reason, for a vacation. But everyone seems assured that nothing cataclysmic is going to happen, and so, I suppose, should I be.

In fact, there's a holiday ebullience ricocheting all over the place here. Like *everybody's* in on the joke. Yeah, we're gonna show those scumbags they can't sell us to some billionaire pimp and get away with it! Get 'em, Velez! We're right behind you!

Among the least worried in our immediate circle are Sally Wallach and Ms. Elite. Sally, you'll remember, is a short-timer herself: her internship is up after the holidays and she's back to, where, Cornell? Yeah, back to Cornell, to finishing school. I wonder: has her old man, E. P. Wallach, been pumping her for information?

"Is her old man pumping her for information?" Velez wants to know.

Nah, I tell him.

"You seen her?"

Nah, I tell him.

"Then how do you know her old man isn't pumping her for information?"

But if anything, Sally seems to be getting a naughty little charge out of our guerrilla conspiracy to sabotage her Dad's business deal. Sally has even volunteered to shepherd our strike team DJ's—all three of them—through the chaos that Monday promises to bring, and today she's on a phone in Velez's broadcast booth calling our finalists to make sure they're going to show up and not pee in their pants on the air. Sally even came up with the suggestion that we bring them in for a run-through after the Velez & Oldham Show tomorrow, but Velez himself would have none of it: spontaneous combustion is what he's after. The worse things go on Monday, the happier Velez will be.

Mischief seems to be blossoming in Sally, and from where I sit she wears it well. A harmless way to give dad the needle, I suppose, though I have no illusions about where Sally's loyalties lie; she knows Poppa Wallach can smite us at his leisure. Meanwhile, Velez is absolutely drooling at the irony; he's even given Sally an underground *nom de guerre*: Agent Orange. We've had a couple of calls from the p.c.'s who harbor unpleasant recollections about the real, jungle-frying Agent Orange that once upon a time was dumped in murderous quantities across Southeast Asia by Colonel Elmo's low-flying colleagues, but most people think it's pretty funny.

"Coolie," Velez crows out over the city, "time for a Veterans Day update from our official secret strike coordinator, Agent Orange."

"Right, Roberto," I say, and on comes a voice over a crackling line that sounds like a World War II walkie-talkie, thanks to the artful doctoring of Enginette Casey. It's Sally, of course, and she's sitting right here beside us.

"Agent Orange?" Velez says. "Come in, Agent Orange!"

Sally giggles. "Um, hi, Roberto—"

"Careful, Agent Orange, the forces of darkness might be listening. The Thunder's new owner might even be listening. No names, please."

"DUH-uh! Hello?" says Sally, I think by way of apology. "Okay, um . . . what do I call you? Wait—I know: Fuzzy Dice." Fuzzy Dice! This giddy ad lib tumbles headlong from the lips of my very own Sally. I howl; Velez howls. Enginette Casey spills her yogurt. Sally Wallach blushes and recrosses her legs—oh, the sweet unconscious body language of the ingénue—and I suddenly find myself rethinking things in earnest.

Velez pulls himself together. "So, how's the strike team shaping up, Agent Orange?"

"Well, Fuzzy, everything's coming along just fine. We're ready for action."

"Yeah?" says Velez. "These clowns gonna do it good, eh baby?"

"Clowns?" I jump in. "Clowns? Careful there, Fuzzy, you're talking about the post-Velez & Oldham future of the Thunder. How 'bout a little respect?"

"Oh, right. I forgot," Velez says. "Well, all I can say is, don't miss Monday, boys an' girls, 'cause you gonna hear what rock's gonna sound like after Oldham and I take the big stroll just four days from right now. An' if you walkin' aroun'"—Velez is evidently feeling truly Hispanic this morning—"an' you trip on a rock an' find the new owner of WRTR hidin' under it, you be sure to remind him to tune in an' enjoy his new toy on Monday, so he can find out how much fun it's gonna be bein' the hotshot owner of a rock radio station that his own children won't listen to unless he ties them to chairs in front of a radio an' won't let 'em go to the baffroom or nothin' until their old man dies of embarrassment at owning the worst station in the history of the world, to match his newspapers and magazines and porno movies an' whatever other sleazy stuff he makes his billions on, an' while you're at it—"

Which is where I jump in and cut to a commercial or two, while Enginette Casey turns Velez off so no one out there in radioland can hear any more of him howling and thumping his console. I, in my bare glass news coffin, can't hear any of this myself, which is the whole idea of having a separate place beyond Velez's manic orbit. Sally Wallach has edged back away from Velez and is now looking through my window at me with something between bemusement and alarm—she's never seen Velez let fly quite like this before, and now, looking past the stiff-lipped voluptuous Sally at my panting, florid partner, I'm not sure I have either.

Enginette Casey is signaling to me. I turn myself on. "Your daughter's on the phone," she tells me, but Velez overhears and intercepts and now Jane Oldham is live on the air.

"Hey, who's this calling the Velez & Oldham Show?" says my partner.

"This is Jane Courtenay Oldham," my daughter says with endearing formality. I listen from my news coffin through my headphones.

"And who is this Jane Courtenay Oldham chick?" says Velez.

And my daughter dutifully recites, "New York's number one junior killshot, Uncle Roberto." Velez busts his buttons; he and Jane rehearsed this at some length two weeks ago. I hear Jane Oldham giggling too; she's pleased to have gotten it right the first time.

"Joo betcha, *chiquita*," says Velez. "*Numero uno*, my sweetheart. You coming up here to see your poppa and me soon?"

Through my headset I can faintly make out Sarah grinding out some impatient coaching. Ask for your father, I think I hear.

"Tomorrow, Uncle Roberto," says my daughter. "Can I please speak to my father?" Ah, Christ; what five-year-old talks like that? C'mon, Sarah, give us a break. Give us all a break.

Now it's me and my daughter, while you one-point-three stay with Velez. Jane and me, and Sarah in the background force-feeding Jane her dialogue. "Hello, dad?" And what's this 'dad' business? Two weeks ago I was 'daddy,' goddamn Sarah's harpy heart. If she calls next month and says, "Hello, father," I'm going to waffle my stand on gun control just long enough to shoot her mother right between the eyes.

"Hi, baby," I say. The first 'hi baby' of the visitation weekend is always the throat clutcher; good thing it happens over the phone.

Tell your father you'll be at his place at five-thirty tomorrow.

"I'll be at your place—" insidious cunt, feeding her *your* place, not *our* place—"at five . . . five-thirty. Tomorrow."

"Yeah? That's great, baby. What do you want to do this weekend?"

"I don't know."

"I have an idea. Let's go have fun."

"Okay," my daughter says uncertainly, and I know Sarah's trying to give her the big rush. I should just say goodbye instead of tugging at the wishbone. "Can I talk to your Mom?" I say instead, but I know what comes next.

"Mommy's busy now, dad. Bye." Click. One can already see Sarah's telephone genes manifesting themselves in our daughter. I sit in the coffin and watch Velez and Sally Wallach cackle back and forth.

# 14

FROM up here, the plaza looks gilded in this morning light. There are so many people. So much motion but none of it hurried, just a circular folding in of pedestrians upon one another—polite, graceful and unhurried. No one is in a hurry. There must be no business to do today. A sultry day, perfect for milling around in the brightly-painted truck whose one side folds out into a broadcast platform. Everyone mills around for a look at Velez and me—except I'm up here, not down there.

Silly people. They've formed themselves into platoons; neat ranks and files. Men, women, children with balloons, all lined up before the broadcast truck as before a reviewing stand. Everyone smiling.

I must get down there. But I can't figure . . . can't figure out how.

At the edges now the ranks are breaking. Those precise little squares of people are quietly disassembling and moving away. Melting, actually. The sculpture is melting from the edges inward toward the truck where I'm supposed to be. How come they're in such a hurry all of a sudden? Slow down! Jesus, your children can't even keep up!

Oh, baby. What was *that* all about? Okay, okay. I'm awake. Sorry about that. Guess we don't really have to bother Doctor Freud with that one, do we?

Well, it does turn out to be sultry; a sultry late afternoon at the threshold of city winter. Another city lie.

Outside Jane Oldham's occasional bedroom window lies the orange-pink reflections of the last of this day. Inside, everything seems to be on around here: television, radio—actually, a few radios. Tea kettle scorched dry and screeching for mercy, the green enamel actually peeling off the aluminum. Not the first of these to go. A tea kettle with a failsafe switch to detect snoring is what this world needs. Remind me, please, to invent one.

What did I tell people the weather was going to be like this morning? I believe I predicted a clear, cool night. On local television, the news readers blame the weather reader when the weather's bad. And sometimes they *thank* him—or her, for weather's no longer too scientific for a woman to predict—when the weather's good. How about just an occasional pat on the ass for guessing the weather correctly, and not straying over the sanity line and implying that the weather reader has some voodoo influence over the weather? Don't they know how dangerous this sort of humor is when you're serving it to a *television* audience?

Because there are people out there who believe that the goofy fat guy who comes on at twenty-four past the hour, after the girl on the gang-rape beat and right before the ex-jock, determines what the weather will be. With such empowerment comes accountability; can blame and retribution be far behind?

Come with me just a step or two into fantasy land, where a high-strung young man is watching the weather on TV the night before his wedding. The fat guy reports to him that the morrow will dawn placid and pristine, which is a good thing because this guy's getting married outside. To save a few bucks, he calls the VFW hall and cancels his contingency booking. Next day just rains its ass off, but by then there's a shuffleboard tournament going on in the VFW hall and the wedding has to be postponed. This guy's girl gets buggy and calls the whole thing off, figuring the monsoon for an omen. Our bridegroom hero marches down to the local news station and waits hunched down in his Jeep Cherokee for the fat weather guy to come out, and gives him over *and* under from the old Winchester.

Never happen, huh? Like hell. For outside this crusty window, open-armed to our incongruous dreamy dusk, lurk just such citizens, and not just a handful. You know what they look like. They look like you.

Tomorrow at this time, my Jane will be perched right here, observing another disappearing day from this, her four-day-a-month home; does she watch enough television to sense what's out there behind the stacks of orange window panes, peeking like so many smiling candles in at her? Has her mother given her to understand that there's more in life to beware than just her father?

There are messages on my machine. Velez says they will be here for me at nine-thirty or ten o'clock tonight. Who's they, and what do they want with me? Did I get talked into something for tonight that I don't remember? From there the message tape turns malignant: Morton the bookmaker and Sarah's lawyer.

Morton sounds agitated and for good reason: I'm in arrears. Sunday pushed me into quadruple figures for the first time this year. Morton will say something like: "No more action until I see some bread, pal." Ho ho. As if Morton is the only bookmaker in town. Hell, Morton isn't even an establishment bookmaker; merely a franchisee of the few *bona fide* guidos left on Mulberry Street. A personal friend of Vincent the

Chin, so goeth the neighborhood lore; Vincent the Chin, a fat Mafia don who prowls Sullivan Street in bathrobe and slippers and talks to the lampposts. Vincent has an airtight defense against any and all prosecutorial efforts: he is as crazy as a blue-assed fly. And yet business goes on in his name; business in a field where crazy is an asset in upper management circles.

It was Rose's sister who told me that Morton the nine-fingered delicatessen impresario and bookmaker is a childhood pal of Vincent the Chin. In the time-honored neighborhood tradition, Rose's sister plays the numbers with Morton. I prefer more participatory sports. But things have not been going at all well lately; even less well than I've been letting on to you. I better go see Morton.

"Hey, Mister Radio," says Morton, without looking up. He's not smiling. "What you got for me, eh?"

I hand three one hundred dollar bills over the salad counter to Morton, who wipes chicken scum off his fingers to count. Before I can look away, the bills come flying back at me.

"C'mon, Mort," I mutter under the general clatter around me.

"You need some money, young man," Morton says. He is not shouting; more like scolding, I hope. "Rose's sister always said you was a good boy, heh? So, good boy: where's my money?"

"Hey, Mort," I grin, "I didn't realize the deli business was so bad."

And before the words are out I know I have overstepped the situation.

Morton sets his chicken corpse down and gives me his attention. "Don't you smart-mouth me, sonny. You on the radio, big deal? Heh? You make lotta money? Whaddayou, buying drugs with all that money?" And now Morton's amplitude is sliding upward and we have an audience. "Well, I don't give a shit you do drugs. I give a shit about my money."

"Geez, Morton—"

He waves me quiet. He scribbles a note and jabs it over the counter at me. "You need money? There. You go see my cousin's husband. He give you money for me. Then you're his problem."

"Morton—"

"Go on. I'm busy," says Morton, and I'm off, avoiding stares, picking up speed, sweating, light-headed from the sauce smells, scrambling for the street.

All right, I know what you're thinking, but forget it: I'm not stupid enough to call Morton's cousin's husband the loanshark to get money to give to Morton the nine-fingered bookmaker. I watch television. I know where such expediency leads.

I have the money. I just don't have every penny of it tonight, not *right this second.* But Monday's payday.

Morton can wait until Monday. He's never had a problem with me.

At home there awaits a silence that Jane Oldham is about to cure. For two days she's going to pack this place full of dopey kid sounds, like questions I don't know the answers to and general giggles of wonderment at whatever we decide to pass the time doing. Jane likes the headphones we bought for her a few weekends ago; she plugs in and scans the receiver and sings along with everything, although I think her musical preference at this stage leans, under Velez's influence, to rap.

"Who you listening to?" Velez or I will ask.

"Cool J!" my daughter will squeak. The headset fairly engulfs her beautiful face; sends her flaxen hair out in manic directions.

"Who's on there now?"

"Puff Daddy!" my daughter will say.

She knows them all. How? Because one feature of our visitation weekends is that Jane Oldham and her father and godfather will throw a raid into Tower Records or another local disc emporium, and send Jane home to her mother with a dozen or so new CD's every two weeks. I imagine her sitting quietly in a cranny of her real home, up with the Westchester white folks, wired into her Walkman and running through the mountain of CD's she has accumulated by now.

But that's tomorrow. Tonight—now, in fact—Velez is coming for me. The buzzer buzzes, and I buzz back. Moments later the previously unspecified 'we' are mounting the stairs; there seem to be three pairs of footfalls, not just the two I expected.

"My father and I never talk business."

That's what Sally Wallach has to say this night about E. P. Wallach.

Bright-colored Japanese food glows under recessed spotlights, and everything else surrounding us four is black and white. The flowers are black and white. The oriental waitresses are all dressed in black and their faces are geisha white. The champagne bubbles colorlessly under Ms. Elite's colorless nose. Clothing that walked through the door with any type of palette is drained by the sly conspiracy of lights. Even the most courageous reds turn gray at the entrance.

Sally and I are seated together in the banquette; Ms. Elite and my partner Roberto Velez are across from us where they can keep a wide-angle eye on things all the way out to the door. The auburn glory of Sally's hair is lost in here but in its place is an intriguing web of shadows that play like a black lace veil down over her face. The spotlights reflect back up off the table to illuminate the soft-focus facets of Sally's face from below, lending her the one aspect that I don't think I've accused her of yet: sophistication. She is a presence that brooks no resistance and yes, I will report without embarrassment that I am holding her hand under the table.

As for Ms. Elite, she bears scant vestiges of Kansas this night, unless there are vampires in Kansas.

"So he's going through with this," Velez is saying.

"I guess. I mean, I don't know. I mean, he hasn't said anything to *me*."

*"Nothing?"*

Sally sighs. "Look, it's not up to just him. He's just one stockholder."

"Bullshit, Sally," my partner says to this, and he's right—though I'm not about to jeopardize this evening of glorious resurgence by taking up for him. "He *is* that company. Everybody knows that." Everybody does know that; E. P. Wallach is a low-profile legend who plays his vast and various holdings like a Times Square three-card-monte magician. And it always seems to be his deal.

Velez looks at his watch and excuses himself. Ms. Elite wolfs sushi like she caught and gutted it herself. Sally Wallach takes a healthy hit of champagne and lays her head on my shoulder and I'm rocketed back to the Bowl-Mor Lanes when first I mainlined the aroma of Sally from such range; when first I felt the full weight of her against me. Now she bounces back up and dives into the sushi pond with Ms. Elite, but the damage is done.

And then Sally says this: "So, you guys really going on strike?" And all I can hear is my partner Velez: Her old man pumping her for information? Huh? Huh?

I say, "So it would appear."

"What're they gonna do?" Ms. Elite asks me. Ms. Elite and I are pretty well pals by now, I should report. We seem to have decided: I'm no threat, she's no threat. Of course, she's never been a threat, but she didn't know I knew that until recently.

"They?" I say.

"I mean, the station. What're they gonna do if you go on strike?"

"Nothing. Wait us out."

"My dad says they're going to suspend you," says Sally Wallach.

Suspend us? "Velez know that?"

"I guess. I'm pretty sure dad told him."

Pretty sure dad told him. Wait—what's going on? Is it remotely possible that my partner is in cahoots with E. P. Wallach? I must think this through. Not here, though. Not out loud. Because it's sounding very much like I know less about what's going on than anyone else at this table, and I don't feel like letting that on.

Velez is stalking back to the table now in a sudden black cloud.

"Gotta go."

Brimming with sushi, Ms. Elite garbles, "'S'matter?"

"My brother is in fucking jail. My fucking brother is in jail."

Uptown now go me and my partner Velez. We are heading not to jail but to the home of Immaculata Velez.

The stairs are dark and crooked and unsteady but they are swept and neat; Immaculata Velez would have it no other way. Inside is as I left it on my last visit—what, six months ago? A year? Maybe a year. There are virgins and crucifixes enough to sanctify every cranny of this place. Above the television—the place of honor—resides a picture of a beneficent madonna caressing a miniature world. A world in her blessed care. The furniture beneath her beatific gaze is weary but clean.

Margareta Velez leaps into her brother's arms. She's not crying; just relieved that her big brother has arrived to take charge. Behind her, Michael sits in gold-trinketed and basketball-sneakered defiance, staring at the mute television. And here comes our Immaculata, out of the kitchen at the charge, wringing water and worry from her beaten hands.

What happens next happens in Spanish far too hasty for my digestion. Velez ushers his mother back into the kitchen, as if that would give them the slightest privacy. Margareta, meanwhile, gives me the outline: Nicolo is spending this evening as a guest of TNT—New York City's Tactical Narcotics Team. This is Nicolo's third visit with the authorities but this time the lad has hit the big time: caught with the goods.

"Margareta," I say, "how come your brother's got a Greek name?"

Little Margareta, beautiful young Margareta, has endured much in the last few hours. More than usual? Who knows, but she needs a distraction. "Huh?" she says.

"This name, Nicolo. That's not a Spanish name, is it?"

I've got her now. "I don't know." She's looking to see if I'm serious.

"Any kids in your school named Nicolo?"

Margareta thinks. "Nope. Not that I can think of."

I try Michael, though I should know better. "How 'bout you, Mike? You know any Nicolos?"

"So what?" is what I get from Michael, staring steadily at the television. "It's my brother's name. Ahright witchoo?"

Margareta gives me a wink. "That's my bro. He's gonna be bad, just like Nicolo."

"I see," I whisper to Margareta, and now here come Roberto Velez and his mother.

"So," says my partner, "What you want me to do? Get a lawyer?"

Immaculata Velez looks up at her son. Could I in a million years figure out what's going through this woman's mind right now? "I want," she says, "I want you to go an' get him out of the jail."

Velez stands and considers the situation. I know what's going on in *his* mind: There are no men in this family but me. I am the man.

He throws up his hands. "Okay, Momma. I'll go get him out of jail. Then what?"

Immaculata Velez says, "Then what?"

"Yeah, Mom. Then what do we do with him?"

I'm suddenly aware of silence. Margareta wants to hear this. Even surly Michael cocks an ear our way. Here's the question that's been on everyone's mind, hasn't it?

Immaculata Velez studies her son and wishes, I bet, that her tragically depleted wellspring of wisdom had one more cup left at the bottom. It doesn't. And they both know it, and so does Michael and so does Margareta. "We don' do nothing with him. He does it with himself."

My partner nods respectfully at the bleak truth. "Okay, Momma. But this is the last time. Next time that little creep gets busted—"

"Next time," Immaculata Velez says softly, "you go down an' get him again."

"Why?"

"Because you're his brother, Roberto. Because he's my son."

We summon Fat Tom the Lawyer from the Velezmobile. Fat Tom wants nothing to do with this business, and whines to Velez about not being the criminal kind of lawyer. Velez hints darkly that Fat Tom better be down at the hoosegow when we get there.

The first thing Fat Tom the Lawyer finds out is that Nicolo, now eighteen, will have the privilege of being arraigned as an adult. The second thing is that the charges, serious enough to earn Nicolo Velez time in most cities, will probably not place him anywhere near the head of the class in New York.

"Court appearance, in and out," says Fat Tom, visibly relieved to have a way out of this.

"Where is he?" says Velez.

"He'll be out in a while. We appear, we plead, we're outa here."

"You talk to him?" Velez asks.

"Yeah, sure," says Fat Tom.

"What does he say?"

"About what?" Tom dodges.

"About what. About what do you think? The fucking bust, Tom."

Tom calculates the chances of finessing Roberto Velez; this both Velez and I see in the slot-machining under Fat Tom's eyelids. But Tom knows better by now. "He told me to mind my own fucking business, Roberto."

We don't do much for the next hour-and-a-half. Tom shuttles in and out of a hearing chamber to check Velez's blood pressure while an endless procession of our fellow citizens parades its way past the heavy-bearded duty magistrate for a dollop each of what substitutes for justice this far down.

Velez and I stake out a bench pretty close to a payphone; not close enough, however, for me to be within earshot. Tom is spending as little time as possible in the courtroom itself; just long enough to see that Nicolo's number hasn't come up yet and then back out with us. Tom doesn't like it in there. Are we surprised? Can we blame him? Can Tom picture himself hauled up before this weary little judge to answer for narcotics transgressions of his own? Does cocaine make you paranoid? Huh? Huh? You talkin' to me?

Tom's part in the proceedings turns out to be seven words: Guilty, your Honor; thank you, your Honor.

We are in the hall again. Night is deep and no longer sultry but just damp: pneumonia weather. Tom is tired, anxious to be dismissed. Nicolo Velez is sullen and bellicose. We stalk toward the solitary red exit sign that seems a mile away at the other end of this echoing hall.

"Hold on," says my partner. Tom stops. I stop. Nicolo keeps right on walking. "Hey little brother, I said hold on."

"I'm tired, *big brother*," says Nicolo to the empty corridor ahead. Velez jumps out ahead of us and grabs the boy's arm and only now do

I notice that Nicolo Velez has his older brother by a couple of inches and maybe fifteen pounds.

"Lemme tell you something, my little friend," Velez snarls. "I ever have to do this again, I'm gonna whip your ass, an' I don' give a fuck what your Momma says about takin' care of her poor little baby—"

Nicolo elbows Velez far enough away for a swing and buries his fist into Velez's gut. Fat Tom and I each take an involuntary step forward before the politics of the situation sink in: this is between Velez and his brother, a family matter. Intervention would humiliate Velez beyond redemption.

But Nicolo Velez has scored heavily. Velez can't draw a breath; can't stand up straight. And now Nicolo backs away down the hall, launching in his wake a Spanish fusillade to the effect that white-boy Velez isn't whipping anybody's ass, that Velez should stay where he belongs with the rest of his radio faggots, that Nicolo Velez takes orders from *nobody*—not his little Momma, and not his asshole, ass-kissing white-boy brother.

And here we stand. Me, Fat Tom. Roberto Velez, who doesn't know what to say.

# 15

OUTSIDE the Palace of Justice, night is a trench. The door thuds behind us and Tom the Lawyer scurries for cover. I walk my measured steps with Velez, who even now is trying mightily to feign normal breathing. I try to sneak a look at Velez's face but there is no face there; only this boiling cauldron, black and sooty on the outside, roiling and steaming and ominous on the inside.

The driver of the Velezmobile is asleep.

It suddenly occurs to me that this, the municipal bowel of Manhattan, is merely a brisk walk from my house; a little north, a little west, following the upward, outward taper of the mighty Hudson. Good, because I won't have to keep trying to think of something to say to my partner Velez, beyond: "I think I'm going to walk it."

Velez nods, barely, and disappears into the Velezmobile. As I swing my solitary way up Church Street, the Velezmobile roars by. No goodnight beep. Velez is in the back seat, blind.

There's much more to tell you; so much more to catch you up on. And since I don't know how much more time we'll have together after Monday, this twenty-minute slink through the craggy halogen pools is as good a time as any. After all, Sarah—I mean Jane; Jane will be here in fourteen hours. Sarah, of course, will be dropping her off, is what I meant; what I started to say. Let's rest our minds, you and I, on simpler days. Just until we get to, say, Hudson Street, when I promise I will return us to the morass of our present preoccupation.

There was a moment when radio held the same romantic intrigue for me that it does for the countless acolytes who scrape against Velez and me every day for a taste. For a Baltimore boy of solitary and unimaginative upbringing, radio was neither political, cultural, nor generational; it was where you listened to the O's games, and the Colts, when Colts could still be found in Baltimore. The rock music was a diverting conveyance to, through, and from school, but the tribal, incantatory seduction was beyond me. Much as I might have yearned for it to be, the music was simply not in my blood. To me it was merely a fabric of colorless anthems and passages to no effect, for a boy who had nothing important to rebel against.

But oh boy, did Ellen Larkin change all that.

Through Ellen Larkin's eyes, radio became a window into a delicious, promiscuous, subterraneum inhabited by people and notions and possibilities alien to the likes of the former me. Radio was a precipitous dose of electromagnetic aphrodisia, and Ellen Larkin, girded in her patchwork jeans and cloaked in her ratty blue airman's coat and haloed with her anarchic, anthemic splay of red hair, was my own personal priestess.

In the hours and days following my own sacramental initiation into the wonders of radio—sound like Alicia the poetess?—I dared to dream dreams of enduring union between Ellen Larkin and me. Hadn't we, after all, together pulled our guzzling audience through its little ersatz revolution? Had we not borne the banners for Jane Fonda and against imperialism? Weren't we the center of the universe, as far out as we cared to be aware of it? Were we not both the focus of all this intoxicating foment and, for that matter, its principal instigators? If we had really been crazy, what havoc could we not have wrought? Do you think we couldn't have set off looting? I say we could have. For about forty-eight hours there—twelve pre-Jane, thirty-six post.

From my seat, shoulder to shoulder with my Ellen, no end seemed in sight to this grand prankish euphoria. From my position as surreptitious outsider just days before, I was now a major player in a game of unexpectedly seductive power. I exercised my newfound dominion in two ways: by saying anything, no matter how idiotic and irrelevant, on the radio, and by blustering all over the members of the official antiwar organizing committee—the legion, that is, of my Ellen's former lovers.

Oh, I could have stayed in that little broadcast booth forever. I could have sent out for sandwiches and beer three times a day and napped while my Ellen carried on our crusade. We were comrades-in-arms, my Ellen and I. We didn't need anybody, least of all the petty, self-aggrandizing crypto-poets who formerly partook of Ellen Larkin's favors. I basked in the opportunity to turn their arrogance on them, drowning them in their own triviality and irrelevance.

But what, you may be wondering, about the more personal aspects of my relationship with Ellen Larkin?

Ellen, I can't deny, was a physically impulsive woman, and I was not so naïve as to make anything sentimental out of our first frenzy. But I had every reason to believe that something had begun there in that booth—something of promise beyond the exhilaration of hit-and-run sex.

And yet even in those early, out-of-breath hours when we together engineered our stream of revolutionary exhortation and brain-pickling music, I had a hard time picturing Ellen Larkin and me outside this jumbled conspiracy of events. Ellen and I over burgers at the local beerhall? Ellen and I at the movies? Ellen and I taking a walk on the windward side of the Raritan? These and other Baltimorish notions crashed against our frantic circumstances with embarrassing dissonance, I must tell you. And so our uncontested occupation of the WRSU broadcast booth took on the amorphous desperation of a dream so intensely pleasurable that you fight in some cranny of the unconscious against waking up and losing it, because you know you'll never find it again.

Still, for this Baltimore bumpkin plenty went on at first for me to interpret as encouragement. There was, for example, the fact that Ellen seemed uninterested in dressing following our first broadcast encounter. I mean, sure, she pulled her jeans back up. But that was about it: she padded around in those wrinkled, holey socks of hers, and the airman's coat stayed where it had landed in a rumple at our feet. Picture, then, the dead of night. Phones are ringing and we are answering and pumping our music out into the enervated remains of our audience. We are taking calls from some of the members of the official organizing committee and to my delight Ellen Larkin seems inclined to blow them off too. Ellen's hair presents us a private, flouncing metaphor for the glorious rebellion that we are ministering, both in here and out there. Ellen's tee shirt is less a covering than a provocation; her breasts swim audaciously under the threadbare cotton, demanding attention out from the scooped armholes and down the misshapen neckline with every dip and unceremonious spin my Ellen makes. This night is a promenade of heedless sensuality on Ellen's part and could I think anything else but that more, much more, was in store?

So I was reluctant to acknowledge the hunger that overtook us both at about dawn of the first day; I didn't want to leave the broadcast booth, and I didn't want Ellen to, either. But we hadn't eaten anything in a long time—who knew how long, but certainly way before Jane Fonda. Something had to be done.

"What's open?" I said, leaning close to the cantilevered form of Ellen. Her tee shirt dipped toward the microphone, a ragged obeisance to the instrument of our shared power. I followed the lines of her neck, down her smudged throat and down, down into the freckled sanctum of her bosom, to which, by the way, I had not actually been granted complete license yet. I leaned into her and hazarded a caressment; Ellen, soothing out over the air to whatever handful of faithful might have been left, stopped mid-sentence and just kind of *blew* into the microphone—what did you make of that, out there in radioland? But then she gently pushed my hand away and pointed at the door and then I was on the street, brown and dusty in Jane Fonda's aftermath, looking for food.

It was midday before we surrendered the booth. By then the mutiny of air regulars was in full, self-righteous fettle, and I found myself installed as a provisional disk jockey at WRSU by *fait accompli.* My first solo show was to begin late that night, and Ellen promised through a departing yawn to be there to show me what to do.

The campus looked like Steinbeck's bleak Route 66. Cars, vans, the occasional truck and plenty of motorcycles, strapped high and hastily for the outbound migration. The occasional organizing committee scruffian could be spotted pasting signs around—fresh proclamations and announcements of the next rally. But even the most blindly quixotic of these guys couldn't ignore the obvious: that *this* little corner of the revolution was smoke and ash. The prevailing sentiment seemed to be this: Jane's out of here, we're out of here. Summer awaits, and the miraculous reprieve from exams and papers furnished by this evanescent politicization of ours was a horse not to be examined too critically. Let's just hop aboard and gallop her on out of here before somebody up there changes his mind.

But what did I care? There'd be people around. People to listen to the radio, which in the space of hours had become my vocation and my cause. I was overtired for actual sleep and besides, there was work to be done. There were summer courses to register for. Yes, I decided on the walk home from my radio debut, I'd stay here for the summer. The radio, I guessed, would be mine. And Ellen could tutor me at our leisure. We would hang out at coffee houses and listen to music and arbitrate the movement from our electronic citadel.

Next, to inform Richard 'Buddy' Oldham that he'd have to weather this particular Baltimore summer on his own.

"I'm switching majors, dad," was the dodge I used. "My advisor says I can catch all the way up if I take a few courses over the summer." I can hear myself saying something along these lines. Buddy allowed as how that made sense, and would have said so even if he didn't think so.

Okay, okay. Communications. Plenty of courses here. Nothing exactly about radio. Here's one: Foundations of Modern Communications. Ho ho. And here: Introduction to Advertising. And another: Television Production. Done. As for the freight on this new educational pilgrimage, send the bill to Richard 'Buddy' Oldham; the defense electronics business was fucking booming back then. Even better than now.

Then, straddled one leg in and one leg out of my wide-open window, high above the raucous, beeping, full-tilt exodus of my former co-revolutionaries, I let the air out; I let the commingling summer insinuations wash around me, the cut-grass and blossom smells entrance me. I slept and did not dream. In the blink of an eye it was night and, miraculously, I hadn't fallen out my window; hadn't, I think, moved infinitesimally in all the hours that the campus hurriedly and stealthily deflated under me. I awoke suddenly and utterly, shot full of Ellen Larkin and the new boundaries of my previously dopey little life. I showered off the sticky aroma of the day and night before, and hurtled out into the next night of my radio career.

All was much as I'd left it at the broadcast booth. A horn-rimmed, big-boned boy in a knitted yarmulke was winding down his program. I listened for a moment from outside in the deserted lounge; he was deep and smooth and colorlessly proficient. I didn't remember seeing him before but then, you never know what the people on the radio look like, do you? And this one didn't seem any more the antiwar organizing committee type than I did. I'd probably passed this guy a dozen times before; maybe sat with him, maybe even taken class with him. That was before he was a radio guy for me. That was before.

Ellen was not there.

The boy in the booth held up five fingers to me. What was that? Did that mean I was on in five minutes? Jesus Christ, what was I supposed to do in those five minutes? Music? Did I have to find music? Yesterday it was just there, laying all over the place. Ellen had pulled all those records. Where was I supposed to get records?

I eased into the booth as the DJ went to his last tune. "You're the new guy," he said without enthusiasm.

"Ellen around?"

"Haven't seen her."

This was no time to bluff that I knew what I was doing. "She, ah, said she'd be here, to get me started."

"This your first show?" I nodded. "Got your music?" Nope, I shook my head. "Got your spots?" Spots? Oh. Commercials. Uh uh. "See, Ellen said—"

"Forget it," he said. "C'mere." What followed was a four-minute lesson in radio broadcasting—except for Ellen Larkin, the only training I've ever had, before or since.

We pulled things together and found my spots and he showed me about logging and helped me pull music. Working the electronics was a different story; that I had down from my marathon of the day before with Ellen. The buttons I knew; it was the protocol and the business I didn't. I learned it—he taught it—in four minutes. That was all we had.

And then, in I dove. "Hello," I said—and froze. A hairy, unswallowable pineapple had suddenly materialized in my throat; I couldn't even gasp. The sound of my *hello* echoed emptily up at me from this crevasse over which I suddenly, pathetically swung.

The microphone, so agreeable, so willing just hours before, jutted up at me now from its littered nest with obscene, merciless hostility. Oh, where was Ellen, my security blanket? How could I not have recognized that Ellen had been the sole source of my nerve? I stared at the microphone. The microphone stared back. The room inhaled to the verge of implosion; I could hear tickings and thumpings and sirens and the coursing of electricity through the building. I could feel the building sinking into the avenue, into an ocean of private quicksand. I stared at the microphone, and the microphone stared back.

The door opened behind me. Ellen!

But no. It was the yarmulke boy, cinched into his backpack and ready to go. "Don't you think you better say something?" he said—loud enough to goose the needle.

I stared at him in terror so abject that he laughed right out loud. "Say this," he told me. "'This is WRSU . . . '"

I stammered, "This is WRSU."

"Okay," he said. "Now say: 'My name is . . . '"

"My name is. . . ."

"What's your name, guy?"

I stared at him for another second. Then, when something *had* to happen, couldn't *help* but happen, what happened was that I laughed—a great involuntary cathartic cackle that jolted my tormentor back toward the door in horror, his eyes betraying the sudden suspicion of insanity. I liked that. And when I turned back to the microphone, its own daunting belligerence had wilted; it looked up at me with a new and docile subservience. It was mine. I owned it. Just like Ellen owned it. I didn't own *them* yet—the ones out there on the other end—but at least I knew how to get to them now. On my own.

I finessed myself through the program thanks to a number of factors: one, I had something immediate to talk about: Jane and the strike. I painted Ellen Larkin as a heroine of the revolution, the bare-breasted Delacroix *Liberty* of the shopping-mall left. I figured she'd like that, and that she deserved it, and that it would piss off any members of the official antiwar organizing committee who happened to be tuned in. Two: you don't have to say much on FM radio, and even less on college FM radio. The less you talk, the more music you play; the more music you play, the hipper you are. I kept my rap minimalist. And three: I knew nobody was out there listening. Oh, maybe a couple of dozen people. The student center *had* to play our radio station; it was the rule. Nobody liked that rule, including me up until forty or so hours ago. But beyond that, and absent the creamy mellifluence of Ellen Larkin, you could smother in hay trying to locate my audience that night. I was sure of it.

But where was Ellen?

I occupied myself by ransacking the booth looking for effects of Ellen. Her number and address were easy: a roster was pinned to the wall. No one had crossed out the mutineers yet; no one had added my name, either. I handled both.

And I called the number listed for Ellen Larkin. Probably every fifteen minutes for the five overnight hours of my shift. It rang and rang with unconsoling monotony. Three hours or so into the night it occurred to me that the number might be a hall phone; not even in her room. I persevered.

In five hours I got three callers. One was a music request from a sleepy girl. One was a wrong number in search of pizza. The last was for Ellen Larkin and went like this:

"Ellen there?"

"Nope. Can I—"

"I'll find her." Click.

By my last hour I badly needed to see Ellen Larkin. Her absence had spun an unbearable tangle of uncertainties. Had I made some assumptions?

My excuse materialized in the form of a book with her name on it. A text, stamped for resale on several of its sides and showing the burden of its travels. I thought you might be missing this, was the ploy I tried out on myself for plausibility. I thought you might be missing . . . I thought this might . . . I thought . . . .

She lived off campus, but just—a once-handsome family home now subdivided into student apartments and left for dead. There was a porch and despite the hour—dawn—somebody was on it, reading a newspaper. "Ellen Larkin?" I asked, and a thumb hooked me around the side of the house to a fire-escape stairway that drooped its way from upper landings downward to this narrow alley. There was nothing in evidence on the ground floor; I climbed.

The door on the second landing was locked.

On the third floor was a kicked-in and tattered screen door. I pushed quietly inside and stepped down into a beer-swabbed hallway. The first two doors were securely closed. I heard low sounds from the third, and crept closer.

This door was open a crack; rancid vapors of burned marijuana seeped out to me. A conversation of sorts was transpiring in a giggling hush. I tapped on the door.

The face that greeted me was all too familiar: an assistant *poohbah* from the official antiwar organizing committee—small; flaying hair and beard wreathing a blanched, bloodshot face; shirtless in glorious display of his motel tan, a roach pinched between his fingers. He struggled to pull me into focus and then gave up and swung the door open for me.

And yes, it did prove to be a convocation of the entire society. One giant, shapeless room, strewn with orphan furniture, books, toppling reams of mimeographed antiwar posters piled on every available surface. In the center of the room a wide column of back-to-back bookcases stacked to the ceiling gave the apartment its only architecture.

I stepped into a soporific haze, hovering over and around the sleeping or otherwise barely animate forms of the official organizing committee. Most of the room's energy seemed invested in the guy who let me in, and who now was pulling on a shirt and stuffing it into his jeans. A female snored wetly in the corner of a beaten sofa; a mottled head lay buried face down in her lap. A despondent blue suffused the room— narcotic vapors filtering the first game light of day.

Now I heard soft rumblings from around the bookcase column, hoarse giggling whispers. Male. I turned back to the wiry figure scrabbling into his clothes. "Ellen?" I asked.

"You want Ellen?" he grinned. I nodded, not at all certainly. He shrugged. "Sure. Why not?" He pointed me around the center column.

On the opposite side of this column the bookcases formed an alcove, into which two or three mattresses had been wedged. Pillows and tangled threadbare blankets and strewn linen and casually discarded clothing formed a human-scale gerbil cage. As I rounded the corner a heavy boy in boxer shorts looked up from a corner at me; he had an ashtray perched on his belly and a reedy misshapen joint smoldered under his nose. The boy nodded noncommittally at me. A labored rustling of sheets drew me further around the corner; below me, broad naked shoulders, a head of dark blond hair—now an arching back and arms stretched down under this form—and a rocking, rocking, to low muted panting. I was this far now, so on with it—even though I absolutely knew what was coming.

My Ellen was asleep, as far as I could tell. Her arms were stretched over her head, her hair a ferocious, billowing red snakes' nest. She was nude except for that same tee shirt, gathered like a scarf at her throat. Her body was at rest, her being detached from the earnest workings between her legs. The boy supported himself on his knees and hands, I could see now, so the only contacts between them were a lubricious friction of thighs and the point of entry itself. Ellen lay peacefully, undulating not of her own but in unresisting, unconscious compliance. I probably tried to read distress in her face, duress—I don't know, anything that would justify my intervention. But it wasn't there. Nothing. Just simple repose.

Then the heavy boxers spoke: "You here for Ellen?"

"Yeah," I must have managed, because he said, "Sit down. Have a hit. Joe's almost finished." He stretched a fat pink leg toward the blond boy and jabbed him with his toe. "Hey, c'mon. You been at it for ten minutes."

The blond boy, also a minor functionary with the committee, looked over and weezed out a giggle. "Yeah, yeah. Feels so nice. Awright. In a minute." I looked around the room. The unextraordinariness of things disarmed me to my bones. Without deciding to do it, I sat down next to the boy in the boxer shorts and took a draw from his joint and watched Ellen Larkin being fucked in her sleep.

The boy said, "We had you on before." In her sleep, Ellen turned her head slightly toward us. I watched the almost tidal movement of her breasts; each measured thrust of the blond boy's hips would for a tiny moment send the heft of Ellen's pink unfreckled breasts up into a lovely bulbous cleft under her chin, only to recede into a generous, shapeless softness across her chest. Her nipples, so gloriously prominent through her shirt as I grappled with her from behind two nights before, were themselves in repose: tiny pools of color floating, I remember thinking, like two lily pads on a rippling pond.

"These guys," the boy said with a directionless wave, "they was rankin' on you pretty bad. Said you don't know what the fuck you're doin'."

"I don't," I said. I noticed a bead of perspiration on the tip of the blond boy's nose; perspiration or snot. I'd never watched anybody fuck before. This boy's hair swung grandly down over his shoulders as he hunched into Ellen. Humiliatingly, I felt myself getting hard.

"Ellen, she stuck up for you. Told 'em you were gonna be a radio man."

I looked at the boy but he stared straight ahead, an unenthusiastic observer to the sex transpiring in front of us. I wanted to hear more. "She did, huh?" I said.

"Yeah." He toed the blond boy again. "How 'bout it, Jose? Give it to her." He turned to me. "I was listening too. Not so much tonight, but the other night, when Ellen an' them was out ridin' aroun'. You want to know what I think?"

The moisture on the tip of the blond boy's nose had now reached critical mass, and strung its glistening way down onto Ellen Larkin's belly.

"What do you think?"

"I think, first, that you obviously don't know what the fuck you're doin', but shit, you been—what—two days on the job? 'Course you don't know what the fuck you're doin'. *Hey!* Let's do it, Joe. Somebody's waitin'." Somebody's waiting? "But," said the boy, "I think you should *learn* what the fuck you're doin', 'cause lemme tell you: you sound *true* over that radio. You could be real, real good."

Before us, blond Joe was bracing for the sprint. My fat friend rooted him on. "That's it, Joe. Give her the bat, Joe. You know she likes you best. She told me so, Joe. Make her dreams sweet, Joe." Now blond Joe went for it, his eyes clenched and the musculature up and down his flanks clenched and his hair flailing across his face. And such now was the rawness of him that Ellen Larkin awoke, her eyes falling first upon me, unrecognizing, and then turning up into the face of her lover. She grinned, I think, sleepily, and said, "Oh, you guys . . ." but otherwise she remained utterly passive of body, as much an observer as my fat companion and I at her side.

I watched her watching. Her eyes were still heavy with sleep; through red slits I could see pleasure of a remote and solitary kind. It was a pleasure that mocked even the notion of jealousy, of possession; the idea, lately and intensely mine, that Ellen could *belong* to me in any Baltimorian sense seemed so wildly absurd now that I think I even laughed out loud, because the fat guy beside me said, "What?" And I just grinned stolidly and watched blond Joe pump himself finally into the dark and magical depths of Ellen Larkin.

"Ahright, Joe baby, I knew you could do it," said my fat friend, but

Ellen Larkin said nothing, for she was asleep again almost before blond Joe's thrashing had completely subsided between her legs, and Joe had retreated from her with a meek and exhausted little moan. And it wasn't another moment before Joe was on his feet and pulling on jeans, trying not to stumble on Ellen Larkin. "Who're you?" he asked me.

"He's the guy's on 'RSU tonight," my friend interceded.

"Um," blond Joe said, and shuffled around the bookcase rampart and out of sight.

And now the heavy boy beside me heaved himself aloft. He took a final draw on the crumbling joint and pinched it out. Then he extended an arm down in Ellen's direction. "All yours," he said. "I'll give ya some privacy. Starvin' my balls off, anyways. But look: you remember what I said. You got a voice for the radio. You got a *sensibility,* is what you got. Can't teach that. Ellen, she got it. She got the touch. You too, I think." He grinned and waved. "See ya."

I sat motionless and presently I heard the opening and closing of the door, and then nothing. Blond Joe and my friend had evidently left. I rose and tip-toed around the bookcase, and yes: everyone who was still there was fast asleep. Girl on the sofa, guy in her lap, others in piles of limbs.

I returned to Ellen's alcove and knelt down beside her. It might have been different if we'd *made love.* Not what we'd done in the booth that first night—that naughty little tippy-toe broadcast coupling. I mean something with a little romance behind it. I mean, to me, there'd been plenty of romance to it; it had been the most romantic goddamn thing that had ever happened to me. But now, in this sorry apartment's rising light, kneeling behind the freshly used Ellen Larkin, I looked at it from her point of view. Was that night much different from this one for Ellen? You may have your opinion, but as I knelt above the soiled softness of her I doubted it. "Oh, you guys . . ." That's what she'd said. *Guys.* How many? Blond Joe, for one. The guy who let me in? Wasn't he dressing just at the moment I arrived? He didn't look too surprised, did he, that some guy was arriving at dawn and asking for Ellen. What about my fat friend in his boxer shorts, my pothead career advisor? Him, too? What about the entire goddamn absolutely official antifucking-war organizing committee—the whole pompous guitar-strumming poetry-spouting army of them?

I knelt quietly and listened for movement in the apartment, for something in my brain to put up a fuss. Below me lay Ellen Larkin, about whom I had indulged myself in a wild landscape of delusion these past days. There she lay, completely blameless for my stupidity. In fact, I *owed* Ellen. Because there was something, I'd discovered in the solitary night of my just-ended broadcast, something to this radio deal quite apart from the seduction of Ellen Larkin. She'd given me the radio and even though it was an experience in its smelly-diapered, wailing infancy, it was the first time I'd ever felt in possession of something—something powerful over which I could have power.

The quiet had thickened in the apartment. The sleep beyond the bookcase was the sleep of the dead. Here, in Ellen Larkin's nest, lay the final moments of my imaginary romance, my silly delusion. I brushed my fingers lightly down the outside of Ellen's leg. Her heat was the heat of the Jane Fonda incursion. Images arose of moments before: blond Joe, working out on Ellen's supine acquiescence. Sweat from blond Joe's nose dripping down among these fine freckles—these freckles that were everywhere but the undersides of Ellen's breasts and the luminescent whiteness of skin above her patch of damp red pubic hair. *"Oh, you guys . . ."*

I unbuckled my belt and slipped one leg of my pants off and eased Ellen's legs apart—even breathing, not a movement of re-emerging consciousness—and, hovering above her, I eased myself into her thinking, blond Joe didn't need a rubber . . . and I came immediately, before I had even settled my weight down onto my hands, I came like I never have before or since, and I pulled out of her and wrestled my pants back on and my shirttail in and myself out of that apartment and up and out of the funny little window-door and down the clattering iron fire escape stairs and into the morning sun before the quaking in my legs had even subsided from this, my second and final orgasm in the actual presence of Ellen Larkin.

I'm not asking you to approve of this. I simply report it. I simply report it.

# 16

How far past the equinox are we? No need for a calendar. The alarm that
summons me to the first tentative levels of consciousness far, far pre-
cedes the dawn. There is chestnut scratching on the front windows, and
there is this ching-a-ling little alarm in the pitch darkness. For a moment
I reconnoiter the corners of the silence for the presence of Jane
Courtenay Oldham but no: that's tonight. I mean, this coming night. Not
the one that hasn't ended yet except for my meager ration of it.

I punch buttons and what's going on? My jabs do no good, the
ching-a-ling goes on, a different kind of warning that something is
required of me; something I'm not quite up to at this particular moment.

Sit up. It's too dark. Oh ho, the phone.

"Coolie?"

I can't find anything to tell me what time it is. Don't I have a clock
around here somewhere? Where's my watch? Where's my alarm clock?

"Hey. Coolie. You there?"

"Where are you?"

"Ridin' around."

"Riding around," I say.

"Yeah. Goin' for a ride."

"Time's it?"

"I don't know. I'm, like, ridin' around."

"Okay," I say. I listen into the tinny, scratchy box that the
Velezphone sounds like. I can't tell whether the Velezmobile is in
motion or maybe parked somewhere, like out in front of Immaculata
Velez's place in Washington Heights.

"You all right?" I try.

"Yeah. Sure."

"Okay," I say.

There's nothing for a minute, and then my partner says, "Look,
Coolie. There's some things I ain't tol' you yet—about this strike and
everything. But don't you worry. I got some plans an' we gonna fuck
'em over good. It's just I can't say anything because there's some guys
involved don't want their names in the news."

"You can't tell me?"

"Hey, man. If it was up to me. . . ."

Now I'm awake. "I hear they're gonna suspend us."

A cackle. "Yeah? Who told you that?"

"E. P.'s bouncing baby girl, that's who. You hear anything about that?"

"They gonna *suspend* us? Good. Perfect, in fact. Let 'em."

"You know anything about—"

"I shoulda kicked the shit outa my brother," Velez says.

Ehh, I say.

"How come she won't move outa that, that *shithole* . . . .? I could move her—anywhere . . . I could give her a big fuckin' house an' people to clean it . . . What she expect gonna happen to that stupid bastard Nicolo they stay in the neighborhood? Nothin' but dead people and their killers in that place now. But no, no. 'I ain't gonna be chased outa my own house . . . ' she says. Yeah. So I gotta get the little fuck outa the can. 'He's your brother,' she says." Velez snorts. "He ain't shit."

"Can they suspend us?" is what I want to know.

"I don't know," Velez says. "Who cares?"

*I'll* tell you who cares: Morton Nine-fingers cares. My ex-wife's sledgehammer attorney cares. I live on a flinty enough margin as it is, after the vultures get finished with me. I don't have a mattress full of money in case this suspension business gets out of hand.

"I'll be in late," my partner tells me.

"You want me to tell anybody anything?"

"Nope. You don't know where I am." And Velez, wherever he is, leaves me.


Friday. I'm in early. Some new guy is finishing up the overnight; has Hendy Markowitz been relegated to substituting for the substitutes? This guy looks about college age. Don't worry; I'm not going off on another maudlin tangent. There's no time.

The Velez & Oldham Show starts without Velez. Read the news, play the music, sell the stuff. Read the news, play the music, sell the stuff. I'm going light on the strike business; leave that for my partner. Read the news, play the music, sell the stuff.

Enginette Casey. A sturdy plugger; we met her, you and I, the night that finished itself off at the Empire Diner. You may not recall, because Enginette Casey found herself somewhat overshadowed that night by Sally Wallach and the mysterious outlander Ms. Elite. Casey doesn't miss a beat or a day. When something has to happen, Casey makes it happen. Nobody tells her how. She just does it. Not manic, not your impenetrable technoid. She's—ah, what's that word I can never quite summon without breaking out in hives?—oh yes: professional.

161

Enginette Casey, all five-foot-three of her sitting in virtual darkness, silhouetted only by the goosenecks and the blinkings of her flight deck with her black aviator shades and her pinched-together fronds of weedy brown hair, is an absolute, total professional. It's time, perhaps, that I begin to regard that as a compliment.

Three tunes in a row give me a chance to compose some non-stale news. The election—that the Democrats will win is not news in any dramatic, late-breaking, this-just-in sense of the word, but a matter of local course to be read into the daily record. Wall Street gave birth to an army of fanged mutant kittens again yesterday; more of the avaricious young will be sacrificed to the gods, and the survivors will hit big again and forget anything ever happened. The Giants and the Jets will be playing as usual this weekend and I must make my fearless picks for the benefit of my listeners, but it just isn't the same this week because I'm cut off. I could go elsewhere, but bookmakers are a cozy fraternity and Rose's sister, the West Village's minister of protocol, has warned me against trying to outsmart anyone.

And now to the blotter: rape, incest, a war on drugs. Maybe we should nominate Fat Tom the Lawyer to be the judge advocate general for the war on drugs. A girl pushed in front of the Canarsie train; surgeons sew her fingers back on and she's expected to play at Lincoln Center in about a week. Surgery's great: before the operation, she didn't know how to play a thing. That's what Velez would say if he were here, which he isn't.

And this: marine cops pull unidentified black male from East River downtown. More grim tidings from Wall Street.

Unidentified black male.

Out of the Velez & Oldham broadcast booth and down into the pen. But it's not nine o'clock yet; Raylene McDonald wouldn't be here yet anyway.

Oh, Raylene. Oh boy.

I read some commercials and ask anyone in the audience who has information leading to the apprehension of Roberto Velez to call their local precinct house, and then on with the music. Raylene McDonald, that occasionally seduced and impregnated but adamantly unmarried way-uptown Mom and Thunder Rock program assistant, is, I reflect as I sit in Velez's elevated chair and stare through the bullet-proof glass portal into my own empty news coffin, one of the only people in this whole place with whom I've spent private time, of my own volition. Occasionally, of my own initiation. She is a silly drinker of cheap wine, this one, and the jaded tissue that encases her heart gives us a common constitution. We have gotten drunk and shared stories of romantic stupidities, and of course her youngest and Jane Courtenay Oldham are occasional playmates here at the Thunder. And then there is the matter of Lyndon McDonald, to whom only so much symbolism can fairly be attached without incising the bleeding heart of sociography. I'm not interested in that; neither is Raylene McDonald, whose approach to Lyndon, her half-brother or something, is old-time family: do what you can, and accept the rest.

But what if the unidentified black male that just washed up on the shoals of Wall Street turns out to be Lyndon McDonald? What then?

Read the news, play the music, sell the stuff. Almost two-and-a-half hours into this. No Velez. And now, the shock troops slosh onto the beach. Enginette Casey looks over to me—no expression of her own, just an adroit little reconnaissance to see if I'm still with her. Yeah Casey, I got it.

First it's Arielle, barreling out of the elevator like the human cannonball, battering innocent early-morning bystanders. Now I see she's running interference for a scrum of suits. One is familiar to me: Sanford Fry, the general manager of the Thunder. Arielle's boss. My boss. On paper, Velez's boss, but in brutal reality a warm body in temporary residence on the seat of authority; Velez has ruthlessly deposed more than one of his predecessors. No one who actually works in this building can fire Velez. I'm not sure who could fire Velez. Someone could, I suppose. E. P. Wallach could.

Here they come. Now I catch sight of Sally Wallach bringing up the rear. Steering clear of this bounding management phalanx. Sally has managed to submerge herself so deep in the Thunder underbrush that nobody except Velez and I seem to remember just exactly who she is. To muscular little Arielle and her potato pickers, Sally is just a babe intern passing through.

Sally swings wide of the cloud of suits clustering toward me, and treats me to a delicious comic face that passes for a review of the mood in the elevator on their way up. Sally's hair—ah, never mind. Enginette Casey gives me a *pssst!* to alert me that words will shortly be required of me. I jab the lock button on our door; it's me and Casey now.

"They look pretty pissed," is Enginette Casey's assessment.

"Cyanide capsules are in Velez's top drawer, Case," I tell her. "Don't let 'em take you alive."

Now Arielle is knocking on the broadcast booth door; such is the soundproofing in here that Arielle could be spraying the office with an AK-47 and we'd never know. I'm using my headphones as blinders but I know I'm not fooling anybody: they know I know they're here. But now Enginette Casey gives me the precious one-point-three and the suits settle down, momentarily. It is as if the suits have just been reminded what the game is all about: those one-point-three. No suit will pee on the one-point-three. The one-point-three get itchy tuner fingers, the suits cease to exist. I love this.

Arielle and the suits pitch camp outside the booth while I hawk the following: McBurgers, McMasterCards, and the suburban metastasis of the *Friday the 13th* flick that Velez and Ms. Elite and I took Jane Oldham to see two weekends ago. Jason is now officially everywhere. Look out. And let's not forget the Korean cars; Korean cars are a Velez & Oldham specialty, Korean cars in a volume to further savage the old Pacific Rim trade balance; Asia-bound profits enough to finance the takeover of every single corner store in town by those multifarious grindstone-nosing clans of Korean grocers.

And there at her desk beyond the war party sits Raylene McDonald, fit and trim. Fingers flying and familial smile at the ready; I can only assume that news—if news of Lyndon there be—hasn't reached her yet.

Enginette Casey has crept into my earphone. "Line o-five, Dennis. Guess who." And sure enough, my partner—he breaches.

"Where the fuck are you?"

"I'm, uh . . . you mean, specifically? Where am I exactly? Let's see . . . Third Avenue and . . . ah, I don't know. Fifty-something."

"No, Velez. I mean, where are you in relation to getting your ass to work? You remember: radio? Rock & roll?"

"I don't know, man. I'm not sure. I'm in too good a mood to be in that place right now."

"Hold on," I say, and Enginette Casey gives me back my one-point-three. "That was a couple of tunes," I tell my listeners. "Here's a couple more. Don't go away. Please. This will get better." And now back to Velez. "Well, you might as well stay right where you are, baby, 'cause you couldn't get in here anyway."

"What you talkin' about?" says Velez.

"I'm talking about every Indian in the world camped outside this booth, partner. I'm talking the French Revolution on the other side of this door, an' they've got a guillotine with a hole in it just the size of a Puerto Rican penis—"

Music to Velez's ears. "Yeah? Who?"

"Fry. Buncha other guys, Fry's fluffers, I guess. And our girl Arielle—real pumped up out there. Got those bi's and tri's and quads and everything fired up this morning, that girl."

"Reason with them," says Velez.

But I say, *"You* reason with them. Hold on—the next voice you hear will be the enemy. Now don't you hang up, you son of a bitch. . . ." I signal Enginette Casey, who rings a phone just outside our booth. I saunter over to the glass door and push my nose up against it and grin. The suit platoon regards me in the fashion of humans peering into the gorilla cage. Arielle, on point, snarls up at me but there's fear in her eyes, lurking under that untamed landfill of electrified hair. I point to the phone in their midst; Arielle picks up.

I can't hear the conversation and don't need to. Arielle promptly hands the phone to Sanford Fry, a young man who may have majored in tennis and blow-drying at some fine southern college before strapping himself into Armani regalia to try his hand at managing a radio station. What transpires between Sanford Fry and Roberto Velez takes about ten seconds and Sanford Fry's contributions are minimal except for an entertaining change of hue that brings to mind a standing-up embalming: what was peachy and preened is now ashy and addled. Sanford Fry hands the phone to Arielle and retires; the siege has been broken.

"What'd you tell him?" I ask.

"I just told him not to be too sure whose ass he's going to be kissing from now on."

"Meaning?"

"Meaning Harold Fish doesn't own that dump yet."

"Meaning?"

"Meaning the forces of darkness come in many sizes and flavors, Coolie. Can't let Fry be too sure he's ridin' the right horse just yet."

"Gimme a hint, partner."

"Ho ho," says Velez.

The coast is clear.

No sign of Arielle or the upstairs contingent. The Stevie Joe Adams Show is entertaining about three hundred thousand people out there somewhere—three hundred thousand got the last three of Stevie Joe's predecessors fired. That's a cool million citizens, allegedly, who blow off the Thunder as soon as me and Velez get through with them. Gotta do better, Stevie Joe.

My theory, in case you're interested, is that nobody, including Velez

& Oldham, could do much better than three hundred thousand on late morning. My theory is that the extra million have something better to do than listen to the goddamn radio all day. My theory is that the Thunder is *lucky* to have two hundred thousand people out there who are so brain damaged that they listen to the same radio station hour after hour, day after day, year after year, without once contemplating life's late-morning alternatives. Sally Wallach, media major at Cornell University, might have a different view of our listener profile and the septic-tank dive we take at ten-o-one every morning. She may be right.

I sneak out to the Thunder *pissoir*. On Arielle's bulletin board over urinal three is the roster for Monday's Veterans Day remote broadcast. Raylene McDonald is the field honcho, as she usually is for these outings. Raylene will have an eye out for Lyndon, though she will not expect to see him. Agent Orange and Enginette Casey will be on hand as well. Agent Orange—Sally, you remember—is listed as entertainment coordinator. What entertainment? Surely Arielle isn't talking about the finalists of our strike team auditions, for whom Arielle must right now be wishing a weekend of biblically hideous misfortune.

Sally is waiting for me back in the official Velez & Oldham broadcast booth, which Velez wound up choosing not to grace this morning after all. "What entertainment?" I ask Sally.

"This is going to be a real extravaganza," Sally beams. "Comedy, music, and an allstar '60's rock band. Not to mention the strike team DJ's." Sally grins us into a creeping intimacy. "You won't want to miss it."

"I don't intend to. Our boy . . ." I hook a thumb at the conspicuously empty seat usually occupied by the rump of Roberto Velez, ". . .him I'm not too sure about."

"Speaking of him, what about our meeting?"

"What meeting?"

"You, me, Raylene, Fuzzy and Arielle—although I think Arielle will probably skip it, don't you?"

"What meeting?"

"You know, our meeting where we figure out what to do on Monday. Our pre-broadcast production meeting."

"Where'd you hear about that?" I ask—not condescendingly, I hope.

"Well, you know . . . Radio 101. At Cornell."

"We don't have those here."

"How come?"

"Don't believe in 'em. No spontaneity if we do too much planning."

"Yeah, but we haven't done *any* planning."

"That's already borderline too much," I tell Sally. Strange to say but Sally's words have an actual aroma to them; it smells good talking to her. It makes me light in the head, as if I were kidnapped and taken to the suburbs and dropped in the middle of a field of poppies. "Look, Sally," I say, "maybe you're right. Maybe a pre- . . . pre- . . . what'd you call that thing?"

"Pre-broadcast production meeting."

"Yes. You're absolutely right. We should definitely have one of those. Maybe Velez and I can learn something. Only thing is," and I nod to the vacant seat of Velez. "Where you gonna be later?" I say, in a tone I'd hoped wouldn't let anything on but which obviously did because from Sally I get the kind of high amplitude Cheshire smile that business meetings don't normally elicit.

"How much later?"

"Your guess is as good as mine. Maybe *late* later."

"Call me," says Sally Wallach, officially opening the last stretch of the highway to hell.

Sleep on arrival afternoon for Jane Oldham is a preposterous notion; I choose, as usual, to pace. This entire old building of mine seems to have high blood pressure. I can feel the pounding in its temples. Impatience is my morbid prelude to this twice-a-month descent of Sarah from the sublime wooded grandeur of her Westchester aerie into this belly of depravity that she so recently and so willingly called home.

Momentary diversion materializes in the person of a giant roach. This is the creature that New York restaurateurs and all Floridians refer to as a water bug, but for us laymen the word 'bug' is ludicrously inadequate. In size and cunning and speed and athletic ability and sense of humor this animal is the sentient peer of the wiliest shithouse rat.

This guy has been around here awhile. I've spotted him in the bathroom and in the kitchen and have gone as far as to lay out some of those roach motels. But even if he could wriggle his gargantuan girth into one of them he'd probably just get himself laid and then check out first thing in the morning, just like we humans do.

How do I know it's the same roach? These big guys don't hunt in packs like hyenas or little brown roaches. They are the Siberian tiger of insectdom, lone predators lurking in life's shoe-level crevices for a nice, chubby, unsuspecting kitten to gambol by. A quick, merciful wrench of its jaws and the kitten's spinal column is snapped; then the roach can drag its prey into a corner to nibble or, at its pleasure, to swallow kitty whole.

I would kind of like to rid the place of this beast before Jane Oldham's arrival. I don't need another report filtering its way back to Sarah's attorney that the girl's father's place is a roach-infested flophouse; my Jane already befriended one of these guys and carted it home to show Mom. Sarah wishes to be rid of the burden of visitation rights; she wishes to be rid of the burden of me.

But what armament? To every chemical short of Verdun mustard gas or Saddam's anthrax, the creature has already proved contemptuously impervious. A big, heavy magazine might do him, but I'd actually have to catch him out in the open for a point-blank shot. You don't get as far in the roach business as this fellow's obviously gotten by being stupid. He's watching me pace and knowing that I'm plotting against him. Something long but more wieldy than a broom. I have a golf club—a putter Velez stole from a miniature golf course during a respite from the Atlantic City gaming tables—but no, my apartment is too breakable and if I couldn't aim the goddamn thing playing miniature golf, what makes me think I'd be any better at big game hunting? Nah. A cruise missile, radar-guided, nuclear-tipped. The kind drug dealers use in Immaculata Velez's neighborhood.

Now he's gone. He's gone and left me with other unresolved business: unidentified black male. Fished out of East River. Unidentified black male.

It's a full four hours before Jane is scheduled to arrive. I wonder where the cops take unidentified black male floaters. I wonder if I have the nerve to find out.

# 17

POTTER'S morgue. A stone's throw from the Palace of Justice. I'm assuming nothing.

"I'm inquiring about . . . I saw a note in the paper . . . somebody—black man fished out of the East River." I start things off this way with the innkeeper of the Motel Necropolis.

"Here to identify?" Eastern Mediterranean. Turkish? Not a bureaucrat; not working here just because he's not smart enough for Motor Vehicle.

"Uh, yeah. I mean, I might know who it is." And I am studied for any visible signs of connection with whoever lies beyond the heavy doors.

He pulls out a form; Xeroxed to an illegible generation. "Name?"

"*My* name?" He smiles the smile of the bored but indefatigable in reply.

"Oldham," I say. "Dennis Oldham."

"Family member?"

"Of the deceased? I thought we were talking about a black man." Again he smiles, but differently, and I think I've just passed a secret test.

"How do you know the deceased?"

"I don't know that I do know the deceased yet." We're both enjoying this now.

"How *might* you?"

Rose's sister: don't try to outsmart anybody. "Might be a relation of a friend of mine."

"How come you didn't bring this friend with you?"

"It would be . . . difficult for her."

"She gotta come anyways," says the innkeeper, not unkindly.

I shrug. "Not if it isn't him." And the innkeeper shrugs.

Now I'm led through a very quiet and disinfected antfarm of a hallway labyrinth. The commingling of odors is comical and sickening at once: bologna sandwich, that one was; and here's the stuff they pickle frogs in to prepare them for amateur mutilation in high school biology class. Now out of the silence I hear laughing, but far removed from our progress; possibly this frivolous horseplay is seeping in from a wing where less grisly business is conducted. We're circling, slowly, into the dense core of the building.

The destination of my dread is exactly as you've seen it on TV: rows of rectangular icebox-type doors lining both sides of a scrubbed and shining no-nonsense space; gurneys at the ready, a long work table in the center, relentless fluorescence bleaching every municipal molecule. Surprisingly, no smells. The smell, I think, is what I'm afraid of. I've read about how death smells, before the spice merchants ameliorate the decomposition. Lyndon—if he's here, I keep encouraging myself—will not have been thus serviced yet.

Something comforting has come over the Turkish innkeeper. Having qualified as a legitimately interested party and not a ghoul, I am now an object of professional compassion for this fellow. This new kindliness makes my skin crawl; can this ordeal be so gruesome that he needs to *fear* for me? But no. Look, most of the people who come here are hysterical relations of one or another of this man's guests; of course he's apprehensive about the layman's queasiness. I consider reassuring him but he's already checked his roster and moved to a door. I angle in behind him.

The bag on the slab takes me by surprise: it's not black like in the cop shows but semi-transparent, so that I can make out fearful intimations of what's inside; not just nondescript mass. The innkeeper rolls the dolly all the way out but lets the bag lay untouched and turns to me.

"How well you know this guy?"

"The guy who this might be," I correct him, "is an acquaintance. But I've, uh, been in his company plenty of times. I know him well enough."

"Yeah," the innkeeper says, "well, maybe. But I. . . ." He searches for words and I would like very much to be out of here. Will this little exercise make things any easier on Raylene McDonald? No, it will not. Like the innkeeper says: she'll have to come down anyway. My nose is someplace it doesn't belong. ". . .been in the water three, four days, maybe longer. But the worst part is, how they found him; I mean, how they found out he was there. Screw sucked him in." He looks at me. Do I follow? What is he saying? Can we get this over with?


There's a diaphanous hissing surrounding me—soothing me, holding me aloft, defying the cloying determination of grim coldness to summon me back down. Whatever's down there is too cold for me; up here, I'm closer to the sun and more secure in the embrace of whatever fragrant jetstream is whooshing blissfully past me.

I bolt upright. A green room. An office—no, a waiting room, but small and unoccupied except for a tall angular man with long, curly, dark hair and pale blue eyes popping in petrified disorientation from their drawn and dark-circled cheeks. Shirt opened, sweaty chest pounding, this featureless chest white under folds of a stained purple shirt. Long arms, God look at how weirdly long those arms are, and white fingers clenched into the soft edges of this table. Shoulders broad but beaten, hunched, awaiting the next blow. Legs hover inches above the floor, long legs, not dangling but viced together, drawn up, wary. Jaw wide and clenched; a whole clenched man, sitting across from me, staring at me, breathing with me, lost and cold, wearing pain.

I ease myself off the table and cross to the mirror for a closer look. Something wants urgently to be remembered but not yet, oh no. Not yet. Let me discuss things with my new friend here, who chose the very moment of my reluctant awakening to spring up himself. Considerate company; everyone here is so considerate.

The Turkish innkeeper swings in. "Ah! You're back. Sit. Sit down." And I let myself be maneuvered back onto the padded table. There's a banging behind my left ear. I must investigate.

"So," says the innkeeper. "How you feel?"

But I have forgotten how to speak for the moment. Too many questions at once may make the condition permanent, so I stall by feeling around my head. It doesn't take me long to discover a brand new feature of my topography—long and bulging and oddly intriguing to touch.

"Back edge of the transfer table," says the Turkish innkeeper and those prove to be the magic words, because now I remember this fellow stepping aside and unzipping the translucent bag and me stepping forward and being physically assaulted by a stew of revulsions that reached up and seized me, immobilized me and transfixed me. And there I stared at this bestial, green, faceless meatloaf that used to be a human being, yes, just enough clues: coarse, crusty, clumps of hair, an assemblage of sinew and slick slimy sheets of, Jesus, skin. And the worst was this: the sense of movement, minuscule tidal movement, under that green, scored, tortured membrane across the thing's belly.

And then the smell. My legs refused to support the inspection of this abomination and, according to the Turkish innkeeper, the edge of the transfer table reached up to greet my collapse with the same callous dispassion that it shows the innkeeper's transients, and that was it.

The Turkish innkeeper has a quick clinical look into my eyes and smiles a yellow reassuring smile. "Won't need this," he says, fingering a little white stringy thing. "Never can find 'em till people wake up on their own. Don't like to use 'em anyway; killer on the sinuses."

Now I look around to see if maybe I'm still in the cold room with the innkeeper's guests. No. It's warm in here and it doesn't smell like anything I don't want to be near. A cup of water materializes in my hand and down it goes. And stays down, tender mercy.

"Listen, I'm sorry," says the innkeeper, "but I gotta ask this, for the record: can you identify the deceased?"

The deceased. Too human-sounding. I stare at the Turkish innkeeper. "May I take that as a negative response?" he asks gently, and I grunt my thanks that nothing more, apparently, is going to be required of me.

The Turkish innkeeper walks me all the way out into the chilly afternoon, now, amazingly, leaning well into evening. "How will you . . . ." is as far as I get, but the Turkish innkeeper anticipates me.

"Without the teeth," he says, "it'll be tough. Theoretically we could dredge for the, the, you know, the rest." We walk together. I feel droplets of rain, and they feel glorious; cleansing. "We send him to the county coroner. From what I saw, there's no sign of gunshot or stab wound. They'll do toxicology and the rest, just so they can pronounce it an accidental death. Nobody claims him after that. . . ."

"So you might never know who this guy is."

"If we wanted to bad enough, we could find out eventually. Unless he's a drifter. But, you know. We got too many anonymous dead guys, and too few hours in the day. Besides, city don't want to pay thousands and thousands to find out exactly *which* derelict that is. It's sort of academic. Different thing if somebody was to come looking for a missing guy who fits the general description." Now the Turkish innkeeper asks me, "This friend of yours—he missing somebody?"

"She. And I don't know." But what's the use, I've already decided, of treating Raylene McDonald to that thing in there, even if that thing *was* Lyndon McDonald? Which she wouldn't be able to tell any more than I could, I assure you.

And so I haul to a downtown bar the weight of this afternoon, the weight of another uncertainty heaped upon the rest.

Not too much, now. Just a wee dram for decompression purposes. And messages; gotta call. Then home to greet Jane Courtenay Oldham.

Dial in my code. Sarah's lawyer. Again. Please return this call, or have your attorney return it if you're currently retaining one. Yes, yes. Velez, twice. Eleven calls from assorted Cathys and Bobs. In all the excitement, I've neglected the Cathys and Bobs, something I have vowed never to do. Morton the Nines. And Sally Wallach.

I need money for Morton.

At the automatic teller machine I run my cards. Visa and MasterCard together limit out at just about six hundred dollars. Halfway there. Cash card: three and a quarter. And I have three or so at home. That covers Morton. And, except for walking-around money, taps me until Monday.

Morton's deli is a lively place on Friday night, but Morton makes time for me. I'm here for redemption, and Morton will welcome me back into the hoary bosom of the gambling fraternity. I pay Morton his twelve hundred dollars and bet two hundred on the New York Jets. Dennis Oldham and Leon Hess, the incurable romantics.

Another thing Rose's sister always says, besides 'don't try to out-smart anyone,' is this: Never fall in love with the hometown team. But this isn't sentiment. The Jets are the *men* this week. Those boys are there.

Even though it's after five, I walk home from the cellar tap room. There are raindrops but only the good kind, the kind that awaken you and take your mind up and out into loftier wonders; the kind that touch your face like cool tongue-tips and invite you out of your box and into the world. If it doesn't get any colder I will walk this neighborhood of mine this evening with my beautiful daughter Jane, who shines through these close and mysterious lanes and alleyways and bestows light when she passes; I will therefore do my neighbors the honor of walking my daughter through their forlorn midst and, for some brief hours, will ennoble everything for us all.

Jane started out as hope. My own solitary desperate hope of binding Sarah and me, that matchstick marriage that, to what little of the outside world cared, must have seemed over before it began.

Sarah and Velez had been fast and furious after Montreal, as was and is Velez's custom. There were about two months when Sarah was Velez's proprietary interest but we three were together everywhere but in bed. Velez knew I was in love with Sarah. Sarah knew I was in love with her. In spite of this they made sure I was around, where more compassionate people might have told a fellow to beat it. Such was Sarah's fascination for Roberto Velez that his predilections became hers— among them the mostly benign self-indulgent tyranny he exerted over me.

It was probably as much my imagination as fact that Sarah's more lascivious displays were aimed at my exclusive discomfiture. We clubbed and beerhalled ravenously; we backstaged by gilded invitation. Velez, after all, was New York's brand new *Señor* Rock & Roll, and the

Thunder made sure he was at every major concert to introduce every major band. Those nights were, in fact, the genesis of the Velezmobile; WRTR would limo us to this arena and that one in advertisement of Thunder status, so at contract time Velez's lawyer just penciled it in and there we were with our own personal, permanent, twenty-four-hour-a-day land yacht to take us to work and to play.

And Westchester Sarah absolutely wallowed in the decadence. She delighted in this unbridled existence of ours and tried with much success to eclipse the outrageousness of all around her. She was deadly competitive in the public display of her body; she drank and drugged and vomited and snickered defiantly at the slightest conventional suggestion—usually mine.

True: I was worried about her. That comes with being in love, does it not? But beyond that it was clear to Velez and me—for we said as much—that this Sarah was an invention of recent vintage. Because no matter how undauntedly she blazed and careened with us, there was no way she could submerge completely her thoroughbred bloodline. This was a Westchester girl on a decadent glamour binge. Such sudden immersion has killed plenty of her kind; I worried. Velez did not, and that about sums things up.

But so . . . so *drunk* was I on Sarah that I didn't permit the slightest filtering of rationality to dampen things. If her rock regalia, the leathers and the plunging, taunting necklines and the whory make-up and crazily mauled and tinted blonde hair, merely titillated and amused Velez and his scurrying minions, the package enflamed and utterly spellbound me. It may have been the simple playful rebellion, or something more: the molting of one personality into another by sheer willfulness. It was certainly the physical Sarah, both the intensity of her beauty and her own flaunting delight in its provocative potency. There was the highborn conceit, calibrated for just the right tactical impact. Jesus, I have said nothing good here about Sarah; how can I expect you to understand how I fell in love with her, and how I *stayed* in love with her while Velez had his adventure with her, and later, when his attention flagged and the wild called?

As my dogged presence was the vehicle for my own torture during this gambol of theirs, I became the vehicle for Sarah's futile breakneck campaign to hang on to Velez once her time was up. First I was her ride, then her pal, then her companion and pretty soon her nominal date; all this served to keep her within Velez's field of gravity.

"You and Sarah an item?" Velez would ask casually, or this:

"Stealin' my babe, huh?" But all in a cautionary frame, telling me without *telling* me that something stupid was going on and I was its author.

I know what you're thinking. I wanted Sarah because she was Velez's; because she wanted to be Velez's. You may even be making some Freudian suppositions, fluffing up some tantalizing subtext. Have fun; think what you want. But don't forget: sometimes the simplest explanation is the right one.

Anyway, Sarah and I suited each other fine just then: she got to be near Velez, I got to be near her and to play like we were together. Hanging out, but *together*. Yet this was an arrangement with, for Sarah, a disconsolately brief half-life; Velez, you see, was making no bones about the finality of things between him and Sarah. He leaped right in with some Englishwoman who, if I remember, played cello with the New York Philharmonic and came harnessed to a seemingly bottomless cruet of cocaine. And so I'm sure you can picture with great accuracy any number of restaurant or club tableaux in which Velez and this woman played dueling tongues while Sarah listened to her heart break and I sat, dopily and moonily attentive, cruelly grateful to Velez for thus slamming Sarah around. But Sarah, unlike me, would not ignore life's little signposts forever, and soon enough accepted that things with Velez were irretrievable.

Yet she couldn't let go of his presence, and so she perpetuated our companionship. And, in fact, I was permitted more and more boyfriendly moves along the lines of hand-holding and kissing—just public in the beginning—and finally, after a party to warm the sprawling and ridiculously unaffordable apartment I'd secured in her pursuit, there was sex. Drunken acquiescence would probably overstate Sarah's efforts but I hadn't expected a single ounce more because she was, for Christ's sake, in love with my best friend. And even if she saw the possibility of gainful intrigue in fucking me, that didn't mean she was going to let herself enjoy it. As for me, it was something quite unlike making love, if that makes the slightest sense. It was, as I sit here and remember it, waiting for her to arrive and drop off the five-year-old product of this union of the damned, like some twisted fantasy stew, concocted of sneaking under a circus tent and diving off the high board and smoking under the church stairs and hearing yes just once after an endless chorus of no's; creeping downstairs in the dead of Christmas night to see what Santa Claus had left for me.

It is past six. Where is my Jane?

The first time I asked Sarah to marry me was about four weeks after the night of our inaugural intimacy. A Sunday morning in my apartment after a night of misdemeanors in the company of Velez, some record promoters, a few nameless members of the choir and others. Sarah awoke slug-headed and pasty and mascara-smeared; I made love to her immediately and panted something scathingly romantic like, What would you think about getting married? At which she laughed and said, "I might be depressed, sweets, but I'm not *that* depressed."

So what changed her mind? Did I batter her with a relentless stream of proposals? Did I threaten, grovel, rant, cajole? Did I offer to give her things? Ho ho; I couldn't afford things she already had eight of. No, I let it drop.

Not the idea, of course. I thought about nothing else. And this was a solitary confinement, this marriage notion. Who was I going to talk things over with? Roberto Velez? I knew what he'd say: She may be depressed, but she's not *that* depressed. And there was no one else who wouldn't channel the news back to Velez instantly. If only Raylene McDonald had been around then. She'd have tried to reason with me confidentially. She would not have been successful. But she would have tried.

Things stood pat for a time. Sarah took to staying with me more frequently. Contract time came up and Velez bludgeoned WRTR into paying me almost enough to afford my apartment if I didn't eat more than absolutely necessary. We hunted in a pack: Sarah, me, Velez, the Englishwoman and others. Occasionally Charly would join us—Charly, you remember, of the fateful Montreal excursion; Charly of the sticky pantyhose. Charly seemed favorably disposed to the arrangement of Sarah and me, and in fact took me aside once to tell me how good I seemed to be for Sarah; how Sarah didn't seem quite so wired since she'd switched from Velez to me. Switched—as if it had been *her* idea. So I had grounded Sarah; so spoke her friend and running mate Charly.

It was actually Velez who closed the Sarah deal for me. Surprise, surprise.

Not that such was his intention, oh no. Velez knew plenty about Sarah and his was the dispassionate eye; he tried in not so many words to steer me away. Velez tends to develop an instant allergy to ex-girlfriends; a psychoimmunology peculiar to Velez's chemistry. Gotta be cruel to be kind. But as Sarah settled more acquiescently into the new alignment, a curious thing happened: Velez started being nice to her again. Not nice-intimate; just nice-companionable. In deference, I reasoned, to my own dire straits. Velez accepted Sarah as a fixture, and that, as it turned out, was all the encouragement Sarah needed to institutionalize the proximity.

So she began to show some enthusiasm. In bed; out of bed. I had died and gone to heaven.

And then in the depths of some night on the prowl, blood still fresh on all our lips from the evening's kills, came this from Sarah: "You still interested in getting married?"

To which I think I said, "You depressed enough yet?"

And Sarah smiled and said, "Guess so."

And so, in the presence of Roberto Velez, standing for me, and Charly, standing for Sarah, we were married. Downtown. Municipal fast-food ceremony. Richard 'Buddy' Oldham was in the Middle East just then and I wasn't about to give Sarah time to come to her senses. As for Sarah's family, they respectfully declined to have anything to do with the proceedings; I was, for them, a rebellious phase best gotten out of their daughter's system. The sooner the better.

Where is *my* daughter?

I pass some time by returning calls. Sally Wallach has gotten to Velez and somehow sold him on the advisability of discussing Monday. "A pre-broadcast production meeting?" says my partner. "Who's she get this stuff from? You?"

Please, Velez. You know better. But let's humor her—and me.

And so it comes to pass that Velez and Sally and Raylene and even Enginette Casey will convene here for the first pre-broadcast production meeting in the entire history of the Velez & Oldham Show later this evening.

My Bobs and Cathys want to talk radio and music. This soothes me temporarily, but where is Sarah? Where is Jane? And now I am finally out of notes except for the ominous bidding of Sarah's bullmoose attorney. Could an explanation for my daughter's absence lie in this woman's crusty, man-loathing bosom? I call Sarah's first, but there's no answer. I turn on the radio for a traffic report that might explain things: a giant earthquake, say, that has severed Manhattan from the mainland and cast us adrift. No ferry service from the continental United States to the new island-nation of Manhattan. That would explain everything.

And as I am about to relent and dial this lawyer-number, knowing it's far past lawyering hours, my buzzer rings.

"Messenger!"

Messenger? I don't expect anything.

"From who?"

"Ah, hol' on, lemme see. Yeah, here it is: Erica Armstrong. Attorney at law."

You can run, baby, but you can't hide.

# 18

IN the years that have separated Roberto Velez from the improvidential reaches of his childhood, plenty has happened to Velez and to the world; for Velez, you'd have to say, most of it good. Better than good. For Washington Heights, though, a different ballgame altogether: things have been unremittingly bad. No, worse than bad: evil. Bad, as even we who come from Baltimore know, can happen by accident. The history that closed in over Velez's wake, that obscured his footprints and blew his traces into the river, this was not happenstance.

It isn't far from the flintiest guerrilla trenches of Washington Heights to a river confluence known as Hell Gate. Unlike Hell's Kitchen, where Irish werewolves still go around disemboweling their neighbors' children at the pleasure of Italian paymasters both incarcerated and at large, and sometimes just for the practice, Hell Gate was not named for the children of the damned. The name, in fact, derives from a Dutch homage to the scenic splendor of its overlook; chances are the Dutch, if they should ever happen back this way, will want to reconsider this particular vestige of their brief and profitable colonization. This can be said for the Dutch: they are a people who know when to pack their valises and go home.

But could we dream up a more perverse piece of serendipity than a name so apt in accidental English for this filthy convergence of lifelorn waterways? For this is indeed the upstream gate to hell; up from the sullen brown rivers, north beyond its clogged autobahn overstreaming with the lucky anointed fleeing for kindlier ports, a fifty-foot neon sign should read thus: Abandon hope, all ye who enter.

But nobody enters; not to stay. And only do those lucky few manage to effect their escape. Hell, as Roberto Velez can attest, does have its unguarded moments and its porous interstices; the chains have their rusty links.

This is a hell that is bestowed as a birthright. Slavery in the grim back alleys of that celebrated shining city on the hill, behind the walls where the voters can't smell it.

Who ventures here, to the crumbling flatlands above the Hell Gate eddies? Those in search of commerce—for even hell has its industry, its own cold peculiar engine for damnation's amusement. The hell of our own years deals in the manufacture and distribution of the Fleeing Rapture. Thirty dollar bag. Five dollar vial. Ain't got fi' dollahs? Hey, come heah. We do bi'ness anyhow. Heah's watcha git fo' ya free dollahs. This'll do the thing; free dollahs. No? Go home in' git it from yo' sis. She got it. How do I know? 'Cause I give it to her. Never you mind, homey. You come on back heah witcha free dollahs. Or maybe I let you work fo' it. Ha'd 'at be?

These are the Holy Orders for the novitiate of the Fleeing Rapture. In the barrenness beyond Hell Gate the Fleeing Rapture is a street banquet of desperate counterfeit exaltation in which all things are possible—especially the things you know are not possible, which in this place means everything. Grandeur and conquest and immortality—these are the heartless beguilements of the Fleeing Rapture. Guaranteed, but no money back. The money is gone. Yeah, and then, quick as shit through a goose, the rapture is gone too, ain't it? But oh baby, here comes more: in the pail comin' down from 'at third story window, through the fence, from that little kid stan'in' over there with his sister the ho. Pretty one 'cross the street with no scars or nothin' on her face an' them plaid skirts the sisters makes 'em wear to school. She ho'in' and he runnin' an' that's good, 'cause that way it'll kill 'em bowf before they's old enough to understand what's been done to 'em.

Can Velez be blamed for pretending all that was and is part of somebody else's life? Wouldn't you, in Velez's shoes, consider yourself redeemed, or at least off the hook, once and for all? How long, my partner surely thinks, do you have to carry that around?

We inside the fortress gates are blessed that personnel witness is not demanded of us. All this stuff is on the news—the local news, where thrusting microphones and leering, bullying minicams twist neat clips of howling torment from the survivors of the damned for our evening delectation. We can flip on the news and partake of death throes, and so insidious are the cameras and the microphones that the more jaded of us—me, an accredited newsman, for instance—come to suspect that the victims are in collusion with the news producers. Hey lady, 'member how you were crying a few minutes ago? Y'know, when you first heard that your kid got blown away in a drug deal—innocent bystander, yes, hey, I know, a good kid—anyhow, here's the thing: our RealAction News mobile unit is here now, yeah, all the way up here just so people can share your grief. But now here's the thing, ma'am: do you think you could, like, sort of *relive* those first moments for us, yeah, the whole emotional thing? And can we get your kids over here again, standing like they were when your neighbor first told you that your little boy had been gunned down, that's right, that's right, I know how painful it must be, but for the television audience, they need to understand, to appreciate your anguish—this way, toward the lights, your loss, that's right, let it go, your boy's blood on the sidewalk, your devastation . . . .

On the radio news, even real radio news, there's no need for such sadism. No one has to be turned into an actor because what good would it do? Listening to someone howl unintelligibly in the aftermath of spilled blood just doesn't make it; watching, though, is even better than being there. If it bleeds, it leads.

News from the law firm of Erica Armstrong, Sarah's attorney, has caught up with me on the very cusp of this expectant evening: legal maneuvering is afoot, with the one immediate result that Jane Courtenay Oldham won't be making her appearance this weekend or, if Sarah and her attorney and her family and everybody in Westchester County have their way, anytime soon.

The issues are served up in a bucket of ponderous language, but behind it all is a petition on Sarah's behalf to void the current terms of my visitation rights and to cut a new deal. Erica Armstrong, a woman whose parenthood context can only be professional, who views my Jane as a lead-lined truncheon in the grand gender police action, who, presented with a child of her own would build a fire under her cauldron and reach for a recipe book, appears to think she has the upper hand. Late child support payments. Late alimony payments. Custodial irresponsibility. Reckless endangerment. High treason, piracy. Horse thievery. Oh boy.

But no outright ransom demands. No hint about what comes next. Just the snide, unwritten intimation: Get yourself a lawyer, pal, and gird your loins, because you as a race are expendable and you as a particularly pathetic species-sample are about to be exterminated.

Sarah is too smart and, in her own Velez-like way, too calculating to be answering her phone this night. Hers is a strictly detached brand of bullying; that's what Erica the bull is for—hand-to-hand bullying. Sarah will lay low. As we reflect, she is en route somewhere; her ancestral holdings give her plenty of hideouts to choose from. Erica Armstrong has no doubt advised Sarah to let me stew in my juice. No reason to think it won't work again just as well as it did in the past. There's nothing passive about retreat as orchestrated by old Armstrong. Together they engineered a groundless divorce, did they not? Oh, of course; how would you know? Well, I'm telling you: they did. Trivial personal details stewed in Orwellian treachery until they came out making me sound pretty unworthy, let me tell you. I denied nothing, hoping that amelioration was the wise long-term road. The Neville Chamberlain school of divorce.

And now the scratching at my front window begins to take on a more winterish timbre; for Mrs. McMichael and Rose and Rose's sister, another stooping season has wound to a close. I'd thought Jane and I might squeeze one more afternoon together on the roof before we, too, are shunted inside. Now, who knows.

But in a self-flagellatory sort of way, this might be for the better. For this week, I mean, because upheaval looms on at least one front and prudence demands that five-year-olds be shielded from the lines of fire.

There goes that gigantic cockroach again. Up the brickwork and into one of the holes that Time Warner Cable outfitted this place with. The search for worthy prey will be hardscrabble tonight, my friend.

Which brings me to Velez.

Between us there is something that I've chosen, not altogether naïvely I think, to call friendship—the kind born neither of affection nor respect, I understand that, but not mere inertial convenience either, I'm sure you're willing to grant me. We more than work together but there persists a mire of ambiguities, not the least of which centers on our work—for example, the assumption on my part, made somewhere along the line and utterly without substantiation, that there is more to Velez and Oldham than the Velez & Oldham Show. This, of course, is the thing: that when you dwell intimately in the turbulent backwash of somebody like Velez, you pretty much buy into his proposition that the universe is in fact centered on him, an abrogation with consequences both good and bad. The imbalances are set in stone and are not negotiable. In the kindest of situations, like ours, the assumptions are locked away—unchallenged by the one, largely unexploited by the other. Not the worst of social contracts as long as it lasts but the side-effects—laziness, somnolence, outright indolence if you don't watch out, which I'm afraid I haven't—can, it's starting just now to dawn on me, put one in pretty abysmal straits if the superstructure ever decides to give way.

This cluttered, empty apartment seems to want to entertain my muddled inventory tonight, this unscheduled intestinal inspection. Time before our first-ever official pre-broadcast production meeting is to convene. Too much time.

So how come this is bothering me now, you may well wonder. This is hardly the first time we've flirted with catastrophe, Velez and I. We've provoked and endured all sorts of suit opprobrium, for Christ's sake. We've walked out, we have cussed on the air and called into public question the sexual orientation of people with power—on paper, at least—to step on us. Nose-thumbing is our trademark. It's one of the reasons one-point-three million of you live with us, because most of you can't thumb your own noses *without* getting stepped on and you know it, and for most of the hours of your days it claws at your noble, subservient hearts, all except for those hours in the morning when we, Velez and I, can be your surrogates in rebellion. So, come on, this strike—just another nose-thumbing stunt. I think I know this.

But somehow I'm not so sure this time. Because Velez is playing this cagey, and making more out of it than a usual gag, and sequestering the provinces of his that are not, and never have been, any of my goddamn business.

So, my little friend, peeking out of your TV cable hole up there to reconnoiter, I put it to you: is there any enterprise so futile as trying to hold onto a simple existence?

That Velez has sheltered me and taken care of me—professionally, and at times personally—is undeniable but unreassuring. Did he ever actually go out on a limb? Was his intercession ever nobler than his own interest, assuming my partnership as his interest? Sure, plenty of program managers have wanted to trim me from the roster, and Velez has stuffed them every time. But are we talking genuine allegiance here, or have I been just one more fragmentation grenade for Velez to slip under the suits' tent?

So if this hairy little gremlin of suspicion, second cousin to the size-9 waterbug encamped under the ceiling above me, bears tidings of truth, how come I'm not panicking?

Perhaps because Velez isn't the only one getting bored with the old Thunder. I don't know. But what then? Huh?

The Velez & Oldham Show's pre-broadcast production meeting is on its way to stillbirth.

"You gotta carry on without me, Coolie," Velez tells me from the Velezphone. How come? I ask. "Gotta slay us some dragons tonight, Coolie. Gotta kick some ass."

"Jane's not coming this weekend," I tell Velez for no good reason.

And only after a peculiar pause does he say, "Yeah? How come?"

"Sarah's lawyer's come up with a hustle."

To which Velez says, "Sarah's lawyer's doin' what she's told, pal. Don't you forget it."

"How do you know?"

"I know. I know because that's all any lawyer does: what he's told. 'Swhat they get paid for; 'swhat they were born to do."

Which is Velez's way of telling me to quit covering for Sarah, the true handmaiden of evil.

Then Raylene McDonald, who has been much in my thoughts. In the matter of Raylene I have a plan, or rather a dodge: to haunt the Memorial for a while and watch for Lyndon; if time passes and Lyndon doesn't show, then I will present Raylene the grisly possibilities, pretending that I just found out. No, even better: just say there's been no recent sign of Lyndon, and play dumb. By that time maybe the Turkish innkeeper will have shoveled the alleged Lyndon into some unmarked outer-borough pit and sweet Raylene will never be the wiser; her hopeless, wandering, crazy half-brother—or whatever he is—will simply have faded away, which is the best that could be hoped for.

Raylene calls. "So what's this meeting for?" Raylene asks, as if I have the answer. "You know I got to find a babysitter, Dennis, or either bring my Charlene." Nah, I tell Raylene. Skip it. It isn't anything.

And so I call Enginette Casey, who sounds minutely disappointed. "Business as usual on Monday, Case. Done it a million times, right?"

"You guys gonna walk?" Casey, in her junior-high whiskey voice, asks. Nobody else has come right out loud and asked, up to now. Casey seems in need of some reassurance and so I make some up: "Velez has a plan." Casey pretends to believe this, or, worse: believes it.

Now for Sally Wallach. But no. I think I'll let Sally Wallach come ahead to this misbegotten meeting of hers. After all, it was her idea. Anyway, if Sally doesn't come, it's just me and the cockroach. Maybe Mrs. McMichael could be persuaded to whip up some emergency cookies.

"Mrs. McMichael, this is Sally Wallach. Sally works at the radio station."

Sally surveys the place. She's been here before, hasn't she? No, I guess she hasn't. "Hello, dear," Mrs. McMichael is saying in the same grandmotherly tone she uses with Jane Courtenay Oldham. Mrs. McMichael is herself fuming at Jane's absence, not entirely out of loyalty to me; such are the powers of Jane that even lives as tangential to hers as Mrs. McMichael have come to depend on my daughter for a periodic dose of delight. I wonder if the good citizens of the West

Village could be mustered into a class-action custody suit against Sarah and her hairy-armpitted mutant ninja attorney . . . .

Sally Wallach is momentarily crestfallen that her pre-broadcast production meeting has vaporized. "I'm supposed to be learning how a real radio station works, you know," she says, and I rush to assure her: "You are. This is exactly how one works."

And it isn't merely cookies that Mrs. McMichael has rushed into the breach with, oh no: my kitchen is like a nuclear power station churning out a mutant Irish pudding of spaghetti and veal sausage with the high-yield fuel rods just like Rose's sister taught her a decade or two ago. And while Mrs. McMichael isn't sure she approves of someone Sally Wallach's age and carriage and manifest delectability arriving here unchaperoned, she is delighted to have another appreciative mouth to feed. So here's a Martha Stewart moment for you: Mrs. McMichael, bountiful-hearted widow of a high-diving Irish bridge painter on her own upper-story mission of mercy, hip-to-hip with her new bake-off partner Sally Wallach—a comically nubile contrast to Mrs. McMichael. Yes, but think ahead thirty-five, forty years and maybe this ripening generous body, full of its promises, could by then very easily have settled itself into the good-humored hefty contours of Mrs. McMichael here, her own congenial corporeal reward for a youth of promises kept; Sally, scuttling with due deference around our maestra, pitching in without meddling, winning Mrs. McMichael in record time. Churning domestic, in a studiously unpredatory way.

It is unlike Mrs. McMichael but tonight she stays, for a while, to dine with us; to give us the opportunity to ooze admiration, naturally, and perhaps to take a precautionary sounding on what this girl is doing here. But talk at the table rifles right in on the Thunder remote Veterans Day broadcast and its burgeoning ancillary circus, and soon enough Mrs. McMichael, satisfied that my scruples haven't finally sunk entirely beneath the threshold of Christian propriety, takes her leave.

Meanwhile I'm trying my best to assimilate the bewildering incongruity of Sally Wallach's presence in this apartment of mine, stocked and accoutered as it is for impromptu invasions and for the twice-monthly evanescent residence of Jane Oldham, but otherwise just strewn about with the desultory disregard of a man living alone as, for all I know, a permanent proposition. Such a place must surely seem cranky and unappetizing to the likes of Sally, which explains why I'm bouncing around here trying to soften the alien environment with rambling overdoses of good cheer and dopey blather.

But presently and unprompted, Sally nestles down into a corner of the couch and asks if I have any beer, and the realm of the possible suddenly takes on splendid new colors and bountiful proportions.

"So," beer fetched, I ask Sally, "what's supposed to happen at a pre-broadcast production meeting?"

"You're asking me? How the hell should I know? I'm the intern, remember?" This Sally accompanies with the sly, self-effacing curlicue grin that has oh so ingratiated her throughout the hallowed halls of the Thunder, a not quite ingenuous smile that manages to say some or all of the following: Jesus Christ, I'm supposed to be here to learn about radio and I already *forgot* more than these alleged superstars here will ever know; but yes, it is fun in a harmless, spring-break sort of way. And besides, I'm not taking this any more seriously than you people, so don't any of you get the idea that the joke is on me, because let me tell you: it isn't.

Sally makes herself at home, an easing-in suggestive, I allow myself to believe, of profound new possibilities. I watch her trying the place on, sniffing for clues to another form of existence and finding things not entirely inhospitable to a girl of a certain age; an adventure among many on the road back home. Meanwhile, her exploration of my unprepossessing West Village existence has taken on an almost archeological curiosity: what peculiar creature could possibly inhabit such a place? is the expression on Sally's face. And so I take the opportunity to study her—what, am I not supposed to? Is this not what just such a promenade is for?

So where shall we stand on the beauty issue? Is this the Pictionary definition of beauty, this occasionally giggly chrysalis of flawless geometry and unconsciously poetic fluid dynamic? Or can true beauty crystallize only as life voraciously lived gradually imposes its relentless self—its ceaselessly compounding traces of evidence—upon such a creature as is currently prowling breezelike around this tatty, unassuming rest stop of a home, radiating and receiving radiants in return, taking casual soundings from corners so taken for granted, so unappreciated until now, the ignored surfaces and salients that Sally seems to find pregnant with clues? If this is a foreshadowment of enduring beauty—the authentic, Greek sculpture and Italian painting kind—instead of one of those nasty tricks of the mind's eye propagated by manufactured illusions of perfection, then what, I'm trying to get at, is the proper perspective for one such as me, with my storied talent for self-delusion in the swampy realm of romance, wandering around with a chromosome arrangement tragically grafted from that other love-flagellated Baltimorian of a simpler generation, Richard 'Buddy' Oldham? It's not that I see in this Sally Wallach girl what once I saw in Sarah; oh no. But the array of mirrors that separates women from what we make of them is, I think, as impenetrable for me as it ever was, because Sally has lighted on a perch and the time has come to admit that I have granted myself provisional leave this night to stalk her, in my diffident, club-footed way.

Velez would say, "Don't pity the young. They're resilient," and in Sally Wallach's case not only would he be right, but in this particular sortie, at this particular moment, I'm plenty more at risk than Sally Wallach of self-destructive entanglement. There. That dispenses with the rationalizations. As for the rest, Sally wears around this skin-tight force-field of ingenuousness and inscrutability and so, for all I can anticipate, may consider this advance of mine anything from an amusing, harmless adventure to pathetic lechery—not that either would necessarily preclude her compliance, if as nothing more than a souvenir of her WRTR Thunder internship to write about on the Cornell Communications Department ladies room wall.

But oh, how each first time never fails to summon forth goblins of the other first times—the significant few—their leery-eyed, condescending audience heightening the conspiracy of goofiness attending each faltering, fluttering new seduction. And so it is that Sally's silent and somehow disappointingly unceremonious shedding of clothes, and the mandatory, time-honored rituals that ensue, are attended by the ghosts of dimly hopeful lovemakings past, and I hear Sarah and this one and that one—no one's idea of an estimable roster to be sure—all the way back to Ellen Larkin of my radio baptism, whispering their gentle imagined warnings of inflated expectations and delusive infatuations and maybe, this time, I'll listen.

# 19

AND so the improbable and inevitable has once again come to pass.

Sarah once, near the end, had this to say in review of my lovemaking: that sometimes a manic eagerness to please is misplaced in bed—or rather, *should* be misplaced once in a while. I, naturally, took that throwaway crumb of deprecation as a hint that maybe things weren't quite yet over the falls, that it was only a question of fine-tuning a few aspects of the relationship that, inconsequential by themselves, had bloated collectively into a toxic food fight of a marriage. And so I took to ambushing Sarah, whenever the level of small-arms fire temporarily subsided, giving her these heaving, half-undressed two-minute drills on the floor or standing up or bent over a handy piece of furniture, all designed to demonstrate whatever it was I hadn't previously demonstrated.

So okay: maybe I was guilty of over-compensation. But what else do you have to go on, for Christ's sake, except what you're told? I was looking for any kind of emergency brake at that point, something to dig my heels into; Sarah, meanwhile, had taken to calling Velez on the telephone. It is not unreasonable to assume that Velez was treated to a blow-by-blow of my grasping attempt at sexual reinvention; maybe they shared an intimate chuckle—I can hear Sarah: God, I don't know what to do with this friend of yours, all of a sudden he's like turning into the hallway rapist, yanking up my skirt and haulin' it out and bouncing me around, I mean really, it's like trying to imagine your parents fucking, I know, and yeah, he's trying so hard but . . . .

Did it go like that? And *where* did it go like that—in a coffee shop, at a bar, in bed? For yes, I have my profound suspicions that Velez and Sarah took up again, in a completely different context but featuring the same old bodily fluid transmissions, even as my own campaign of marital resuscitation was hitting its turbo-hysterical peak.

The old Velez dagger. He had given it to Sarah—picked a couple of ribs and buried it to the hilt just to snuff any lingering misapprehensions concerning their arrangement. That English cellist babe was on the scene in a flash, wasn't she, and Velez staged an abundance of public tit-fondling, always zeroing in on the one that Sarah had the best view of. The dagger. Neither Velez nor my Sarah gave any overt signs that they were screwing behind my back but from Velez I began picking up these small solicitations on Sarah's behalf: 'She probably feels as disappointed as you . . . I know she felt—*felt!*—very deeply about you . . . Try to see it from her point of view . . . .' No conclusive evidence of betrayal there, you say, but so goddamn unlike my partner Velez, who, if something clandestine wasn't going on, would have been saying things like, She's nothing but a snotty spoiled Westchester cunt out to roll around in the mud, Dennis, so fuck her, let her go back where she came from, she ain't worth gettin' worked up about, we throw four or five lawyers at her and make a clean break. She don't like it, we give her a Drano job, we chop her up and feed her to the African red ants, just like all the others . . . .

Meanwhile, we have reached the point in the Veterans Day remote pre-broadcast production meeting where Sally Wallach, assuming me asleep, is sniffing to no apparent purpose around this apartment of mine in specialty-store panties and a shirt that I believe I recognize as mine.

Now, I've tried as a matter of policy not to burden anything with expectations but in the matter of Sally Wallach how could I help myself? I was sure Velez was right that Sally had a history; this is a girl too open-eyed and curious to be hauling around a cherry at the ripe age of twenty. And even during our early bobs and weaves I sensed no particular apprehension on Sally's part for what might transpire. Neither could I convince myself that Sally had spread herself around; what did she have to rebel against? But how about love? Had love yet napalmed Sally's otherwise clam-happy path?

I will lay here quietly for a moment, partly because the tiny sounds and the delicate vibrations emanating from Sally's tip-toe excursion are pouring a syrupy buzz over me, warming my belly and floating some narcotic string sonata-with-a-backbeat up into my frontal lobe. And here I lay, damnder than Faust, a first-degree defiler of impressionable girlhood because let's face it, Oldham, you idiot: this is not the same as mutually experimental intercollegiate athletics no matter how you slice it, there's something a lot less innocent about this than most of the episodes that probably make up Sally Wallach's romantic résumé to date. I can't for the moment even try to figure out what new meanings to impregnate our coming eye contact with; composure, at the bare minimum, will be expected of me and that will be easy enough to fake.

Give me some room, okay? Give me a minute.

Meanwhile, this might be a good time for me to give my deposition of the events of the last hour. For Sally's part, the casual observer could not help but be touched by her sincere vehemence, a treatment of her own body as something of a recent and intriguing discovery; a new

Christmas bike that refuses to await spring thaw for a tryout or, I don't know, a new stunt for show-and-tell concocted for the sheer ear-ringing glee of exhibition. And while I didn't allow myself to buy for a nanosecond either of the howling banshee flourishes that Sally was sweet and respectful enough to stage for me, it's hard for me laying here in these quizzical shadows not to feel an ominous spasm of sentimentality about the still-reverberating proceedings, laced as they seem to be with this revelatory bonus: that although it wasn't too good, this irresolute, mismatched little communion of ours, somehow it doesn't seem to have mattered much to my dear Sally; provisionally, no penalty points seem to have been assessed.

Sally is on the phone. Out by my chestnut window. Her voice, like her body, is soft and musical and buoyed by a lazy low tidal rhythm. I can't make out what she's saying or who she's saying it to. I can, however, hit the old playback button for another undercover second and wonder at the rudderless conspiracy into which I may have just stumbled; it would be easy enough to cook up a fairy tale of assumptions here, which would, as you know by now, be entirely consistent with encounters of mine past. Has this evening, still young and in different ways just as unsettled as before, altered the balance of allegiances? In other words, what would Velez make of this?

Velez will make much of this development; he'll see much merit . . . .

But later, for hither comes Sally Wallach, and what Sally wants most to know right now is, "You have any coffee here?" Okay Sally, I'm not asleep, and if coffee is the price of skipping the analysis for right now, I'm buying.

Of course I'd like to be in a better position to sort out the intergalactic implications for you but everything, as usual, seems tauntingly contradictory here in the murky upcurtaining onto yet another awkward burlesque. Take, for instance, the expression on young Sally's face— can you see the slightest impression that the last hour has made on it? Can we spot even a pixel or two of deeper attachment lurking behind those eyes? Nope. Just the unpretentious, restless insouciance of fresh sex.

Now, Sally stands above me in the patient expectation of coffee. I pause long enough in my creaky, close-range ascent up the north face of Sally Wallach, just about halfway between her knees rubbed red by our recent floor exercises and the seamless, convergent curvatures of her fine-downed thighs, to try to divine veiled meaning in the lingering intimacy of this casual, unclothed promenade. But wait: could this be one of those cruelly camouflaged instances where the simplest interpretation is the right one? That she's simply having fun parading around this older guy's apartment, basking in the storied afterglow? Can we all buy this suspiciously uncomplicated version of reality for right now, for tonight at least? I say, yes we can. Or, with your kind indulgence, we shall.

Sally sits above me sipping black Sanka and hugging her bare legs; I, floor-bound, conduct a mute, surreptitious reconnaissance of the firebase. Sounds tick off the moments; the decibel level of the city's white noise ratchets its way up as, out there below Sally and me, mischief of many stripes prepares to engage. Sirens provide the perverted comfort of familiarity—things aren't much better or worse than they were last time the sun went down, we are assured; the essential context hasn't been tampered with by unseen forces. The same sketchy canon of rules, celebrated in antiphonies of Darwinian attitude, will apply for the time being. Sally Wallach may or may not be hearing any of this little symphony of moral physics and I have no intention of pointing any of it out. These are the observations of generation to generation; we don't need too fine a point on that line of subtext just now, thank you.

The rose-petal angularity of Sally's hips abruptly dismisses these intrusions—these exquisite curvatures with depths not seen but sensed, textures with power to caress the fingertips through the eyes of the beholder.

The rest of Sally, meanwhile, sits nestled within my shirt, not buttoned but wrapped and tied at her stomach, revealing a plummeting sliver of Sally from her throat downward, disappearing down behind her upward-folded legs. I could take her again right this second—that much threatens to make itself evident—and maybe this time even earn a little of that polite ecstasy of hers, but not now, not before the dumbfounding vapor surrounding Sally and me has a chance to land somewhere and I have a chance to decide what she's supposed to make of me, and far more to the point: how I'm supposed to engineer the proceedings to come.

This started out as my evening with Jane Oldham; I haven't forgotten that, and the irony, if that's what it is, isn't lost on me. Because it wasn't so long ago in my early ruminations upon the girl Sally Wallach, you remember, that certain disquieting parallels insinuated themselves and what I'm trying not to get at is this: what if Jane Oldham finds herself, at some cloudy future waystation, in just such a situation? Will I, still occupying the nominal office of father emeritus, approve? I'll at least appreciate the preposterous ambiguities that led Sally to this evening; let's hope that'll be enough.

"This pre-production broadcast—"

"Pre-*broadcast* production meeting," Sally corrects me.

"What, exactly, did you have—"

"Y'know," Sally exasperates, "format, what happens where, who does what to whom, what we do with those strike team finalist guys, how we emcee the entertainment, what music we bring along; all that, y'know."

"Um."

"So? What about all that stuff?" Sally demands.

And so suddenly the night sprouts wheels. "Okay. Music, my sweet. Let's go." I hide long enough to let Sally pull on her pantyhose and skirt and locate her bra and shimmy this whole glorious assembly up into her sweater, suspecting, no doubt, but not knowing for certain that I'm watching. For whatever else has or hasn't happened here tonight, something from the shadows of antiquity has been reignited, a giggling wild-eyed gremlin has escaped; in short, the thousand-ship-launching genetic vestiges that dwell in the bosom of Sally Wallach have wrought their timeless sorcery again and blood, for good and ill, feels like it's flowing. Sally girl, if only you had a clue about your own magic power.

There are few signs of life up ahead in Too Tall Jones—a couple of lights here and there, just a sprinkling of late-night candlepower up the faceless chiseled curtain of blackness below the teetering smooth-angled precipice, and now I can make out the WRTR slice of Too Tall up there on the eighteenth floor, not much, none of those miserable smothering fluorescent ceilings, just a few lamps and goosenecks. In the, what, six? yeah, six years since we seized a chunk of floor eighteen of Too Tall for our very own, my late-night visits have not been frequent.

Sally, probably for reasons of her own, has elected not to acknowledge any broad reconfigurations for now, no hand-holding or nuzzling initiatives, no instant christening with pet names, no sly smiles or turbo-sighs. There are grown-ups at work here, friends; if anything has changed, the collegial playing field has been slightly regraded in Sally's favor. Fine with me. Sally's taken enough Junior Bluebird shit from Kenny Appleton's producer and from Kenny Appleton himself when her scavenger hunts in the cobwebbed Thunder vault didn't yield the particular crap of Kenny's momentary obsession. Not to mention our little iron-pumper Arielle, who started out figuring Sally for a *primo* brown-nosing opportunity until her old man announced his universe-warping intention to dump WRTR. So if Agent Orange all of a sudden becomes a temporary force to be reckoned with, even with horsepower borrowed against rumors—since that's all they'll be until Sally's safely back in her ivory tower where she won't give a shit what anybody thinks, presuming she does now—I say screw 'em. Velez, after all, has elevated far less worthy petitioners than my Sally on the flimsy credential of services and obeisance willingly, even giddily, performed upon the person of the star.

Too Tall inhales and we are sucked up through the silent floors with pneumatic-sounding stealth. Sally is neither looking nor looking away.

We awaken the Thunder security guard and sign in.

Furtive cleaning is occurring in Thunder corners; wheeled industrial tubs shadow a pair of professionally paced sweeper-dusters. I don't smell the disinfectant; the nocturnal air strike apparently waits until the sweeper-dusters secure the area and complete ground-level reconnaissance.

A tune, piped and filtered down into the lower registers of our consciousness, now announces itself by ending and the air around us aligns its molecular chaos for the optimal dispersion of Grandfather Rock, Adrian Boe.

Sally Wallach and I creep our way through the shadows until, from the underbrush, we can peer through the glass window into Adrian's booth. Somebody's in there with Adrian, we can hear, but it's Adrian, the voice that may have urged you, too, to your first adolescent atrocities—tales of the bygone days—who's communing in the night with that ambivalent but lucrative audience segment that refuses yet to consider itself an oldies crowd even though that's exactly who they are. And it's Adrian, timeless Adrian—my partner Velez calls Adrian Boe's show the closest time gets to stopping entirely—who sits up here night after night and decade after decade, laying down reassurance that the passage of time hasn't slipped completely out of control, children and corporate tyranny and mummified parents and alcoholism and baldness and all manner of physical and emotional betrayal notwithstanding.

Which is an important service, isn't it, now that I explain it out loud. Can you imagine the raging hopelessness that would engulf this city in the absence of Adrian's sentimental anesthesia? The rampaging epidemic of desperate acts? For Adrian's is the age when lies begin to play indispensable life-support roles. Leave it to Grandfather Rock. As long as Adrian's still rockin', baby, we must be too.

Now as I'm about to nudge Sally on about our business, I find her staring at the Adrian tableau in something approaching rapture. This, I suddenly and sadly realize, is what she came to the Thunder for, whether she realized it or not: a glimpse behind the curtain of the grand alchemist in his chamber, shuffling his magic secrets in the gothic solitude of his midnight realm. It occurs to me, sadly, that Sally will understand more about radio by our spying on Adrian for these small minutes than she will from a whole semester jerking around here every morning with the rest of us. I wish I had more to offer; I wish I'd realized sooner that she was serious.

So for a moment it looks like we'll stay out here in the dark and watch Adrian. Sally nestles back against my chest; my innards whisper to me approvingly.

Adrian has an elegant spareness of effort and sureness of voice; an awareness, I guess it comes down to, of what he represents. And he has a high-order affinity for the air—the microphone distills and enriches the simple notions and recollections with which he strings together the music of other, more romanticized times. In fact Adrian is, as much as anybody else, the author of this fraudulent infatuation with the sixties, that mystical place in time that managed to think of itself as spiritual, uncorrupted, and guilty as sin all in the same breath. But we can't blame him; nobody is more taken in by Adrian's whimsically muddled version of history than Adrian himself, the pied piper of a race trooping wearily off to hell in a nostalgia handbasket.

Adrian's elder-statesman presence doesn't come without its sacrifices. While the record company boys revere him, nobody, I'm sure, drives up with dumptrucks of money and drugs and guaranteed female companionship to shuffle Adrian's playlist the way the Kiwi Corcorans of the world flock to, oh, Roberto Velez, for example. Nobody's interested in promoting music via Adrian Boe—how many more copies of *Stairway to Heaven* and *Watchtower* do you think the world is going to buy, once you've all replaced your vinyl with CD? WRTR doesn't care, of course, because Adrian still sells advertising in handsome piles, and he doesn't need new music to do it. The Thunder has Velez and Stevie Joe and Kenny Appleton and Cheryl Mann and the swings like Hendy Markowitz to shill for the record companies in our unholy mutual interests.

There's something familiar about the back of the head bobbing congenially at Adrian's side, but I don't make a positive identification until the longhaired figure fishes from his leather vest a squeeze bottle of nasal spray and cranes backward for maximum firepower. Yes, it's none other than Judd Tate of the legendary Standard Band—right up Adrian's alley, timeline-wise—and I'm not the only one who's just made a positive identification of this fossilized rocker.

"Hey! Know who that is?" Sally semi-squeals. "C'mon," and I'm being pulled into the throw of Adrian's low lamps.

But Adrian and Judd Tate don't see us right away because it's dark out here and even Sally is by now enough of a veteran to know not to thump on the glass while Adrian's live. We watch quietly through our own reflections while Judd Tate fondles and tweaks a road-ravaged acoustic guitar and swaps chortles with Adrian Boe, trading obscure fragmentary references to rock festivals and road wars from their dope-addled astral files. "—first time I heard you an' the boys do that was—"

". . .Nah, man, we was doin' this one before, before. . . ."

"Oh yeah, that's right, I remember, 'cause you did it at that big gig in Chicago, just before the Democratic convention—"

"Yeah, that was the one—an' 'member that babe climbed up on the chandelier 'a that place, that ol' theater—what was it called? I don' know—anyways that chick climbs up, 'member? an' hauls off her tee shirt an' the chandelier's swingin' like crazy, God, I thought she's gonna come down right on top of us." Chortle, chortle.

"Oh, man," says Adrian from somewhere long ago and far away, "oh man." And how can you doubt him?

Now Judd Tate is picking diffidently at his guitar, tuning a string, and the people out across the night can hear, can *feel*, Judd Tate and Adrian Boe, two wizened, wrinkled survivors up in Adrian's deep-night aerie, remembering the voltage and scents and flashes of light, and the pops and thumps and crashes and whines, the stratospheric wail, the seismic thrash, the sweaty, sacramental chants, the fists and peace fingers flying, the willingly discarded childhood, the guileless uncalculated sex freely given and freely taken, the purity of art and the passionate innocence of its politics, young bodies painted and ornamented and anointed for the rock pageant. And Adrian can make all those people out there in the night—the accountants and lawyers and cops and trainmen and mothers—feel like *they* were once the stars of the long-ago pageant, swinging from that Chicago chandelier, doping in a Newark balcony, dancing at night in a park with a girl you never saw before dressed only in a pair of tattered hip-slung jeans, offering her sunburned breasts to the music and the moon, and the ultimate fantasy: bathed in white light, sitting under a speaker tower on the edge of a stage, expecting never to hear normally again and not caring, not willing to trade the transcendental levitation of the human wave at your feet, being, yes, *being* a rock star, making all the little girls out there scream and dance and fuck and cry—yes, you remember how it was, don't you? Great, huh, while it lasted, before the rockers who made the Thunder thunder grew crow's feet and creaky knees, before we drank off the last of the pageant and had to grow up. But we remember, don't we—me, and Judd Tate here, and you—wherever you are, it'll always be a part of us.

Fucking sorcerer, Adrian.

You know the Standard Band's music. Three gigantic Nixon-regime hits, a few others you hear on our New Year's Day top-five-hundred-in-the-history-of-the-world survey show. White-boy walls of boom trimmed with Judd Tate's slashy guitar, short on finesse but enough steel-tipped crunch to peel off the wallpaper. And yet here, in the parlor privacy of Adrian's broadcast booth, with no electronic armament or the delirious rantings of the Standard Band's sweaty, idolatrous throngs of old for cover, unplugged, as they say, is Judd Tate, offering whoever might be listening and care, a small inkling of what the music sounds like to him, inside him, minus the rock machine. It is sweet and sad and funny and yes, even wise, this soft one-guitar reading of trite-but-true oldie rock anthems—the battle hymns of generational warfare, of sexual revolution. And for this moment there isn't a sound in the city except for the solitary elliptical melodic poetry of Judd Tate. Who'd have guessed? Well, Adrian of course; Adrian, he knows where all that stuff came from, and knows where to find it again, when he needs it—when his people in the night need it most.

After, silence. Adrian knows enough to leave his friends out there in the dark with a moment or two more—just a moment to say goodbye to what they would like to remember as their youth, before the voices of two old men bring them back to this night of their own lost circumstances. I watch Adrian Boe give Judd Tate one of those peace-and-love sixties handshakes and I watch Judd Tate hold onto it for a moment; they grin at each other and to me it looks like they're both thinking, Thank you, my friend.

Then Adrian goes to commercials and Sally Wallach bounds into the booth; there's a hug and a kiss in it for Judd Tate, the kind you probably wouldn't expect from somebody you only laid eyes on twice in your life.

"Hey," Adrian says cordially, "It's our soon-to-be-former morning newsman and his lovely daughter." Judd Tate reaches up and shakes my hand with the ashen look of the unexpectedly busted, but I grin it off and now Judd Tate remembers me. "Yeah, sure, man, couple weeks ago." To Adrian he says, "Ain't a whole lot sink in at that hour, man," and Adrian chuckles in sympathy.

Sally, meanwhile, has wheeled a chair over beside Judd Tate. "So," she says, "You ready for Monday?"

"Monday?" Adrian asks for me.

"Yeah," Sally says proudly, "the Veterans Day broadcast! We're gonna wind up with a noonday outdoor concert and guess who's playing!"

"Janis Jop—"

"Right! The Standard Band! First New York appearance in, in . . . ."

Sally looks to Judd Tate for help, but Judd guffaws wetly at this assault on his memory. "You kiddin' me?"

And Adrian Boe says to Sally Wallach, "Since you were doodlin' in your diapers, darlin'."

"Anyway, the best sixties band ever, *ever*, right here on the Thunder for Veterans Day. What do you think of that?" Sally trumpets.

"This for real?" Adrian wants to know, as the commercial winds down. Judd Tate grins uncertainly, as if this is news to him.

"Back with Judd Tate and a couple of drop-ins from a different time zone," Adrian tells his children. "In person, in the flesh, we've got Dennis Oldham, who rides shotgun for Roberto Velez while you and I are asleep, from six to ten every morning here on WRTR, and a world-class-looking babe who I think you know as Agent Orange—" Does Adrian actually listen to our show? How else would he know about this Agent Orange business? ". . .bringing us a great piece of news. Judd, you sumbitch, you've been holding out on me, man—it's okay to tell, right?—Well, it looks like the Thunder broadcast from the Vietnam Veterans Memorial downtown on Monday will have some extra special horsepower, gang, because I've just been told by Agent Orange here that there's gonna be a noontime concert featuring—are you ready?—the Standard Band its very own, original, honest-to-God in-the-flesh self!"

Well, from the look on Adrian Boe's face I can tell he's having a hard time believing this even as he says it, and Judd Tate doesn't look entirely convinced either. The only person displaying any degree of certainty is my Sally. Has she engineered this? Does she know what she's gotten herself into? Can she, specifically, fathom the odds against four acid-addled sixties burnouts presenting themselves under the noonday sun, not to mention remembering to bring their guitars and remembering how to use them? Oh, Sally.

But Adrian, no doubt sharing my misgivings, is making discreet inquiries. "How long since you've gigged with the guys?" he's asking Judd Tate, and, "You guys going back into the studio?" And in between his barely coherent aw-shucksing, Judd Tate gives us to understand that the four members of the Standard Band, whose names I'll bet you've been trying to remember, have in fact gone as far as rehearsing for this reunion engagement, and contract talks are in the wind.

"Hey, man," Judd Tate offers by way of explanation, "we ain't any older'n the Stones, right?"

# 20

"WHERE we going?"

Downtown, I tell Sally.

"Yeah? Where?"

"Is this still the pre-production broadcast meeting?"

"The *pre-broadcast*—forget it. Anyway, you're the boss. I'm the intern. Remember?"

"Then we better do a location check."

"It's one-thirty in the morning."

"Oh, I'm sorry—I thought you wanted to be in radio."

We're crackling down beyond lower Manhattan's deepest outposts now. Skirting the crypts of finance, nosing down to where it all began, to the swine-fouled plots that long-forgotten Dutchmen had way more sense than to spill their blood defending. "They want it that bad?" Peter Stuyvesant's colonial security advisor probably whispered to him as they peered over their crummy stone fort at a horizon-full of British sails. "Fine. I say, let 'em foagin' choke on it." This is what raw news sounds like before the sanitary engineers get hold of it—you know: history's first draft. "Anyhow," somebody must have pointed out to Governor Peter, "They'll always have old Hell Gate to remember us. Get a kick outa that, wont'cha, British cuntwaulers!"

Well, much to my surprise—since this trip downtown was a blind-shot scam on my part—things have actually happened down here in this sunken riverside crater, shouldered around its periphery by upsloping brickwork and slabs of concrete and stone, all a reasonably reverent concentricity around Lyndon McDonald's Wall, etched with the iridescent ravings of the soon-to-be-damned.

Ah, but I don't need to describe this place to you; we've been down this barren trail before, you and I, at similar times of the day, so you'll be as surprised as I am to see an erection in progress—a grandstand of metal piping, its back to the steeples, that reaches, seatless so far, up through rows of virgin treelets into tonight's halogen-tinted nebula. Blue police-line sawhorses lay piled, ready for assembly and deployment. And cleaving the grandstand barricade is a mini-canyon of a center aisle just begging for a parade to happen by and bustle through it.

Sally and I pick our way over the deserted clutter and into the plaza on errands of our own.

Beyond the grandstand trusswork, canted slightly downriver of

Lyndon's Wall, sits a bare elevated platform. Nothing elaborate; not, at least not yet, even an overhang to shelter the stage. Stairs on either side. One of those Ingersoll tow-along nuclear generators pulled up behind one stair.

Figuring the grandstanders and the squatters and the accidental wanderers-through, I'd say this place is laid out for about a thousand people. This Veterans Day deal must be a serious parade.

Sally has hoisted herself up onto the stage now. From my vantage point she's silhouetted by a lone free-swinging high-wattage safety lamp; the slickest music-video producer in town couldn't have confected a more sensuous apparition than my Sally, hair flaming up into the night sky, wind molding this fluttering sweater of hers across her fulsome upturned contours, legs planted wide for balance and probably because it feels good. Up there. Where no one is immune to seduction. Probably not even me. Surely not Velez, who gave in a long time ago, before you and I even knew him.

I patrol the perimeter for signs of Lyndon McDonald. Down by the wall I find a couple of humble tents—military jobs but pitched without the anal military fastidiousness—and as I move closer I can make out an orange glow. Not a fire; some species of stove. Kerosene, or maybe electric. Maybe a forty-dollar Sears coffee-for-life job, or possibly a sixteen-thousand dollar McDonnell/Douglass autograph model from Air Force surplus. Either way, there's a pot of coffee in the works; the river breeze carries this intelligence my way.

And now, I hear a guitar. Tiny, down-home picking. Inside one of the tents. I pull up a granite slab and listen.

Sounds I associate with the rural south. Bluesy and unhurried, seeking no audience but itself. Carrying its owner from one stop to the next. To here from Vietnam; to Vietnam from, where? Tuscaloosa? Tupelo? Nothing more than names from songs to me. Names to build a different brand of fraudulent, pussy-dampening romance around. I move close enough to draw attention.

"Hey," I hear from inside one of the tents—not a challenge, just that swayback southern substitute for 'hello.'

Unconcerned rustling emerges, like I was expected. I am not surprised to find faded variations on the jungle camouflage fashion theme wrapped around unshaven and red-eyed masks of terminally disillusioned narcosis. A short, stringy man in a black bandanna and lots of sleeve stripes thrusts out a hand. "Haya doin'? 'Nother early arrival, uh? What outfit?"

I resist the urge to invent some more illustrious military *bona fides* than the paltry tale I have to offer. Wouldn't fool these guys anyway. Look at them: they know where every platoon spent every day and every night. So I opt for the old truth dodge: "Logistics."

"Where?" they want to know—Bandanna, and two others who introduce themselves as Sentry and Airborne.

"Way down south," I say. "The Manila vicinity." For this effort I am granted a conditional chuckle. Wait. I know. "I also did a little radio over there."

"Yeah?" Sentry sort of sneers. "Did the official body count report, did you?" And now something deep and uncongenial threatens to descend on us. Armed Forces Radio, of course, was a particularly insidious part of the swamp of military deceit that helped turn these guys by the end of things into the bitter functional dead of Vietnam's homefront epilogue. Bandanna and Sentry and Airborne and the other one, the one they simply call The Grunt, are not, unless I miss my guess, going to find Sally's code name too funny either.

But as I shake hands around the little circle I detect no visible traces of contempt. "I'm with the radio station. The one's gonna be broadcasting from down here Monday?"

Which is news to these guys. "Radio broadcast? Here?"

"Hell yeah," I say, hoping enthusiasm is the proper tactic.

"Wha' for?"

"You know, Veterans Day, the parade. . . ."

A conference of eyebrows. One says, "You gonna broadcast the parade?"

"Yeah. No," I say, but suddenly no one's paying much attention because the collective thousand-yard stare has ranged in on Agent Orange, Sally Wallach. I turn to find Sally waving and clambering down from the stage; I wave back. "She with you?" they all want to know. Yeah, I tell them, not too smugly.

"Whew," offers the black bandanna, "Radio business mus' be purty damn good."

"These gentlemen are here for the parade," I tell Sally by way of introduction, but Sergeant Bandanna puts us both straight. "Sheee, we ain't either." He eyes us both, Sally and me. "You ever seen one 'a these Vet'rans parades?" Sally looks at me like it's my play.

"Not really," I confess.

"Ain't nobody else, neither. Mos' pathetic-ass parade y'ever saw. Two, maybe three hun'erd guys clumpin' down the street, coupla crappy school bands, the local recruiters, is it. Nobody out to see nobody 'cep family."

"Tell 'em about the Civil War dudes," snuffs their heavily patched sentry.

Civil War.

"Oh, hell yeah," Sarge says. "Got these guys dress 'umselves up like Yanks and Rebs, musket rifles an' ever'thing. Guess so ain't no vets feel left out."

Sally, so far, seems undeflated but wary. "So, you mean, not many people come to these parades? Is that what you're saying?"

"'F they'd knew'd you was comin'. . . ."

"'F this is a 'lection year, mayor'll pro'lly show up if the weather ain't too bad. Hey, this an election year here?"

I stand by and wonder what Sally Wallach makes of these four—the whole troop, it appears, unless there are more hiding out inside the tents. Does it occur to her, as it does to me, that these guys have a lot in common with Adrian Boe? That there's a certain commerce being transacted: trading along the circuitry of a pathological karma—only difference is that Adrian's is the pleasure button, but for these guys . . . no. Heartless and untrue. These guys aren't asking for anything except the morphine of these reunions. Private services.

Sally shifts her positive-thinking module into overdrive. "Let me tell you guys: there'll be *plenty* of people here for *this* parade. We've been talking about it for weeks on the air. Y'know, these guys," hooking a thumb at me, "are the top-rated rock radio program in New York City. Wait'll you see all the people down here."

This news is not, I pick up right away, greeted with glee among the waterfront platoon. Suspicion descends. "You guys figurin' to cash in, that it?" is what I pick up from the undertow.

"How do you mean?" I say, as if I didn't know.

"Vietnam's been hot stuff las' some years," says Bandanna. "Movies, books, Oliver fuckin' Stone—look at us, gone from dog shit to hot commodity, an' it on'y took twenny-fi' years."

"Nobody meant anything," I apologize. It seems to work.

"Want some coffee?" This in the raspy baritone of a proud-bellied brewmeister type with Airborne plastered all over him. I look at Sally and she seems game.

So here we sit: Sally Wallach, me, and the four-man waterfront platoon. Sally is being regaled with war stories of time-burnished poignancy, but sanitized, I can tell, for Sally's consumption. No doubt there are scalier, grislier versions of each man's jungle saga but these are reserved for those who've earned a place at the table with exploits of their own. The coffee is good. The night is quiet but in some subterranean, reptilian way unsettled. The steel and marble and limestone citadels above us stare down with glowering incomprehension. As for me, this gurgling turbulence of Sally Wallach's authorship continues to warm and disturb me in ways that I hope will not subside. All things seem possible.

Now Sally is promoing Monday to our new friends. "Lotsa live stuff . . . some comedy, a concert—you guys ever heard of the Standard Band?"

"Holy shit! You mean Judd Tate gonna be here?"

"Wait—din't he—"

"Naw, that was that other guy . . . that one that was married to the—"

"Oh yeah. . . ."

"Whatdya thinka that? Ol' Judd still around! Goddamn!" The boys are pleased.

"Where do you guys come from?" Sally jumps in and asks. They don't want Sally to go; I can see that. Airborne drives a truck sometimes. Interstate; long hauls. Lumber, livestock, anything that needs hauling, we're informed. Bandanna has a little fishing boat he charters out of Gulfport, Mississippi. Grunt and Sentry supplement their permanent disability checks doing a little of this and a little of that.

The coffee's gone, and we take our leave. Sally seems not quite to believe that these guys have encamped here for the weekend but says nothing to pluck the flimsy membranes of sanity. We get as far as the grandstand skeleton before I make my move. "You wait here. Be right back."

At the tents I make inquiries. But no, nobody's seen a big crazy black guy hanging around the wall this night, nor last night when they pitched camp. Sure, they'll keep an eye out. Yeah. See ya Monday. Nah, we don't need nothin'. But thanks.

We pitstop at the Moondance for coffee and I try Velez's place and the Velezmobile cellphone, without luck. "I thought he might be going out of town," says Sally Wallach.

"Which out of town might he be going to?"

"Aruba."

"Uh huh."

"Kendall's in Aruba."

"Oh."

"Working. She, like, got this Sports Illustrated-kinda bikini gig? Anyhow, I'm pretty sure I heard her tell Fuzzy to come down this weekend. I'm pretty sure he said he would."

Heard her? Pretty sure? "Kendall's been rooming with me. Thought you knew that."

Aruba.

"What about the station?" I decide to try.

"Kendall needed a place. While she looks. Actually, while she waits for Fuzzy to decide to move her in with him. I said she could stay till after the holidays—till I go back to school."

"Velez isn't moving her anywhere," I say. Sally shrugs like she knows better.

"Velez and your old man up to something?"

"What are you worrying about? I'm hungry."

"Who says I'm worried?"

"Pancakes. What do you think?"

"About what?"

"About pancakes."

"I have no opinion about pancakes. None whatsoever. I am in a completely pancake-neutral frame of mind. What about your old man?"

"Dennis, jeez. Harold Fish wants to buy WRTR. Who knows why—maybe just for the hell of it. My dad thinks Harold Fish is a pig. My dad and Harold Fish like to screw each other every chance they get. WRTR is just the handiest appliance at the moment. That's all. See?"

No.

"Well," says Sally, "I need pancakes. C'mon, Oldham. I'm declaring a pancake emergency."

I greet the daylight portion of Saturday from my roof.

The night haze surrenders early to the portent of another New York autumn aberration: today will blaze. The old lawn furniture up here has taken another ass-kicking this summer, between Jane Oldham and me and weather and neglect. Jane would be up here with me, arranging her mangy mustard-stained raveled blanket over the lounge chair in fort configuration; her bobbing blonde head would be peeking out right now to inspect the sunrise with her father. This, Saturday, would be our good day; many hours away from Sunday's customary pre-partum psychosis.

Over the rusty railing, a spy-satellite view of Mrs. McMichael's and Rose's sister's garden; thoroughly scavenged remnants now, except for some obstinate fall blooms.

Somewhere to the north and east, Sally Wallach slumbers.

Somewhere to the south and west, Velez may be dozing off a Margarita migraine wrapped in the sun-dappled tentacles of Ms. Elite, another womanchild inheritor of all the earth that's still worth inheriting.

No he's not. I don't believe it. Velez, play tag-along on a photo shoot? Not a chance. Where then?

Sally playing it so close to the vest last night under my ruthless interrogation leaves me with the big question: Have deals been made?

To suspect Velez of treachery at this convoluted juncture is both easier and harder than I would have imagined. Loyalty, I suddenly realize, has seldom been tested between us. The train, pretty much from the start, has been pure gravy. And yet we do have eleven-and-a-half years between us, don't we? Doesn't that, day in and day out, entitle someone to certain expectations? Even as I ask this, I think I know the answer. So: has Velez cut himself a deal?

Just pretend he has. It's not so hard to imagine. Okay, the part about Velez being in cahoots with E. P. Wallach—*that* part is hard to imagine. What does Old Man Wallach have that Velez would want? What does Velez have that E. P. would want?

And why do we still mine other people's harbors when Bandanna and Sentry and Airborne and the Grunt could tell us it doesn't work? Where is my daughter? What's the capital of North Dakota? Where do we start?

Where, while we're at it, is the hard evidence of a supreme being, a master blaster behind the scenes? Who can we pin things on? Can this much blundering be the production of anything premeditated, even sixteen billion years ago when Big allegedly Banged? When so much news crosses your desk, you can't help but search for deeply concealed patterns, for fingernail scrapings that could, in the right hands, point the way to conspiracy. I will dispense with such futility some day soon.

Bennie. Late of Bennie's bar; late of many former Bennie's bars that were never Bennie's except in some abstract expressionist frontman sensibility. A late morning call.

"Party," says Bennie. "A 'So Long, Velez & Oldham' party." So long, Velez & Oldham.

"Don't you want to know where?"

"Jesus, we're not exactly retiring, Ben."

"My new bar. Right around the corner from you. Small fuckin' city, huh?"

Bennie. Fountainhead of irrational resilience. "What's it called, Ben?"

"I don't know yet. Pre-opening party Monday, honor of you an' Velez. Word's out, man. Be the ultrababe festival of the western world."

"Jeez, Ben, I think Velez's out of town and I'm not sure—"

"No, no, forget about it, man, you gotta be here. Gotta. I awready told every babe in the galaxy that you an' Velez were gonna be here. Giant, serious stuff, Dennis. A night that dreams are made of."

Maybe I should get out of town, too. But what then of Sally Wallach?

But first downtown for a little more scouring, although this is hardly Lyndon McDonald's witching hour. I figure that Lyndon may be suffering from disorientation, due to the squatters who've commandeered his Wall.

But there's no chance that Lyndon, if he were still alive, which he's not, I sincerely fear, would show himself in the midst of what I find down here in all this salty smarmy autumn resplendence—New Jersey, it would seem, has been evacuated, a civil defense drill, no doubt—and everyone seems under orders to hang a camera around his neck and flee to Manhattan. If one of those MX missiles secretly cocked under the Federal Reserve building down here decides to detonate *in utero*, New Jersey would stand to lose a number of congressional seats.

The South Street Seaport, in case you haven't had the pleasure, is an out-of-town pirate's plot to remake Manhattan in the image and likeness of modern-day Baltimore. Once upon a time, you see, Baltimore built a retailing siege wall around its harbor in the folly of glamorizing the City Where Cousins Marry; the developer beheld what he had done and saw that it was good. The rest was just a matter of keenly targeted dollars and cents.

And so a visiting Baltimorian, like Richard 'Buddy' Oldham, could wander the cobblestones down here and as long as he didn't happen to check the prices or glance up to see what's about to happen over his head, he could convince himself that he was right back home on the squished-crab-cobbled Inner Harbor.

And what, I wonder in the idleness of this too-bright and optimistic touring hour, is Buddy up to these days?

It's been a while. Perhaps a visit to Buddy, after this weekend blows over.

Beneath the general shuffling and scolding of the migrant army I hear a familiar nasal drone. Could it be—yes! Hendy Markowitz, manning the Thunder mobile rock broadcast booth, a sloop-nosed Mitsubishi armored cruiser with one side rigged to fold outward and downward, and FBI surveillance-quality banks of sound electronics. People walk up and wave at Hendy. Someone in torn jeans is hawking brand new WRTR Thunder sweaters; a grab-bag of worthy causes are being hyped.

You cannot escape us. We are everywhere. We are in your brain. Want to buy a sweater?

Where had Lyndon lived?

If you recall the desertedness of our previous visits down here, you'd have to wonder about the supply of hideouts. Crannies are apparent, abundant. But not the kinds of places where even one as impervious as Lyndon McDonald could hope to survive a city winter. The wind alone would flush him out and slice him into lunchmeat. Besides, this is territory firmly in the control of the financial wizards who rule the invisible legions of the damned and who don't tolerate them cluttering up the sidewalks with their stink and their open-sored portents of apocalypse.

But you don't have to look far, even if you aren't, as I am, an accredited journalist, to begin to see the nethercity. Between the river, for instance, and the hexagons of blacktop that masquerade as Olde New York streets is a pocket of briny tidal space—five feet high at best, and washed out of existence in an angry high chop—that plenty of our forebears called home. More congenial to rats, I'm sure your opinion would be, and you'd be right, but none of the lords would begrudge you a rotting crossbar perch above river pilings during the day, especially if the accommodations would get you out of their genteel vision. Could Lyndon have wrapped himself in enough purloined swaddling to squirrel himself safely and warmly away down there? Why not.

And there are always the creaking alleyway shells that once were dwellings and still, furtively, are.

Down to Lyndon's wall. A few more tents have slung themselves up around the waterfront platoon's original two. Beginning to look like Tomkins Park's homeless villages in between police bulldozings. Except for the tiny unit flags, whose bright licks of color are set off nicely by the diaphanous neutrality of the etched wall.

Not that many tourists wander this far below the Seaport's pseudo-suburban security zone but some Ralph Lauren adventurers happen upon Bandanna's platoon; children have questions that Sentry and the others look willing—eager—to entertain. The grandstand is well on its way to completion; the city crew is hoisting seat planks into position and bolting them down. A multi-peaked canopy has sprouted over the stage and two simple banks of lights stand at attention on either side, ready for the triumphant return of Judd Tate and the Standard Band.

All right. I've looked. He's not here. That doesn't make him dead yet. The weekend is young.

# 21

DON'T ask me what's sucking me back up into Too Tall again today. There is nothing to do here; no one is waiting for me here. One of the swings is on. New. A black man about half my age, non-confrontational flattop and Lennon specs. Plodding through a playlist about which I doubt he had much say.

Raylene McDonald sits at her desk. She has headphones on; tuned elsewhere. Housecleaning seems to be happening. In fact, selective packing seems to be happening.

Charlene McDonald, pigtails tucked up under a Mets ballcap, is standing tip-toe on a swivel chair and graffitizing Arielle's scheduling board with DayGlo magic markers. On another Saturday afternoon, Jane Courtenay Oldham would be on hand to help Charlene firebomb this place; today, Charlene is the Lone Marauder. She can handle it.

I cheek a corner of Raylene's desk. "So?" I ask.

"They's rumors," says Raylene.

"They's *always* rumors," I remind her, before it occurs to me that she might be talking about Lyndon. I search. No signs. Uh uh.

"Charlene?" she calls into space, and a squeaky "What, Momma?" finds its way back to us.

"What you doing, baby?"

"Nothin', Momma."

"Good. You keep on doin' it, and don't raise any hell." To me she says, "Where's your baby? This your weekend, idn' it?"

"A secret island," I say as lightly as I can, "inhabited by a race of female attorneys who kidnap because they can't procreate." Raylene doesn't need to be told any more.

I'm just about to ask again what Raylene is up to when the elevator vomits Arielle and a mini-phalanx of her personal junior-varsity suits our way. We go unnoticed as the conga line two-wheels it around the corner but Charlene McDonald isn't so lucky.

"Ah, 'scuse me, *'scuse me,* but what the *fuck* is this kid doing to *my* scheduling board?"

"Ah, damn," Raylene whispers mid-catapult, but I beat her around the bend.

"Hey, boss," I say, hustling Charlene away from the scene of destruction, "New programming assistant?"

"You," is all Arielle has to say to me. To Raylene: "You wanna bring your kid in here, *watch him!*"

"Her," says Raylene.

But Arielle is back to me with the kind of red-eyed rodent malevolence that keeps exorcists in business. "Where's your asshole partner?"

"Don't you mean, 'Where's your partner, asshole?'"

"Where?" Arielle grits, her hair curling tighter with every alien-like brain contraction.

"Wasn't my turn to watch him."

"Fine," says Arielle, "great. Incredibly fucking funny. But lemme tell you: things are getting ready to start flying up *your* ass, too, hotshot." And with a final portentous bovine snort, Arielle barrels back through her suitlings, setting them spinning like a formation of Giorgio Armani dreidels for the moment it takes before they're sucked up and away into Arielle's malignant draft.

Raylene gives me the Coliseum Christians' eye of doom, but I assure her thus: "She knows nothing. If anybody's going to hell here, it's her." I make a hasty pile of her stuff. "C'mon. Let's get out of here. Hey, Munchkin," I growl into the belly of a high-flying Charlene McDonald, "we're history."

"We're history!" crows the littlest Met, and we roll, leaving the Thunder in the innocent hands of a black man wearing John Lennon's glasses, who right now couldn't be blamed for sensing some long-term employment opportunities.

We—Charlene, her Mom and I—find ourselves presently at a rear table in a place called the Broadway Deli. Here's what the Broadway Deli is like: the beasts of the earth sentenced to appear on the menu here are led down a ramp into a plague-infested medieval dungeon, where a rabbi with a chainsaw quarters them live and prays over their twitching carcasses until a union crane operator hoists large chunks of their remains into place between slabs of bread. These hellish abominations are known in local circles as sandwiches, and in places like the Broadway they are given the names of celebrities embalmed in the special immortality that comes only after centuries of performing ethnic humor for audiences of the vacationing deceased.

"Maybe this is the best thing," Raylene is saying. "It's time we left anyway. Past time."

"Sure," I say.

"I got a sister in Philadelphia."

"Philadelphia? You'd do that to your little girl?" The little girl in question, meanwhile, is burrowing tunnels and sowing horseradish mines into what was, in happier times, a fully assembled and functional pig.

"Neighborhood's closing in, Dennis. All the time, closer. You don't know. Girl Charlene's age two weeks ago got shot dead right through her front door, *inside her house,* Dennis. Couple of those crack gangs chasin' each other down the street, everybody shooting an' this little girl's all of a sudden got a hole in her head."

Add to the list of things that here hold no horror this: it is the children who are the killers.

"Maybe if the police sponsored some firearms training, y'know, teach the druggies to hit what they're shooting at. . . ." I try.

But Raylene is in no mood. "It's worse than just crazy, Dennis; it's *random.* If it w'unt for Lyndon. . . ."

Whoa.

"Don't think I can leave with him out there."

"Can't do anything for him."

"I can worry about him. Even if. . . . You seen him?"

Ah, Raylene.

Raylene's eleven-dollar porcine autopsy lays undisturbed on its rye gurney between her elbows. "He was such a man, once. He was such a man." Her jaw clenches and unclenches. Won't give in. "He was so proud of his uniform. I remember. So proud. Fool." She straightens her silverware again and dabs a napkin to her mouth and I think she wonders why she can't just think all these thoughts one final time and be done with them. Ah, but that's not the way it works, is it?

"I wish I could have 'im with me again. Way he was before they took him off to fight. God, he was such a fine father."

Ho ho, there's a concept. "Lyndon has kids?"

Raylene looks me in the eye. "Lyndon has *my* kids, honey." She taps the bright blue bill of Charlene's ballcap. "Not this baby. My grown ones. Lyndon was my husband, once upon a time."

So. One of us after all. "I thought you told me—"

"Yes. Yes, well, I suppose I did. Don't take it as a personal lie. I just, just couldn't manage with Lyndon in our life. Not the way they brought him home. Not the way he . . . is."

And now Charlene and I watch her mother fold herself silently into her Broadway Deli smiling porker napkin. I look around; Charlene looks around. Nobody catches on. We're by ourselves in the eye of this oblivious frenzied munch, as we should be.

"They took my man," Raylene finally manages to whisper, "and they brought me back . . . junk. Just old thrown-out Army junk." And the years—the centuries, I guess you could say in Raylene's case—threaten finally to brim down her cheeks. "He was so bad, Dennis, he was so dead, he was—I couldn't even *mother* him. I'da done that—I'da mothered him the rest of my life. I didn't care he peed himself every time a loud noise went off but . . . but they wasn't even enough left of him to mother."

She wipes sandwich leavings from Charlene's mouth. "Couldn't keep him in the hospital forever. But every time I bring him home, he'd run off. Just wander off. You know how he is; what am I tellin' you? After a while, I let him wander. But I can't—can't just—I gotta be around, don't I?"

"His kids—"

"Lyndon's boys think he died." She shrugs. "They forgot all about him by now. Y'know it's been a lot of years. They were just boys. They still have pictures of him in his uniform, and some bullshit medals got sent home pinned to him. It was a good lie. I think. There's times when a good lie is best. Don't you think so?"

Well then. Sounds like permission to me. "Lyndon's dead," I say.

ALL the voices on my machine sound like they're in a hurry; like something's getting ready to leave and none of them want to miss it.

Sally Wallach: "Hi it's me—callmebye."

Alicia: "Don't do this strike thing. Trust me. It's Alicia."

Bennie: "Name of the new place—ya ready? *Graceland.* It's gonna be outrageous. I'm at home."

Sally: "I forgot—555-1881. I didn't know if . . . right. G'bye."

Bennie: "For the bar, I mean. Name for the bar. Don't forget Monday night. Countin' on you."

And then, after easily a half-tape more of this, after the Bobs and the Cathys have had their say, comes another. "Uncle Dennis? Hello. This is Margarita Velez. Do you know where my brother is? Anyway, please tell him to call home—I mean, to call us. I left a message at his place too. Thank you. It's important. Thank you. It's important."

I find the locks on Immaculata Velez's door broken. The jamb is a jaw of angry splinters.

Inside has the smell and bruises and undischarged static electricity of hasty, incomplete domestic triage. Things have been churned in anger.

Margareta Velez leads me inside.

"Your Momma okay?" She nods, not vigorously enough to shake the confusion from her eyes. She's tall now, this girl, this unlikely miracle of Immaculata Velez's twilight. We sit beneath the slightly cock-eyed inspection of the smashed television and the Virgin. "You called the cops, right?"

She shakes her head.

"How come?"

Well, how shall I put this, Uncle Dennis? Am I even supposed to be telling this to you? Momma said to find Roberto. All this darkens in the heart of her eyes.

"Come on," I say as softly as I can.

"It was Nicolo did this." And now in a rush, like everything needs to be said first, comes the plot: Nicolo is in trouble with some guys. Nicolo needs money. Nicolo demands his Momma's money but Immaculata Velez for once says no. Nicolo starts throwing things around. I got cut, see here? It's okay, didn't bleed much, he didn't throw at me, exactly, but a glass smashed and part came and cut me. Then Momma, she tells him to get out, leave his house keys, not to come back. Later we go out for a minute, we had to go to the store and Momma didn't want me or her to go alone and when we come back we find it like this. And Momma's money—it's all gone.

"Where's your Momma?"

"She's inside—she's trying to sleep."

"Can I talk to her?"

But Margareta says, "I think . . . I think it would be good to leave her alone."

The first thing I can think of is, "We got to get you two out of here, kid."

Margareta shakes her head. "Momma won't go. Anyway," she laughs hopelessly, "Nicolo won't be coming back; nothing here left to steal."

But oh, yes there is. I call around and finally get a Manhattan locksmith who, for a hundred dollar front-end bribe, will see his way clear to make the trip to Washington Heights. We wait, Margareta and I; she makes us soup. Immaculata Velez remains behind closed doors, even through the drilling and hammering and chiseling as the locksmith installs one of each kind of lock ever invented. She's not asleep. She is humiliated.

Now late in the afternoon, after much silence, there's nothing left but to go. "You know you can come stay with me, you and your Mom," I say to be polite. And, "Hey. Where's the other one? Michael?"

Margareta Velez looks out through the curtains of the barred window and down into the street. "Out there. Hangin' out somewhere. I don't know." She smiles a secret smile. "I've seen the limo outside, you know. Late, when he doesn't think we're awake."

We practice once to make sure Margareta has the drill straight on all this new security hardware, and I'm nearly out the door before she grabs my arm and says, "Guess what? Tomorrow's my birthday."

"Get out. Which one?"

She shines proudly and beautifully and for a beatific moment the reality of this existence of hers vanishes. "Thirteen," she says. "I'm gonna be thirteen years old tomorrow."

I am body-slammed by my alarm clock. Monday, four a.m. Club-closing time. The lucky and the damned file shoulder to shoulder out into pitch black, differentiated only by an irremediable string of accidents that could just as easily have fallen the opposite way. Some of these people will be tuning in to what may be the last official Velez & Oldham Show on the Thunder. Or just another gigantic bluff on the road to radio ever after.

In the course of my stumbles I manage to find the right remote control and raise the Thunder. It's Hendy Markowitz, but I leave it anyway. ". . .all hoping things'll hold off until after the big Veterans Day Parade broadcast, live on WRTR—the Thunder—from the Vietnam Memorial downtown . . . all the way downtown, just keep goin', it's on the East River side, just before you fall in. 'Course, don't forget this is the big day for the Velez & Oldham Show, too—will our boys make good on their threat and go through with this strike? Well, hey, I don't know what those crazy guys are up to—guess we'll all find out together at Velez & Oldham's special holiday show starting at eight o'clock this morning—but all I know is that WRTR has been the spiritual home of rock longer than any other station in New York and I know that whoever winds up owning WRTR will want to keep that tradition alive, will know how important. . . ." And on and on. Just give us the fucking weather, will you, Hendy?

" . . . beautiful right now, but the weatherdude's calling for all heck to break loose by this afternoon, thunderstorms, cold moving in, maybe *flurries* by nightfall, *come on!* Hey, boys and girls, it is November, you know, but I mean, gimme a break, right?"

Whether or not Roberto Velez shows up—that's right, I haven't heard word one, and my call to Aruba yesterday brought pretty plausible denials from Ms. Elite—the Velez & Oldham Show will hop today. Someone has shaken the celebrity tree and all the usual suspects—you know, the activists ready to bleed for whatever cause is about to be televised over worldwide satellite hook-up—have been conscripted for special appearances this morning; every actor who ever scammed a few million dollars off Vietnam in the late, great John Wayne *faux* leatherneck tradition will be emoting with Velez and me, or at least me, sometime this morning. We have folkies and rockers to furnish the gray-haired, drug-desiccated authenticity, and some stand-up comics for in-between. And at high noon, just in time for the Wall Street lunchtime jailbreak, comes our grand finale: the legendary Standard Band.

Oh yes. There's Agent Orange and her strike team DJ's.

There is no news from Washington Heights, I am happy to report. Margareta Velez and her girlfriends seem to have found non-life-threatening ways to usher in her adolescence. Today, a school holiday, they'll take the subway downtown to lower Manhattan so she can show off her brother doing his radio thing; I have promised to put her on the air as a birthday present. Nicolo is underground. It's always possible that Nicolo is literally underground; Margareta had no details about what kind of trouble the little slimebucket is in. We watch television, though, don't we. We won't be taken by surprise.

Here's another region where the news blackout remains in effect: Westchester County. I called, listened to the ring-buzz, hung up, vowed the hell with it, called again almost immediately, got a busy signal, put the phone on automatic redial for a couple of hours and listened to the electric boop-beep-boop and its faithful response, the busy-buzz. Phone off the hook? I've read of a new spy gadget from Japan: you can program a particular incoming number to get a busy signal every time it tries to beep-boop-beep its way in until the end of time. I bet Sarah has one of those.

It's only paranoia when it's not true, you're thinking.

Oh, but Sentry or Bandanna or anybody of Vietnam vintage could tell you that's not necessarily the case. It could be true and also be paranoia: say you harbor a handsome set of conspiracy theories, based on nothing more than random cosmic alignments and the drooling insanity of your own convictions. But say that somewhere, under some secret rock or maybe in that parallel state of existence they talk about in Justice League comics and at the Massachusetts Institute of Technology, the very conspiracies you instinctively suspect are *actually* taking shape. Paranoia? All right, technically, but only on the same grounds used by people who choose to disbelieve UFO sightings despite exhaustive supermarket documentation. Narrowminded, I say, and shamefully unworthy, in this fully accredited reporter's view, of the boundless promise of post-Modernist retro-alienation.

None of which matters this morning. What matters this morning is whether Velez will be showing up and whether we'll be slicing Velez & Oldham's scrotilia as part of the Veterans Day festivities.

Casey the Enginette greets me on the scene. It's a little before six-thirty as the oily industrial-red gloaming groans its way up from behind Brooklyn. I can never remember which red sky means we're in deep trouble—you know, that sailor thing—but the sky is decidedly red-assed and the wind is confused and agitated and up there at Colonel Elmo's CAP altitude the jet stream seems on the verge of decisions with potentially unhappy repercussions.

What brings Colonel Elmo to mind—besides the obvious—is the surface-to-air-missile-sized coffee thermos Enginette Casey is wielding from a high discreet cranny of the WRTR Thunder Mitsubishi armored-personnel-carrier broadcast booth. "Careful," Casey warns, "there may be small traces of psychoactives in there." She wipes her mouth on the sleeve of her fatigue jacket—even the Case is in theme this morning—and asks, "Won't be any pop urine quizzes today . . . ?"

"Nah, Case. Stoned is the only alternative. Anything less would be unpatriotic."

Casey has business to attend to: WRTR has evidently posted bail for a small squadron of local between-engagement roadies to button up the stage—union cards won't be checked too carefully today—and so Casey is swapping walkie-talkese with an emaciated body-art billboard who seems to be in charge of the crew.

The tent village of my waterfront platoon hasn't grown much; accommodations for no more than a dozen cozied up around the base of the ghostly glass slab. The effect, startlingly, is of the monolith rising cold and inhuman out of this grim little furrow of ruined wasted human-ity, all encircled by the absurd stone battlements up there near the floor of the sky, a scene, I feel compelled to report before it slips my mind, of almost unspeakably heartbreaking eloquence. Much nonsense and kitsch and hypocrisy and counterfeit sentiment will attempt to swamp us this day, I fear. So now, before the avalanche of treachery commences, let us, you and I, pause in dopey tearful incomprehension at the ancient pathos being reenacted for our private benefit in this first light of oblivion.

# 22

In the hour before final countdown, I sprint across the six-lane southern terminus of FDR Drive to the river. Here, I figure, is more or less where the frogmen hooked Lyndon McDonald. I can't help scanning the rotten, tarblack, urchin-encrusted pilings that somehow still manage to keep the old ferry terminals from collapsing into the river for suspect forms, and there are plenty of those: an infinite selection of New York detritus, come home to the river for final disposition. More crud blows off the top of garbage scows into this river in a day than most towns manage to manufacture in a decade.

And that is the true endearment of this city: that it foists no embarrassing civic affectations. New York doesn't give a fuck what you think about it. The highway splasher revulsion-attraction syndrome is what we feature here. That's what keeps you coming back for more. The fragrant, sticky glisten of freshly-spilled blood; the deliciously terrifying chance that this time it might turn out to be yours.

Traffic has already roiled itself into a murderous frenzy; predators are slinging themselves off the FDR in satellite-guided Bavarian units. Veterans Day, of course, is a holiday only in the department store sense; the gamesmen down here who haven't yet been sacrificed to the market goddess by their unindicted superiors are in a hurry to strap themselves into their rigs and sink into another day of silent icy terror wondering what became of all the credulous little customers of yesteryear.

But one man's ceiling, as they say; and by lunchtime these people will have despaired of fencing corporate ownership notes to strangers and will be ripe for a harkening to the innocent days of youth—not necessarily *their* youth, since many on the hustle down here are the very children inadvertently conceived under the clanging spell of the Standard Band. Borrowed anthems, we'll call them; the soundtrack of eternal youth. Which just happens to be on the menu today out in Vietnam Memorial Plaza or whatever they call this place, courtesy of WRTR—the Thunder.

I reinfiltrate from the north, right into the tiny tent village at the Wall. Bandanna and Airborne are arranging a small cache of Vietnam memorabilia out where passers-by can have a look. The boys will be anxious to share their stories today at this, their permanent traveling museum of mutilation. Kids will ask about the NVA hardware; Bandanna and Airborne will be eager to please.

One of the two portals through the Wall has been blanketed off for a tiny mess. Sentry is, as usual, on coffee duty. The odors of illicit consumption are much in evidence. Bandanna reports no sightings of a big crazy black guy, and they're all pleased that Sally Wallach has already been by to visit with a load of bagels and donuts. "Oh yeah," grins the chorus, "ol' Agent Orange. She been 'round. Good girl, that Agent Orange. Jesus Christ, man." And they howl in harmless and even perversely endearing lechery.

And then there, conferring with Enginette Casey and Raylene McDonald in front of the Thunder battlewagon, is Agent Orange herself. Sally has scrounged some kind of high-visibility military rescue jumpsuit in a temperature of orange that threatens to scream right off the infrared end of the visible-light spectrum. Zippers and patches surround many of my very favorite curvatures. At her waist Sally is corseted into a cartridge belt chock-full of giant, purposeful-looking bullets the size and disposition of Lyndon McDonald's fingers. Her hair is twined severely into a single thick braid down her back, and her face is all but concealed by ludicrous flying-saucer sunglasses—our undercover operative in deep-incog.

Seven-forty-three.

I climb up into the booth; Enginette Casey headphones me back to the studio so I can savor the last gasp of Hendy Markowitz's program.

Now Sally is back with three prisoners in tow. "Here they are!"

Yes, the strike-team DJ's.

Sally does introductions. A gawky, bespeckled travel agent named Miriam, featuring metal-detector earring assemblies. An art student of Asian extraction and uncertain gender; Chang is as close as I will get. Rounding out the crew is Mike, a regular, thin-hair-and-beer-belly Judd Tate-era guy.

The seven of us—Sally, Enginette Casey, Raylene, me and the scabs—just about pack this broadcast rig. Enough room for Velez and that's it. Once the celeb interviews get happening, somebody's going to have to get the hell out.

Seven-fifty.

Miriam is the one with the questions. "Where do we sit? Shall I get coffee? What do we say?" Then she nails us with the big one: "Where's Velez?"

I look from Sally to Casey; we all zero maliciously back in on Miriam. "Isn't he with you?"

Now Casey's on with the studio engineer and flagging me to the microphones for soundcheck. I chirp and meow the familiar mantra into my mike and then Velez's. "Going live in five, babe," Casey whispers, fingering me down, and I listen to Hendy back at Too Tall: ". . .just another few minutes we'll be cutting down to the Vietnam Veterans Memorial on the East River and right now, here's Dennis Oldham on the scene . . . Dennis? Are you there?"

Okay. "Right, Hendy, thanks, yeah, we're here, wired and ready to go, at least most of us are, if you get my meaning—Agent Orange is on the case with our three Thunder strike team DJ's, you're gonna meet them in a little while, and our Enginette Casey is at the stick."

"How 'bout our man Roberto?"

"I give up, Hendy—how 'bout our man Roberto? Isn't he with you?"

"Whoa, I—what?"

"Yeah! Thought he said you were gonna bring him down here."

"Well, jeez, Dennis—"

"'Kay, Hendy, back to you." I kill my mike but the Case waves frantically. "The asshole's still talkin' to you—" and so I flip back in time to catch: ". . .bet there's already a big crowd down at the Plaza, huh Dennis?"

We all peer out of the Thunder mobile booth into the Plaza. There's my waterfront platoon, the stage crew, a sprinkling of sleeping, demented, vomit-encrusted street people and a bunch of scurrying comatose briefcases who couldn't care less. The trees outnumber the audience. "Nah," I tell Hendy. "Nobody here yet, man. People gotta work for a living."

"Yeah, uh, okay, Dennis Oldham, well, we'll be going to you guys live in just a little while now for news, music, guests, vets, and at twelve noon, the Standard Band!"

The news. Oh boy. I forgot the news. "Who's got a fucking newspaper?"

Nobody.

"Miriam," I say, taking her trembling hands in mine, "I've got a mission for you. You have a hundred and twenty seconds to find me a newspaper or we're all screwed, Miriam. Ready? Go."

Sally fumbles around in a sheaf of garbage; she emerges with dog-eared sheets and tosses them my way. "Friday's news," she says. "Just in case."

Okay. Relax. We're pretty settled in; this is going to work.

The studio reported only six calls from listeners complaining that the Velez & Oldham Show was trying to put Friday's news over on them again; the dead giveaway was my football picks for games that were contested yesterday, with outcomes not, as you might expect, entirely consistent with my analysis. Whoops. But by the eight-twenty-five newscast our guest jock travel agent Miriam returned with a few late-breaking items courtesy of the *New York Post* and, even better, a *National Enquirer* retrieved from a trash bin. Imagine the morsels that are making up my newscast today. Miriam especially liked the UFO barbecue story datelined someplace in a truly dangerous section of the great American Southwest, exclusive to the *Enquirer.* Those inquiring minds are getting a bellyfull today. I've decided to let Miriam handle next hour's news chores.

Here's an updated list of things there's no sign of yet: an audience, Roberto Velez, and a parade. Only the last surprises me.

According to Raylene, who I notice is keeping a weather eye around the firebase perimeter, we're supposed to start the live stuff during the nine o'clock hour. Sally is massaging our three strike team jocks, and they're starting to crank. Regular Mike even takes me on about my absolutely guaranteed weekly football picks: "No offense, Dennis, but an ignoramus could make a pretty steady buck bettin' against your picks." Yeah, well maybe, Mike, but didn't those Jets spot me a couple of day's walking-around money yesterday with a four-point cover? Huh, Mike? Can I pick 'em?

So I turn things over to Casey, Sally and the scabs, and I take a little walk. The Plaza is not exactly deserted—maybe a hundred empty-eyed itinerants with time on their hands have scattered themselves around on the otherwise barren bleachers, hot on the scent of indiscriminate largesse.

The coffee is hot behind the tent shared by Sentry and the Grunt. Someone has come up with a portable radio tuned to WRTR, a bit redundant considering the megawattage pouring our every inanity out over the few tons of Marshal stadium speakers ringing the stage; but radio, as these guys and I know, is a highly personal medium. Radio is meant to be shared like a joint—among a small circle of accomplices. I go as far as to crawl inside Grunt and Sentry's tent, the psychotropic hall of fame; there are traces of smells in here that most earthlings won't have the chance to sample in a lifetime.

The parade is on the platoon's mind, too. Specifically: "When'd they move the parade down here?"

"Isn't it always down here?"

Airborne drains a Bud heavy. "Fi'th Avenyah," he informs me. "Long's I can remember. Fi'th Avenyah."

"Yeah," says Bandanna, "Down'a that little park with all 'em little colored kids sellin' dope."

Well, *I* don't know when, or if, the Veterans Day Parade was moved but somebody would have checked, don't you think? I mean, whose idea was it to stick us all down . . . Arielle. Arielle, my little pumper.

Back to the booth. "Raylene," I say, "Call somebody at City Hall. Find out where the parade is. And not a word to the bad guys."

And as I sit in a fast-forward ponder, what should career into view but the Velezmobile, hopping a modest curb or two on its collision course with the WRTR mobile broadcast vehicle. It's one of those situations that leaves no time for screams, just eye-popping wonderment at the imminence of particularly cartoonish death. But then, at the last second, the Velezmobile hits its brakes and ass-ends sideways in a maneuver best left to professionals; moments later my partner Roberto Velez steps from the carriage, pulls up his socks, and saunters our way.

Untanned.

I'm out onto the tar.

Velez surveys the empty plaza. Arm around my shoulders. "Nice fuckin' turnout, Coolie."

"Yeah, well, they all heard you were coming. Where you been?"

"Ridin' in from the airport listening to my last show. Ain't too funny yet. I thought you and Agent Orange had this deal zipped up, man." He pinches my cheeks together infant-style. "Where's the parade?"

"Yeah, well, we're looking for it."

"It's lost?" Velez snorts.

"Yeah. Well, nah. It's around somewhere. It'll turn up. Tell me about the airport, partner."

But all Velez gets a chance to say is, "We gotta talk, Coolie—" because halfway up the steps to our booth-on-wheels Agent Orange hurtles out the door chest first into my partner's nose. "Whoa!" hoots Velez, extricating himself from Sally's orange-encased bosom, "careful with those things." Presently we're all crammed up into this Japanese submarine-on-wheels, and Velez wants to know, "Awright, children, what the hell's going on in here?" But our strike team jocks are already up and slam-dancing toward the great Velez and right about here is where Raylene McDonald shouts *"No fucking parade!"* And that pretty much brings all kowtowing to a halt as everyone, even Regular Mike, tandem-shrieks "Whatdya mean, *'no fucking parade?'*"

Meanwhile, the limousine stunt driving has roused my waterfront platoon into action: Bandanna, Grunt, Sentry and Airborne come barreling up the stairs. "Where is he? Where's Judd?" Velez has me by the collar whispering "Who the fuck are these guys?" Miriam, Chang and Regular Mike would be scurrying if there was anyplace to scurry but four military cranium cases have corked the only way out and now I see Chang dive for cover into the official WRTR mobile airplane-style crapper just as Casey, kneeling up on her stool, catches my eye and starts fingering me down from five. I can't even see my microphone and the intelligence seems now to be seeping in that there's no parade coming anywhere near here today, rendering my Sally momentarily apoplectic; at two I shake my head furiously in the Case's direction but something of hers has quit and as one becomes zero on the Casey fingerometer and this bedlam blows out live to one-point-three million sleepy hostages Casey slams her fist into something electronic and I sink to my knees and crawl among fatigue-clad legs toward where I think I remember last sighting a microphone.

From the more promising perspective of the floor I wedge myself in under our mini-console and fish my mike and headset down under here with me. We're on the air. "Well, friends, it's an official game now: the one, the only, Roberto Velez, *Señor* Rock & Roll, has just landed. But first, this just in to the Thunder newsfloor: there ain't no parade down here on the old waterfront, kids. Yes, friends, Rolling Thunder Radio has assembled a Veterans Day extravaganza complete with everything except veterans. . . ." Listeners with superior sound systems will probably also be picking up pieces of this in the background: ". . . so who the fuck said there was a. . . ." "Hey, don't look at me, Fuzzy, it was goddamn Arielle—" "You mean that wu'nt ole Judd come flyin' up in 'at big ass limousine . . . ?" And from Raylene, elbowing a circuit through this sweating forest, "Would everybody please *shut the fuck up* so we can do a radio program?"

I grab a high-visibility-orange leg and a lizard boot and pull them down under the console for a mid-broadcast production meeting. Sally and Velez and I breathe into each other's faces; the range is unfocusably short. "Where's the parade?" Velez says.

"Fifth Avenue, somebody said," reports Agent Orange, whose rescue jumpsuit, I can't help noticing at this angle, is beginning to come unvelcroed in the melee.

"Can we be just a little more specific?" I say, concealing the live mike for spontaneity's sake. You one-point-three million fans have stuck by us through good times and bad; might as well be in on the bloody finish. Sally pokes her head out but Raylene is unflaggable; I grab Airborne and pull him to the floor. "Where'd you say the parade is?"

Airborne, apparently propelled by all this into an eye-popping flashback of sulfurous deck-hugging slaughter, can only stammer "Some park . . . colored kids . . . selling dope. . . ." Great, Airborne. Thanks. Sally shoves him up and away.

I hear Casey whispering, "Go to the spots, Dennis, c'mon," into my headphone. Ho ho, somebody's sponsoring this clusterfuck. I hoist the mike up to where it's inches from my lips, Velez's and Sally's all at once. "'Morning, Roberto," I say.

"Well, well, Coolie. Guess you got me by the weasel this time, eh, baby? Been tryin' for almost twelve years, and now, last chance . . . okay. One for you. Hi, everybody. Roberto Velez here, in a stirring Veterans Day re-enactment of the Tet Offensive here inside our broadcast trailer, guess you can hear the gunfire in the background but don't worry 'cause Velez is on the case now and soon as we find this friggin' parade—" Now Casey crawls into my ear with "Madison Square, y'know, where Broadway crosses Fifth Avenue."

"Hey, 'scuse me, Bobby," I blurt, "but this just in to the Thunder mobile newsroom: the stealth parade has just been located, making its way to Madison Square, just about sixteen thousand miles from where we are right now, due to arrive in about an hour."

And here's where inspiration strikes Velez. "Oh yeah?" he says. "Well, that's great. Because that will give the WRTR program manager, our dear Arielle—you all know her from the gym, right, guys? She's the one can't quite keep that Brillo pad tucked up inside that little Cindy Crawford rig of hers—anyway, Arielle, if you're listening to this, babe, you've got one hour to figure out how to get every veteran in the parade from Madison Square down here, or Harold Fish's first official act as new owner of WRTR will be to boil your eyeballs. . . ."

Like a hippopotamus ballet, feet suddenly stampede past us and out the door and before you know it there's nobody left in here except Casey, Raylene, Velez and me; even Sally has disappeared. Velez and I hazard a look out the door in time to see the strike team and the waterfront platoon stampede a newly arrived limousine. The platoon is hoping for Judd Tate but Judd Tate will more likely be taking the subway here, assuming the Vietnam Veterans Plaza has even managed to make its way onto ol' Judd's itinerary today. Whoever's in there has more sense, apparently, than to get out, and now Raylene's hollering our way: "Velez! Arielle would like a word."

"Yeah? Here's one: *fired!*"

Guess I better turn the microphone off for a minute.

Velez listens into the phone for a second or two and then bombs Arielle. It is a rabid symphonic fusillade of anatomical slander and bare intimations of corporate sabotage; the type of synthetic hysteria that Velez does better than anybody in the business, winding up with words to the effect that either Arielle finds a way to get the vets from midtown down here to the Plaza by Standard Band concert time or Velez goes public with WRTR's top-secret 'screw the vets' policy. Velez cuts Arielle off and gives Raylene and me the air-pump of victory and it seems that, at least from now until noon, we are holding the Thunder hostage.

A quick check outside reveals this: limousine number two has deposited in our midst a young lad named Patrick Elmsford. That's right, *the* Patrick Elmsford, the one who starred in that Vietnam epic a few years ago where he plays the idealistic journalism student whose father shames him into signing up and who gets over there and turns into the best thing to hit the Expeditionary Force since the daisy cutter, a regular one-boy genocidal battalion, and then finds Jesus and shoots himself in the foot so they ship him home where he figures to straighten out his father, but just a week too late because the old man, in the meantime, has discovered some Nixonian truths of his own and shoots *himself* for packing the kid off to the jungle, leaving his son's pyschic healing in the delectable hands of the movie director's child bride, who somehow landed the role of the long-suffering girlfriend, whose only job in the movie is to slather her beach-bunny brand of physical therapy all over Patrick Elmsford's peanut-oiled loins as we fade to credits. You remember that one. How Patrick Elmsford managed to summon tears in the middle of that last scene, laying there with the director's wife on top of him manufacturing one plausible, Sally-Wallach-quality orgasm after another like a Swiss watch—it's possible, it occurs to me just now, that Sally has seen this movie and taken notes—baffled the Academy of Motion Picture Arts and Sciences into a nomination and apotheosized the lad as one of those new men who's *not afraid to cry.*

Anyway, this guy's here for an interview. Since the movie he's the new Vietnam vets' MIA poster child, and yet Airborne and the Grunt and skinny old Sentry and tattooed Bandanna take one look at this kid and turn back for their tents shaking their heads and talking behind their hands.

Hope they don't think this kid's appearance this morning was my idea.

But look: if you have a compassionate bone in your body you can't help but want to tell Patrick Elmsford to get back into his limo and make a run for it, because the events of the morning—not to mention the events as yet unrevealed to me of Velez's mystery weekend—have set my partner to salivating for unsuspecting prey.

But now Agent Orange is leading Patrick Elmsford up toward our booth, arm hooked through his, and the screaming orange jumpsuit is making an impression.

Velez misses nothing. He fingers the retreating platoon. "Who'd you say they are?"

"Some Vietnam vets. Camped out."

"You tell 'em you did the 'Nam?" Velez asks.

"Well. . . ."

"Get 'em," says Velez, and before you know it Patrick Elmsford is pinned in between the Grunt and Airborne, with Sentry drooling down the back of his neck and a microphone stuck up his cosmetological wonder of a nose. The Case has rigged a few hand-held mikes so at this point anyone who wanders in here could scoop one up and talk to one-point-three million people, more or less, if they feel like it. "Here's a treat," Velez says maliciously, "Five guys swapping Vietnam stories . . . ." And we turn the platoon loose on Patrick Elmsford, who may, up until this moment, have allowed an adoring public to convince him that he is, in fact, a war hero, just like that delusional ballerina John Wayne back in the day, that those things they gave him all that money to pretend, and the hardships, the bout of malaria we all read about, actually qualify him to share a beer with the likes of Airborne and Sentry. "What was it *really* like . . . ?" Airborne breathes into Patrick Elmsford's flushed face; "Were you *scared* when they blew up all them fake grenades an' stuff?" Sentry fires up a crumbly joint and close-quarters us all into toxic shock. "Tell us, Mister Elmsford, sir, did you have *nightmares* after you finished makin' yer movie?" I take a peek at the formerly star-struck Agent Orange and note with small-minded satisfaction the deflation in her eyes. Owe ya one, Sentry.

Outside, the curious and the aimless have finally begun to assemble; our megawattage can no doubt be heard ricocheting through the downtown canyons all the way across the foot of the island to the mighty Hudson. We—listen to me: we!—*somebody* has aimed enough speakers upriver to hijack a few thousand Seaport lunchers in another ninety minutes or so. Since there's no room for me in the WRTR mobile broadcast unit, I make my way to the stage at the opposite end of the Plaza. Our renegade roadies are *check-check-checking* and re-rigging the canvas stage canopy against an increasingly foul-tempered river breeze; I can even hear snaps of canvas echoing back from the limestone cliffs above, the way, in the darkness of past mornings, I could sometimes hear that crazy Lyndon baritone bouncing its way in and out of the land of reason.

Who knows what Lyndon would have made of this circus. He'd probably be trying to raise Colonel Elmo, ready to call in the air strike that this enterprise so richly deserves.

# 23

HERE'S a perfect chance for you and me to sit back and watch some vintage Velez—maybe our last chance, it suddenly occurs to me—Velez, blustering around our mobile broadcast bunker, pockets full of ripe Thunder plums; Velez, feeling loose and looking invincible. Velez is dewy with conspiracy; he is wired to something gold-plated. He's palming all the good cards this morning. Playing with house money.

If the old Druid saying is true that nothing lasts forever, especially the stuff you didn't deserve in the first place, then this last tango of the Velez & Oldham Show should be playing at Stonehenge.

Don't forget: it wasn't so long ago that he was trying this act on for size, back in Albany, under the dope-seared sinuses of fat Molly, that severed root at the withered extremity of the rock family tree; secure, was Velez, in the meaninglessness of the stakes we were playing for— who cared if we got fired? We didn't want to be there anyway, did we? Anyhow, a couple of early-on firings were just the thing to stoke that bad-boy persona. Daring something that the old white boys didn't have the *cojones* to try. Make a name.

But still. Who'd have guessed that a big-time outfit like WRTR-FM would coincidentally find itself clutching the edge of the toilet bowl, looking for something, anything. So we got it, Velez and I. Did we deserve it? Irrelevant. Did we *want* it? One of us sure as hell did.

What does Velez want now?

All right, I've found a spot where I can keep an eye on things here at Vietnam Veterans Plaza, site of a non-parade and the final—maybe— broadcast of the Velez & Oldham Show. I'm sitting on the edge of this stage that the City of New York has been magnanimous enough to produce for the festivities this day. Before me rise the twin banks of stands with their tentative sprinkling of audience. To the left—downwind— hunkers the Thunder recreational vehicle. To the north lies the scrabbly bivouac of the waterfront platoon. The stream of the idle curious and the war morbid is building by the minute, encircling the encampment of Airborne and Grunt and the others. From here I can plainly make out a show-and-tell by Sentry; he holds what looks like a hand-hewn pipe or reed to his lips, gives it a grand, red-faced, gland-busting toot, and then shifts roles from assassin to victim, demonstrating for a pocket of high schoolers the ghastly effects of whatever's supposed to fly out of the lethal jungle straw. Look, now: I believe one of those kids is none other than the adorable Margareta Velez. On her birthday outing. The boys want to check out the ninja hardware. Figures.

There is a stir. Partly the weather; didn't Hendy Markowitz quote the weatherdude, which most of the time is me, to the effect that Arctica was about to descend? I, the authentic weatherdude, should investigate. But I have appointed a surrogate weatherdude for the balance of the morning: Chang, the hermaphrodite art student who Sally Wallach finally managed to coax out of the mobile Thunder pooper once the eye of Hurricane Velez had settled in upon us. I have encouraged Chang to handle the weather with the same professional demeanor with which I have comported myself during the eleven-and-a-half-year run of the Velez & Oldham Show on WRTR. He hasn't let me down so far.

It's more than the weather, though. Something at the subatomic level is trying to manifest itself; to deliver a warning while there's still time. Even here on the edge of this stage, with the stacks of Marshals looming above humming in hopeful anticipation of the Standard Band or some representative fraction thereof, I can feel quanta being leapt in abject terror: new elements are on the verge of spontaneous generation and who'll know what to do with them once they show up? Who'll step up to take responsibility?

Lizard cowboy boots are sticking out of the Thunder broadcast booth. The pointed toes are lazing and looping back and forth to the tune slurping out of the speaker towers behind me. The red sun of impending doom has chromed out all the details down here: everything, from the previously ghostly green of the Vietnam Veterans Memorial Wall to the grungy tents leaning to, to the steel tips of my partner's lizard boots are all the color of the reflection from a cheap pink neon sign.

There's boozy scurrying over and around me, meanwhile, as the gray-flecked and tattooed chain gang of freelance roadies prepares for the triumphal resurrection of Judd Tate and the Standard Band. East Village punks and headbangers are beginning to turn up; howls of recognition echo down from the frail catwalks of this makeshift stage to the motorhead pool below. The river wind threatens now to heave an incautious roadie clear off the scaffolding; less spectacular than the storied Queensborough high dive of Mrs. McMichael's dearly departed Duane, though a dive of any height would get plenty of TV play tonight. Even the towers are beginning to do some rocking.

But the wind and the chaos are no match for the seduction of rock delivered at sonic boom amplitude; people fitting most descriptions are finding themselves pulled into our little riverside pocket for reasons few, I'm sure, could explain. It's Veterans Day—ahh, bullshit, it's just the handiest Monday—and here's a chance to steal some absence without official leave from handcuffed lives, all in the name of some stale commemoration of forgotten battles waged in other people's yards.

Above me, around me, through my bones and entrails, Velez waltzes and taunts, giggles through the stacks. Snarls. Velez is willing Lower Manhattan to tilt slowly our way; more and more people are tumbling helplessly into our vortex. And out in the shadowy canyon a mechanized convergence begins to take shape: I can spot the baby blue armored divisions of New York's finest cruising up and down Water Street, pulling over, taking up positions, figuring, bitching, moving on. Local TV news vans, with their *War of the Worlds* antennas and satellite dishes and Krupp cannon microphones are jockeying like kids at a bike rack to see who can score the most pathetic vet shots in the name of the people's right to know.

"Okay, Arielle, my l'il *chiquita*," Velez says to the world, "where's my mofo parade, babe?" Velez is taking no prisoners this morning. The tactic is public vivisection, one of Velez's favorites. No doubt Arielle has an army of underlings calling every horse-and-buggy operator in town to haul this parade from *up there* to *down here*. The point of all this? Just to kick the shit out of the suits one more time. That's all.

But it's apparent, isn't it, that Velez is in collusion with suits of *some* stripe.

So . . . we'll be moving. Or we'll be staying and the Arielles and the Sanford Frys will be exiled to maybe Albany, where they can lick their wounds and hide their humiliation for a while. Or forever, like Molly, who never set out to be a boondock radio derelict when he grew up but that's just the way it worked out, and at least Molly had the reptilian sense to know when his ass was kicked. Arielle and our butter-tan station manager Sanford Fry have no such grasp of reality, and their unembarrassable ambition will float them both back to the top sooner or later. History will revise itself, as it always insists on doing: Sanford Fry and Roberto Velez will one day be on the same dais, accepting broadcasting awards—lifetime achievements, philanthropic sainthood, you know the drill—and they'll shake hands for the trade press and Sanford Fry will still break out in a cold sweat to think of how this smart-assed little Puerto Rican bastard once squished him like a cockroach into the tone-on-tone carpet of WRTR in front of all the little people who feared him.

Sanford Fry should by all rights be on the way down here with a loaded gun. Who'd blame him for blowing a hole in Velez? But Fry will wait behind a rock to see who wins before he shows his cards to anybody. As for Arielle, she loses either way. If Velez stays, Arielle will be out of WRTR so fast that the wallpaper will peel off in her wake. If Velez goes, so goes WRTR; Sanford Fry will make sure Arielle hangs for it. The pumper will be teaching low-impact aerobics at a blue-hair spa by Christmas. Just like I told Velez from the very beginning.

Word of the parade fiasco is spreading fast; people are streaming into the Vietnam Veterans Plaza. Maybe every one of our listeners—all one million, three hundred thousand of you, more or less—will stop down here at noon to see for yourselves just how out of control things will get.

There are helicopters overhead. News radio rigs, plus a big clunky Coast Guard job from a New Jersey outpost hovering out over the river. My waterfront platoon boys are freaking—eyes roll heavenward with every chopper pass; there's a general inching toward cover. The East River, which so recently swallowed and then surrendered Lyndon McDonald, has regained its appetite; a spirited chop waves up at the circling helicopters, perhaps mistaking them for the tourist runners that ditch on a regular basis. But the river's optimism is not unfounded in any case—today there'll be food enough for each and every predator.

People are figuring me for an authority, sitting here as I am in feigned tranquillity on the very boards that less than an hour from now will groan under the glorious resurrection of the Standard Band. Hawkers are scoring with American flags in your choice of sizes. Margareta Velez and company are making their way toward the broadcast truck; her shoulders are straight and her head is high, her eyes sparkle with festivity and in the interest of full disclosure I will also report that her body is beginning to take a shape, a terrific little behind in tights peeking out from under a giant white shirt, wearing lacy anklets of the type that figure in kink of the intergenerational variety. She's going to be a beauty, this girl, this young lady who was just one year old and already fatherless when Velez and I hooked up for our first provisional out-of-town tryout.

The audience has reached a critical mass, a couple of hundred and multiplying like Dutch rats, waiting for something weird to happen. These folks too might be under the delusion that a parade is due, and Velez is doing nothing to soften the disappointment. "Do we think the Thunder is going to let our vets down?" he happens to be howling at this very minute. "Hell no! WRTR promised our vets a concert, well, dammit, WRTR's gonna come through! Right Arielle?" The crowd hoots encouragement and now here comes Agent Orange blazing a tangerine comet-tail through the crowd, all of whom get the symbolism because here and there I catch "Hey, that babe must be Agent Orange, whoa!" And pretty soon the whole gang is hooting and whistling and my Sally's grinning from behind her spy shades and now even waving—waving!—to the crowd like *she's* a goddamn rock star. This little girl is going to wind up with an epic headful of herself today . . . ahh, so what? Let her.

I help Sally up onstage. She makes it a point to rub against me; she holds on way after we're sure she's got her balance. She presses into me. Much is in evidence down inside her orange flight suit; she's showing me secretly in front of these hundreds of faces that there's nothing on underneath. If there was ever any distinction in Sally Wallach's mind between rock radio and sex, it's gone forever.

And if I believed in reincarnation, I'd know it was Ellen Larkin standing beside me.

Don't get me wrong; I don't. But what I'm saying is: If I did . . . .

But now Ellen—I mean Sally; Sally has official business to conduct. At her bidding a microphone and a stool materialize: the tools, as everybody knows, of the stand-up trade. Agent Orange waves through wind-bent treetops to the Mitsubishi amphibious assault craft, Velez rips a tape off the air—"Never did like that song"—and launches. "Ladies and gentlemen, while the vets' parade makes its way down here to join us—we hope—let's get this show deal started. So right now, here she is, the glorious Agent Orange herself. You got it, baby."

For a second I think I spy mike fright, but the Bob Hope USO-quality whistling that greets this introduction melts it away in an instant. "So glad you all could come," says Sally. If the crowd's reception is making her blush, she's covering it well; all I can think about right this minute, I must confess, is tearing her out of that jumpsuit at the earliest possible opportunity. ". . .and if you're looking for something to do, you still have time to come down to the Vietnam Veterans Plaza and join. . . ." Like a radio pro, squeezing out every promotional drop. Is this a clue? "Right now, direct from every cable station on your box . . . ." Up climbs a faintly familiar comic, young, not ethnic in any discernible way; Sally plants a kiss on his cheek and then hauls me down the side stairs after her.

I would have had no hand in the course of the morning's events— not even a decent enough vantage point to report what happened—had it not been for the intoxicant effect of live rock radio on Agent Orange, combined with the animal imperatives ignited in me by Sally's moist inflections and the joyously salacious caressments of *the jumpsuit.*

By the time Sally had introduced that first comic to the fast-gathering horde, the morning had already roiled itself an avalanche of momentum. Unconfirmed reports poured in to Raylene McDonald and the Case that limousines were spotted converging by the score on sleepy Madison Square, scooping up unsuspecting handfuls of veterans and spiriting them downtown in our direction. Raylene, meanwhile, floated in some altered plane of consciousness where disbelief fades in and out, juggling shameful hopes and grim obligations behind her nearly defeated eyes. She didn't want me to see her hoping I'm right, that her Lyndon is finally gone. I gave her room.

I'd pretty much resolved to stay out of the way; listen to the music, stick my head in once in a while in case somebody was taking attendance. The Thunder strike team DJ's—Miriam of the Pentagon earrings, regular Mike and Chang the truly inscrutable—had all but chained themselves to their consoles, bantering back and forth, bathing in their own banal little witticisms, just exactly like Velez and Oldham do on the Velez & Oldham Show. Velez played madman, slicing into whatever was taking place at his fancy, raving his pro-vet platitudes. Making short-timer noises; burning bridges. Pelting Sanford Fry with allusions of sexual preference; blistering Arielle with the sixteen-inch guns. Giggling madly. Hauling microphones out of one scab claw and into another like a demented amateur night at the Apollo. Running through a random litany of appreciation and damnation for everyone we've crossed paths with during eleven-and-a-half years at WRTR. Sabotaging commercials with glee. Quintessential Velez; maybe his best ever.

Sure enough, at about eleven-fifteen a cavalcade of limousines began pouring into every available inch of Vietnam Veterans Plaza, careening down like Valkyrie from the FDR, from around the Battery, from the torturous cowpath labyrinth of Wall Street City, nosing each other out for any available spot, some blustering, eyes closed, right through the breach between the now-teeming grandstands, some bouncing up onto curbs, some bouncing into each other, all disgorging a mismatched scraggle of vets and wives and children of vets who squinted around with the look of instant lottery winners. Airborne and Sentry went bounding from one stretch to the next, certain that one of these boats would be hauling Judd Tate. Agent Orange dispatched the strike team DJ's to give every reasonable facsimile of a former fighting man his very own Thunder sweatshirt, free for nothing; sixty- and seventy-year-old men could be seen pulling rock sweatshirts over their ancient pin-encrusted VFW caps and accepting beer from the WRTR hospitality trailer, wherever *that* came from. And just as the waterfront platoon had sworn, into the middle of this sauntered a half dozen assorted hard-case battle junkies all got up in Civil War gear, furnishing us, just in case we needed it, a final layer of surrealist lacquer.

Things were, in short, approaching the nuclear-fueled critical mass for anarchy, whipped along by the crazed ringmaster Velez. Beer vendors and drug peddlers were rushed to the scene. As the dense darkness of noon approached, ties were seen being unknotted, hauled off and tossed into the river. Secretaries poured out of buildings, prepared to break vows. And then, in a ragged phalanx led by Airborne and a beaming Bandanna, the arrival of the legendary Standard Band.

As near as I can recall, a pair of local folkies were spinning out Arlo Guthries and Harry Chapins to a crowd increasingly more in the mood for Mardi Gras or a Haitian election when word began to spread that Judd and the boys had beached. Airborne and his troop had evidently appointed themselves the band's bodyguards, like Hell's Angels at Altamont back in the days when Judd Tate was royalty. Grunt was dispatched to seek out Agent Orange, who the boys had sensibly decided was the only Thunderer worth a collective damn. Sally leapt with glee and allowed herself to be swallowed whole by the leather and camou-flage-bedizened troop lumbering its way through the standers and squatters and on toward the stage. I climbed up onto the roof of the Thunder battlewagon, from where I could observe the progress of this delirious pocket of lost youth, an undulating, ugly brown lily pad, Sally riding high in their midst, their adopted blazing orange blossom.

The folkies knew when they were licked. They grinned and waved their acoustic guitars. The river wind blew one's granny glasses clear off his nose and into the crowd. No one noticed.

The outlaw roadie battalion crawled out of the woodwork instantly, helping Judd and his three boys up onto the stage, plugging them in, shaking hands, hoping to be remembered. I wasn't close enough to tell you what transpired among the members of the Standard Band beyond an initial floor-walking numbness at the sheer unlikelihood of this time-warp resurrection. But it must be like riding a bike, this rock business, because pretty soon the usual sauntering and stomping and tuning and drum-thumping, this ritual prelude, right down to the mandatory passing of beer bottles and a joint in full view of the world, kicked itself in as naturally as if more than twenty years of descendence and disillusionment and banishment from the music heart, the idolatry dissolved, had only been a weird vision stewed up by a tab of nasty acid after last night's gig. Here we are. Right where we belong. And there *they* are, down there, all of 'em, right where they're supposed to be; right where we remember 'em.

Sally was out front, then, drawing the crush of celebrants to her, glowing when the spots, now swaying and heaving ominously in the gathering storm, managed to hit her. Sally, waving her arms in a futile quieting gesture that only stoked the roar, now peeled off her sunglasses to give the crowd a good look at her, the strapped-up hair and the splendid unbuckled body thrust out into the maelstrom like a lightning rod, like she may possibly have been imagining just two nights ago, alone, with only me and the outriders of the waterfront platoon for an audience, backlit by that one safety light. Like that night, the river wind now caresses and exhalts her, but today she's scaling far loftier heights: it's the ultimate rush, coming from all those eyes down there—*drinking me in from just a safe enough distance, but I can feel what they're thinking: if only they had the chance, every single one of them would die for the chance to fuck me. So this is what gets Kendall off.* Did I imagine that Sally, up there introducing Judd Tate and Keith Bollinger and Fringe Johnson and Michael James Johnson, was sucking all this into her veins and her sinuses, or am I projecting Ellen Larkin, my first near-fatal brush with addiction, on her again? You think so, huh? Wait.

Sally and Velez did a mini-banter from the stage to our broadcast booth roof, where Velez had now joined me with a hand-held mike. As Sally vamped and hollered back and forth across the plaza with Velez, my partner gave me the evil eyebrow and the circled-finger poke sign; I declined comment but fucking Velez knows all. Velez hollered a couple of applause lines for the benefit of the vets who by now had spread out around the plaza; the older, wiser ones had already fled. When it looked like the Standard Band was ready, Velez stuck the mike in my face and said, "Looks like this is it for the Velez & Oldham Show, Coolie. Any last words?" I looked at my partner Velez, into the black eyes that revealed nothing. He looked back long enough to confirm the fact: this really *was* it. Velez & Oldham was history, as of right now.

Velez pulled back the mike, shouted a goodbye to the plazaful of fans and strangers and to one-point-three million of you, more or less, and signed us off with, "Orange, it's yours, *chiquita.*"

"Right now, ladies and gentlemen, and especially all you vets—we love you!—and everybody out there in WRTR land, here they are: the Standard Band!" Those would be Sally's last words in this particular spotlight; a couple of drum bashes you'd all recognize from oldies shows and that wall came tumbling down in all its ear-punishing glory, flooding the plaza and the canyon beyond with passionate sonic time travel. The crowd, tiny by old-time Standard Band standards but more people than these guys had seen in very many years, held up their end of the bargain, clapping and fist-thrusting and, as darkness congealed and the temperature dove minute by minute, even waving their Ronson butanes over their heads in homage.

It was then that Raylene McDonald scrambled up with an armload of champagne bottles and plastic cups. She crawled over to me and hugged me hard from behind; I thought I felt wet smear my cheek but when she let go and I turned to her, her eyes and her conscience looked clear. We drank champagne while Velez waved to his minions below and I watched Sally Wallach make her slow, glowing way across the plaza toward us.

What has stayed with me is this last half hour or so of the real, old Velez, up on the roof of the Thunder mobile broadcast booth, overlooking the windswept waving crowd, listening absently to Judd Tate and the Standard Band, being observed and envied by faces in the windows up under the clouds, guzzling champagne with me and Raylene McDonald.

Velez, it turned out, had, as we suspected, been in conference with henchpeople indentured to Sally Wallach's old man.

"Television, Coolie."

So.

". . .hadda have our meetings at night, 'cause E. P.'s lawyers sleep in their coffins during the day. . . ." Velez spins his tale of clandestine Hollywood deal-making. "This woman—takin' care of me, you know, showin' me around, blonde maybe six, seven feet tall, got on this flower print dress makes you want to stretch her out an' have a picnic all over her. . . ." Velez waves to his fans below and pontificates at Raylene and me. "This is the perfect woman—someone with no romantic illusions at all; somebody I can go out with at night to pick up chicks, and who'll know how to work the video camera when we all get home, and who'll cook everybody a champagne breakfast before I kick 'em all out. And my babysitter for the weekend, she doesn't even get upset when I tell her this—I think she kinda likes the idea. . . ." Raylene has tuned out by now.

"Then she asks me if I have herpes. Ho ho. In this day and age, she's worried about *herpes*? I says, 'Whaddaya, kiddin'? Course I have herpes! I'd be embarrassed *not* to have herpes!'"

But in the middle of this cultural orientation, some business must have found time to transpire. I hope I haven't represented Velez's existence as haphazard, random, arbitrary—oh no; it's just that it seems to lurch from inconsequential farting around to redline spikes the same way New York changes from downtown Beirut into Oz and back again every twenty paces and this power weekend appeared to have been no exception, because as I watched Sally Wallach picked her enticing way through the crowd toward us Velez wrapped up his monologue with the announcement that he signed that very night somewhere over the nation's snoozing heartland on the coast-to-coast redeye a personal-services contract with E. P. Wallach with an eye to TV superstardom. "Late night, variety," Velez was saying as I eased away to join my Sally, to sneak away for a secret deal of my own. "Studio band, comics, video, fluffers like that peachtree in the flower dress, El Lay at my feet, the whole mofo, man—"

Did I figure into this West Coast assault? There'd be time enough to find out, I figured; for now the wind just about blew me off the roof into my Sally's arms and off toward the Velezmobile like some giant invisible croupier's stick sweeping us out of Velez's field of radiation and on to a mad, half-dressed, stardusted coupling, sweet young Sally on velvet, *the jumpsuit* parted to the crotch and half shed for serviceable access, don't kick over the decanters, babe—such were the mind-bending phantasms smoking out of my ears at the moment Margareta Velez swung into view.

How did I get off the roof and into Sally's flushed embrace? Who was leading whom away from the WRTR broadcast booth and toward the Velezmobile? Was I the one who decided to capitalize on the irresistible craving to do each other in a frenzied glut of shared celebrity? These details are too trivial to occupy us now; the details to come all but consume them. Leave it this way: Sally Wallach and I were making our way with no small urgency toward the black-windowed sanctuary of the Velezmobile to re-enact a treasured rock sacrament at the very moment when Margareta Velez and her friends approached from beside the broadcast rig. I stopped and reached out for her when suddenly she looked beyond me with uncomprehending eyes; I turned with her to see a black-and-way-too-chrome Mercedes back in within yards of us and an almost comically terrified Nicolo Velez launch himself from the back door. I looked up; Velez was oblivious.

I stepped toward him. Why? I don't know. But he pushed by me. "Look out, man. Gotta see my brother." He stank of fear; sweat putrified the air around him. Now Velez looked down and began to take things in.

"Hey, Roberto, need to talk to you." Choking throat.

"Get outa here, punk, before I come down there and whip your ass." Did Velez know about Nicolo's latest plundering of Washington Heights' humble *Casa Velez*? I know I didn't tell him. Who could have? No.

"Hey look, man. I need your help real bad. No bullshit, bro."

Velez peered down. "What you need?"

"Money."

"You need money? Sure. How much you need?"

Nicolo Velez was almost ready to throw out a figure before the venom from his brother's eyes hit his blood stream. New sweat beaded. "Look, man—"

"Fuck off, crackhead."

"I'm beggin'—"

"Away," Velez said quietly, and took a sip of champagne. Nicolo backed slowly away, toward the open rear door of the blacked-up Mercedes. He turned and lifted hands and shoulders in petrified, penitent submission.

Judd Tate and the Standard Band pounded around us. Real thunder rolled in above us. When the inside of the Mercedes lit up, we didn't hear a thing.

I didn't exactly see what happened, except for the puffing out of the back of Nicolo Velez's shirt, and then that one tiny pinkish explosion about halfway down Nicolo's back, the one that managed to find its way clear through the monkeyishly recoiling Nicolo with just enough resistance that by the time it got to me it was just about out of gas; just enough to wedge itself a half-inch into the outside of my thigh. Then I was down, not from my wound, which I didn't even *notice*, but from the dead-flying weight of the late Nicolo Velez—former aspiring street entrepreneur, suddenly on the catching end of an occupational hazard. We made a pile of ourselves: Sally on the bottom, me, and Nicolo on top, leaking all over us with the rank smell of seeping innards . . . and then, the thing I least expected to hear on the occasion of my being shot: horse hooves.

As for the rest of the details, you know as much as I do. On Channel Seven's tape you can catch a momentary glimpse of the pimped-up black Mercedes snaking and squealing through the mess of limousines, fishtailing out toward Water Street. But that's all from Channel Seven, folks, because on Channel Two's tape you can see a police car crunch the Channel Seven truck; can see the minicam flying through the patrol car's windshield. The horses under the mounted cops, finding themselves in a hysterical swarm of stampeding humanity, lost their own composure as their masters wrestled them in toward the center of the shooting—the vicinity of me and Sally and dead Nicolo and careening, screaming strangers; for myself, from pavement level, I couldn't help flashing for a deranged instant on the Ayatollah's funeral but I didn't have the luxury of dwelling on historical curiosity because Sally was pulling me out from under Nicolo—how did Sally get out from under *me?*—and toward the Thunder broadcast trailer; the horse hooves so loud in my ears, all I needed was to get trampled by eighteen-hundred pounds of peace-keeping horseflesh, but somehow we made it *under* the booth, wedged in behind the rear tire and the little tin stairway. It was then that we, my panting, wide-eyed Sally and I, became aware of the blood on my pants, blood that looked somehow more insistent than the blood all over the rest of me—Nicolo's blood—a stain still modestly spreading, I guess, instead of the rest, dabbed and blotted-looking. I smiled to reassure Sally, which I suppose she took as the onset of delirium and maybe shock; I think I heard her whisper "Jiminy fucking Crickets!" and there she left me to pinch closed my leaking thigh and hug the deck.

It may have been a minute or two—no more—before people started to pile out of the Mitsubishi. I made my move and gradually hauled myself to a seat on the booth steps. Judd Tate and the Standard Band were of course way out of the sound range of automatic gunfire and so played on, even as the crowd began to peel, layer by scrambling layer, away from the shivering stage. There was an apocalypse-soundtrack quality to the Standard Band's earpump, massaged and spindled around the melee by a wind that by now was issuing final warnings. I became aware of Enginette Casey standing beside me with a hand-held mike in her fist; "You're bleeding," she informed me coolly, "and you're on live in five . . . ." She handed me the mike and leapt back into the trailer and one second later I saw four Casey fingers become three out through the window.

What could I say? "There's been a shooting. . . ." This I must have repeated a half-dozen times before it occurred to me that aside from the identity of the target—hey, Raylene, finally some druggies who can hit what they're aiming at!—I didn't know much. But wait—I'm an accredited newsman; okay, time to investigate. "There's been a shooting down here at Vietnam Veterans Plaza, a young man"—should I name names? I *have to* name names; it's my job—"a young man named Nicolo Velez has been shot and seriously killed—" Listening to myself on five-second cranium echo, I froze and looked back at Casey who gave me the 'fuck it, keep going' signal; ". . .one other injury that I know of—me—it's not serious, oh look, the bullet just fell out, no, I swear, fell right out, nothing to worry about. . . ." And then I was up and wandering and blathering as far as my microphone tether would let me.

More signals from Casey: hands cupped in prayer? Were things that desperate—oh, yeah, the wind, okay; I shielded my mike as best I could from the squall. No sign of Sally Wallach. The horses have moved off. Sirens everywhere now, but not much police action yet; not too many cars going anywhere. And here we have Nicolo Velez, punctured, saturated shirtfront, bloodsoaked pants, curiously unattended—the police either haven't spotted him yet or figure he's not going anywhere, so what's the hurry? "The crowd," I remember observing in what must have sounded weirdly catatonic, "doesn't know whether to run or stay and gape." The gunplay seemed over; that much was clear. And then a ring of observers, a gaggle of my fellow accredited journalists elbowing for space with the common citizenry anxious for an eyeful of gore, closed in on me, looking at me, looking at the blood, wondering God knew what—that a delirious almost dead guy had commandeered the Thunder? A terrorist, perhaps, making demands? Did this have anything to do with Pan Am 103? Was I crazy and, more important, was I armed?

I moved—strolled, really—past Nicolo Velez, in no definite direction, in search of nothing in particular; a blood-spackled ringmaster encircled by masks of fascination and horror. People standing, kneeling, pointing cameras. Minicams already rolling, tiny piercing floodlights teeming in from the darkness, Judd Tate whining down from the stratosphere; I tried to concentrate, to relay a logical sequence of observations but, well, *you* know what came out—you saw it on TV every goddamn night for a week.

I snuck a peek at the Case. She bobbed her head out around the circle; I didn't get it, and meanwhile a helicopter descended, compressing dust and dankness in on the scene, obliterating sound, stirring great plumes of city crud out and upward on all sides. I stopped talking. To my right, the cops had now begun staking out the territory where the Mercedes gunship had slid in and out of the firebase perimeter. At my feet, a congealing puddle with Nicolo Velez in the middle. My eye followed the line of fire beyond where Sally and I and Nicolo had piled up. Sitting on the pavement, leaning against the front wheel of the Thunder rover, surrounded by her horror-stricken uptown daytrippers, was Margareta Velez, an oozing black hole where her left eye used to be.

# 24

PEOPLE would have stayed around all afternoon. As it was, plenty of closet ghouls were willing to take a drenching for a pulse-quickening whiff of spectacle. It was only after the boys in blue threw a couple of plastic sheets over Nicolo and Margareta that the fun drained out of our Veterans Day celebration.

After that, it didn't take long for the Vietnam Veterans Plaza to flush itself out. My newscast had ended mid-sentence when I sighted Margareta, sitting there, sort of expectantly it looked at first, just like everybody else squeezing in for a view of Nicolo. I'm not sure if her friends had even realized what had happened until I froze, gaping, dumb. Not ready to believe. There wasn't that much blood; maybe it's not—? Then everybody looked, and the back of Margareta's head. . . .

By the time it occurred to me to check the roof of the radio roadster, nobody was there; Velez had vanished. Raylene had climbed down too, taking charge inside, bustling Chang and Miriam and Regular Mike back out through the looking glass into real life, cranking things hastily back uptown to the sanctuary of Too Tall Jones once it became apparent, I guess, that neither I nor anybody else down here could continue; reeling me in, taking my microphone, pulling me up into the booth. Buttoning up from the wind and, now, the downslaught of rain. Taking care of business.

It may have been fifteen minutes or so before Detective Sergeant Peter Corollo scrambled up into the Thunder booth for a chat.

Did I know the deceased? Did I see what happened? Have a seat, officer. Oh, boy, have you come to the right place.

But Corollo the Cop noticed right away a minor detail I'd forgotten in the aftershock: I'd been shot. Well, yeah, but a junior-varsity battlescar at best, a nick, I tried to tell him. "Fuhgetaboudit," Corollo overruled; we'd talk on the way to the hospital.

What, I wondered, had become of Velez?

Outside, the thousands had vaporized. The stage was bare; the speakers abandoned to the roiling thunder revue. The limo squadron had scrambled; stranded vets—we said we'd get 'em here, we didn't say we'd get 'em *outa* here—could be seen fleeing the Plaza in disarray. Soaked seatboards were already working their way loose from their grandstand architecture; crude aerodynamics contemplating lethal flight. News vans stood by, awaiting the arrival of their first-string correspondents to contemplate the corpses. Van-top dishes and antennas swiveled like giant lances and shields—champion of the mechanized joust getting the ooziest gore shots.

The Velezmobile sat in confused solitude right where it had been moments—*moments!*—before as Agent Orange and I, temples pounding and assorted glands distending, had prepared to tuck ourselves into its secluded embrace for some furtive shenanigans; the windshield wipers were on now, doing their duty, trying to ignore the steaming indignity left on the car's hood right next to the Cadillac emblem by a backed-up and intestinally distressed police mount. Corollo the Cop was angling me with some persistence toward an EMS truck but I had to check on Velez.

Inside was nobody but the driver. No Velez. No Sally. No sign. No instructions. I told the driver to follow me to the hospital. "Your name Velez?" he asked.

"Uh uh. I'm—"

"Then take a walk, pal."

From inside the EMS ambulance I looked back. Two blue puddly plastic lumps; one mobile radio station, motor running, escape imminent. A hunkered circling of officialdom, press-wise and cop-wise. Angry reverb from the stage canopy, well on its way to self-mutilation. A furious gust rose up from the river just then and engulfed the plaza in sound and darkness; I watched, stupefied, as the truculent gale tore Margareta Velez's blue plastic comforter from her and hoisted it high into the air, cartwheeling it up over the Mitsubishi and away toward the tent city at the foot of the Memorial Wall, finally snagging it high up on the Wall's corner, plastering it profanely over the glass iridescence.

Just before Corollo the Cop swung the door in on us, I caught a last brief look at Margareta Velez, still sitting up against the wheel, a tiny blood trickle no bigger than a tear stain down her cheek, looking after me with her one eye, wondering where I was going and why she couldn't come too.

Even before I was discharged from the hardly-worth-treatment ward of NYU Medical Center, evidence had begun to accumulate that a certain primal reordering was underway in the outside world.

"So this kid, this Nicolo, he's Roberto Velez's kid brother?" Corollo the Cop was making an effort to complete his dossier under the clamor of reporters and TV reptiles who'd tailed us up the FDR to this place. Before long, Corollo was relegated to taking turns with my accredited-journalist colleagues wedging questions in on me. If I were him I'd have locked them all in a giant vat full of honey and fire ants but Corollo didn't seem to mind, and probably figured to kill two birds: let 'em all in here now, and he might get off without a press conference rerun later on.

"Yeah," I said. "Velez's brother."

"How 'bout the little girl?"

How about her.

The press, as you saw for yourself, had a Richter-scale orgasm when I identified the second decedent.

Funny. I had stopped wondering where Velez had got to.

A double-jointed Pakistani medicine man was busying himself slathering my thigh with something from the home country, milked, it felt, from the fangs of a fugitive from the pre-Cambrian-rainforest corner of hell. My reaction accounts for that beeped-out audio moment on the news that night and the inexplicable chorus of laughter that followed. I gave my self-censored account over and over. No mention of Agent Orange, of course. No revelations for public consumption about the abortive pharmaceutical career of Nicolo Velez. Nope, didn't see the license plate. Yep, Mercedes. What kind? How do I know?—the big pimped-up kind. No, nobody got out. Shots from the rear gun turret. *Clack-clack-clack.* Yeah. Just like that: *clack-clack-clack.* Real fast. What kind of gun? How the hell . . . don't ask me; check with the National Rifle Association, Washington Heights Chapter. Well, no, I don't *know;* I just mean that's where the Velez family lives. No, not Roberto. His Mom and—well, now just his Mom and another kid brother. That's all.

None of which gave me much time to plan my next move, which turned out not to matter because just as this Pakistani guy was waving an ostrich feather over my numb bandaged thigh and appealing to the prophet on my behalf, in marches the one person I most hoped and even, irrationally, expected to see: Sally Wallach. Accompanied by probably the last person I expected to see: her old man. E. P. Wallach. In the flesh. Their mini-entourage I took to be heavily armed corporate security types; some cold hip-checking quickly cleared a space for E. P. and Agent Orange.

So guess what Sally has told her old man. "Son," he says to me, "I understand you saved my daughter's life today."

E. P. Wallach is a trim, athletic type; if you've seen him on TV you'd say he's shorter than you expected. He has a big-money tan. He has cufflinks. His cologne comes from the same family of creatures that my coagulant thigh-balm does; this I can tell from the remarkable similarity of their effects on the central nervous system. We live in a world where a single animal can kill you, heal you and make you smell good, so no more demands for proof of God's existence.

There was blood on Sally's jumpsuit; deep amber on reflector orange. Maybe mine, who knows, but probably Nicolo's—I mean, after all, he did donate plenty more than I did to the afternoon's festivities. But the stains, darkening one zippered breast pocket and most of Sally's lap, no doubt lent grim immediacy to whatever story Sally had shoveled onto her father's plate on my behalf, and gave the minicamsters jammed into this room a perfect excuse to zoom in on Sally's deeply revealed bosom for the evening news.

Corollo leaned in. "That true? You save this girl's life?"

"Too early to tell," I told Corollo.

Corollo snuck a peek. "Great-lookin' chick," he whispered to me.

"Well. Detective school wasn't a total waste," I said; fortunately, Corollo just grinned.

After that, Corollo the Cop and I pretty much let E. P. Wallach commandeer things for the time being, and E. P. seemed to be having a splendid time chatting with the press until somebody said, "How does this affect Roberto Velez's status at your radio station?" Which stopped E. P. cold for a strobe-flash; I could *hear* microelectronic gates popping and slamming frantically behind E. P. Wallach's eyes. If Velez's story on the Mitsubishi roof was true, then E. P. Wallach was the proud new owner of his own personal drug-smeared celebrity. I could see the *Daily News* headlines already: *Velez's Druggie Bro Bumped* and *Did Rockin' Roberto Doublecross The Mob?* I could read on the jagged graph-line of E. P.'s eyebrows the weight of catastrophe that just may have landed on my former partner. I could still hear Velez: "Television, Coolie."

But then Corollo was tapping my shoulder. "Anything else?"

No, I can't think of anything. "What happens now?" I whispered to Corollo. "You go catch the bad guys?"

Eyes went skyward; head sagged. "We can look for the car. We can talk to people in Velez's neighborhood, who'll tell us to go shit in our hats. Maybe someday we bust some mook and maybe he gives these guys up to save his own ass. It happens. For all I know, the guy responsible for this might already be in the can."

"Huh?"

"Sure," said Corollo, tucking away his notepad. "Lotta drug operations these days run right out of the Rikers Island slam—just a dime away from retail franchisees when they fuck up."

What else happened at the hospital? I don't remember. One minute everybody in the world was in this patching-up room with me; the next minute it was me and the Pakistani, who I suspect had extramedical intentions. I do recall the leave-taking of E. P. Wallach, who said, "I'll want to talk to you later, young man," and his daughter, who mouthed, "Me too, young man," so her father wouldn't catch it. E. P.'s Brooks Brothers prætorians engineered E. P.'s getaway out without firing a single shot that I could hear. The posse of journalists figured that they'd about wrung me dry by then but their straggling departure featured a peculiar chorus: congratulations. For me. And not for getting in the way of a used bullet.

Downstairs—yes, I got my wheelchair ride—waiting for me was Raylene McDonald. "Why didn't you come up?"

"Oh, I did," said Raylene. "I had enough crowds for one day."

I hoisted myself out of the chair and batted my eyelashes goodbye to my personal Pakistani fakir. "So?" I asked Raylene, "what was the final score?"

"Wasn't my turn to keep score."

Outside, the ugly underside of autumn had bellyflopped all over Manhattan. We waved Veterans Day greetings to blind taxi drivers fleeing up First Avenue. Finally, a pullover.

"Where you goin'?"

"Washington Heights," I said.

"Yeah?" cabbie said. "Have a good trip."

"Hold on—" Raylene began, but the cabbie bit her off. "Hey, nothin' racial, lady; I wouldn't take you two to Washington Heights even if you was *both* white."

Even as I warmed to the battle, Raylene shimmied past me and waved down another cab, and in a minute we were cruising uptown. "I'll drop you," I said.

"Where are you going?" Raylene asked, before the obvious registered. "Want company?"

Thanks, Raylene. But no. Immaculata Velez will not be in the mood to entertain, despite the new vacancies at her dinner table.

I heard them halfway up the stairs.

"Don't wanna hear you talk about your brother that way!"

"Mom—"

"No. No more. You had the chance to leave here, Roberto. I love you an' I'm happy for you. Nicholas din't have the chance. Never had the chance."

"Why do you make excuses for him, Mom? Huh? *Momma!* Momma, come on. You know that kid was nothing but—"

"I know he's your blood an' my blood an' Jesus doesn't care—"

"Oh wait, please, how 'bout we give Jesus a break just this once an' leave him outa this" and then a crack of palm on cheek. This I heard from the landing below; the creaking would have given me away if I'd climbed any higher. So I crouched and listened. And after a little more of the same I heard this: "Will you at least do what I been asking you to do for years, Momma—get outa here? Look: you take Margareta. . . ."

Take Margareta. He didn't know. Velez must've freaked and bolted so fast after Nicolo went down that he never even saw Margareta sitting there against the tire, down below his swinging lizard boots.

So I am the messenger again. The bearer of tidings. Here I am: the *newsman*.


The rains have come.

It was hard to tell where afternoon had left off and night had begun. The rain had settled into dismal permanence. Such was my own state of mind that I had actually wandered alone around the neighborhood of Immaculata Velez looking for a cab to effect my escape but that wouldn't have been an easy proposition on the best day of the year; pretty soon I found myself ducking down into the subway, picking my way over the unlucky and the malignant, puffing up some fake invincibility, squinting as menacingly as I dared from side to side. And so it was— not inattention, no accident, the tracks just happened to point there— that I found myself at nightfall back in Vietnam Veterans Plaza, Pakistani spirit-serum burning a putrid hole in my leg and fairly soaked through but otherwise spookily placid, considering.

It is so dark now that you couldn't tell how far the afternoon had progressed; the sky is a grisly pallid slate heaving ponderous sheets of water and, I swear, even a little sleet across the deserted Vietnam Veterans Plaza. The rain comes and goes but the wind, whimsical and malicious, barrels through our little copse as relentlessly as age.

So quickly had the weather descended that the temporary architecture down here sits in bludgeoned abandonment: the stands, here and there adorned with soggy lumps of stuff forsaken by panicky spectators in their flight; the stage, from whose solitary shelter I can see the whip-ping yellow police tape—*crime scene, do not cross*—circling painted white Keith Haring human outlines on the pavement just feet away from where the Thunder broadcast van was anchored hours ago. But now, it's just me and the pathetically tattered remnants of the canvas vaulting above the stage, snapping like the report of gunfire out into the leaden afternoon—a sky too treacherous even for Colonel Elmo, whose lethal 20-millimeter ground-cover intercession we could have used today.

Who's left? I see light in the tents along the base of the Memorial Wall. Diffident orange hurricane lamp light, blue sterno cooking light, but enough to make its way into and up through the Wall's green iri-descence, hearthlike; a warmth and transient humanity that the Wall's designer couldn't have had in mind. The boys—Sentry, Bandanna, Grunt, Airborne and their comrades—have battened down for the night. Inside the canvas they lay, listening to nature's comforting fury thump-ing over and around them, smelling the coffee, nursing the beer and sucking what's left of their hash up into the recesses, anesthetizing the events of the afternoon and retreating into their worn and storied months waiting out the monsoon nights in dugouts and tents on the banks of the mighty Mekong.

Sentry and the Grunt were asleep; a walled-in comatosis apparently way beyond reach of all but the most powerful antitoxins. Airborne worked quietly with an oilrag, rolling and packing each artifact from his 'Namorobilia collection. As for Bandanna, he was making notes in an unlined leather-bound book with a beautiful, almost feminine handwrit-ing. He seemed glad to see me, if just for news of Agent Orange.

"We got to her right after the shootin' started," Bandanna said. "Headed for Judd'n the boys but no time, y'know, an' 'sides they was plenny'a cops 'round the stage. We just grabs the little girl an' hustles her down behin' the wall here, 'til, y'know. . . ."

I knew. Or hadn't, but I did now. Just then Airborne looked up from his labors and inspected my mottled pantleg. "The hell happened to you, man?" And while I aw-shucks'd myself through an accurately self-effacing account of the gunplay, I privately indulged myself in the notion that perhaps, a few decades late, I may in a small, accidental way have earned the momentary comradeship of men like these, in service to a cause at least as noble as theirs.

"Where you guys going?" I asked.

Airborne looked up from his packing. "Vets' convention. Down to Fort Myers. Ever' year." He looked from Bandanna to me and back again. "Not much shootin' in Fort Myers. 'Cept gator season. Which this ain't."

Outside, I watched the rain dance around the painted outlines of Nicolo and Margareta Velez until it got too dark to make them out from the ruins of the very stage where Sally Wallach had done her cryptostrip to intoxicated acclaim; where Judd Tate and the Standard Band had somehow resurrected their magic, if just for one no-account *touristo* afternoon.

Mrs. McMichael ran a bath and dumped in handfuls of salts for which she credited the Little People; they did not entirely disagree with the Pakistani potion, though, and pretty soon something encouragingly scaly began to take shape over my wound. Mrs. McMichael, meanwhile, bounced around the apartment with a breathless account of the breathless accounts she'd been watching on television all day.

"What'd they say on the radio?" was what I wanted to know.

"Dennis. You know I never listen to that radio station of yours."

Mrs. McMichael's views on rock remain as uncompromising as ever. If I weren't such a transparent fraud of a rock 'n roller, she'd have kept plenty more distance between us all these years, I have no doubt.

Of a whole tape's worth of phone messages, I returned one.

"Hi, Dad."

There was a touching dollop of relief in Buddy Oldham's voice. "Heard this wild story . . . you all right? Is Roberto okay?" Buddy has always liked my partner; liked the way we'd pal him around and not treat him like somebody's old man.

"Yeah, Dad, we're okay." I figured I'd spare him the details for now. But Buddy seemed to want to talk. Okay. "You coming to town?" I asked.

"Ahh," Buddy said, "New deal. No more dragging my butt all over the world—"

"You didn't retire—?"

"Nah. Got promoted, sort of. Gonna spend my time in Washington now."

"Doing what?"

"Buying senators lunch, mostly."

"Get out. A *lobbyist?*"

This cudgelled Buddy, but just for a minute. "Well, yeah. I guess you could say that."

"There go all the frequent flyer miles," was about all I could come up with.

"I could already go to Mars free," Buddy said.

And then I had the otherworldly impulse to ask Buddy, How's Mom? Natural as that, it would have come out: How's Mom? She change her mind about things yet, Dad?

Buddy might have gotten a kick out of that. No more international gunrunning; more time to keep Elizabeth Reilly company. Buddy could have made anyone else happy. Still could. By anybody's lights Buddy is a dead-cool guy for a sixty-something-year-old former defense-indus-try pimp—his words during an outing last year with me and Velez, not mine.

"You moving to Chevy Chase, Pop? Gonna start partying with Ted Kennedy?" But you and I both know that Buddy isn't moving anywhere now. After all these years in Perpetual Help Cemetery, Elizabeth Reilly Oldham is far too set in her ways.

I awakened well after midnight; the rain had gone but vapor-breath cold had seeped in from the door to Jane Oldham's rooftop fort and spread itself out around me. Over my head, one of Jane's cockroach friends was making solitary dinner plans; even these creatures can't help missing Jane when she's not around. This lad's aimless prowling seemed to foreshadow the onset of a general dispiriting malaise; a bleak realization, like Peter Pan before him, that Never Never Land might soon have seen the last of Jane Courtenay Oldham. This guy has been poking around in my mail, no doubt, and has spread the word around the neighborhood that the day of reckoning with Jane's mom is drawing ominously nigh. The next time we see New York's number one junior killshot, they and I fear, she'll be allergic to fairy dust.

With the terrifying dislocation of time on my hands, I dressed and hit the street. Steam issued from streetlights and sorrow-wrinkles and manhole covers. The sudden closing-in, the old mysteries just out of reach, the tip-toeing through snoozing peril, somehow brought me up and out and crackling; I could hear everything, from behind every window, under the sidewalk, the conversations in front of radios where Adrian Boe would have kissed everyone goodnight by now and left them, all of them, to the longest hours. I loved it. I wanted never to sleep again.

Around a shady corner and into an unfamiliar fan of pink light, deepening the crevices underfoot. Twenty-foot-high white Southern-plantation-style columns flank the gaping grill of an old white Cadillac grinning maniacally down at me from above the front door. A Tennessee license plate glowed in the dark. Music wailed low from inside. A sign with the legend *Graceland* encircled in guitar-shaped pink neon.

Inside was a welter of replica detritus from what I took to be the King's movie sets: the jailhouse, the beach, et cetera. The crowd—no, the smattering—huddled and drank and smoked and vogued Fifties.

Bennie was leaning over the bar, deep in conversation with two youngsters in ponytails and torn fishnet stockings and underpants-length skirts. Above Bennie, above the bar, dominating the proceedings, sat a giant glass sarcophagus, glowing pale blue from inside, containing the Vegas-satin-clad remains of Elvis Presley.

"Can't take your eyes off it, can ya?" Bennie said triumphantly. *"Graceland.* Get it?"

"Business looks like it kinda sucks," I pointed out to Bennie.

"Well, yeah, people sorta gave up on you an' Velez showin' up. By the way, hear you got shot." Bennie's bluebird companions took some small notice of this; it was, from their perch, an evening that could only be redeemed by a blush of violence.

Bennie hit a blender and soon enough a row of frosty deals appeared in tall glasses, each imprinted with the image of a mausoleum marked 'Graceland.' Above us lay Elvis, in his batwing collared, sequined jumpsuit. He looked cool, unperturbed. The burdens of the world were clearly all behind him. Have I mentioned that Bennie is, in his own small, inconsequential way, a social-engineering genius? If Bennie were in Moscow, he'd steal what's left of Lenin and build a club around him.

A television at the end of the bar kept clicking between MTV, British underground hour, I think, and the cable porn station. Women short on career alternatives worked out on their meaty breasts and invited you to call and chat. Eight bucks for the first minute; *please, now, I can't wait you make me so hot.*

"You ain't gonna believe," Bennie seemed to be saying over and over, and finally I wrenched myself to attention.

"What? What?"

". . .who was in here tonight. Marnie!"

Who?

Meanwhile, "Can we call?" one of the young girls at the bar asked Bennie, and only then did I figure out that they were the ones in command of the TV remote control. Bennie made a face, you know how

Bennie does, but one put her hand on his hand and puckered up to his face and said, "Please, now, I can't wait, I'm so hot," far more convincingly than anything we'd seen on the tube; Bennie caught his breath and fetched a cordless from under the bar. "This is on your tab, girl," Bennie tried, but the girl sighed her theatrical aphrodisia and said, "Bennie, we told you we don't have any money," and Bennie surrendered without further resistance.

Elvis Presley, meanwhile, seemed to have shifted ever so slightly in his glass tomb. I studied the body. No movement at all. He didn't look bad in there, I must report, but then neither does Lenin from far enough away, I hear.

"You rip off Madame Toussaud?" I asked Bennie.

"Better," Bennie said. And then, "So, c'mon! You remember Marnie! Living with me, sort of, when we was at that blue-Margarita place on Broadway?"

Ah yes. "Went back to school, you said."

Bennie snorted the snort of the older and wiser. "I told her, didn't I? Didn't I? Wanted to be a million-dollar Wall Street asshole? I told her."

"She coming to work for you?" Beside me, the two ponytails had by now made direct contact with representatives of the psychosexual netherworld; they pulled the phone back and forth and pretty soon I heard one say, "Ooooh, yuck," under spellbound eyes.

"Work here? Nah. Too much pressure on the relationship. She learned her lesson. Anyhow, she's in acting classes and dancing classes and everything. Takes up all her time."

"Sounds expensive," I said.

"This place takes off, I can handle it." *You* can handle it? Goddamn it, Bennie. But I kept my mouth shut.

Beside me, girl one to girl two, this: "Try another one. See? I told you we can do this. They must make some good bucks! Here, here: try this one." Dialing. "What? Huh? Wait—wait." To her companion: "Shit! She says we need a credit card. Bennie!"

"No way," said Bennie, who might have felt differently had it not been for the return of his beloved Marnie, who for all I know might have ditched the fast track even without a sureshot sucker like Bennie wallowing in the wings. Okay, I'm the first to impute manipulation to the likes of Marnie the Method waitress, or Ms. Elite, as another classic example of the crafty New Age ingénue. And what, you may have been wondering, had become of Ms. Elite, last heard from laboring under reflectors on an Aruba beach in a peanut-oil froth? As I sat under the corpse of Elvis Presley, eavesdropping without shame on two aspiring young phone whores with Bennie here—Bennie the delusional romantic, whose life, like more than a few in this company of fugitives, pirouettes on one trivial fucking epiphany after another—I have to confess that I've been wondering exactly the same thing.

Ms. Elite—Kansas Kendall just Kendall of the killingly beautiful eyes—fronts, I suspect, an impenetrable wall of contrivance, even giving all possible benefits of doubt. My own suspicion is that in Kendall's case the nipples are not, as Velez would have us believe, the window to a woman's soul; that behind her manifest genetic serendipity there is cold-blooded calculation and not just ethereal hyperconsciousness gliding upon halcyon winds.

Ah, but Ms. Elite would have to wait to be taken account of, if indeed she turned up at all after what has transpired. All depended, it seemed obvious to me, on what happened to my partner Velez now. E. P. Wallach, for one, must already be calling in his 'sell' orders on his Velez stock—*dump it all, get rid of it.* The E. P. eyebrow action up in triage this afternoon left little doubt. In the matter of Ms. Elite, none of this mattered to Velez, I think we all realize; Ms. Elite's face value was—is—valuable indeed: not just in the cash-commodity sense by which she herself accounts, but in the reflective splendor that made Velez want her around. Love is just something that Sally Wallach in her ingenuousness had projected on Velez's deal with Ms. Elite. As Velez has instructed me on many occasions, and not only in reference to his former girlfriend and my former wife Sarah: "You have to learn how to fuck without falling in love, Coolie."

Bennie couldn't find his wallet. I offered my American Express card to the two girls beside me; the luridly contagious intrigue had, on this pulseless night, hooked me. The nearer ponytail read the number into the receiver and panted "Yeah, it's okay, go 'head!"

They listened and giggled, and occasionally one or the other would whisper back into the line—they'd apparently managed to summon themselves a live human being on the other end—playing along, trying out their own ditzy fantasy rap. "Yeah, my girlfriend and I are here, we're all alone—giggle—oooh yeah, I know, we like to do that too!" I thought I detected some extra-tight crossing and uncrossing of torn fishnet legs; maybe not. Up past them on the flickering screen, a naked bearded fat man was interviewing an emaciated girl with a nastily tattooed shoulder; her leg was angled out over his pasty lap, grazing him in spread-eagled indifference. I couldn't hear over Bennie's dance mix. Above us, Elvis slept the sleep.

The girls' phone date was evidently still on the line. The far pony-tail clenched the phone; she covered the mouthpiece with her palm. "Ask her," her friend kept saying. "C'mon! *Ask her!*"

"Awright, awright, wait," said the other. They listened. I caught a glance and flashed a don't-forget-whose-credit-card scowl that seemed to register; she offered me the phone. As soon as I waved her off, Bennie was all over her. Enough light seeped its way down from Elvis Presley's iridescent coffin so that the ponytails and I could watch Bennie's pupils dilate.

He shoved the phone into my face; "You gotta, you gotta . . . ."

I plugged my other ear and tuned inward. The voice inside was sleepy, dreamy, no doubt lightly narc'd for the long numbing night ahead, gently ridiculing this filmy passion charade that my American Express card was sitting here financing without complaint. I could hear her sly, winking invitation to chuckle along with her kinky recital, but then, something else: something more deliciously conspiratorial, per-formance narcissism of a sincere and generous brand. And the power—a potion redolent of . . . what? Something. Oh, how a voice like this could twist you and intoxicate you and finally, with your own willing connivance, satiate you; the dark and wonderful places it can take you. But then I suddenly, stunningly recognized this voice as it whispered out to me from my own longest shadows: ". . . being with me, in me, deep in the night, just be here deep inside me," Ellen Larkin said to me, "because baby, I love to fuck for you."

Above us, the back wall of the glass sarcophagus swung open, and Elvis Presley disappeared.

# 25

My body, not yet attuned to strike time, insisted on waking up before dawn. Net post-Elvis sleep logged: four hours. This deal that was supposed to have been a prank strike would take some getting used to.

I turned on the radio. WRTR-FM. The Thunder. Thunder Rock. Rolling Thunder Radio. New York's *numero uno* rock music machine. Maybe I expected to hear Velez's voice, expected some twinkly-assed taunt: "Hey, Coolie, you raggedy-behind mofo, who gave you the day off, baby? I gotta cover for you *again?* C'mon, man, these shoulders a'mine gettin' weary, newsman!"

No. Somebody named Hendy Markowitz was sitting in for Roberto Velez. Hendy would be enjoying this even more if the Veterans Day Massacre hadn't given Velez and me a dignified leave of absence; couldn't very well chew on us under the circumstances. But Hendy was already exacting some overripe vengeance: I listened and listened, and didn't hear one single solitary reference to the Velez & Oldham Show. Just Velez. No Oldham. It might not have sounded like it to you, but trust me: this was a personal and profoundly gratifying kiss-my-ass from Hendy Markowitz to me. I'm here, Oldham, and you're not. How the mighty have fallen, and so forth. Hendy Markowitz's Sermon on the Mount: The arrogant insiders shall be tossed out on their ass and the shat-upon shall prevail; the nerds shall be hip and the hip shall be square; the previously anointed shall wake up and find out it was all a joke . . . .

The Church of the Intercession, West 155th Street. A street in need of much intercession.

Matching white caskets lay before the altar. Like a bride and groom: pristine, serene. God's own. There were candles at the head of every other pew. Many people were in attendance. News coverage was morbidly enthusiastic; you wouldn't have settled for less, would you?

In front was Immaculata Velez, supported at either elbow by her oldest son Roberto and an old-country-looking gent in a baggy black suit. Son Michael ass-knelt at the far end of the pew, slumped, sullen and unmoved by the proceedings, contemptuous of the hypocritical reverence frothing around the casket of his dead-end brother, unable even to look upon the companion box. The priest, once he got through swinging his incense thing around and fiddling with the rest of his rigmarole, had a few things to say about neighborhood violence and wasted lives, but wanly and with threadbare conviction; with such a broken-record sermon of futility, even this indefatigable soldier of Christ must surely by now have begun to figure the hell with it.

Outside I kissed the cheeks of Immaculata Velez. Her face was dry. She introduced me to the rumply man, who turned out to be her brother, as her son Roberto's best friend.

"Your Mom looks pretty okay," I said to Velez later.

"Yeah, well. She's gonna go stay with her brother now. Finally get outa . . . this."

"And Michael?" I asked, but Michael was already doing his homey slink-strut off across the street to a waiting car, a jump-shocks drive-by gunship model pounding out angry, high-octane *Latino* rap. "I don't think so, Coolie. I think that boy's history."

I stole a look at my suddenly former partner, hoping, I suppose, for an invitation to do whatever friends are supposed to do at times like these. For once, Velez looked his age; hints of recent ravage betrayed him badly this miserable morning. He's been around longer than you think, you know. Almost as long as I have.

But all we could wring out of eleven-and-a-half years was a long minute or two shuffling and looking aimlessly over each other's shoulders, while Velez's two departed family members were gurneyed out of the church and loaded into their twin hearses. "Bobby," I started, wanting to say something brotherly about sweet, beautiful, laughing Margareta and the incomprehensible conspiracy of demons that—ah, you know; but the words wouldn't sort themselves out. And so I stood there with my mouth open, seized by the terror of sounding trite at a time like this. Finally Velez rescued me. "Listen, I gotta . . ." with a nod toward the hearses.

"I know."

"Don't—you don't have to. . . ."

"Thanks." Velez knows I don't do cemeteries; it's been a policy of mine since Elizabeth Reilly's final bow in Baltimore. "So—see you later?"

Velez managed a game facsimile of the old Hollywood Velez smile. "I don't . . . don't think so, man. Headin' out tonight. Right after . . . right after I get my Mom an' my uncle out to La Guardia. Supposed to start kickin' L.A.'s ass tomorrow morning."

Los Angeles. So E. P. Wallach was sticking with his new media property Roberto Velez after all. In the worldview of E. P. Wallach, notoriety is its own reward. "Television, huh?" I smiled wearily.

"That's what the man says, Coolie," said Velez, gazing as close to tears as I've ever seen him toward the hearses, wincing hollowly at the twin muffled thuds of the doors closing on his prematurely damned brother and his sweet, martyred baby sister.

A summons. Power lunch.

I duly presented myself at the mouth of a pink-linen Central Park South sanctuary whose waiters were clearly among the original furnishings. The Wallach table, please. A slight incredulous stiffening of the old boy's tuxedo at the mere mention. In a prescient touch of whimsy I had worn a tie, thus denying this stony guardian of the great his most obvious pretext for turning me back out into the elements among my own shantytown kind.

I was led to a fat round window sumptuary iced with a ransom of crystal. Outside, daylight had failed miserably and the park was fast surrendering what little fall blush remained, reducing the whole scene to one sullen, undulating, tidal mud puddle. Twenty leagues or so of gathered green tapestry poised above the table to ring down just in case things in the real world outside got too dreary.

Who, I couldn't wait to find out, would be here? The call had come from E. P. Wallach's appointment android; clarification queries had not been entertained. So who will the contestants be: a corporation-munching high roller, his auburn-tressed sorcerer's apprentice of a daughter, and a hobbled-up radio exile? Place your bets, ladies and gentlemen.

And sure enough here sat Sally Wallach. Dressed like a grown-up. This was not the sort of detail I'd have overlooked even under the most strained circumstances. She wore a suit, a dark one over white silk with ruffled collar and cuffs; her hair was cotillionish. This was, in short, an E. P. Wallach production—a howling omen of unwelcome diplomatic realignment.

But it was the old Sally, sitting by herself, who jumped out from behind the afternoon's *Town & Country* camouflage; her eyes were again for a fleeting moment the eyes of playful anarchy, precocious death-defiance. Of meaningless childish conspiracy, which, it suddenly and sadly became clear to me, just about summed up me and Sally Wallach.

Three chairs. Two settings. Can I take a hint? I eased myself down under the bare outside edge.

Hi, how's your leg, glad you came, yeah I'm fine. A bit about Velez and the funeral— "yeah," sadly, "wish I coulda been there but, y'know . . . ." Then: "Dad's got a deal for you."

Years seemed to have passed since the afternoon a few days ago when this girl and I were interrupted sneaking away for a Velezmobile backseat bonk by the *clack-clack-clack* that suddenly turned the hands on everybody's watches way ahead. This, perhaps, is what a twenty-year high school reunion feels like: cobwebby recollections passing between sad-aged eyes of oaths sworn one glorious night behind the old gym; of small enduring lies told in the shadows the night before graduation. I felt my throat, that irrational, humiliating organ, tighten.

"How come you told him I saved your life?"

"You did. I mean, you would have. On purpose, I mean, if you'd had time to think about it."

Real talk wouldn't come, so I commented stupidly on the day outside and watched Sally Wallach sip bubbling orange juice and drew designs with my tongue on the dry roof of my mouth.

"Want something to drink?"

"Am I staying long enough to finish it?" In other words, Sally, I won't be offended if we cut to the chase.

"Dad will be here shortly. He said he wanted to talk to you for a minute. That's the kind of thing Dad means literally."

"The one-minute deal. . . ." But Sally wasn't biting; she knew better. It was her old man's play. So I tried this: "Are you going to be around?"

Just a slight pause; a momentary glance out into the heavy, looming day. "'Fraid you and I are part of the deal, Dennis."

My involuntary cold-water pucker won't surprise you. "You *told your father?*"

Sally smiled, mostly to herself. "My dad's not the kind of man you can bullshit and hope to get away with it."

And then E. P. Wallach was upon us.

"That was quite an afternoon you had Monday," E. P. offered, along with his business hand. I chanced a peek Sally's way, but Agent Orange had developed a sudden obsession with her menu.

"Tragedy," he pressed on. "Well, anyway. I must apologize, Mister Oldham. This day, like most of mine, has too few hours in it. So here it is: You may have heard that I'm planning to sell my interest in WRTR."

"There's been talk," I tried to say lightly; I think E. P. smiled but his is the kind of face where you can't be sure.

"Yes. Well, that's exactly the case. The transfer happens in . . ."—he actually checked his watch—"about forty-eight minutes."

"Congratulations." Was this a stupid thing to say to E. P. under the circumstances? I don't know; I was just trying to lubricate his monologue with an occasional response to show I was paying attention. But I swear E. P. gave me a momentary look of interrogation, searching, I suppose, for the one last piece of inside information that he may have overlooked. Just as quickly, he convinced himself there was nothing to it; that *I* couldn't possibly be holding any cards. A drink I hadn't seen him order appeared at his elbow.

"My daughter thinks very highly of your work. And Roberto does too. You have a very loyal friend in Roberto."

Which shoved me, I suppose, past the nothing-to-lose threshold. "What about Roberto?"

"He comes with me."

"Even after Monday?" What answer was I hoping for? Did I want Velez to lose his shot?

"Especially after Monday," said E. P. Wallach. "America likes to forgive its celebrities. Am I right?" I suppose I must have given a goofy nod. "Of course. Roberto is going to be huge. You should be proud to have helped him get his start." Past tense reverberated off the ceiling, rattling the crystal.

Then he asked, "What are your plans?"

Ah, Oldham, what's the right answer? If only he'd given me a multiple-choice instead of an essay question. "For now, I thought I'd—"

E. P. pulled a blue-bound document from his breast pocket. Sally had turned to stone, feigning interest in the sullen row of sodden horses hitched to hansom cabs that would have no takers this day in the park below. "Here's the best I can do," said E. P. Wallach.

It was clear he didn't want me to sit there and read. I looked up at him.

"Three years guaranteed as news director at WRTR."

Ho ho. "I thought you said you were selling the station."

"Oh, I am. This is your insurance policy."

"So when Harold Fish—" I began; E. P. shot a look Sally's way and then let it pass. Even his daughter is a suspect.

He finished for me. "When Harold Fish takes over the station in"—time check—"forty-five minutes, he inherits himself an extravagantly paid news director with a nuclear bomb-proof contract."

"But how about if he wants—"

"He can do whatever he wants. He can fire you; probably will, just like he's going to fire everybody else at that place. Only thing is, he has to pay off your contract. Think of it as three years of severance pay, compliments of Harold Fish."

I couldn't resist. "Is this because I happened to be standing in front of your daughter Monday afternoon?"

Sally looked my way warily, as if she expected cutlery to levitate at my impertinence. But E. P. was cool. "Nope. Figured it was an accident; most heroism is. I fought; I know. Show me a hero, and I'll show you an ordinary guy who couldn't get his ass out of the way fast enough. No, this is because Roberto made me promise to set you up, and this way it doesn't cost me a quarter."

Well. "What happens to WRTR?" I asked.

"I don't know. Maybe talk radio. My daughter tells me that smut and right-wing politics is the cash cow now. Harold Fish enjoys cash. Likes it a lot. Pretty fond of right-wing politics, too, last time I heard. Anyway, what do you care? News is news, right? What do you care if it's wrapped in—Fish?" He beamed suddenly at his daughter. "Get it? News, wrapped in fish? Like they used to wrap fish in the. . . ." But Agent Orange's blank stare deflated E. P. Wallach. "Ah, hell with it," he grinned.

As E. P. Wallach held out his hand to me now in symbolic dismissal, I noticed the same cufflinks he'd been wearing during his emergency room personal appearance. I wondered if maybe he only owned one pair. Must jot it down: a good Christmas gift idea for E. P. Wallach. His out-stretched hand finessed me smoothly but decisively out of my chair and onto my feet. Interview over. "Good luck, Mister Oldham," said E. P. Wallach, and his daughter chimed in with sentiments in the same vein. Nothing left but to head for the street.

"Dennis," E. P. stopped me; looked like we'd part on a first-name basis. "You might want to sign this before you go." The contract. I had-n't read a word. But then, I've never read any of my contracts. Why start now? And then this, even as I backed away from the table: "Roberto tells me you might need a little family legal help. Here," he held out a card, "call this guy. He's expecting to hear from you."


Family court.

Oh yay, oh yay, gather near all ye petitioners. . . . Nah. They don't say that. Very businesslike operation here. Antiseptic civility; histrionics discouraged up here in Westchester. The chairs are austere but comfortable.

Not that Sarah needs the home-court advantage, but here we are.

In this corner, wearing something offhandedly Chanel, is my former bride. Her hair is pinned up neatly in the back, the way a serious Mom would wear it. Beside her are her parents. This may be the half-dozenth time I've laid eyes on them. Sarah's dad has a golf course tan even as December looms; I bet he's been hauled back from Florida under protest just for the day's grim proceedings. Sarah's Mom, sporting a hat you could fake a UFO snapshot with if you frisbee'd it out at just the right angle, has been given charge of patting her daughter's hand anytime the magistrate's gaze sweeps the plaintiff's bench. And of course Erica Armstrong, with whom you've already made acquaintance.

In my corner is me. My original plan had been to have Fat Tom the Lawyer represent me, notwithstanding his severe allergies to courtrooms and children, but that was before E. P. Wallach had slipped me the magic card to my daughter's salvation. Unfortunately, I have yet to lay eyes on my new legal team, and, as the clock strikes the witching hour, they are nowhere in evidence.

Although I haven't actually seen her, I am given to understand that my daughter may be somewhere on the premises, sequestered beyond the pale of my toxic influence, here to give testimony in the event that I don't play ball. "A court appearance can be a real, lasting trauma," Counselor Armstrong warned me on the way in, "often leaves lasting scars, but I don't think it will be necessary . . . do *you?*" Leaving me here in my solitary pew to ponder the pathos that Erica Armstrong knows goddamn well I'd drink powdered glass to avoid.

The interests of the State of New York are being looked after today by Judge Yolanda M. Watson, a gray-streaked black woman who, judging by her rapt attention upon Erica Armstrong at this shadow-lengthening hour, is blessed with a bottomless boredom threshold. Judge Watson has had little to say but much to write; Counselor Armstrong talks, Judge Watson takes notes.

At issue this crisp blue pre-Thanksgiving afternoon is whether Jane Courtenay Oldham's father should ever be permitted the sound of his daughter's voice during this, his current lifetime.

Let's tune in for a moment and see how Counselor Armstrong is getting on. ". . .repeated admonitions, your Honor, for the child's safety. But Mr. Oldham has consistently shown an utter disregard. . . ." The child's safety? ". . .allowed a five-year-old girl to play, unattended, on the roof of a six-story building with not so much as a guard rail—"

"Your Honor," I try—Fat Tom would have jumped in here, and I'm quickly dispairing of the promised legal reinforcements—but Erica Armstrong outjumps me. *"Your Honor,* Mrs. Oldham's daughter *herself* has told her mother about such episodes. And if the child's safety weren't concern enough, Mr. Oldham fails to observe even the remotest responsibilities of parenthood, dragging the child around all night with him and his music cronies, feeding her *beer. . . ."* How'd she know that? Did my Jane spill the beans? ". . .on one particularly upsetting occasion, when Mrs. Oldham picked Jane up from her weekend visitation the girl was carrying a live, three-inch waterbug in her pocket—*in her pocket,* your Honor, and told her mother that her father"—she looks at me like I've just risen from the primordial slime pool and assumed human form for purposes of depredation—"told her she could carry it around!"

Well, sure, but I can explain. "Your Honor—"

*"Your Honor,"* insists Erica Armstrong. I get it. Every time I say, 'your Honor', Erica Armstrong immediately says, *'your Honor.'* They must have taught her that in law school. I'm not fooling; it's like clock-work. Watch: "Your Honor?"

*"Your Honor. . . ."*

I'll get my chance. We'd been to the Museum of Natural History. Me, Jane Courtenay Oldham, Raylene McDonald and Charlene-with-the-pigtails McDonald. It was a Saturday and everything was cool. Jane and Charlene got wind of the bug collection, the finest bug collection in the universe. We spent the afternoon down with the bugs while the dinosaurs cooled their heels upstairs, waiting in vain for our arrival. So? Jane got crazy for bugs. Looked at one under the microscope and decided the bug's face looked like Jason from the *Friday the 13th* movie that Velez and Ms. Elite and I took her to—remember? So that night we'd been sitting around checking out a *Simpsons* episode that Jane had taped in her rear-room electronic wonderland when the biggest cock-roach in Christendom sauntered out of that cable TV hole by my ceil-ing where they all like to hang out. And while I foraged for a surface-to-cockroach missile my daughter snuck up on the thing, caught it with her Mickey Mouse cup, adopted it and named it Jason. What the hell, I suppose I figured at the time: the kid's got to have a pet. The apart-ment's too small for a pony.

Well, we stuck it in a Tupperware thing and poked some holes in the top so it could breathe and Jane fed it some Cheerios and linguini; I figured it'd be dead before dawn. I didn't give it another thought but it took Jane exactly one day to train the thing to ride around in her pocket. She even took it with us to Too Tall Jones next day to show Charlene McDonald, as if Charlene and her Mom needed some little white kid to show them what a cockroach looks like. So the two of them spent the afternoon playing with Jason the cockroach; let it horse around in my official news booth and munch on a slice of vintage pizza. I guess what happened is Jane decided to take Jason out of her pocket to show her Mom on the way home on the Cross-Bronx Expressway. I never knew those things could fly.

". . . frankly fear for the moral environment that Jane Courtenay Oldham is being exposed to during her visitations with her father—"

"What?"

*"Your Honor,"* Erica Armstrong sweeps the boards, elbows flying with grievous intent, and fires this outlet pass: "Mr. Oldham has recently entertained a female minor in his home, engaging the girl in an intimate relationship. . . ."

I'll be damned. I *am* damned. But, how . . . . ? Did Sarah put a goddamn detective on the case? I fumble around for a delaying tactic but Erica Armstrong flourishes her ostrich folio and removes a manila folder—a *manila folder*—what's in there? Pictures? Everybody's looking at the manila envelope. Judge Watson can't take her eyes off it. There it sits. Counselor Armstrong drums it lightly with her fingertips. Do I want to up the ante? Is there any use?

There's more. The hardships Sarah endures shuttling Jane back and forth every two weeks. The expert opinions from school counselors and a family therapist and other shadowy accomplices that my evil ministry has pushed little Jane to the brink of madness. The well-documented Satanism at the heart of rock music and my collusion as a high-profile practitioner. I hazard a close look at Judge Watson from my deserted quarter before the bar and I see this: she looks like she decided to grant Sarah's petition about one femtosecond after I walked in here.

I sit, fingering the worn wood of this chair crafted for the utilitarian comfort of cornered Presbyterians and their mercenary advocates, and the great calm of the damned seeps up into me from these highly polished, unsympathetic floorboards—a karma of serene hopelessness, a reprieve from the futility of further resistance. My disenfranchisement is about to become complete and neither Fat Tom nor Johnnie Cochran nor even that bullethead who used to get John Gotti off the hook all the time, *nobody* can do anything about it.

But now, even as the final triumph of the family legal system descends and I wallow in my soiled trousers feeling irrational stirrings of remorse, doors fly open behind me and the winds of righteousness pour in.

E. P. Wallach's Flying Legal Wallendas set upon the proceedings like a Mafia hit squad's company picnic: three nastily intimidating suits take up triangulated firing positions while a short, fluffily packaged but steely-eyed Ma Barker type slides down beside me and snaps open a briefcase that I fully expect to conceal something of at least semi-automatic capabilities. I think: these guys are on *my* side.

Look at my Sarah over there. Look at Erica Armstrong. They have the hollow look of recognition that seismic shifts have occurred under their feet; that somewhere—Manchuria, perhaps, or the Bikini Atoll—a rogue meteorite has just slammed home and altered the trajectory of planet Earth just enough to ruin their day profoundly.

"You're Dennis Oldham?" Ma Barker whispers sweetly.

"Yes."

She stands. "Evelyn Ashcroft, your Honor. White, Stanford and White. Representing Mr. Oldham. May I approach?" Yolanda M. Watson checks her watch and notes to her dismay that it's much too early to call it a day and head for cover, and under the peeling echo of *"your Honor!"* ricocheting from Erica Armstrong to various corners of the room, my attorney Evelyn Ashcroft scoops out of her briefcase not one manila envelope but a whole armload of manila envelopes, enough to dwarf Erica Armstrong's one measily manila envelope, and stalks purposefully up to the bench of justice.

What's in those manila envelopes? Pictures of the old Sarah, the rocker in the torn-assed jeans and the black lace bras that used to serve as her outerwear; the boots and the *"Too Drunk to Fuck"* tee shirt in which she managed to beguile half of Montreal the weekend I fell in love with her? Wonder how that picture would sit with the prim Justice Watson, whose job it is to decide how much of a danger I am to my daughter's very existence.

The curtain descends like a lethal injection. Judge Yolanda M. Watson raps on her desk with her gavel, mutters "continuance granted," and heads offstage. See how far my legal education has advanced in just these past moments? It's all so clear to me now: the team with the most manila envelopes wins. The only person in the room more dumbstruck than I am at this whiplash turn of fortune is Erica Armstrong, who sits holding like a severed head the defeat she has snatched from the jaws of victory here in Westchester County Family Court, without even realizing that someone had hauled down her drawers.

I stand and shake hands with Evelyn Ashcroft, who is already packing up to leave. I feel reluctant to ask what happened, fearful that knowing the details would break the spell. But I do manage, "What happens next?"

"How old is your daughter, Mr. Oldham?" my attorney asks.

"Five," I say, but no, wait: "Six next week."

"Six. Twelve years until she's eighteen. Okay. We do this every six months for the next twelve years. Or until your ex-wife chokes on her own legal bills. Which will happen way before your daughter turns eighteen."

"Speaking of legal bills. . . ."

"All taken care of. Courtesy of Mr. Wallach. Keep in touch."

Outside in the quaint, autumn-dappled town square, I spy Jane Courtenay Oldham. Hunting for bugs.


That just about catches you up, doesn't it?

It has been a fortnight of mostly suspended animation. Much has happened—oh boy—but the deadness of the in-between hours, days, has schemed to intensify this eerie sensation of weightlessness, of transparency.

Coverage of the Veterans Day Massacre, as our blood-addled local scoops immediately christened the events in the Plaza, has just now started to let up. It is fortunate for, among other people, my former partner Velez, that no story—not even this one—can stay fresh enough for Page One of *The Post* forever; soon enough, stories begin to stink just like the fish wrapped up inside. Bodies have been located in a Staten Island sewage treatment basin; foul play, says the police spokesperson, is suspected. Page One. Guys in artificial breathing apparatus and Martian strolling suits digging through gunk that might, to the febrile imagination, look in this murky black-and-white *Post* photo like human remains.

There's still a story every day; you just have to look a little harder for it. On TV, you might have to wait ten or fifteen minutes into the broadcast for your Veterans Day Massacre update. Not that there's any new news. Just a rerun of the wild video collages you've surely grown sick of seeing by now; all those still-frame Zapruder-style shots that not even a NASA analyst could make anything out of, with maybe a new chunk of interview overdubbed for ersatz newsworthiness.

Just two days ago, buried in the belly of still another Veterans Day Massacre follow-up article, you may have spotted this:

*"Police Detective Sergeant Peter Corollo of the City's Drug Enforcement Task Force said that no evidence has been found linking radio personality Roberto Velez, who recently and abruptly left his top-rated morning show on WRTR-FM, with the alleged activities of his brother Nicholas, one of the deceased and the presumed target of the gunmen. Nor, Detective Corollo said, was there any reason to believe Mr. Velez knew the assailants.*

What do I hear from Velez? Same as you; I watch *Entertainment This Evening* too. Velez—host of this year's Billboard Music Awards show. Velez—producing and starring in some MTV-type thing. Velez—talking to Fox and Warner Brothers about a sitcom; no doubt a heartwarming chronicle of a slick-ass Puerto Rican radio dude. Like this story was supposed to be, before things went out of control.

Snookered by my nefarious three-year guaranteed contract, Harold Fish seems to have decided to stick with me for the time being as his provisional news director. Meanwhile, outside my new glass office, WRTR is fast descending into flaming chaos as Harold Fish disembowels the beloved, legendary Thunder like Sherman through Atlanta. This turn of events is not, as you may imagine, without its petty satisfactions for me, watching from my temporarily secure bunker as the likes of Hendy Markowitz and Arielle the buff little program director and even Sanford Fry, our general manager, are marched single file to the gallows by Harold Fish's new programming squad of young Republican haircuts with that watertower-sniper gleam in their wide righteous eyes, clearing the counterculture underbrush for the newly minted Heartbeat of Talk Radio.

I have, in fact, seen the secret plan. Soon, the only trace you will find of our former glory will be a nostalgic four-day-a-week, midnight-to-three artifact: *Adrian Boe's Rolling Thunder Revue*.

Yes. Adrian has outlived them all.

I have so far spent about eight minutes in the company of Harold Fish, who turns out to bear demented genetic kinship to E. P. Wallach, except for the nose and the flat ugly British croak. I am under no delusion here: I am a pernicious mote in Harold Fish's eye, planted there by E. P. Wallach. I am a walking fuck-you card. I have no doubt that

Harold Fish is already plotting his revenge; his lawyers are already dissecting my allegedly guaranteed three-year contract for microscopic structural impurities. Count on it.

But here I am compelled to make a confession: I have begun a cautious reappraisal of broadcast journalism as a not entirely dishonorable vocation. This may be a sign that my protracted period of adolescent denial, suddenly bereft of its young patron saint Velez, is at long last about to dissipate. I've reached no definite conclusions, mind you; I'm just thinking about it. Because despite my newfound legal firepower, it's clearly time to establish some modest *bona fides* in the eyes of the Westchester family court system. That much I owe my daughter.

Besides. Velez & Oldham are history. I have to do *something*.

Bennie, I find one fine night, seems to have a hit on his hands. Fortunately for Bennie, New York has no immediate shortage of part-time Elvis Presleys. Since last we checked, Bennie has refined the stagecraft: now Elvis splits his time between lying in state in his glass sarcophagus and gyrating on a suspended stage from where he lip-syncs his greatest hits. The transvestite trade alone will keep this place in business for centuries.

You won't be surprised to learn that I have examined my American Express bill for the telephone trail of Ellen Larkin's ghost. The more I replay the sex-phone voice in my mind, the more I am certain that it was her. Like the dear departed Nightbird, it's not a voice you can forget in one lifetime.

It was late on Wednesday, Thanksgiving eve, when I arrived back in Penn Station from my Westchester Family Court victory. Tomorrow morning, another train takes me to a long-overdue visit with brand-new hotshot D.C. lobbyist Richard 'Buddy' Oldham. Buddy will no doubt try to lure me back home to Baltimore. "There's plenty of radio here," Buddy will say. But no thanks, Dad. New York City *is* my home. Sure didn't plan it that way; it just turns out to be the perfect place for the permanently homeless.

When I come back from Baltimore, we'll have a birthday party for Jane Courtenay Oldham. Mrs. McMurphy will bake chocolate chip cookies. Morton the nine-fingered bookie, with whom my account is current, will furnish the cannolis, and Rose and Rose's sister will cook enough pasta for every man, woman and child in the West Village to celebrate not only a birthday, but Jane's liberation from the forces of evil. If only every other weekend.

Velez's birthday present for his goddaughter arrived yesterday, and sits parked in my living room: a three- or four-thousand dollar F.A.O. Schwartz miniature electric Ferrari, with fuzzy dice hanging from the rearview mirror and a very authentic-looking California vanity licence plate that reads: JR KILLSHOT.

I find a message on my machine. It is Agent Orange, who you thought you'd heard the last of, hadn't you? Just like I had.

The wind down here is cold and strangely musical tonight; starting like a whistling serenade somewhere out over the black river, swirling its way inward, folding around itself, confecting eerie harmonies, and then storming the Vietnam Veterans Plaza in all its Wagnerian glory.

My hopes of finding Sally Wallach down here were not high, and sure enough she's not here. I'm several time zones late. Her message said could I meet her at nine-thirty; it's already almost midnight. Even if she had actually showed up here tonight, she has long since given up on me.

And what do you suppose had been on Sally Wallach's mind? Probably just a final clipping for her scrapbook, and a symbolically thumbed nose at Old Man Wallach. Sentimental lass, that Agent Orange. I guess she just wanted to ice the cake on another frolicky episode of her young life. For Sally has already learned, perhaps at the knee of Velez: you have to learn to fuck without falling in love.

I hang around for maybe an hour, pacing in the footsteps of recent, already fading drama, before the cold closes in on me. The Memorial Wall glows on. The platoon is long gone. I must remember to come visit them down here next year.

As I turn to leave, from the corner of my eye, a shadow. Down by the Wall. In and out of the twin portals, lumbering but stealthy. Silent. Casing the joint. Then suddenly the apparition rises up and spreads its tattered arms to the heavens, and the voice peals majestically up into the night, echoing from the crevices and the stone glacier faces and the netherplaces, summoning a phantom rolling like thunder across the floor of space:

*"Colonel Elmo, don't let dese boys down!"*